THE GRULLA PAINT MURDERS

OTHER BOOKS BY DAVID HUEBNER

CHILDREN OF THE RIFT: CHEMONE
COWBIRD*
BUSTER'S GOLD*
HEART OF A BEAST, SOUL OF A WOMAN
WHISKEY RUNNER
THE PREVAILING WESTERLIES

* A Sheriff Evan Coleman novel.

THE GRULLA PAINT MURDERS

by

DAVID HUEBNER

Copyright 2003
All rights reserved by the author

Dedication

For Corinne, who gave me a love for Equus.

THE GRULLA PAINT MURDERS

"He will by no means leave the guilty unpunished, visiting the iniquity of the fathers on the children and on the grandchildren to the third and fourth generation."

Exodus 34:7

1

"Telephone, Evan," said Suzy, "There's a sobbing woman on line two who wants to talk to you."

Evan regarded the phone contemptuously. *Can't be any woman I know*, he thought. *I haven't made a woman cry in a long time. Smile either come to think of it.*

"Evan. Please," begged Suzy. "I'm late for lunch."

The sheriff was on vacation. Evan Coleman, Saguaro County, Colorado, deputy sheriff, was taking his turn in the office.

"Deputy Coleman," he announced flatly. "Can I help you?"

"Hello, sheriff?" asked a timid female voice.

"Yes, ma'am, this is Deputy Coleman. What can I do for you?"

"My husband is missing," stated the woman.

Evan waited for details, but there was only silence punctuated by a muffled sob. "Yes, ma'am, when did you last see him?"

"He left yesterday morning about ten to go elk hunting and he isn't back yet."

This could be tricky. The rifle hunt for elk didn't open for two more days. Perhaps the man was archery hunting. That season ended tomorrow, but in any case, a one-day elk hunt starting at ten in the morning was hardly normal. Maybe the guy had a girlfriend somewhere and overslept.

"When did he say he'd be back?" Evan tried to get some sense of perspective.

"This morning. He was only packing some supplies into his camp. One of our sons is coming out tomorrow and they're going hunting the day after."

Okay, this is a little better. Evan looked at his watch. It was five minutes past noon.

"Well ma'am, it's just barely afternoon. Why don't you sit tight and give him a few minutes?"

"Oh no, Deputy Coleman, you don't understand," she protested, her voice beginning to quaver. "His horse just came back without him."

Could be something, could be nothing. Evan cracked a smile. The guy might have been careless and let his horse stray, or maybe he fell off when the horse spooked. Then again, he might have had a heart attack and tipped over—permanently. "Ma'am, I'll need your name and address."

"This is Ruth Pike and I live..."

Evan didn't let her finish. "Is your husband Ben Pike?"

"Yes," she admitted, and her voice broke. She started sobbing in earnest. "Yes, that's him."

Evan wasn't certain if she was crying because Ben Pike was missing or because she was married to him. If there were a nastier man in the county than Ben Pike, Evan didn't know who it was. In his youth, Pike was as close to being a criminal as could be without being locked up. Now, well into middle age, he skipped along the line that defined the edge of the law, stepping over whenever he thought he could get away with it. Arrested many times for many things, including assault, poaching, theft, fraud, and extortion, he usually managed to get off with just a fine. He was a man who always appeared guilty, but the crucial evidence was usually lacking. He had never done hard time.

Evan's history with Pike went back to before he started to work for the county, but Ruth Pike's voice was insistent, calling him back to the present. "Sheriff. Sheriff. Are you still there?"

"Yes, ma'am, I know your husband."

"Can you come out right now? You have to find him. I think something bad has happened. Please help me."

"Okay, you stay calm. I'll be out directly."

"And you'll go look for him won't you?"

"Well that's another matter. I...."

She cut him off. "You have to look. It's not far where he went, just up into the hills behind the house. Please, I'm worried sick about him."

Good grief, thought Evan. *Hard to believe anyone, even his wife, could care that much for him.* "I'll do what I can, ma'am," he promised, "but officially your husband won't be a missing person until tomorrow. I'll be over directly." He hung up before she could say any more.

"Damn, the last guy on the planet I want to look for is Ben Pike!" But nothing else was happening, and this would definitely get him out of the office. He wrote Suzy a note telling her where he was going, and set the phone to roll over to the State Patrol Office in Salida. If anything of consequence came up, Buster, another deputy, would be coming in at one o'clock to take his turn in the office. Evan dropped his Stetson onto his head. As he went out the front door of the courthouse, he flipped over the sign hanging from a hook screwed into the weathered wooden door frame, changing the message from; "Sheriff's Department Open" to "Sheriff's Department Closed." Below was the phone number of the State Patrol in Salida.

From the courthouse to Pike's place was about twenty minutes. If Evan hurried, he could go home, pick up a horse, some supplies, and still get there within the hour. It was a golden day in late September. Ruth Pike's request to find her husband didn't seem so bad when he considered it an opportunity to go for a ride in the hills.

Three years ago Ben Pike had come up on assault charges. The incident involved two men who were elk hunting on the BLM land behind Pike's place. Even though Bureau of Land Management areas were public property, Ben acted as if owned the BLM land behind his place. If he had told them nicely that he was hunting the area, they probably would have left peaceably. However, being the aggressive dope he was, he started shouting, cursing at them to get out. When one of the men gave him a little sass about who owned the land, Pike gave him back a little sass of his own, disarming the two at gunpoint and running them off. It didn't take long for the men to file a complaint with the sheriff.

After a brief hearing, a judge convicted Pike of a gross misdemeanor, and slapped him with a substantial fine. Pike had been lucky. If the judge had convicted him of a felony, his rifle toting days would have been over, but even though he'd escaped jail, Pike resented the monetary penalty. He told the judge he shouldn't be penalized for defending his territory. The judge explained that the BLM land wasn't his exclusive territory and the fine would help him to remember. Since that incident he'd stayed clean. He hadn't even been suggested as the cause of any trouble. *Although,* thought Evan as he sped down the road, *it's hard to believe he's been reformed.*

Evan had been involved in the previous investigation and out of curiosity, more than necessity, had ridden up into the hills behind Pike's homestead to see where the incident had occurred. He found the place to be a tranquil alpine meadow at about eighty-five hundred feet of elevation, heavily forested on three sides with an almost vertical rock wall guarding the back side. There was a good spring at the base of the rock. It was close to the water, tight against the rock wall, that Pike had made his elk camp. His "tent" was a semi-permanent structure with a treated lumber floor, eight foot high stud walls, wrapped with canvas, and topped with a corrugated steel roof. He insisted the canvas walls qualified the thing as a tent.

Evan liked the area. It was private and pretty. He imagined the hunting would also be good. The more he thought about it, the more he was anticipating his return visit to the place. Too bad he had to look for Pike.

At home, Evan swapped the police cruiser for his pickup truck, and backed up to his bumper pull horse trailer. The little trailer was set up to go. Everything he'd need in case he had to spend the night on the mountain was in there.

Evan would take Diablo, his favorite horse. It was on Diablo he'd first visited Pike's hideaway. If his recollection were right, it was a four to five-mile ride from the Pike place. Diablo was surefooted and strong; there'd be no problem getting up and down before total dark. No problem that is, if Pike cooperated. Evan was hoping he would locate him quickly and there would be an easy explanation for his horse returning home without him.

He checked his gear; change of clothes, cook kit, flashlight, lighter, GPS receiver, knife, binoculars, toilet kit, folding saw, and a box of rifle ammunition. In addition, he threw in his oiled canvas drover coat. Rain was unlikely, but weather in the mountains was unpredictable. All in all, it was a fair amount of weight so he decided on his Daisy Wade saddle. It was tough and twenty pounds lighter than any of his other saddles. It would give Diablo a break, and was comfortable enough at the pace they would travel.

Satisfied with the gear in the trailer, he walked through the barn and out the other end to the horse pasture. Even though the breeding season was over, Diablo was in the back of his paddock talking to the mares through the fence.

Evan had acquired Diablo six years ago as a two-year-old colt. He found him at an auction at the Denver Stock Show. Aptly named, he was wild and undisciplined in the sale ring, rearing and running compulsively, eyes flashing, nostrils flaring. The consignor admitted the horse was spirited, but even though he promised the horse would settle down once he was gelded, bidding was almost nonexistent. Evan didn't pay any attention to the colt's behavior; he could deal with that. He was looking at the best conformation of any horse he had ever seen. The animal was almost perfectly proportioned and balanced, and though he appeared wild, his movements were fluid and precise. Evan knew once he had the stallion's trust, this horse would be able to do anything asked of him. He won the bidding for a paltry twenty-one hundred dollars.

But to bring him home from the auction, Evan had to get him in the trailer. He worked Diablo at the end of a thirty-foot line until he was tired. He never raised his voice or used a whip, he merely ran him in circles until he gave up his attitude. Then he walked him on a lead rope until he cooled down. Finally, after offering the horse water, he walked him easily into the trailer. The whole process took less than an hour. When he got the horse home, training began in earnest. A month later Diablo was composed and calm. Three months later Evan was riding him for short periods of time. When the horse turned three, he was a bullet proof riding horse, steady as stone. Diablo also had a terrific foundation quarter horse pedigree, and Evan had been standing him at stud for the past few years. He was well mannered and a willing partner who trusted Evan implicitly. Evan whistled for the stallion. Diablo turned and trotted towards Evan.

Evan opened the gate and Diablo stopped a few steps away, waiting. Facing him squarely, Evan called, "Diablo" and took a step backward. Diablo responded by moving towards Evan until he was a foot away. Stopping there, he stood, waiting. Evan reached out, patted his head, and started back through the barn towards the horse trailer. The ritual had been designed to keep Diablo from being stolen. If anyone approached him directly and attempted to throw a rope on him, he would run off. The stallion followed Evan like a dog at heel. When Evan stopped at the trailer, Diablo stopped. Evan stepped aside.

"Get in the box, Big D." The horse complied without hesitation.

"Nothing like a smart horse," Evan told himself smiling. Inside the trailer, he clipped Diablo to a trailer tie and tossed a flake of hay into the feedbag hanging on the wall.

He patted the horse on the neck. "We're goin' for a ride, Big D, just stand easy." Evan set off down the road to see Mrs. Pike.

Ben Pike called himself a contractor. Mostly he moved dirt so other people could build things. His place was littered with used earth moving equipment. Evan counted three backhoes, two dozers, two skid steer loaders, an old grader, and an ancient earth scraper. Also scattered around were several trailers and a vintage tractor trailer that Pike used to transport the stuff.

It's too bad, Evan thought as he drove down the long drive between the rusting pieces of machinery, *this is a beautiful piece of property and it's cluttered with junk. How could anybody make half a living with all this trash?* He started to speculate what he could do with the place if it were his when his thoughts were interrupted by the sight of Ruth Pike hurrying from the house to meet him. He stopped the truck and lowered the window.

"Sheriff, I'm so glad you're here. I'm worried sick about Ben." She continued on but Evan wasn't hearing her; he was staring at her face. He couldn't help it.

Twenty years ago she must have been stunning. She was still pretty. She had high cheekbones, a straight, thin nose and full lips. Her eyes were wide and deep blue. Her hair was thick and blonde, and Evan could see no evidence of dark roots. But there was an edge to her features, and she looked more than a little harried. That probably came from living with Pike.

As she talked to him he wondered how she came to be with him. "And you're going to look for him now?"

"Yes, ma'am, just as soon as I saddle my horse. Where can I park my truck?"

"Anywhere, it doesn't matter." She flashed Evan a smile. "This is no showplace or anything. You won't hurt the lawn." She gestured with an all-encompassing wave of her arm.

Her smile was big and beautiful. It momentarily took the harsh edge from her features and made her blue eyes shine. Evan smiled back. "As I recall, I want to go up that draw." He pointed to a little valley at the back of the property towards the northeast.

"You've been here before? I've never seen you." Ruth knew she would have remembered him. He was a handsome man with the most intriguing eyes she had ever seen. His eyes were a mysterious pale gray.

"Yes, ma'am, several years ago. Your husband had a disagreement with some hunters about who owned the BLM land."

Her smile vanished. She looked away from Evan. "Ben can be difficult."

There was a brief awkward silence that Evan broke by saying, "Well, I'll just drive down to the back gate and park there. If that's all right?"

"That would be fine."

Evan took his foot off the brake momentarily and the truck crept ahead. He stepped back on the brake. "Ma'am, I wonder if I could look at the horse."

"What horse?" She gave him a curious look.

"The horse that you told me came back this morning without your husband."

"Oh. Yeah, sure. I was a little mixed up. Ben bought another horse and brought it home just the other day. I thought you meant that one."

Evan thought she looked relieved. He wondered. Was there another story here? He made a mental note to check for any complaints of missing horses when he returned to the office.

"I'll meet you over there," she pointed to a building with weathered wood siding, "by the horse barn. I put his horse in her stall."

Examining the horse, Evan found nothing unusual or informative. In fact, the mare looked remarkably fit and well cared for. She was a buttermilk buckskin about sixteen hands, straight legged, with a big hip, and a pretty head. Apparently Pike could do some things right. It would seem he knew how to pick a decent horse. It also appeared he understood how to maintain one.

After looking over the buckskin, Evan glanced around the barn, but didn't see another horse; the one Pike allegedly had just bought. Rather than ask questions, he followed Ruth back out of the barn. *One thing at a time.*

"I'll be heading out now, ma'am," he told Ruth as they left the barn. "I'll be back down just as soon as I can. You should call the office if your husband shows up in the meantime."

2

Riding slowly down the trail, Evan could sense that Diablo wanted to stretch out. He gave the horse the slightest amount of leg pressure. Diablo picked up the pace immediately, going into a trot. Evan allowed him to trot for about a minute, before he gave him another slight squeeze. "Lope!" he commanded.

Diablo went from a trot into a smooth, flat lope. Evan continued in this manner watching the scenery flow by. He thought about Ruth Pike. How had she come to be where she was? What made a woman love a guy like Ben Pike? From all accounts, he started behaving badly at birth, worsening with age. Maybe Ruth Pike had been one of those pretty, young women who thought outlaws were daring, romantic, and glamorous. When he was a teenager, Evan had known girls who favored tough guys. They were friendly to him, but would never date him, and it wasn't from his lack of trying. It wasn't a problem with his looks either. Evan had attributed their behavior to stupidity, but perhaps, in retrospect, they found him dull. Maybe for Ruth, being around Pike was more exciting than being around the average teen-age boy who merely talked tough. Ben actually was tough, and had the rap sheet to prove it.

"Well," Evan assured himself out loud, "I'll bet if she thought he was cool back then, she damn sure doesn't think so now."

For no good reason, he contemplated his ex-wife. She had been one of those pretty young women who are only in love with themselves, very charming and very manipulative. So sweet when you have what they want, and so quick to change when they get it or decide they really didn't want it after all. Ruth Pike wasn't the only one who'd been fooled.

"Damn it!" Evan exclaimed, "I'm still bitter."

He thought he was over her. And mostly he was, at least the loving her part, but apparently not yet completely over the hating her for what she did to him part. It had been almost ten years since Sheila walked away from him, and in the ensuing divorce, either she or the lawyers had taken almost everything he had including their two-year old daughter, Nikki. Sheila had also made it damn near impossible for him to visit Nikki. She moved half a continent away to Philadelphia where her parents lived and he could only visit one Sunday per month, for four hours. Evan still wasn't certain how that had happened except her lawyer seemed to be much smarter than his. Since the split, he'd seen his daughter only once, nine years ago. After that visit, he knew there was no way he could be a father to her from two thousand miles away. He had not been back.

Now ten years later, after much sweat and hard work, he had managed to acquire more dirt with a house on it and a few good horses. "Hey, but what the hell," he announced in his defense, "I'm still relatively young and healthy, and right now I've got a good horse under me."

He gave Diablo another bit of leg pressure. "Run!" The powerful animal responded immediately. Evan leaned into the acceleration.

Thirty seconds and almost a quarter mile later, Evan slowed Diablo to a walk. It had been a good romp, but Evan wanted the horse's respiration rate back to normal before they started climbing. Ahead was a left turn in the trail. Once they turned the corner, they would enter BLM land, climbing as they followed the trail into the hills. Also, Evan needed to be paying more attention to their surroundings.

He began looking for signs of Pike's passage although he didn't expect to see anything out of the ordinary. He was certain Pike had merely been careless. He'd allowed his horse to stray. He was confident he would find the man alive and well reposed, comfortable in his camp enjoying a cocktail while he contemplated shooting an elk before the season opened.

Where the trail turned, starting up the hill, Evan consulted his watch. It was one thirty-five. They had done the first two miles in under twenty minutes. The next four miles however, would take at least an hour and a half. That would put him at Pike's camp just after three. If all went well, Pike might offer him a drink, and he could be started back down the hill by three-thirty. By seven, at the latest, he would be home drinking his own whiskey. It would have been a nice, Friday afternoon ride in the mountains.

As horse and rider moved up the mountain, following the trail in and out of the trees, the afternoon wore steadily on. Just before three, they approached an area where the trail came within fifty feet of a sheer rock face. A rockslide from high above had scoured the path, leaving a slope littered with boulders. Dismounting, Evan held the reins, and led the horse as they picked their way through the rockslide. Here and there in the earth that remained, he found hoof prints. Evan was no expert tracker, but he could tell more than one horse had come and gone through this area in the past few days. This was inconsequential information. He already knew as much. Without a string of pack horses, it had taken Ben more than one trip to get all his supplies into camp.

Once through the slide area, the trail made a hard left, leading downhill. The first time he had been up here,

Evan wondered if he had made a wrong turn somewhere. He'd been told, after leaving the valley, the trail climbed steadily to the southwest. At this point, he was now going downhill to the north. But after a short descent, the trail turned back to the southwest, ascending once again. He remounted Diablo, and followed the trail to Pike's camp.

Five minutes later he was on level ground, and five minutes after that, the trees stopped. He whoa'd Diablo at the edge of a beautiful alpine meadow. Soft afternoon sunlight played lazily across the front half. There was just enough humidity in the air to give the place a slightly out of focus, dreamy appearance. As he dismounted, he thought if he were an elk, this would be the place to live. Or maybe not, remembering Ben Pike and his camp

Dropping the reins on the ground, he pulled his rifle from its scabbard. He moved off to one side of the horse and knelt at the meadow's edge. He could clearly see Pike's canvas cabin, pitched hard by the side of the cliff that defined the back of the meadow. Lifting a pair of compact binoculars, he slowly glassed the area.

Pike's tent was big, at least sixteen feet by twenty feet. Four years ago, when Pike ran afoul of the law up here, conservation officers had dismantled his camp. Obviously Pike had rebuilt it bigger and better than before. Thirty yards to the left of the "tent", a horse was tethered to a tree. *Must be his pack horse. I wonder how long it's been tied to that tree.* According to Ruth, Ben had come up here yesterday morning.

Between the horse and the tent was a pile of gear; a set of panniers for certain, a number of what appeared to be canvas duffel bags, and a large cooler—groceries, Evan guessed. He glassed back to the tent, studying it for signs of life. There was no smoke, but he could see the shimmer of heat waves rising from the metal chimney pipe.

Just like I thought, the damn fool let his horse stray. Evan smiled.

He lowered the binoculars and started to stand, but as he did, movement in the trees, about a hundred yards to his right, caught his eyes. There was a flash of gray and white that quickly disappeared. He lifted the glasses again. Searching carefully back and forth through the area for a least a minute, he saw nothing. *Must have been an elk. You better get out while the getting is still good.*

Satisfied with his analysis, he remounted Diablo, and started through the meadow towards the tent. Half way across he stopped. The high rock wall cut off the westering sun. The back half of the meadow was deeply shaded. When he crossed from sunshine into the shade he reflexively felt a chill. The camp no longer looked as friendly as it had when he was looking at it through the glasses. Imagination or not, suddenly things didn't seem just right. Rifle in hand, he got off the horse. Taking a step forward, he turned to face Diablo and held his hand up, palm out.

"Stand!" he commanded. Dropping the reins to the ground, he started forward on foot, senses on edge. Rather than walking directly forward toward the camp, he angled off to his left toward where Pike's pack horse was tied. From there, if the canvas flap on the tent were open, he might be able to look inside before he had to get too close. Maybe Pike wasn't even around. *Knowing him, he's off somewhere getting the jump on the season.*

He walked slowly, eyes constantly searching for movement in and around the camp. He stopped several times to use his binoculars, looking not only ahead, but also behind. Moving in this fashion it took Evan several minutes to get to the tethered horse. He patted the horse gently on her shoulder, and moved around to get behind the tree to which she was tied.

"Hey, baby," he spoke soothingly to the mare, "how long you been standing here?" She nickered quietly in response. Evan looked her over. A line-backed dun, she was well fed, about 14.3 hands high, and sturdily built. With her physique, Evan figured she should have been cutting cows, not hauling groceries. Promising to untie her shortly, he knelt again, and raised the binoculars to his eyes. The tent flap was partially open and he could see, at the back of the tent, what appeared to be the end of a cot with a pair of feet on it.

"Having a rest, are we, Pike?" he asked out loud. The mare nickered.

"I'll send your owner right over," Evan told her. "Just let me go spoil his nap."

He stood and walked straight towards the tent. Twenty feet in front of the tent he stopped. If Pike's rifle was within reach, he probably didn't want to surprise him out of a sleep. "Pike!" he shouted. "Ben Pike! This is the Sheriff. Come on out!"

No response. Evan repeated the request. Still no response. He considered firing a shot, but decided he didn't want Pike to wake up thinking he was under attack. Instead he cautiously moved closer. About ten feet in front of the tent, he squatted, peering in through the open flap. The feet were still in place on the end of the cot. The interior of the tent was dim. Then he noticed something that grabbed his full attention. There was a large, dark puddle on the wood floor under the middle of the cot. What appeared to be a length of rope was lying next to the cot.

What the hell is going on here? This isn't right. He pushed the safety off the rifle, bringing it to a ready position as he stood. The adrenaline surge had started. Moving slowly forward, he was on edge, prepared to react to anything. When he got to within arm's length of the tent, he stood off to one side. Using the rifle muzzle, he carefully pushed the tent flap all the way open to look inside. There was the definite smell of smoke, molding canvas, and something else. Evan saw a man, Ben Pike no doubt, lying on the cot. He was nearly naked, covered with blood. Blood was on the canvas wall and the floor. It was the source of the something else smell. Evan stepped quickly across in front of the opening so he could see into the opposite corner of the tent. Satisfied no one else was in there; he flicked the rifle's safety back on, and slowly entered.

"Sweet Jesus," he whispered aloud. He turned and ran from the tent. He whistled for Diablo who was standing calmly where Evan had left him. *God, what a fool I've been*, he was thinking as he ran to meet the horse. Swinging into the saddle before Diablo had completely stopped, he turned and galloped back to the spot where he had seen the movement in the trees when he first arrived. Rifle at the ready, he walked Diablo slowly into the woods and began searching. Two minutes later he found some sign. Someone, on horseback, had stood right at this spot and watched him. Heart pounding, Evan followed the tracks through the trees until they reached the same trail on which he had entered. With nothing and no one in sight, he relaxed slightly to consider his options.

He consulted his watch. "Whoever it was," he told the horse, "has twenty minutes on us. He also has a plan. He knows where we are, and where he is going, and we don't know anything." He turned Diablo and rode back to Pike's camp. Dismounting about twenty feet from the tent, he ground-tied the horse and went in.

From just inside the entrance to the tent, Evan regarded Pike. He was lying face up, naked except for a blood soaked T-shirt. There was a pool of clotting blood on the cot between his legs at the crotch. His body was splattered red from his neck to his knees. His forehead was damaged and there was something white stuffed in his mouth, some kind of gag. Evan moved slowly, carefully, not really wanting to be a part of this. Considering all the blood, it would seem as if he had bled to death. His penis had been cut off, the capital letter "R" was branded into his forehead, and the white thing in his mouth was a sanitary napkin. Evan didn't bother to remove the napkin. He knew what else he would find in Pike's mouth.

"Maybe he choked to death," he said out loud.

Without touching anything, he examined the scene in detail, making notes in a small pocket notebook. A Browning BAR in .270 caliber, stood on its butt, propped against the tent wall in the corner opposite the cot. *Must be Pike's elk rifle.* He let it stand. He found another length of rope at the head of the cot, and judging by the marks on Pike's wrists, he must have been tightly tied to the cot. Evan speculated his assailant had somehow overpowered Pike, got him on the cot, and tied him down. No mean feat; the man looked to weigh at least two hundred and eighty pounds. When Pike was secured, the assailant had proceeded with the deed. Other than the abrasions on Pike's wrists, there were no signs of a struggle inside the tent. Pike had no bullet holes in him, and Evan wondered how the assailant got Pike to cooperate; unless he had somehow rendered him unconscious before dragging him into the tent.

The murderer must have tied Pike's hands together under the cot. His fingernails were ragged and bloody, and there were scuff marks on the wooden floor where his hands would have been. His feet were apparently tied together, too, and judging by the length of rope used, the free ends of the rope were passed under the cot in opposite directions before being tied together. Pike had been tied spread-eagle, trussed up tighter than a calf in a roping contest. Evan didn't understand why whoever murdered him, had bothered to untie him.

But that was only one of the things Evan didn't understand. He couldn't imagine why any of these things had been done to Pike. The mark on his forehead was a burn—a brand? It explained why the camp stove was still warm, but what was the significance of the "R", or the napkin in Pike's mouth, or removing his penis? Evan's head was beginning to spin. His stomach wasn't doing any too well either. After ten minutes he had seen enough. He surmised Pike had been dead at least three or four hours. The state crime experts from Denver would have to sort all this out. He was just a county deputy sheriff. He hurried from the tent, tying the flaps shut on his way out.

Diablo was standing patiently where Evan had left him, but he was eyeing the little mare still tied to the tree. First things first, Evan thought as he rummaged around in the saddlebags Diablo carried. He found his cell phone quickly enough, but had to dump both bags before he found the GPS receiver. He was breathing hard, and his hands were shaking. Stuffing the electronic wizardry into his pockets, he looked up at the cliff behind the camp. About fifty yards to the south, was a chute angling up the face of the cliff. From up there, above the trees, he could probably call the office. First, though, he would have to get a satellite fix from the middle of the meadow. He grabbed his rifle, and went for a walk.

Standing in the approximate center of the meadow, waiting for the GPS unit to determine where it was, Evan contemplated Pike's camp. It looked peaceful and cozy, the kind of place where a man could really relax. *Well he's about as relaxed as he's ever going to be. What the hell is this all about? Is it the random act of some psychopath who just happened to bump into Pike on the mountain, or is it a well planned execution of some sort?* Evan shivered involuntarily. Even Pike shouldn't have to die that way. When the longitude and latitude finally came up on the GPS receiver, Evan wrote them down and walked back to where he could climb the cliff.

"Sheriff's Office."

"Hi ya, Suzy, how was your lunch?" Evan asked the dispatcher.

"Evan! Where are you? At the Pike Place?"

"No, actually I'm above the Pike place at a very pretty spot in the hills."

"Did you find him?" Suzy wanted to know. "His wife has called here three times in the last hour asking about you."

"That woman has a real problem, in more ways than one, and yes, I did find him."

"Is he okay?"

"No, he's not. Is Buster there?" Buster was the oldest member of the Saguaro County Sheriff's Department. He'd been a deputy since he was twenty-three and he was now sixty. He'd watched half a dozen sheriffs come and go, and knew more about the job than all of them combined.

"Yeah, he is, hang on. Evan, you be careful!"

"Hello, young partner."

"Hello, old buddy."

"How can I make your day better?" Buster asked him.

"I don't think that would be possible."

"You found Pike?"

"Yup."

"What's his condition?"

"He's been mortally mistreated."

"He's dead?"

"Yup."

"Foul play?"

"The foulest, Buster. Based on his condition, we can definitely rule out suicide."

"That will be hard on his missus."

"Yeah, I believe it will."

"You want me to drive over there and break the news to her?"

"You would do that for me?"

"Yes, I would."

"Thanks, Buster, you truly are a gentleman. Would you also contact the state crime lab? They should get a team up here now."

"They'll never make it before dark."

"Yeah, that's okay. I'll stay here tonight and baby-sit the scene."

"You're not afraid of dead men are you?"

"Not this one, I whipped him once when he was alive. I'm damn sure he can't hurt me in his present condition."

"Tell me about it"

Evan proceeded to tell Buster all the gory details.

"What do you think the 'R' on his forehead signifies?" asked Buster when Evan had finished.

"You think that's important?"

"It's the key to the mystery." Buster said it solemnly as if he were reciting scripture.

"Hell, Buster, I don't know, it could be the killer's initial! You know, like a 'Z' for Zorro, only maybe an 'R' for Ralph."

"I seriously doubt it."

"Okay, how about 'R' for Rapist."

"Makes more sense considering his other wounds, but Pike never raped anyone, or at least anyone we know about."

"True, but what percentage of rapes never get reported for one reason or another?"

"Yes, you're right, but why go to all the trouble of mutilating the body?"

"I don't have a clue," Evan admitted, "but do you know of any woman who could pull off such a deed? Pike was no pansy."

"Women have many methods. Who said it had to be a woman?"

"I don't know, Buster, I'll have to think about it."

"Well, as my old, sheepherder buddy, Woody McPherson, once told me, 'We are certainly doing a poor job of being the most civilized species on the planet.'"

"What the hell is that supposed to mean?"

"Think on it, Evan. In the meantime I'll do your dirty work."

"Thanks, Buster."

"You bring anything with you for supper?"

"I did, but I think I'm going to look around to see what Pike might have. There's a set of panniers and a cooler over by the spring."

"Enjoy yourself. I'll see you in the morning.

"You going to fly in with the state people?"

"You know better than that. I'll throw a saddle on Tick, and ride up there in time to fix you breakfast before those people are out of bed. Besides, I have to see this thing with my own eyes."

Evan laughed. "I knew it. You're not just an old man; you're a perverse old man!"

"Well, just when I think I've seen it all, one of you young deputies comes up with something totally new and different. By the way, you heard there've been some grizzly bear sightings in those mountains?"

"Yes, I heard. They've got nothing to fear from me. If one shows up and wants Pike, I won't argue."

"Don't fret. I'll swing by your place and mind your horses. Well, have a good night and sleep tight." With that, Buster hung up.

"Yeah, and don't let the bedbugs bite," Evan said to no one. He climbed down from his perch on the rock wall and went to work. He felt stupid roping off the tent with yellow crime scene tape, but knew the state people would expect it. Buster, of course, would ask him if he thought mountain lions could read. *Oh well, getting static from Buster is common and constant.* After the crime scene looked official, Evan went to look after the horse that was tied to the tree. He briefly wondered if this was the new horse Ruth had told him about. After untying her, he led her over to the spring welling up into the tiny pool that had been Pike's water supply. He watched as the mare sucked up about four gallons of water without stopping. Diablo was sniffing the air behind the mare from where Evan had left him.

"Don't get any ideas, Big D," Evan told the stallion. "We don't give it away." But Diablo's relative indifference told him the mare was not in heat. After the mare slaked her thirst, Evan called Diablo over to drink. Then he led both horses to the corner where the meadow met the cliff. It was the place from where he had climbed up the ledge to make his phone call. He would camp there. He could watch the tent and see the spot across the meadow where the trail ended. No one could sneak up on his backside, and he wasn't far from the spring. He removed the mare's lead rope, leaving on her halter. She immediately started grazing on the late summer, meadow grasses.   Evan pulled off Diablo's saddle, the saddlebags, and removed the bridle and bit. Diablo moved to where the mare stood, and after a brief introduction of sniffing, squealing, and foot stamping, they were grazing together.

The time was half past four, and soon the sun would soon be behind the mountains. The little meadow was already completely shaded. It would be dark up here in an hour. Evan gathered dry wood for a fire, and went to see what the recently departed Ben Pike had to offer for supper. The boxes and cooler next to the spring surely contained something worth eating. If not, Evan would have to be satisfied with the jerky he carried along. He had no intention of returning to the tent to see what might be there.

The panniers were empty, but still wet, smelling strongly of blood. Evan smiled knowingly. Opening the cooler, he found it full of fresh elk meat. Turning towards Pike's tent, he addressed the dead man, "You did poach one!"

Evan contemplated the timeline. Pike hauled his supplies up yesterday morning, got up early this morning, poached the elk, and boned out the tenderloins and at least one hind quarter. He was ambushed by his assailant back here, after he put the meat in the cooler, before he had time to thoroughly rinse out the panniers. Judging by the size of the backstraps, it had been a young cow or spike bull. Camp meat, too bad Pike never got a taste of it. He sliced half of one of the tenderloins into one-inch thick pieces, returning the rest to the cooler.

Evan shivered again when he thought about Pike's departure from the physical world. He even felt somewhat sympathetic towards Pike, although that could change when the case was solved and he knew the details. That is, if the case was ever solved. He wondered what the state crime lab could discover. A large, outdoor, crime scene was difficult to deal with, but they had some sharp people. Several of those he had met were a little quirky, but no doubt smart enough.

The rest of the boxes from Pike's cache contained canned goods, staples, and whisky. There was even a sealed bottle of excellent single malt.

"All right, Pike!" said Evan when he found it. "You weren't totally without class." The single malt was a personal favorite of Evan's and hard to come by. Had he known the simple facts, he would not have been quite so magnanimous towards Pike. The scotch was for Pike's older son, Abel. Old man Pike hated the stuff, said it was for sissies and "dilly-en-tants." But he loved his "boy". When Abel came to hunt with him, Ben catered to his preferences.

When Evan finished ransacking the grocery boxes, he repacked and secured everything as it had been, minus a few items. He went back to his camp spot laden with steaks, canned potatoes, a can of green beans, a loaf of bread, salt and pepper, coffee, and the bottle of single malt.

The moon was bright in the east when Evan finished eating supper and washing the dishes. His fire was burning low. He offered the horses water and then clipped them to a picket line. He didn't want them stepping on him while he slept. The way Evan saw it; his biggest problem would be a mountain lion or bear smelling the blood and coming to investigate Pike. Crawling halfway into his sleeping bag, he leaned against the trunk of a massive pine to reminisce.

Evan wasn't working for the sheriff's department the first time he made Pike's acquaintance. He was just out of the army and recently returned home. To have some fun, he'd entered a local rodeo. He'd won a belt buckle and a hundred dollars roping steers. It was late when he was leaving the fairgrounds. On the way to his truck, he came across a big man pulling a seemingly unwilling woman by the arm towards an old pick-up parked near the back of the mostly deserted parking lot.

"You're goin' with me!" the man roared.

"Leave me alone, please!" the woman wailed.

Evan sized up the guy with one quick look. He looked to be six-five, maybe six-six, and probably weighed at least two sixty. *He's got four inches and fifty pounds on me, but he's obviously drunk. No problem!*

"Hey, buddy!" he yelled at the big guy. "Maybe you should listen to the lady."

The man stopped to regard Evan briefly. "Buzz off, punk!" Waving his free hand at Evan as if he were a pesky fly on a hot day, he continued pulling the woman towards the truck.

Evan was twenty-five years old, hard as a rock, tough as a rawhide saddle tree, and after the guy's comment, ready to roll. Dropping the saddle perched on his shoulder; he strode purposefully towards the couple.

As he approached, the big guy stopped to regard Evan. "What's a matter, Dipshit? You got ear trouble?"

Adrenaline was surging through Evan at a dangerous level. "Let the lady go, Dickhead!" His voice was clipped and quick.

Shoving the woman aside, the big man snarled, "She ain't no lady." He hesitated, but only momentarily as it dawned on him this kid didn't seem to be afraid of him. Usually his sheer size tended to deter most encounters before they became physical. *What the hell? This punk must be real stupid. I'll give him a lesson.* With a quickness that belied his size, Pike came at Evan swinging his fat fists.

Evan brought up his left hand to block the first punch. The blow hurt his hand, instantly infuriating him. He threw a quick feint with his right fist. When Pike reacted to it, Evan kicked hard and quick to the big man's left leg.

Pike was suddenly confused. Why was he falling? He hit the ground screaming in pain. Evan's kick had dislocated Pike's left kneecap. He writhed in agony, looking for a position that would ease his pain. After what seemed an eternity, he squirmed onto his left side with his left leg drawn slightly up towards his chest and his right leg extended straight out. Cold sweat stood out on his forehead. He was hyperventilating. "I'll kill you for this, you little sonofabitch." Gasping like he was, it was an empty threat.

"I doubt it, big boy, but if you say that again, I might have to hurt you some more just so I'm sure you can't."

"Leave me alone! Get the hell away from me. Oh damn. Call an ambulance." In between demands, he moaned.

"What should I do first?" Evan asked.

Suddenly Evan was slammed from behind. He stumbled forward for a few steps before he could react to this new attack. Recovering quickly, he spun around in a low crouched position to confront none other than the woman he had been trying to rescue.

"You bastard!" She was screaming. "You hurt him!" Lurching drunkenly towards Evan, she swung her fists, attempting to hit him.

Evan grabbed her by both wrists, spun her around, and sat her down hard on the ground next to the big guy who was still blubbering. This gave him a good look at her face. She was probably only in her mid-thirties, but looked much older. Her hair had been bleached to the point it appeared brittle. Her eyes were dark, sunken, and what probably could be a very pretty face, was haggard and drawn. Had he been describing her to his mother, he would have said she looked tough. Had he been talking to his buddies, he would have said she looked like she had been rode hard and put away wet—more than once.

"He was right," Evan had told her. "You 'ain't no lady'. You call him an ambulance."

Evan tugged the sleeping bag up a bit higher. His rifle was lying across his lap, the scotch bottle in his right hand. He remembered Buster's comment about grizzly bears. There was a positive sighting near Pagosa Springs last summer and rumors of one in this area. He hoped there were still some grizzly bears in the territory. The animals in these mountains should be at least as dangerous as some of the wild, life forms in New York's Central Park.

Contemplating eternity, he stared at the stars, sipping whisky. It was not quite nine o'clock when he corked the bottle and fell asleep.

3

Just before sunrise, Evan's eyes snapped open. He awoke with a jolt. Diablo had whinnied. Both horses were standing ten feet in front of him looking across the meadow towards the trees. Evan quickly squirmed out of his sleeping bag. Grabbing his rifle, he slipped behind the tree to his back. It was barely light enough for him to see a horse and rider moving slowly towards him from the far side of the meadow.

I can't believe I slept so soundly. Good thing my horse was awake. He felt foolish.

Half way across the meadow the rider stopped. "Don't shoot me, Evan," a voice called out. "My bride expects me home early today."

Evan laughed. "Come on in, Buster. I've been waiting for you."

When Buster was close enough for normal conversation, he said, "You weren't waiting for me. Your horse had to wake you up."

"Yeah, well, since I have a smart horse, I can get a little extra sleep." Evan quickly pulled on his pants and boots.

Buster dismounted and began loosening the cinch strap on his saddle. "That may be, but your horse won't be of any help protecting you from the Dragon Lady."

Evan regarded Buster. A better friend or partner would be hard to imagine. He would go anywhere and do anything Buster wanted, and Buster would do the same for him, but sometimes he said things that appeared to make absolutely no sense whatsoever. Evan suspected he did it just to provoke a response, and sometimes it was irritating. This was one of those times.

"Okay, partner, I'll play your silly-ass game. Who, on God's green earth, is the 'Dragon Lady'"?

"She's the new head of the state crime lab, and she'll be here in about an hour and a half." Buster was grinning, "She told me to say hello to you, specifically." He finished pulling off Tick's saddle, setting it on the ground next to Evan's, cantle up.

Evan thought hard. "I don't know anyone at the state crime lab, let alone the head Dragon Lady."

"Think again, she knows you."

"Damn it, Buster! Why do you do this to me?"

"Do what? Make you think."

"No, provoke me with stupid questions and esoteric nonsense. You better be nice to me or I'll teach Tick to hop around in tight little circles every time you try to get on his back."

Although Buster believed Evan could train a horse to do most anything, he wasn't worried. "You wouldn't do that to me. You need me too much. Who else would ride up here to your rescue?"

"My rescue? What are you talking about rescue? I have the situation in complete control. Pike is still dead, and nothing, or no one has molested the crime scene."

Buster was still grinning. "Okay, how's this? Do you know a Doctor Nicoletti?"

"What does she look like?"

"I have no idea, but she sounded pleasant enough over the phone."

"Wait a minute, let me think. I once met a very pretty woman by the name of Cheree Nicoletti, but she didn't work for the state, and she sure was no dragon lady by any stretch of the imagination."

"Could it be the same person? When did you last see her?"

"I don't know, six, no, seven years ago. She was in her last year of med school and her husband was a cop. I think she said he was a lieutenant with the DPD. It was coming up on their first wedding anniversary and she wanted to buy him a nice riding horse, but she didn't have a clue about what to look for. She said her father-in-law told her if she wanted to get him a good horse she should look up Bertram Coleman from Alamosa. She tracked down my dad, and he told her to come to me."

"And you sold her a horse?"

"Yes, I did. A very nice buckskin gelding."

"Well, that woman is now the head of the state crime lab, and she is supposed to be a difficult lady, although my source phrased it differently."

"I doubt it. Your source got it wrong. The Cheree I met was very sweet, not to mention beautiful. I can still remember being big-time jealous of her husband."

Buster considered this for a minute. "My source could be somewhat prejudiced. He's been there for about thirty years. Maybe he thinks he should have her job."

"Did you talk to him before or after you talked to her?"

"After."

"How'd she sound to you?"

"Very polite. I explained everything you told me. Her only question was how we had secured the area. I told her it was under constant surveillance by the best man available."

"Did she buy that?"

"Yes, she did, and when I told her your name, she asked if you were the same Evan Coleman who trained horses. I told her you were that Evan Coleman."

"I'll bet she was impressed."

"I don't know about impressed, but she did tell me to say hello for her, and that she would see you in the morning."

"When did you talk to your friend about her?"

"I called him last night from home," Buster replied.

"Why?"

"Why? I was curious about her, that's why. If you recall, the last time we were involved with the state crime lab things got a little confusing. I wanted to find out what my friend thought of Doctor Nicoletti."

Buster was referring to an apparent suicide they had investigated several years back. The sheriff, their boss, had insisted on being closely involved. "The way I remember that affair, it was the sheriff's fault for compromising the evidence."

"True, but if you recall the details, it was you and me the state wanted to blame."

"Only until we set them straight. I doubt if we have anything to worry about from the Cheree Nicoletti I knew."

"I hope you're right."

"You had a busy afternoon. How did Pike's widow take the news?"

"That was hard. I didn't tell her everything. She wanted to come up here with me, but I convinced her it would be best if she waited until the investigation was over. I was surprised when she agreed."

"Yeah, considering her mood when I was there yesterday afternoon, that is a surprise, but you are a smooth talker."

"Flattery will get you breakfast. You hungry?"

"I am. How about elk tenderloin?"

Buster lit up. "You have elk?"

"I don't, but Pike does, or rather he did. We can't let it go to waste."

"I have eggs."

"You packed eggs up here?"

"Of course! I told you I was going to fix breakfast for you. I brought bacon too, but if you have elk, we won't want the bacon."

"Well this is your lucky day. You get a fire started. I'll go relieve Pike's cooler of some more backstraps. We'll have steak and eggs for breakfast."

As Evan started walking towards the spring, he remembered why they were here. "Hey, Buster, you want to check out the scene?"

"Let's eat first," he replied, "I can almost always find a dead man somewhere to look at if I want. I very seldom have elk steak for breakfast. I'll wait until Dragon Lady gets here."

"Good choice," Evan called back over his shoulder.

An hour later they had eaten, cleaned up the mess, and were finishing the last of the coffee when they heard the methodic thumping of an approaching helicopter.

"Right on time," announced Buster after consulting his watch. "Your friend, the doctor, said they would be here by seven-thirty."

"I suppose we had better walk out into the meadow to signal them."

"Yeah, I've got an orange flag in my bag."

After Buster retrieved the signal flag, they walked to the approximate center of the meadow. The chopper made a pass over them at about three hundred feet while Buster waved the flag. It turned to come directly in. Buster and Evan hurried out of the way as it settled onto the grass. The pilot turned off the switch, and the blades quickly spooled down.

"Well, partner, let's go meet the Dragon Lady."

Before they were halfway to the aircraft, the door opened. A tall, dark haired woman wearing a short leather jacket, blue jeans, and cowboy boots emerged. Another woman and three men, all casually dressed, followed her out.

"As I recall, she'd be the tall one. She doesn't look very threatening from here," Evan commented quietly.

Buster whistled softly. "She certainly is nice and tall—and nice."

The brunette advanced to meet them while the other four individuals busied themselves donning white coveralls and removing their gear from the aircraft. The closer they came to each other, the better the woman looked to Evan. He subconsciously quickened his pace. Three feet apart, they stopped. Evan and Buster were staring. She was even better looking than Evan had remembered.

"Cheree Nicoletti," the woman said, extending her hand. "Good to see you again, Evan." Her brown eyes sparkled at him.

"My pleasure." Evan took her hand firmly. "Does your husband still have that buckskin gelding I sold you about seven years ago?"

The sparkle faded abruptly. "Yes, I still have him. He's been a wonderful horse."

Something is obviously wrong. She said "I", not "he". Time to change the subject. "Cheree," Evan said, directing her hand towards Buster, "this is Buster Alexander, the deputy who contacted you yesterday." Her hand was warm, and her grip was firm. Evan hated to let go.

"Hello, Buster. You must be an early riser. I thought I'd be up here before you this morning."

"Pleased to meet you." He nodded towards Evan. "I couldn't allow Evan to handle this all on his own."

"I see." She looked at Evan, smiled, and turned back to Buster. "He looks capable to me."

Evan thought it was a smile he could get lost in if he weren't careful. Buster thought he might be witnessing the start of something. Evan felt his face warming as he tried not to blush. Suddenly realizing he was staring, he directed the attention away from himself. He nodded in the direction of the deceased man's camp, "Are you ready to look at the scene?"

"Yes, I am. Let's walk back to the helicopter first. I'll introduce you to my team. I brought you my best. Buster told me this case would be difficult so I've got all my seasoned veterans. They have over sixty years experience among them."

After Cheree made introductions, Evan led the parade to the camp. "I found him yesterday afternoon at approximately three-thirty," he told Cheree as they walked back to Pike's tent. "My best guess is he was killed four to six hours before I arrived. His wife called me at noon to report him missing, and it took me until three-thirty to get up here. I'm thinking he was already dead when she called."

"When Buster talked to me yesterday, he mentioned you told him you may have seen someone leave the area. Tell me everything you remember about that"

Evan related the details of what happened after his arrival on the scene and finished by saying, "I made a mistake. I should have done things differently. I should have investigated that movement immediately instead of going to the tent first."

Cheree shrugged. "Oh, I don't know, you were alone, and you weren't expecting to discover a murder. I don't think anyone could fault the way you've handled things. I certainly couldn't criticize your methods."

"Well, thanks, but I think I should have paid more attention to whatever it was. I might have gotten a look at the perpetrator."

"Maybe, but you could have been attacked too."

"I doubt it. It seems to me, even though I didn't surprise him in the act, I arrived before he was ready to leave. I think getting away was his main concern."

"Maybe. Or maybe if you'd come too close, whoever it was might have attempted to avoid capture by any means possible." She briefly touched his shoulder. "Give yourself a break. You'll catch him." Her touch was nice and she was right. There was no way Evan could have predicted the scenario he discovered. They stopped at the yellow tape, thirty feet in front of the tent.

"Has anything here been moved or changed in any way?" she asked.

"I was in there for about ten minutes yesterday looking around, but I didn't touch anything. The only thing I did was to tie the door flaps shut when I came out."

"I'd like you to place the door in the same position it was when you first arrived." Evan nodded and Cheree signaled to one of the men, "John, we need pictures."

While Evan untied and rearranged the door flaps, she pulled on a pair of white coveralls. Satisfied with the way the door looked, Evan stepped back. "That's the way it was when I got here."

The man carrying the cameras, a pro HD camcorder and a 35mm SLR, thoroughly video-taped the tent and surrounding area. When he finished with the camcorder, he used the 35mm to photograph the scene from every conceivable angle.

While he was working, Cheree asked Evan, "What are we going to see inside?" She pulled a small tape recorder out of a jacket pocket. "I'm recording your statement, okay?"

"Sure," and Evan described the tent's interior and Pike's condition.

When he finished, Cheree moved to the door. "I'm going in first, with John. After I've looked around, I'll be back, and the rest of the team will get started searching the interior." She nodded to the cameraman. "Let's go"

While she was inside, the other two men and the woman divided up the area immediately around the tent, and began searching. Initially, Evan couldn't tell if they had a method or it was just a way for them to look useful. However, after watching them, he decided they knew what they were doing, and were probably quite efficient at it. Evan and Buster stood around feeling rustic, somewhat useless in the presence of their big city cousins.

Ten minutes later, Cheree and the cameraman emerged from the tent. Pulling off a bloodied pair of latex gloves, she told the three other team members, "It's all yours. Come and get me when you're ready to move the body."

Evan and Buster watched Cheree remove her bloodied gloves, knotting them together and shoving them into a pocket of her coveralls. "Well, ma'am, what do you think?" Buster asked.

She took a long, deep breath and slowly exhaled. "My first estimate as to time of death would be about noon yesterday. That could change when he's posted, and I believe he bled to death, not only from his obvious wound, but the femoral artery on his right leg was severed."

"I missed that," Evan admitted.

"Lots of blood, I didn't see it right away either. There's a small incision about an inch deep in his right groin, made with a very sharp instrument, probably a scalpel. It certainly wasn't made with an ordinary knife. The edges are far too clean. The femoral vein was also severed. The vein and artery are side by side at that point. Pike is a big man, but not obese. Both vessels are only about a half an inch below the skin. The killer knows some anatomy, at least of that area of the body. I can't be certain if the incision was made before or after his penis was severed."

Evan and Buster winced in unison. "Why do you suppose the killer would do that?" Buster asked.

She shrugged her shoulders. "Your guess is as good as mine. You're not asking me to rationally explain the irrational mind are you?"

"Oh no, ma'am, but you have to understand, we don't see things like this very often. Actually we never see things like this. This is the sort of crime that happens in the big city."

"I have to disagree. This sort of thing doesn't happen in the big city on a regular basis. Frankly, this is the most bizarre murder setting I've ever seen. You tell me, Buster, what's your take on the situation?"

"No disrespect, Doctor, but I don't think the person who did this is necessarily irrational. I think whoever did it, held a grudge against Pike. I believe the brand on Pike's forehead is the key."

"What do you think the brand means?"

"I don't know," Buster confessed, "but Evan thinks it stands for 'Rapist'."

She looked at Evan. "Hey," Evan held up his hands, "that's just a guess. I'm not positive, but considering everything else done to the victim, I believe it might make some sense."

"I could go with that. Did he have any history of sex crimes?"

"None we know of," Evan said, "but I think he was capable of most anything."

Buster agreed. "He's been accused of most everything else."

After much discussion and bandying about of theories, none of which led anywhere, Cheree finally changed the subject. "Tell me, Evan, about that horse you sold me, why does he want to buck when I first get on him?"

"It could be any number of things. He could be uncomfortable with some of the tack you're using, or maybe you're cueing him in a way that's confusing. And certainly not to insinuate you're heavy, but if you don't ride him often, he might just be protesting the weight." Evan was watching her eyes. *God, she's gorgeous*! "Or he might just be a little honky and needs a gentle reminder of who's boss. How long has he been acting up?"

"Ever since I started riding him. My husband used to ride him every day or almost every day, but he was killed three years ago. I haven't much wanted to ride until lately. Is there a chance I've ignored him too long?"

"I'm sorry about your husband," Evan said. "I had no idea."

"Yeah, it was a terrible shock." She paused briefly, looking away, across the meadow. "He left for the station, as usual, early in the morning. An hour later there was a state trooper at our door with the news. He was killed in a car accident just five miles from home. It's been a long two years."

"Losing a loved one is difficult," Buster told her. "I'm sorry for your loss."

"Thank you both," she said, and there was the customary awkward period of silence when no one knows what to say. Finally she continued, "I'd like to do more with the horse. Riding him makes me feel good."

"I'd be glad to tune him up for you," Evan offered. "All my horses come with a full warranty. I'm betting all he needs is to be reminded of what he already knows. I'm certain he's not permanently soured."

"Well, that's good news. How do I get this warranty service?" She was smiling again.

"Easy. You can bring him to me or I can come to the horse. It's up to you."

"That's great! Thanks, Evan. As soon as I get back and we get the evidence from this case under control, I'll make arrangements for my free tune up."

One of her techs approached. "Doctor Nicoletti, we're ready to bag the body."

"Okay, thanks. I'll be right there."

"Mind if I join you?" Buster asked. "I came up here this morning to see this, but I haven't been in there yet."

"Of course. You should see it. Maybe you'll find something we missed. The more trained eyes, the better. How about you, Evan, you want to see the scene again?"

"No thanks, I've seen enough of Pike to last a lifetime."

"Okay, I can understand that." She and Buster left him standing in the morning sun.

When Buster returned ten minutes later, he was quiet. "Well?" Evan finally had to ask. "What do you think?"

"The human experience should not be so difficult."

"What does that mean?"

"He died ugly."

"Hell, Buster, he lived ugly! What could he expect?"

"I know that. At the worst he was evil; at best, he was a mean spirited bully who apparently made at least one very dangerous enemy. And I'm not suggesting he didn't deserve his fate, but it's still an ugly demise."

"Yeah, I'd say so, and we have to find the man who did it."

"Or the woman."

"Yeah, I had that same fleeting thought yesterday, Buster, but this was done by a man."

"How can you be sure?"

"Give me a believable scenario with a woman as the perpetrator."

Buster was still thinking about the challenge when Doctor Nicoletti returned to them. "Well, Deputies, is there anything else you can show me here?"

Evan waved towards where the horses were grazing. "I can show you his pack horse and his supply of groceries over there by the spring."

"Did you go through any of it?"

"Yeah, I went through all of it. I even ate some of it for supper last night."

"Really?" She seemed genuinely surprised. "You may have eaten a vital piece of evidence."

Evan was silent. She couldn't be serious? Or could she?

After what seemed to Evan to be a long time, she finally smiled. "I'm joking." She'd had him. "Come on, show me the stuff."

Walking off quickly, he made a mental note. *I owe you one.*

When they got to Pike's cache, next to the spring against the cliff, Cheree said, "What a beautiful place." She looked back across the meadow. "It would be fun to ride up here and camp out some time."

"Yeah, I feel the same way. Even under the circumstances, it was peaceful. I slept like a log."

"Obviously you don't believe in ghosts."

"Strange you should mention that. Buster asked me about Pike's ghost too."

"What did you tell him?"

Before Evan could answer, Buster broke in, "Oh, this guy is very brave. He told me he once fought Pike while he was alive and beat him. He wasn't worried about him leaving his tent last night."

She laughed. "If you two can have this much fun investigating a murder, I'd like to see how you operate on a less serious crime."

"Oh, we can be serious," Buster assured her. "I'm sure before this one is over, we'll have had our fill of seriousness. Not to mention the late Mister Pike."

"Apparently he was rather notorious. What else can you tell me about him?"

For the next fifteen minutes, Evan and Buster told her Pike stories. She watched them closely, moving her eyes from one to the other. She was a trained listener. They could have gone on easily for another thirty minutes if one of the crime lab crew hadn't come to announce they were finished.

"What now?" Buster asked.

"Now we go back to the lab."

"What about the scene?" Evan asked. "Anything special we need to do?"

"Leave the tape up, go home. We've photographed and videotaped it in great detail. Now we have to go through everything we've collected. With some luck we'll find a place to start. If not, we might have to come back in a day or two, but I have a feeling if we didn't get it today, we probably won't find anything else later. Outdoor crime scenes like this deteriorate rapidly. But there is one thing I'd like you to do for me if you could."

"Name it," Buster told her.

"You told me Pike killed an elk yesterday, and you estimated it was probably early in the morning."

"That's correct. My guess would be he shot it some time around sunrise," Evan said. "His wife told me he came up the day before yesterday to haul in supplies for him and his son. If he just blundered into one when he first got up here, he could've shot it late that afternoon, but I doubt it. I suspect he got up early yesterday morning and popped one."

"Okay, makes sense. I'm reasonably certain everything done to him was done once he was in the tent. He's a big man. It would have been difficult for anyone to get him inside without his cooperation, but it's not impossible. I don't know how long it would have taken him to field dress the elk, but there could be a chance he was first assaulted when he was busy with the kill. If that's the case, there may be something helpful at that site."

"If we can find the site, what do you want us to do?"

"Don't disturb it. Just call me, and we'll come back out." When neither of them commented, she added, "It's not that I don't think you're capable, but I believe we're dealing with a very careful, very smart perpetrator. He may have even wanted to know Pike was found, but obviously didn't want to be caught. I think any clues will be extremely subtle."

"What about the body? What do we tell his wife?"

"As soon as we get airborne, I'll call to tell her. We're taking the body to Denver. If she wants to see him, and I suspect she will, I'll make certain she has transportation. Once she's seen him, we'll start the autopsy. When we're finished she can decide on funeral arrangements. We'll deliver the body wherever she wants. I'll also insist she leave this camp as it is for a week. After that she can do whatever she wants with what's left up here." She looked back at Pike's tent. "Frankly, I don't think we're going to get any more from here than we already have."

"Did you find anything of consequence in the tent?" Evan asked.

"We have fibers and hair, probably the victim's. The prints we lifted all appear to be the same, probably the victim's too. The killer most likely wore leather gloves. I think he may have drugged Pike. There's a small puncture wound the size of a twenty-two gauge needle in the back of his upper right arm. There's also a small hematoma on the back of his head, just at the base of his skull. He could have been sapped before he was drugged. I just don't know yet. We vacuumed most of the floor, and we'll go through that back at the lab." She regarded the two deputies. "Not much to go on is it?"

"Drugs could explain how Pike was tied up without a struggle," Evan said. "But not how he came to be on the cot."

"How about a woman?" Buster asked. "Could one or more women have done this?"

"Interesting speculation. Let's hope the fibers and hairs will give some answers."

"We'll be waiting to hear. In the meantime, Buster and I'll start by talking to Ruth Pike. She might have some ideas about who could have done this."

Doctor Nicoletti nodded. "Gentlemen, thank you both very much. Buster," she said extending her hand, "it was good to meet you. And, Evan, it's good to meet you again, circumstances aside. I'll be taking you up on your warranty offer for my horse. Call me if you come up with anything else." She shook his hand and then gave each of them her business card. "I'll be in touch as soon as we get a handle on the material we collected."

She turned and left them. Watching her from behind as she walked across the meadow to the chopper, the two deputies had to admit she was a fine sight. Her crew had everything packed in the aircraft including Pike, and a minute later the blades were churning. As the helicopter lifted, Evan waved, felt stupid about it, and stopped. He looked at her business card. She had added her home phone number.

"Dragon Lady?" Evan grinned as the chopper clattered away.

"My source is obviously confused."

"Confused? How about stupid? Let's hope he's a better forensic expert than he is a judge of character."

Buster pulled off his Stetson and ran his hand through his wavy white hair. "Well, it's after eleven, what do we do first?"

"What do you mean?"

"It's been almost five hours since breakfast. Do we do what the lady requested or do we have lunch first?"

"I suppose we could grill that other backstrap while we looked around. I have a feeling Pike killed that elk close by."

"I'll make a fire."

Before noon, Buster had the tenderloin spitted on a stick, suspended over a bed of embers. In the meantime, Evan had saddled both horses and was impatiently waiting for Buster.

"Which way?" Buster asked.

"I thought you'd never ask. Follow me." Evan turned his horse into the trees to the west from where he had camped. As they picked their way through the timber, Evan kept a close eye on his compass. He wanted to travel due west for approximately a half mile, before turning to the south. He had a hunch he wasn't sharing with Buster. Yesterday afternoon, just before his arrival at Pike's camp, he spotted two eagles circling to the southwest. After discovering Pike had killed an elk, he wondered if the birds had located the spot where he field dressed the animal. At a normal walk, a horse traveled three to four miles per hour. After ten minutes, Evan reined Diablo to a halt. They should have traveled about a half-mile.

"Do you have any idea where you're going?" Buster looked doubtful.

"Yes, I do, I'm taking you to the place where Pike shot that elk."

"Would you mind telling me how you know this?"

"Yes, I would mind. Do you doubt my abilities?" He was enjoying himself.

"Well, not exactly. I don't doubt your abilities in general, but I am wondering, in specific, what in hell makes you think you know where you're going."

"Give me five more minutes. If I haven't found it, I'll go anywhere you want to go."

"I have no idea where to look. I just want to know why you think you do.

Evan turned to the south. "I'm a genius, Buster," he called back over his shoulder, "a damn genius."

"Yeah, right," Buster scoffed, but he followed. Five minutes later the trees gave way to a small alpine meadow, not as big or as pretty as the one where Pike had made his camp, but secluded and carpeted with thick grasses. At the opposite end of the meadow an eagle perched at the top of a tall, standing dead, pine tree. Evan pulled out his binoculars to glass the area.

"Look on the ground just to the left of the dead pine with the eagle parked in it." Evan handed his partner the glasses.

Buster looked and saw what Evan had seen, the remains of an elk. No doubt the one shot by Pike. "Okay. Well, I guess you are a genius. How'd you know?"

"It's like you just said, Buster, I'm a genius. The problem is, now what do we do? Do we check out the area or do we leave it for Doctor Nicoletti and her team of trained professionals?"

"She told us to leave it alone and call her."

"Buster where's your spirit of adventure? What if we were to nose around a little and come up with the clue that solves the case?"

"There aren't any clues here. Pike was ambushed at his camp, not here."

"How can you be so certain?"

"You ain't the only damn genius. Who boned out the tenderloins and hind quarters, and put them in the cooler by the spring? The perpetrator?"

Evan considered this. "Good point. Although, he might have made more than one trip before he got whacked."

"Immaterial, he wasn't ambushed here, and one more thing is certain. If we shag ourselves back to your campfire right now, that tenderloin will be medium rare when we get there."

"Okay, but let's get a fix on this place so we can find it again." As soon as the GPS receiver stabilized, they recorded latitude and longitude before riding back.

"You know, Evan," Buster was spearing the last piece of meat with the small blade on his pocketknife, "that Doctor Nicoletti is one fine looking young lady. Smart too, it would seem."

"Buster, your powers of observation are truly amazing."

"Now don't be a wise ass, I am thinking of your best interests here. You're single. She's single. She is obviously interested in you. I think you should pursue the possibility."

"Which possibility is that?"

"The possibility of you and the lady getting together, of course."

"Yeah, right. I'm a two-bit, county deputy sheriff and she's a Ph.D. with a big state job. What would she want with me?"

"Yeah, you're right. Forget it."

"Oh come on, Buster, you're not playing fair—again. You're supposed to pump me up, tell me what a wonderful hunk of masculine pulchritude I am. Flatter me with all sorts of accolades, and chide me gently for not believing in myself."

Buster smiled, leaning back against a tree. "Got any cigars? We really should have a cigar and a little taste out of that scotch bottle you poached. You realize it's Saturday and it's after noon."

Evan shook his head. "No, I don't have any cigars. I got the scotch; it was your job to bring the smokes."

Buster pointed towards his saddle. "You're younger than I am, look in that saddle bag, the one nearest to you."

Evan did as he was told. Two minutes later they were propped against adjacent pine trees, smoking heaters and sipping whiskey. Thick, rich, yellow sunshine flooded down on them as the temperature wiggled up towards sixty degrees. A gentle breeze, like the loving hand of God, occasionally ruffled the golden leaves on the aspen trees across the meadow.

"Tell me something, Buster. Is this not pleasant?"

"Yes it is. It's generally pleasant to enjoy a good cigar, good whiskey, and the company of a good friend."

"Okay. I'm single and you're married."

Buster nodded.

"Even though you have a beautiful wife with a generous spirit who loves you dearly, you're sitting up here with me."

"What's your point?"

"My point is obvious. I can do this whenever I want. Why would I want to have a permanent relationship with a woman, even a beautiful woman like Cheree Nicoletti?"

"Just as I suspected. You have no point."

"Yes I do! I'm free. You're not! You should be at home or at least headed home. It's your day off, but you find goofing off with me better than being at home with your wife. And by the way, I don't understand what she sees in you anyway."

Buster slowly shook his head. He took a long pull off his cigar. "You're very confused. First of all, we are not goofing off; we're investigating a murder. Secondly, I love my wife dearly. If I had to choose between you and her, you'd come in a miserable third. Lastly, I find many things pleasurable, but that doesn't mean I can or want to do all of them all the time. I can't make love to my wife day and night. Even if I were your age I couldn't. I don't want to smoke a cigar or drink whiskey every day, all day, and I sure don't want to baby sit your sorry ass every day either." He took a drink from the bottle and passed it to Evan. "Although, right now, I find even your company somewhat pleasant."

"Well, I guess you told me. So you think I should contact Doctor Nicoletti?"

"I know you're a shy guy, but you don't have a choice. She ordered you to call her when you discovered the place where Pike killed the elk."

"Ordered is a strong word."

Buster shrugged his shoulders. "She appears to be a strong woman."

Evan tamped the cork back into the scotch bottle. Pushing himself away from the tree, he stood. "Okay, you convinced me. I'll pursue her."

"Good thinking." Buster extended his hand. "Now help an old man up."

4

They came down the mountain single file, Buster leading the way on Tick, followed by Evan riding Diablo, trailing Pike's pack horse behind. They were quiet, occupied with separate thoughts. Buster was contemplating the murder and what the sheriff would have him doing Monday morning. He didn't much like his boss. None of the deputies did. He was a hard man to like, primarily because he was impossible to respect. He was impossible to respect because he consistently failed to support his men. Any controversy or problem within the department was quickly blamed on the ineptitude of one or more of the deputies. The sheriff refused to accept any responsibility for anything, unless there was glory to grab or credit to steal. Because of his treacherous behavior, some of the deputies spent as much time covering their backsides as they devoted to aiding the county's citizens and upholding the law. Buster, however, was not the political type. He did what his instincts told him were right, and damn the sheriff. So far he had not lost a single round. It wouldn't surprise him if somehow the sheriff were to grossly mishandle this case and get his hinder in a sling over it. But if that were to happen, he'd need to find an innocent party to blame. Buster decided he could not allow that innocent party to be him or Evan. The sheriff was predictable. Buster considered options.

Evan, on the other hand, was not thinking at all about the sheriff or Pike's murder. His thoughts were exclusively on Cheree Nicoletti. Until she appeared on the mountain at the scene of the crime he had forgotten she existed. He'd met her by chance and sold her a horse. After that, he'd never heard from her again. She was beautiful, but she was married, obviously in love with her husband. Even though Evan had recognized her as his ideal woman, at least physically, he never considered her to be anyone other than a buyer of one of his horses. But that was then. Now he didn't know what to think about her except she was still his ideal woman. Tall and leggy, with that long dark hair framing her face, tumbling recklessly down around her shoulders, she had practically made him weak. When he talked to her, he had to concentrate to keep from staring into her wide dark eyes. She was sleek like a mountain lion, and moved with a fluid grace he could only describe as feline.

There is absolutely nothing wrong with her, he thought. From the tip of her straight nose, to her well-defined breasts and all the way down her legs she was perfect, and for some reason that made him nervous about his prospects. Maybe she had really ugly feet. That would help to give him something to make her less goddess-like so he might have a chance. However, he doubted the part about her feet. They were probably perfectly formed too, with long, shapely toes.

It wasn't merely her physical attributes, either. She was obviously brilliant, capable and charming. She had a tough, demanding job that by all appearances she handled with ease. *And Buster thinks I should make a play for her.* He shook his head. *How on God's green earth could I stand a chance? She must have doctors and lawyers and all types of big shots pursuing her. I don't have squat. I'm a two-bit deputy from a backwater county whose ultimate aspiration is to be a successful horse trainer.*

Actually, Evan had a great deal of confidence. On the physical side he was tall, dark, and handsome. Handling horses kept him tough and fit. He was an inch over six feet tall and weighed two hundred pounds. His hair was thick, brown, and wavy. His nose was straight and his jaw was square. Attracting women had never been a problem for him. Most women noticed him right off. And once they noticed him, it was his eyes that held their attention. Whether they saw them as pale blue or gray, they all saw something in them they liked. Women of all ages tended to stare at him wistfully.

But now that he was older and wiser, Evan had learned discrimination. He was after one quality woman, not a quantity of inferior women. Right or wrong, his experiences had convinced him most beautiful women were high maintenance, neurotic, or a combination of both. Regardless, the net effect was the same; he couldn't afford them, mentally or financially. He strongly suspected handsome men had similar problems although he considered himself to be extremely well adjusted. He was level headed, slow to anger, fairly intelligent and so far, able to cope with everything that came his way. He wanted a woman who was the same. A flighty woman with an overblown ego, no matter how physically desirable was no longer an option. He knew from experience there were worse things than being alone.

When the deputies came to the border of the BLM land and Pike's property, where the trail turned to the right and cozied up to the creek that spilled out of the hills, Buster slowed to allow Evan to ride alongside.

"I've been thinking," he announced.

"So have I. You first," Evan replied.

"Sheriff Tate will probably have all of us back on the mountain Monday morning searching for clues. He's going to want us to solve this as soon as possible. It won't look good to have a deranged, mutilating killer running loose in his county."

That was obvious, but Evan knew Buster was leading up to something. "And?" he asked.

"Well, it would appear to me, the more we do before Tate gets back Monday morning, the less he'll be able to interfere.

"It's already Saturday afternoon. Other than interview Ruth Pike, what can we do?"

A sly smile settled onto Buster's face. "Well, if you were to convince your friend at the crime lab to give us an 'official opinion' of how to proceed, we might be able to keep the sheriff from running us all over the county chasing our tails."

"Buster, what in hell might an 'official opinion' be? And why would we want the state telling us how to do our job?"

Buster held up his hand. "Easy, Big Fella. Don't get nervous. We don't want the state to tell us how to do anything. Obviously, you and I are going to solve this crime. What we want is the sheriff to think the state is telling us how to solve Pike's murder."

This clarified nothing for Evan. "I'm confused. You want the sheriff to think the state is telling us what to do, but you think you and I will solve the crime. Why would the sheriff accept the state's interference and furthermore, what makes you so sure we're going to determine who killed Pike? The more I talk to you, the less I understand you."

"Listen, the sheriff is a highly political animal. It'll be in his best interest to get this case solved as fast as possible. If someone at the state level were to suggest to him that he detail me and you to work closely with a state representative to resolve this case, I strongly suspect he'll cooperate. In fact, I'm sure he'll be more than happy to cooperate. We're looking at a situation here that could be very difficult. If the sheriff thinks the state is in charge of the investigation, he can always claim he had no control if things go badly. If on the other hand, we solve it quickly, he can claim the glory by saying, 'Because I decided to work closely with the state authorities, my deputies were able to bring this case to a speedy resolution' or some such BS. Understand?"

Buster was probably right. Sheriff Tate was a weasel. He never missed an opportunity to grab the credit or hand off the blame. Whenever you talked to him, it was as if you only had half his attention, the other half was somewhere else, scheming and plotting. Evan considered Buster's proposal. "So what you want me to do is involve Doctor Nicoletti in your little plan?"

"She's already involved. What I'm looking for is a bigger commitment. I want you to convince her to recommend to our boss that you and I work with her department to solve the murder."

"Aw, Buster, you know that's highly irregular. Her department has no authority to work with us other than to provide technical assistance."

"It would if Tate agreed to it. I'm betting he'd be only too happy to oblige."

"Aren't we being deceitful, Buster? I don't mind conning Tate, but I'm not about to be dishonest with Doctor Nicoletti."

Buster slowly shook his head. "Evan," he said in his most fatherly manner, "no one is asking you to be dishonest. In fact, I want you to be completely honest. Just tell Cheree exactly what I've told you, and simply ask her if she'll suggest to the sheriff he allow you and me to investigate the case with her direct assistance."

"It sounds too simple. What's the catch?"

"There is no catch. Look! You and I, but mostly you, have already involved the crime lab and Nicoletti. They would've become involved anyway because even the sheriff would have eventually realized he needed them. You did the smartest thing you could have done by getting them in here as soon as possible. All I'm trying to do now is to keep the sheriff's meddling fingers out of things. I believe we can solve this, but if we allow that moronic, two-bit politician to take control, it could become a disaster for the department. You want to spend the next two weeks on this mountain looking for clues that don't exist? We establish control right now; it'll be a lot easier to solve this thing."

Evan thought for a while. "Is there anything else, anything you're not telling me?"

"I don't know, there might be, but I haven't figured it out yet."

"Sometimes you scare me, Buster."

"Think nothing of it. Sometimes I scare myself, but this is not one of those times. You'll be the second person who knows if I develop an ulterior motive."

"You will tell me?"

"Of course, I just said I would!"

"No, not about your ulterior motive, but when you scare yourself?"

Buster laughed. "It doesn't happen often."

"I hope so. I'd like to keep my job."

"Don't worry your pretty little head. You'll not only keep it, you'll be a hero."

They were silent as they reflected on what they needed to do. Buster genuinely believed they could solve Pike's murder if the sheriff would stay out of it. Evan was not quite as certain, but he knew he'd be a lot happier if he could work directly with Cheree and keep the sheriff at bay. The sheriff was ambitious, inexperienced, and incompetent, a dangerous combination. He was just smart enough to play politics, but too stupid to be a big winner. Being a deputy under his command, you could get hurt bad enough that full recovery might not be possible. In the short time since his election, Tate had already forced one long time deputy into retirement and embarrassed another into resigning. Pike's murder could become a high profile case, surely if solving it took too long. Buster was right, the more they could control the situation, the better for everyone.

"You ever heard the history of this place?" Buster asked.

"What?" Evan was jolted from his thoughts.

Buster waved his hand at the real estate around them. "The Pike place. Do you know how it came to him?"

"No, I guess not. Somebody, maybe it was you, told me it's been in the family for years."

"That's right, over a hundred years. Ben Pike inherited it from his father, who in turn received it from his father." Buster paused while he considered the commitment. "I like that. It's good to have strong ties to the land. Whatever else is said about Ben Pike, he can't be faulted for not loving his land. He didn't chop it up into thirty-five acre ranchettes and sell them to a bunch of scissorbills from Denver."

"Yet another point for the recently departed—or maybe the only point. How did the property come to his grandfather?"

"Well now, there's a little known story behind that, the truth of which will probably never be determined."

"Buster, why is everything about Pike mysterious? And how do you know so much about it?"

"Right now, the only thing mysterious about Pike is his death and as soon as we find the perpetrator, that mystery will go away too. What I'm talking about concerns Ben Pike's great-grandfather. My great-grandmother told me this story, and she was born before Saguaro existed, as a town or a county. I'm not saying my great-grandmother was nosy, she merely tried to be well informed. According to her, Ben Pike's great-grandfather showed up in Saguaro County in the late eighteen hundreds, probably around eighteen eighty-five. By all accounts he was in his mid-twenties, big, strong, and handsome. There were some rumors he was on the lam from the authorities in Kansas City, but they were never substantiated. In fact, he seemed to be a model of industry and honesty. He went to work for a man named Emil Kupfer. Emil was a prosperous, hard working Dutchman. He settled this land to raise dairy cattle. His ambition was to make cheese, lots of it."

Evan regarded Buster somewhat critically. "Cheese? He was going to make cheese? There couldn't have been more than seven or eight hundred people in the whole county a hundred years ago. What was he going to do with the stuff?"

"You have to remember, cheese doesn't spoil as fast as butter or milk. If it's well packed and kept cool, it can last for weeks. Emil could harvest all the ice he needed during the winter to keep his cheese cool year around. He could ship it to Creede. Sell it to the silver miners. It took about five days to get there, but there was a road."

"Okay, Creede was booming in those days."

"Yeah, and the miners had pockets full of silver. Apparently Emil thought they might enjoy a slice of Gouda with their bread."

"Was he successful?"

"Emil was in his mid-forties, but had a young, pretty wife, and a young son about three or four. He put together a small dairy herd, and just started selling cheese when Pike's dashing great-grandfather came to work for him. All went well for about a year, until he was killed in a freak accident."

Evan was intrigued. "The plot thickens."

"Yes, it does. It seems Emil was driving a wagon when he somehow fell off, landed on his head, and was run over by the back wheels. By the time his wife and Pike's great-grandfather discovered the accident and got him to town, he was dead."

"Were the circumstances ever investigated?"

"According to my great-grandmother, the incident was considered an unfortunate happenstance. Emil was buried the next day and in a short time, largely forgotten."

"So much for the cheese baron of Saguaro County. I suppose Pike's great-grandfather took up with the lovely, young widow and everyone lived happily ever after?"

"Not exactly. The plot gets even thicker. After a brief period of mourning, Emil's widow did marry Ben Pike's great-granddad and he adopted the boy. Even had his last name changed from Kupfer to Pike. Everything was fine for about six months, when suddenly the new Missus Pike and her son disappeared. According to Pike, his wife had gone back to Omaha to care for her ailing mother, taking the boy with her. A year later, the boy returned without his mother. Pike explained his wife had contracted influenza and died."

Evan was puzzled. "So, all that seems plausible. How has the plot become thicker?"

"Again, according to my great-grandmother, the boy who returned was not the same boy who went away."

"That's absurd! I'm not buyin' it! How could Pike possibly have gotten away with that? You can't swap kids without someone realizing it. People would know!"

"People! What people? There were hardly any people around here a hundred years ago. This place is ten miles from town and town isn't much even today. There were only a handful of people within a ten-mile radius, and they didn't see each other very often. Kids grow fast! Their looks can change quickly. In a year or two who's going to know, especially if you've only seen the kid once or twice before?"

"If that's true, how did your great-grandmother know it wasn't the same kid?"

"She remembered the boy's eyes. She said Emil's son had the most beautiful blue eyes she had ever seen. The boy that came back had brown eyes."

"Oh come on, Buster, that's way too much of a stretch."

"You doubt my great-grandmother?"

"No, I don't doubt her, but I can't imagine the guy could get away with something like that. Besides, why bother? If his wife and son had gone back east and she died, why bother to bring back a substitute son? What's wrong with the adopted son?"

"Nothing except Emil had a will that left the property to his son. When Pike married the widow and adopted the boy, he figured he was closer to owning the land. But, the boy would no doubt outlive him and get ownership at the age of adulthood. It's my guess Pike worried his adopted son could legally kick him off the property when he turned twenty-one. Now, if the boy and his mother were both dead, he would no doubt get the property. But that's too obvious and would arouse suspicion, especially when people remembered the alleged accident that killed Emil. So Pike murders his wife and adopted son, fabricates a story about them going back east, and a year later, passes his own son off as the rightful heir to the property."

Evan wasn't hearing it. "No way! It's impossible! Where was this 'real' son all that time?"

"Who can say? Not even my great-grandma had any ideas. But about three months after the boy came back, a pretty woman showed up in town. It wasn't long before she took up with Pike. My great-grandmother believed the whole affair was orchestrated by Pike."

"How much time passed from when Pike first arrived in town until the new woman settled in with him?"

"I was told, almost two years."

Evan shook his head. "I still don't like it! Who's going to play a game like that for two years? If the second boy really was Pike's legitimate son, I'd have to assume the woman was his actual wife. I can't imagine her and the boy hanging around somewhere waiting for all this to happen."

Buster gave a shrug that happened to coincide with a snort from his horse. "I don't know, but I'll tell you, it was this story that first gave me the idea I wanted to be in law enforcement. Obviously, Great-grandma couldn't prove anything. All she had were her suspicions, but true or not, after I heard it, I decided I wanted to do something to prevent things like it from happening."

"How old were you fifty years ago, twelve?

"Just about to turn ten, but anyhow the land passed from Emil Kupfer to Ben's great grandfather and it's been in the family ever since."

Trying to comprehend the enormity of the scheme, Evan was silent. It was almost inconceivable to him. A man kills three people including his pretty new wife and adopted son, and lives a charade for two years just to get a piece of property. If it weren't such a foul deed, he could almost admire the determination and intensity of Ben Pike's great-grandfather.

Buster interrupted his thoughts. "It's probably the best chunk of land in the county. There's five hundred acres, the dirt is decent, and there's more than ten cubic feet per second of water rights."

"That's a fair amount." He did some quick mental math. "In fact, it's almost six and a half million gallons a day." A thought teased around the edges of his subconscious, somewhere down around his brain stem. *Is that much water worth enough for somebody to murder for, and if so, who's the somebody?*

"Very good," Buster complimented. "I see they still taught arithmetic when you went to school. Besides the creek, there are several springs and a big artesian well on the property, none of which Pike uses. He tried farming, but didn't like it much so he leases most of the land for grazing."

"Does the property own the first rights to all the water."

"Yup. All the way back to the day Old Man Kupfer got the original deed."

"How do you know so much about the place?"

"About thirty years ago a representative from the Colorado Springs Water Board was here. He tried to meet with Pike to negotiate a sale of some or all of the water and Pike ran him off."

"Good for Pike!"

"Yeah, but even though I agree in principle, it's still my job to uphold the law."

"What law allows the CSWB to make bad offers for water rights?"

"Who said it was a bad offer and not only that, there's no law that prevents them from making any offer, good or bad. According to the fellow from Colorado Springs, Pike assaulted him. He supposedly even fired a shot at his vehicle when he was leaving."

"Okay, there is a law against that. What did you do?"

"I went to have a little chat with Pike to get his side of the story. That's when he told me all about his water rights."

"Yeah, then what?"

"Nothing. The guy from Colorado Springs went home. He never pressed charges. Now, Pike's neighbor leases the land for his cows. He uses as much of the water as he needs to flood irrigate the pastures. What's left over goes into county ditch number forty-two."

"Did Pike really assault the guy?"

"According to him he didn't. He said he told him to go away and stay away or next time he wouldn't be so polite. He fired a shot into the ground for effect."

"For Pike that was polite. Did he ever say how much the CSWB offered him for the water?"

"No, and I never asked. Actually, I don't think they ever got to talking about money. He did tell me though, he had made a will and a prenuptial contract with his wife that dictated upon their deaths, the property would pass to their eldest son. He said, 'Dirt's no good without water. I can't leave my boy worthless land.' He also said his wife had made her will with the same stipulation."

"Thought he was smart didn't he?"

"Yeah, for a guy who abused the law every way he could, he seemed pleased with himself for using the law to pass on the property to his heir."

"What if all they had were girls?"

"I wondered about that too, so I looked up the records. Ben and Ruth were married two months after Abel was born. I'm not sure he'd have married her if the kid had been a girl."

As they rode the final few yards to the gate at the back of the pasture, Evan was thinking. "You know, Buster, I always thought Ben Pike was unprincipled, ill-tempered, bad-mannered, and stupid. Now I'm not so sure he was completely stupid."

"Yeah, I'm not sure he was stupid either, stupid acting for sure, but not totally stupid. He seemed to act on instinct, without thinking. That makes a person look stupid, unless of course, his instincts are infallible."

"Well he's dead now. Neither of us will ever know the real Pike. I wonder if his wife knew everything he was up to. She seemed naive and helpless yesterday."

Buster reined his horse to a stop. "She may know more than she'll want to tell us." Dismounting, he walked to the gate and opened it. After Evan went through, he walked his horse through, closed it and they rode to where their pickup trucks were parked.

Evan dismounted and led Pike's pack horse to the trailer. "Buster, if this horse will load, I'm going to haul her back to the barn rather than lead her. That way I won't have to make two trips. We can both drive back to talk to Mrs. Pike."

The little mare stepped into the trailer without hesitation, and when Evan parked next to the barn, she readily backed out. Evan led her to the paddock behind the barn where Pike's saddle horse was grazing. The two mares whinnied a greeting to one another. Evan turned her out with her stable mate. He remembered Ruth Pike's sudden confusion from the day before when he'd asked to see the horse. She had asked, "Which horse?" He decided now would be a good time to take a look around the barn.

In the shape of a capital L, the barn had a large main section with a shorter section branching to the right at the end. Evan could easily see there was no horse in the main section where he was. Dust rose up from his boots as he walked the length of the main building into the smaller section. It must have been the original barn. The only light came from gaps in the siding and two small windows at the far end. The sidewalls were low, probably not more than six feet high. The air was stale, smelling heavily of rotting hay and musty wood. Evan walked slowly down the center aisle past several box stalls and a large room with a sliding door that at one time must have been used for hay storage. At the end was another small room with a closed door. Evan twisted the dusty doorknob to push the door open. Ropey cobwebs sagged in long loops from the roof. The room contained dusty saddles and mildewed tack. There was no other horse. Evan walked back into the main barn towards the door through which he had entered. Just as he was leaving the barn, Buster met him.

He handed Evan a note written on a sheet of copy paper. "Looks like we'll have to come back."

"Dear, Deputy. Me and my son, Jason, have gone to Denver to see Ben. I don't know for sure when I'll be back. If you found Ben's pack horse, please put her in the pasture behind the barn with the other horse. Thanks for your help." It was signed, "Ruth Pike".

Evan read it twice before handing it back to Buster. "I was dreading it before. I really hate to come back tomorrow."

There is a point in every investigation when you have to get serious. Not that Pike's murder wasn't serious, but until now, Evan wasn't closely involved with the victim's people, the family and friends. When he'd talked to Ruth Pike briefly the day before, as far as they both knew, Ben was alive. Now they both knew he was dead. Their next conversation was going to be different. Judging from her behavior yesterday, she would be grief stricken and possibly in shock. He would have to be sensitive to her grief, but he needed to ask hard questions she could possibly resent. Even though he was good at it, it wasn't something he enjoyed. He had been anticipating it for the last half-hour, but now he'd have to wait. It would be worse tomorrow because he'd have all night to think about it.

Buster agreed, "Yeah, it would have been better to do it now. Let's hope she won't make us wait too much longer."

"Yeah. You ready to leave?"

"I am. You done poking around?"

"I guess. I was looking for another horse, but I don't see one."

"What about another horse?"

Evan explained how he thought Ruth was confused yesterday when he asked to see Ben's horse. "I had this feeling I caught her off guard. I thought it was an easy question, but she acted strange, like I'd asked her something tough."

"Maybe you're just too suspicious."

"Yeah, maybe I am, but knowing Ben Pike, Ruth may have had something to hide. But if there was another horse, it's not here now. I'm ready to go home. I want to take a long, hot shower, put on some clean clothes, and sit on my deck with three fingers of single malt. Maybe I'll even smoke a cigar while I watch the sun go down."

"And what else?"

"Oh, I don't know, I might go over to Gordo's later for a plate of soft tacos and a margarita."

"And then what else?"

"What, 'what else'? It's Saturday afternoon, soon to be Saturday night—nothing else."

"The 'what else' you are forgetting is to call Doctor Nicoletti and put our strategy in place."

"Oh yeah, right. You mean your strategy, don't you? Or did you conveniently forget this is all your big idea?"

"My strategy is our strategy unless of course you have a better one."

"Okay, okay, I'll do it. I'm not guaranteeing anything, but I'll try."

"If you ask, she'll oblige." Buster was grinning again.

Evan considered asking Buster why he was so certain, but he didn't think he'd get a straight answer, or at least one that would readily make sense, so he didn't ask. He was tired. He closed and latched the back door of the horse trailer on Diablo, got in his pickup and simply said, "Thanks for your help, Buster. Talk to you later."

Buster, still smiling, watched him drive away. "I know," he said to himself. "I know."

On the drive home, Evan tried to put the murder of Ben Pike out of his mind. He was successful because his thoughts quickly turned to Cheree.

Once home, he turned out Diablo and looked after the rest of his horses. They whinnied and nickered when they saw him, partly to greet him, partly in protest. They wanted their daily ration of oats. Buster didn't give it to them last night and they hadn't forgotten. He obliged them. An hour later when he went into the house, the phone was ringing. It was Cheree Nicoletti.

5

Evan took his time getting to the phone. He expected a telemarketer or worse yet, the office. He was in no hurry to answer it. After sleeping on the ground last night, he was tired, feeling gritty and ornery. The phone continued to ring until he finally lifted the receiver. "Yes." His voice conveyed irritation.

"Hello, Evan. This is Cheree." In contrast, her voice was warm, melodic, and inviting. "Did I get you at a bad time?" His tone had been unmistakable.

Evan quickly speed-shifted emotional gears. He was suddenly interested in talking on the telephone. "No, no, this is a great time. I just walked in and was going to call you." It wasn't a total lie. He did intend to call her, just not now. But he wanted to talk to her and he was glad she'd called.

"Good, I called earlier, twice actually. I was getting concerned you and Buster were having some difficulties."

"Oh no. We were just moving a little slower than usual is all. It was such a nice morning we took it easy and…"

"And so you were goofing off while I've been working hard, not to mention concerned about your welfare."

She was teasing him. He liked that. *This is one pleasant woman.* "Yeah, that just about sums it up. I'm flattered you were worried about me."

"Well, was my worry in vain or did you discover something else up there?"

"We found the place where Pike killed the elk if that's what you mean, but I doubt there'll be anything interesting left there."

There was a pause. "Why do you say that?"

"Scavengers. The eagles found the carcass yesterday. By the time we get back there, the scene will be somewhat compromised."

"Yeah, you're probably right, but now I'm looking for something very specific."

"Can you be less cryptic or don't I have a need to know?"

"I can be a lot less cryptic if you want to work tomorrow."

"Sure, why not. I'm six for six right now, might as well make it seven straight. What do you have in mind?"

"Okay, good! Here's what I know right now. First of all, it appears the victim was initially incapacitated by a powerful electric shock to the back of the neck, taser probably. Next, I believe he was injected with the anesthetic ketamine in the back of his right arm. We found substantial amounts of the drug in his blood, what little was left. He was tied to the cot and his femoral artery was severed. I determined the time of death was between nine and ten yesterday morning. I think he was branded on the forehead after he was dead."

"What about his other wound?" Evan asked tentatively.

"Oh yes, that. I don't know if his penis was removed before or after his artery was severed, but from the bleeding there, I'm certain he was alive when it was done."

Evan exhaled a long slow breath. "Ouch!"

"That's putting it mildly, however, if he was awake, he would have lost consciousness from the blood loss within minutes. Four minutes is about maximum with a severed femoral and no first aid."

"Thank God for small favors. Obviously his wife has already been there to ID him. She left us a note she had gone to Denver."

"This morning, right after we left you and Buster on the mountain, I talked to her. She told me she would get to the morgue as soon as she could. I was surprised when she arrived here at three-ten this afternoon."

"How'd that go?"

"She had her two sons with her and the younger brought his fiancée. Ruth was obviously distraught. She didn't break down and become hysterical, but she was badly shaken. I told her what little we knew at that time. They didn't stay long, twenty minutes total. She told me she would call me with the funeral arrangements. She said I should thank you for finding him."

"What about the two sons, how did they react?"

"The oldest one, Abel, had tears in his eyes, but didn't say anything. He looks like the strong, sullen type. He's even bigger than his father, handsome in a rugged way. He looks tough, although he was clean and neatly dressed. The younger son, Jason, was very curious and asked a lot of questions, but he seemed detached, as if he were inquiring about just a body, not his father. He's too handsome, almost pretty, looks a lot like his mother. He didn't seem to have a lot of emotion."

"What about the girlfriend?"

"Veronica Valdez. Very pretty, very feminine, very solicitous, almost cloying—at least that was my impression."

"Spanish?"

"She looks more Anglo than me."

"What color hair?"

"Blonde. The color seemed natural. There was no indication it was bleached, but I'd have to get a closer look to be certain. Regardless, I can't imagine her getting her hands dirty doing the type of work we're talking about."

"You don't believe everyone is capable of anything?"

There was a pause. "Possibly, but in her case, not probably. She appeared much too soft."

"We'll make some inquires on Miss Valdez. Notice any tension between the two brothers?"

"None that I could see. Why?"

Evan related the story Buster had told him about Pike's legal manipulations to guarantee his oldest son, Abel, inherited the property. He also told her, according to what Ruth had told him yesterday, only Abel was going hunting with him, not Jason. "I wondered if you could detect any hostility between the two. After all, the property now belongs to Abel, at least technically. In actuality, Ruth owns it until she dies. Abel can't throw her out."

"I didn't see any indication of sibling rivalry. In fact, the boys and their mother seemed as close as they could be under the circumstances. If Jason knows about the legal agreements, and they're bothering him, he certainly didn't show it. Maybe the wills were modified at some point to accommodate Jason."

"Could be, what about clues to the perpetrator? Find anything interesting?"

"We have a few things, mostly fibers and hair. We vacuumed the floor but haven't sorted through all that material yet. Ninety percent of everything else was either on Pike's body or the clothes he was wearing. The perpetrator was apparently wearing suede work gloves. We found sixteen small fragments of brown leather, but no brown gloves. And there are some blue cotton fibers from blue jeans or other denim garments. None of that will be of much help. We also found a few other colored fibers most likely from a woolen shirt and we have some hairs, mostly horse hairs."

"What color are the horse hairs?"

"That's somewhat confusing. I think we have hair from possibly five horses. We're using a color analyzer to classify them, but right now it appears we have white, pale yellow, gray, light brown, and red. Sorrel, I'd guess you'd call it."

She was going to say more, but Evan interrupted, "Gray hairs?"

"Yeah, they look gray. Why?"

"Gray in horses can be really confusing. The coat of a gray horse is a mixture of black and white hairs. The horse looks gray, but has no individual gray hairs. It gets worse. Most experts consider gray to be a pattern, not a color. Actually there are horses referred to as iron gray that look almost red. I'd bet the hairs you're calling gray are not from a gray horse."

"Well these hairs certainly look gray. They have a blue cast to them."

"They're probably grulla."

"What?"

"Grulla," he repeated, pronouncing it grew-yah. "The color is grulla or grullo depending on who you talk to. It's the rarest of all horse colors. Less than one-half of one percent of all horses are grulla colored."

"I have never heard of grulla. What color is it? Explain it for me."

"It's been described as anything from the color of a field mouse to the color of a blue heron. There are at least six variations and more misunderstanding about it than any other horse color. An individual hair could be gray, silver-gray, gray-brown, gray-blue, almost brown or almost black. Typically a grulla horse will have hairs of several different shades and hues."

"Oh, great! And I thought I had something." She sounded discouraged

"You do! Obviously some of the hair you found belongs to at least one, and maybe both of Pike's horses, and I may have even dragged in some from my own horse. We can get samples from those horses and rule them out. If what is left is hair from a grulla horse, we have a break. You also mentioned white hair. Do you think that's from a separate horse or from one of the others?"

"I won't know until tomorrow. We're dealing with very small samples and trying to classify them by morphology. We can't do any DNA testing. None of the hairs have attached follicles."

"Forget the pale yellow hairs. Pike's riding horse is a buttermilk buckskin. His pack horse could be tricky though, she's a dun and some of her hair could look identical to some of the hair from the grulla." He thought for a moment. "You know, if one of the horses is a paint it would explain the white hair." He was getting excited. "If the grulla horse is a paint, it'll make it even rarer. I have a reference book that will make your color analysis easier."

"How so?"

"It's by a vet who did a lot of research on horse colors. According to him, there is only one color of pigment and the reason for different colored horses is the way the droplets of pigment are arranged within the individual shafts of hair."

"Interesting, I'll want to see that. We also found a number of Ben Pike's hairs and one, long, light red hair."

"From a horse?"

"No, human. I'd call the color strawberry blonde, actually."

"Are you telling me a red-headed woman was involved in Pike's murder?"

"No, I'm telling you we found one, fourteen inch long, light red, human hair at the scene."

"Just one?"

"Yes, but it has a follicle. That's the reason I want to go back to the scene. I want to reexamine his tent to search for more red hairs. I also want to see where he killed the elk, but that isn't critical."

"And you want me and Buster to come along?"

"You're both welcome, but I just need one of you."

"Who would you prefer?" He was fishing.

"You, of course."

He wasn't prepared for her quick response, but it pleased him. There was a brief pause while he regained his mental footing. "Well, I'm your man. When do we leave?"

"I'd like to be there now, before the scene can deteriorate any more, but obviously that isn't possible. It'll be dark soon, I'm tired and I'm sure you are too. How about I pick you up at the Saguaro airport at seven tomorrow morning?"

"You'll be the one in the helicopter?"

"That will be me. You're okay with helicopters?"

"It's been awhile, but I've ridden in a few."

"Army, Navy, or Marines?"

"Army."

"Ranger?"

"How did you get to be so smart?"

"My younger brother was a Navy seal. You and he seem alike in some ways. He liked it, but after he saw what happened in Somalia, he decided he didn't want politicians running the show, at least at the shooting level."

"Yeah, that happened a few years after I got out. I'd like to talk to him sometime. I was in for four years and didn't see much of a future either."

"I'll arrange a meeting, but tomorrow you're busy. You and I have to find clues." There was a brief pause. "You know, Evan, if the sheriff would allow it, I'd like to work closely with Buster and you on this case. You think he would agree?"

"He probably would if you requested it. Sheriff Tate is a highly political animal and your department is the big time. I'm betting he'd let us go. The down side is you'd have to deal with him."

"How about if I get the governor to request it from him?"

"You could do that?" Buster's scheme was being realized without his even asking.

"Yeah, he and I are on good terms. In fact he owes me."

Evan suddenly felt a touch of jealousy. The governor was also a bachelor, rated the most eligible in the state. He wondered on what kind of terms he and Cheree were good. "Ah, yeah, I'm sure that would work on the sheriff."

"Good, that's settled. I'll have the governor call him Monday morning and request my department oversee the case, and that you and Buster be the main investigators under its jurisdiction. That way, I can be involved as much as possible."

"The governor must really owe you." Evan was impressed.

Cheree laughed, "Yes he does! I got him out of a big jam with his latest girl friend and I'll make sure he doesn't forget it."

"Okay, it's settled. Buster will be happy." *And I'm relieved.*

"Are you sure this will be all right with Buster?"

"Oh yeah, it'll be just fine with Buster." He didn't tell her about Buster's plan.

"Good. I hate to run, but I've got things cooking, literally. I have to get back to the lab now. I'll see you at seven tomorrow morning."

"I wouldn't miss it for anything." She couldn't know how serious he was.

"Goodbye, Evan."

"Goodbye." He held the phone for a while before he hung up, staring at it with an almost dumb look on his face. "Like no other woman I have ever met," he said out loud.

Later, after he showered, Evan sat on his deck facing the La Garita Mountains to the west. OK, the tomcat with the crippled right front foot that lived in his barn, lounged on his lap. The cat had limped into Evan's life two years ago. He named him OK, short for Old Kitty, but the vet who tried to fix his foot told Evan he was probably less than three years old. Life can be hard.

There was no evening breeze. The smoke from a mild Dominican cigar spiraled slowly up over Evan's head. The spicy smell of Spanish cedar and the crisp tang of the Connecticut wrapper soothed his senses. This was aromatherapy he could handle. The single malt whisky he was sipping didn't hurt either. Slouched in a padded chair, feet propped on the deck rail, he contemplated the events of the last thirty hours. He stroked OK's head between the ears. If he didn't pet him just right, OK would swat him. All was well. The cat was purring like a diesel engine at half-throttle. So much had happened it seemed like three or four days rather than a day and a half. Individual events were blurring together and he was trying to think everything through to establish perspective. He held up the glass, contemplating the setting sun through the silky amber liquid. *I better go easy on this stuff,* he thought, *or I won't remember my own name by the time I go to bed.*

His problem was, every time he concentrated on a particular event, he immediately began entertaining speculations. He'd seen a flash of gray and white in the trees as he surveyed Pike's camp on his arrival. At the time, he thought it to be an elk. Now, he believed it was the perpetrator, possibly riding a grulla and white paint horse. If that were so, how could he track down the horse? There probably weren't more than twenty grulla paint horses in the entire state. *Start by checking the APHA registry, of course.* The American Paint Horse Association would help. Maybe the horse had been stolen. *If its owner had reported it, that would make it even easier to find, or at least it would make the original owner easier to find.* Thinking about stolen horses caused him to remember Ruth Pike's words. *Where was the "other horse" she had referred to, the one Ben had recently acquired? Did he steal it? Did Ruth know that and quickly move it away? Maybe it wasn't even important. But what about the story Buster told him about how Pike's great-grandfather had acquired the old homestead? Had he really murdered three people to get the land Ben Pike now owned, correction, used to own? Now that he was dead, the land would pass to his older son. How would Ruth feel about that?* Evan had not yet met either of Pike's sons. *What are they like?*

Shaking his head, he tried to chase away the multitude of thoughts competing for attention. "I'm hungry!" he announced in an effort to change the subject on himself. He hadn't eaten anything since he and Buster had devoured the elk tenderloin on the mountain just before noon. That was almost seven hours ago. He decided to go to El Gordo Picaro, a small Mexican restaurant with a bad name and good food. At one time the proprietor, a balding man in his late fifties, might have been a rogue. Now, he was just fat. It was one of only two restaurants in Saguaro so it would be crowded and noisy, just what he needed to divert his thoughts from Pike. The sun was slipping behind Mesa Peak as he tossed down the last of the whisky, pitched the cigar butt over the deck rail, and went in to call Buster. The deposed cat limped back to the barn.

  Not surprised when Buster didn't answer, he left a message on his machine. "It's a done deal," he told the recorder. "Come Monday morning we'll be working for the governor." He didn't elaborate, preferring to give Buster something to ponder for a change. He brushed his teeth, put on his best pair of Lucchese boots, grabbed a jacket proclaiming him to be a member of the National Cutting Horse Association, and headed down the highway in his pickup.

  Arriving at Gordo's, he had to park a block away. It looked to be a good crowd, even for a Saturday night. It was going to be tough to find a seat, or so he thought. However, as soon as he cleared the front door, he heard his name being called from the crowded room.

  "Evan! Over here!" There was a slim, attractive woman standing and waving at him. It was Buster's wife, Amy. "Hey Evan, come and join us."

  He waved back. It solved his seating problem, but now he would probably have to talk about Pike. *Oh well, might as well get used to it.* He made his way to her table through the crowded restaurant.

  She greeted him with a generous hug, which from her was always pleasant. "Hello, good lookin', where you been hiding lately?"

  "Your husband has been running me ragged."

"Ha! That's what he said about you. I don't believe him either."

"It's true, the man is a slave driver." Evan glanced around. "By the way, where is he?"

"He's at the bar trying to get us a drink." She motioned with her thumb back over her shoulder. "So, who killed Pike?"

Evan smiled at her. "I don't know, but Buster tells me we're going to find out."

"I hope so. I don't relish the idea of a homicidal lunatic running around loose in the mountains dismembering his victims."

"You don't have a thing to worry about. Most murder victims are killed by someone they know." As soon as he said it, he regretted it. Amy's ex-husband had beaten her badly. It was ten years ago, but Evan was certain that to her, it was still very recent. "Sorry, Amy, I shouldn't have said that."

She smiled a pretty smile. "It's okay, Evan, I'm not worried about my ex. Buster told him if he ever showed his face in Saguaro County, you'd kill him."

"Me?" Evan responded. "I never said that! Buster told me he would kill him."

"Who you going to believe, me or your slave-driving partner?"

"Neither. The longer you live with him, the more you talk like him. I don't know what to believe from either one of you."

"Hey, partner, how about a nice margarita grande?" Buster arrived at the table carrying a tray laden with three large margaritas, three shot glasses of tequila, a big bowl of chips, and three small bowls filled with salsa of varying intensity. "You look like you could use one."

"Yes, I could. Conversation with your wife is as confusing as conversation with you."

Buster set the tray down and placed a margarita and a shot glass in front of each of them. Sitting down, he lifted his shot of tequila and toasted, "Here's to conversation with good friends."

"Here," agreed Amy.

"Here," agreed Evan, and the three of them knocked off the shots in one swallow.

Amy made a face. "Every time I do that, I wonder why can't I just pour the shot in the margarita and drink it."

"It's a brain stem thing," said Evan.

Both Amy and Buster looked critically at Evan. Amy asked, "What, does that mean?"

"It's a behavior related to a deeply ingrained motivational factor. It doesn't come from the thinking part of your brain. It's embedded in your brain stem, basic instinct stuff, like hunting for food or running away from danger. It's left over from our primitive ancestors."

"You mean cave men had tequila?" Amy asked incredulously. "And you said talking to me was confusing."

Evan waved his hand and laughed. "Forget it. I'll explain my theory some other time. It's way too late in the day."

"Did you talk to your new friend at the crime lab?" Buster asked, leaning close so he wouldn't have to raise his voice too loud to compete with the background noise.

"Yes, I did. I called you and left a message. Everything is all set up. Our boss will be getting a phone call from the governor Monday morning."

"The Governor?" Buster was genuinely surprised. "I'm impressed. You were obviously effective in convincing your friend of our need."

"Hey, it was easy. I think she likes me," and Evan told Amy and Buster all about his conversation with Cheree. He originally wanted to make Buster work for the details, but he found himself babbling like a mountain brook full of spring runoff.

When he was finished, Buster asked, "So you get to go flying off with the best looking medical examiner who ever existed, and I get to go interview the deceased's widow?"

"I'll trade with you."

"You sorry sack! You know full well I hate flying; especially in planes with wings that flap around in circles."

"Sorry to hear that, Buster. Then, yes, I will be flying off with the most beautiful medical examiner in existence while you interview Ruth Pike."

They continued to talk through another margarita and dinner, not getting too serious and avoiding the case as much as possible. With the noise level in the saloon it was just as well. At ten-thirty, they a made a decision to call it a night. Evan was home in bed by eleven hoping to fall quickly asleep. He did. There were no dreams of dismembered corpses to disturb his rest

6

Evan's alarm startled him at five AM. He was lying in the same position, or so it felt, as when he had gone to bed six hours earlier. He would have preferred to lie in bed for a while to give himself some time to get used to the thought of getting up, but he remembered he was meeting Cheree. That gave him the impetus to move. An hour and a half later he had fed and watered his horses; fed, watered and showered himself, and was north bound in the cruiser to his rendezvous. He was looking forward to it. After talking to her last night, he'd developed a sense of optimism. He was beginning to believe they would solve Pike's murder and maybe solve it quickly. He arrived at the little, seldom used, municipal airport ten minutes early. He was surprised to see the helicopter already on the ground. The blades were stopped. Cheree was standing outside the cabin, leaning against the fuselage.

He parked a hundred feet away and walked over, "Good morning. Am I late?"

"Good morning. No, I'm early." Her smile was devastating. "I woke up early and couldn't get back to sleep so I got up. I thought I'd take my time with breakfast, have a leisurely second cup of coffee and all that, but I couldn't relax so I got to the airport ahead of schedule. The pilot was early too, so we took off as soon as he finished the preflight. The local weather forecast is predicting rain and snow in the higher elevations. I'd like to get up there before it gets wet."

Evan looked to the west. There was a dark blue layer of high cirrus clouds over the mountains waiting for the daylight to turn them white. "Let's wake the pilot and get the blades turning. I didn't bring any rain gear."

As they climbed aboard and buckled themselves in, Evan asked about the test results on the white horse hairs. "They must be from two separate horses," she told him.

"Must be?"

"How much do you know about DNA testing?"

"I know the basics. When I registered my stallion, I sent a hair and blood sample to UC Davis. I was curious, so I asked how the tests were done. A very patient veterinarian explained the process to me. I assume you use the same basic methods."

"Yeah, pretty much, we have all the latest equipment and methods so we can get results from a very small cellular sample in a little more than twenty-four hours. The problem is, none of the horse hairs had any attached roots so DNA testing was not possible. Actually, I could have tested mitochondrial DNA and that would have told me if the horses were at least maternally related. However, the morphology of the hairs indicates they came from two different animals. There's also a disproportionate number of one type hair compared to the other type."

"Does two horses mean there's more than one perpetrator?" Evan asked

"That's your job. I was hoping you could tell me."

"I'll have to think about it. The hair was most likely carried into the tent on the killer's clothes. At least, I didn't see any evidence of a horse being in the tent. If there were more than one killer, maybe one spent more time in the tent than the other."

"Maybe. Or maybe one of them rode bareback and had more hair on his clothes."

"I doubt it. Either way, we could have as many as five horses involved or only three horses, if two of them are paints."

"You certainly are quick to reach a conclusion." She was thinking fast, considering the possibilities

"Are you implying I'm leaping?"

"No, not exactly, but you seem to have a lot more confidence about it than I do right now. Tell me what you think." She was thinking perhaps it hadn't been a good idea to get involved in this case with Evan. Working closely with him could get complicated

They were sitting close together in the small cabin of the helicopter. The smell and light pressure of her next to him was almost making Evan weak. She was, at least at this point in his life, the most desirable woman he'd ever met. He took a deep breath, and started in. "Okay, here's my leap. I think Pike was murdered by two people. There may have been more involved behind the scenes, but I think two people came to his camp, incapacitated him with a stun gun, subdued him with drugs, restrained him with ropes, and killed him. I think these two perpetrators were riding paint horses, one a grulla and white, the other a sorrel and white. I also think what I saw in the woods when I got there Friday afternoon, was one of the killers making his getaway on the grulla and white paint horse." He looked her in the eyes. "What do you think?"

She was thinking he was very handsome, but that isn't what she said. "What about the other horse hairs and the red human hair?"

"Pike had two horses with him, his riding horse, a buttermilk buckskin and his pack horse, a dun. That accounts for the other horsehairs. As far as the human hair, I don't have a clue. Pike could have brought it up there on himself. It could be from a girlfriend. I don't think for a minute he was a faithful husband."

"That's a possibility. After meeting his wife yesterday, I know it's not from her head. She appears to be a natural blonde with no gray and at her age that's a rare thing."

"Like a grulla colored horse?"

"Maybe even rarer."

"How about a strawberry blonde? How rare are they?"

"I don't know. Obviously it isn't common, probably less than one percent of the overall population."

"This case should be easy, all we have to do is find a strawberry blonde riding a grulla paint horse."

"How about the second perpetrator, the one on the sorrel and white paint?"

"That'll be a little tougher," Evan admitted, "but when we find the strawberry blonde, we squeeze her until she coughs up her accomplice."

"You think it's a woman?"

"I haven't seen many strawberry blondes with fourteen inch tresses, but the few I remember were all women. When will you have test results on the human hair?"

"They should be in sometime early this evening. I have every available technician working overtime."

They continued speculating during the short flight to the mountain meadow crime scene where the pilot made his descent. After landing, when the blades stopped rotating, they got out. Pike's camp looked forlorn in the pale, early morning light. The cloud cover was noticeably heavier up here and rain, if not snow, seemed possible. There was a chill in the air Evan had not felt at the airport. He hoped any precipitation would hold off until they were finished.

"Here, Evan, put this on," Cheree told him, holding out a pair of white coveralls.

"Do all crime scene investigators wear these things?"

"I don't know. We do. It prevents stray fibers from our clothing from confusing the issue."

"Well if I ever decide to commit a crime, I'm wearing a pair," he told her as he struggled to pull the coveralls over his boots.

"You're not going to commit a crime. You're going to solve one. Take this and follow me." She handed him a black, hard-sided case and started across the meadow towards the scene. Grabbing the handle of the case, he followed behind as he tugged up the zipper of the white suit.

The smell of decay from the congealed pool of blood was thick in the darkened tent. "Inside the case you're carrying," Cheree told him, "are some high intensity flashlights. We're going to need them."

He opened the case and removed what looked somewhat like a cordless drill with a flashlight head where the drill motor should be. He pulled the trigger. A brilliant light stabbed through the gloomy interior of the tent. "Damn! This isn't your ordinary flashlight!"

"No, it's not. It's a lot more powerful and the color temperature of the light is the same as natural sunlight." She reached for the light he held. "Give me one, you take one, and we'll start looking. We want to search the entire tent."

"What are we looking for?"

"Primarily long red hairs, or anything else that will be helpful in solving the case."

"Sounds simple enough. Where should I start?"

"You can start in that corner," she pointed to the corner of the tent to the right of the door," and work clockwise. I'll start on the other side of the door and go counter clockwise. We'll meet in the back and keep going. That way we'll be looking at everything twice."

Evan moved to his corner to start searching, looking at the floor from the center to the outer edge and up the wall. Moving forward about a foot at a time, the search soon became tedious. After about thirty minutes, they crossed paths at the back of the tent. Another thirty minutes later they were back at their respective starting locations. Neither of them had found anything significant.

"Looks like your people got everything the first time around."

"That's good. It means they were doing their job, but not good because it leaves me in doubt about the red hair."

"How so?"

"Finding just one clue is a tease. It makes me wonder."

"What, if it's a plant?"

"Maybe, but if it was deliberately planted, it raises a whole new set of questions I don't even want to consider. I told you we vacuumed the entire floor, or at least all of it that wasn't covered with blood. The only human hair we found most likely belongs to Pike. We found the red hair under Pike's body. Something about that bothers me and I don't know what."

"Okay, I can understand that, you've got a hunch. Where to next?"

"Can you find the spot where you saw the movement in the trees on Friday afternoon."

"You mean where the perpetrator ran off? Sure, let's go." They started off across the meadow, moving quickly away from the depressing tent with its heavy stench of death.

"Same rules?" Evan asked when they arrived at the spot.

"What do you mean?"

"Look for everything and anything."

"Oh, that. Yeah, as long as it's meaningful to the successful resolution of the case." She said it with a straight face, but her eyes were laughing.

"Okay. I'll go ahead and take the left. You follow and take the right."

They moved slowly, Evan following the trail of hoof prints still easily discernable in the soft earth. They searched the ground, the low vegetation and the tree trunks, finding nothing until just before they reached the edge of the trees and the trail that led away from Pike's camp. At a spot where the horse and rider had passed close between two large pines, Evan spied several long black hairs, about five feet off the ground, stuck under the bark on one of the trees. "Cheree, we have something here."

She quickly joined him. "Good job, some of these still have the roots attached. What do you think?"

"I think it's hair from the mane of the horse ridden by whoever I chased out of here." He gently pried up the bark, removing the three long hairs from the tree. He held them against the leg of his coveralls. They were jet black. "I'll bet these are from the mane of the grulla paint." He handed them to her and reexamined the tree. A little farther down the trunk he found several short white hairs. "Here are some more, but these are white body hairs."

"Move over, I'll start looking from the ground up."

They spent the next ten minutes using their flashlights to examine every square inch of the tree from the ground up to six feet. When they were finished, they had amassed a grand total of twenty-three horse hairs, three long ones most likely from the horse's mane, nineteen short body hairs, ten white and nine varying in color between gray and brown, and one additional long black hair, no doubt from the horse's tail. Cheree put them all together in a zip top plastic bag.

"I thought you told me grulla was sort of a gray-blue-brown color," she said as she tucked the bag into the case Evan carried. "Why is the hair from the mane and tail black?"

"Remind me to show you a grulla colored horse sometime. When the Spanish Conquistadors first came to the Americas, the horses they brought with them were of a breed called Sorraia. It's an ancient breed of particularly athletic horse that the early Spaniards trained to herd cattle. The horses were always grulla or dun colored. They were short, never more than fourteen-two hands high, and never had any white markings. But, they always had black manes and tails as well as black dorsal stripes and black around their eyes. The tips of their ears were black too. A lot of them also had black horizontal bars on their legs, sometimes as high up as their shoulders."

"They sound beautiful."

"They were, but now they're mostly extinct."

"That's a shame, what happened?"

Evan shrugged. "Who knows? There are still a couple of small private herds in Europe and some wild ones left in Oregon, Nevada, and Utah, but even though they're mostly gone, their genes are in every modern breed. That's why grulla colored horses pop up in every breed even though they're rare. According to several experts, the Sorraia gave the American Quarter horse its ability to work cattle."

"Okay, that explains the black mane and tail, but you said the Sorraia never had any white on them. This horse appears to be loaded with white."

"Paint horses are a color breed. Horses with white on them occur in most every breed. American paint horses and American quarter horses share most of the same ancestry, but as far as can be determined; Sorraia horses were never painted. You know a lot more about genetics than I do, you tell me how it works."

"Like everything else, it's more complicated than it appears. I'll figure it out as soon as we solve this case."

"Just think of a grulla as a blue dun."

"Yeah, that really clears it up for me."

"You'll see what I mean when we find the horse that lost the hair in that bag." He was excited. "I'll also bet this horse is a tobiano paint or a frame overo."

She looked at him and started laughing.

"What?"

"You should see yourself. You look like a kid who just found the map to a pirate's treasure. And what's really funny is that I don't have a clue."

"I'm sorry, I can explain."

"I'm sure you can. What's the difference between a frame overo and a tobiano?"

"Well, there are two major paint horse color patterns, overo and tobiano. Very simply, in an overo pattern, the white starts on the bottom and goes up. In a tobiano, the white starts on top and goes down. There are also sabinos and toveros, but enough for now."

"I don't get it."

"If the horse has white that crosses its back, it's a tobiano. If the white starts on the horse's belly and goes up its sides without crossing its back, it's an overo. We found some white hair high up on that tree."

"Got it. Now what's a frame overo?"

"A frame overo has lots of white. Sometimes they have almost completely white sides, but the top of the back and part of the legs will be the body color. That's not an official definition, but my point is, this horse has a good percentage of white and it has it high up on its body."

"Okay, see if this is right. One of the horses used in the commission of Pike's murder is a grulla paint horse, either of a frame overo or tobiano pattern. And this color paint horse is quite rare."

"Perfect! You got it! We find that horse and we're well on the way to finding Pike's killers. And," a raindrop splattered on his arm for punctuation, "if you want to really be confused, there are only two horse colors, black and red."

She looked at him like she didn't believe him. "What?"

"All horse colors can be genetically explained as either dilutions or modifications of either red or black."

"Yesterday you told me there was only one color of horse pigment."

"Yeah, I did and I'm not contradicting myself. The genetic theory of two colors compliments the one pigment theory. He looked up. Another drop hit him on the forehead. "I've got some books that explain it beautifully." Several more drops pelted him. "What more do we need to do here?"

"Nothing right here, but I want to see the place where Pike killed the elk. I doubt we'll find anything of significance, but we should look. If we hurry, we won't get too wet. I also want to see those books later."

They hustled back to the chopper as the rain began to intensify. By the time the pilot dropped them in the meadow Evan and Buster had found the day before, ice pellets and snowflakes were mixed in with the light rain. The pilot was concerned and when they left the cabin he told them, "I don't like this weather. I can't give you a lot of time." He kept the motor running.

Evan hastily led Cheree to where Pike had butchered the elk. As they approached, they saw hide and bone scattered across a wide area. The carcass had already been thoroughly scavenged. "Obviously we're too late," Cheree said.

"Hey, give 'em a break. The critters up here are hungry. For them this was the equivalent of Thanksgiving dinner." Evan pointed to the trees closest to the kill site. "Let's look over there. If I had ambushed Pike, I would have done it from those trees."

They moved past the remnants of the elk and into the trees. Half dozen steps into the woods, Evan spied a bright shell casing. He bent down to push a small twig into the end of the spent cartridge. He sniffed the open end. "A .270, recently fired." He offered it to Cheree. "Most likely from Pike's rifle. This is where he stood when he shot the elk."

The casing had a small dent in the edge of its open end from the extractor during ejecting. "A semi-automatic?" she asked.

"Yeah, Pike had a .270 BAR propped up in the corner of his tent. You must have seen it."

"I never saw it."

"You didn't? I never touched it. I assumed it was Pike's. Since he hadn't been shot, I let it stand. I thought you took it back with you yesterday."

"If one of my crew picked it up, I don't know about it. Could Buster have taken it?"

"No. He would have said something. I would have seen it."

Cheree looked around. "There's nothing more we can do here. If I had fifty people we might find something, but I doubt it. Let's go back to the tent to check for the rifle."

The proportion of snow to rain and ice in the sleet had been increasing. Visibility was beginning to fade. Evan and Cheree had to beg the pilot to give them five more minutes. He wasn't happy about it, but he flew them back to the tent. "You've got five minutes," he told them when they touched down, "after that I'm leaving with or without you."

"It'll only take two," Cheree told him before they ran for the tent. A hasty search yielded nothing.

"I don't get it. It was in that corner." Evan pointed to the corner of the tent closest to the head end of the cot. "It was standing where he could grab it in a hurry,"

"Well, it's gone now. Let's get out of here before we have to walk home."

They ran through the thickening sleet for the chopper. Visibility was dropping fast. The opposite side of the meadow was swallowed in a sloppy gray mist. If the aircraft's engine wouldn't have been whining, they might have missed it.

The pilot was doing some whining of his own. "We shouldn't be up here in this crap. We're too close to the ceiling of this aircraft to tolerate any ice."

He started spooling up the engine before they had the door shut. Just as he pulled up on the collective, a sharp gust of wind hit them from the side. Barely off the ground, the chopper skidded sideways across the wet meadow toward the trees. Cheree grabbed Evan's arm. Evan braced for the worst. The pilot cursed, spinning the plane's nose back into the wind. He regained control, slowly climbing the chopper over the trees.

They were quiet on the flight back to Saguaro, both of them thinking about the missing rifle. Evan soon came to the conclusion someone had come back to the tent sometime between when he fell asleep and when Buster arrived Saturday morning. If Buster or one of Cheree's people hadn't taken the rifle, it was the only scenario that worked. He was positive Buster hadn't packed it out, and if one of Cheree's crew had removed it, she certainly would have noticed. It wasn't something that could be easily hidden. Also, Cheree was the first and only person in the tent after him, and she said she hadn't seen it. It could only have been removed at night while he was asleep. *Cheree must really think I'm incompetent, allowing someone to sneak in to steal Pike's rifle right from under my nose. Whoever I chased away must not have gone far. He just circled back to wait for me to go to sleep. Damn, I've been hosing this case from the start!*

While he was beating himself up, he also considered why the perpetrator wanted the rifle. *Why risk your ass to come back and get it? It obviously wasn't the murder weapon, although the rifle and scope were worth at least a thousand dollars. Maybe the guy just wanted a trophy.*

Sitting next to him, elbows on her knees, chin in her hands, Cheree was equally baffled. She had not seen the rifle and was certain none of her crew had taken it. That could only mean it disappeared while Evan was sleeping. She didn't like that thought. It meant the perpetrator had been very close to him, close enough to hurt him. *What is going on here?* Evan suggested he might have interrupted the perpetrator. *Obviously, Pike was already dead. Why was he hanging around in the trees when Evan got there? What was he waiting for? Why come back for the rifle, or did Evan's arrival scare him off before he was finished? What significance was the rifle anyway; it wasn't used to kill Pike.* Then she had another more disturbing thought. *What if the perpetrator wanted to make certain the murder was discovered and had waited for Evan to arrive? That might indicate Pike's wife was involved. According to Evan, she had begged him to find Pike. No, that's too obvious and still doesn't explain why the rifle was important.* Her head was spinning faster than the helicopter blades.

Racing east down the slope of the mountain, they quickly flew out of the precipitation. It was only a line of squalls moving through, merely a harbinger of things to come. Back on the ground at Saguaro's little airport, the pale sun was still shining. Cheree walked with Evan back to where he had parked the patrol car.

"Thanks for your help." She told him

"Yeah, such as it was." He smiled but he was still mentally kicking himself and it showed.

She put a hand on his shoulder. "We know a lot more now than we did four hours ago. Do me a favor. Go home, take it easy. Get your mind off the case for a while. We're doing everything we can. Tomorrow we'll have more information."

"It's a deal, just as soon as I talk to Buster to find out how he did with Ruth Pike. Maybe he learned something." Evan's statement carried the insinuation they hadn't learned anything.

"Well, okay. I almost forgot about Ruth. Talk to Buster. If you learn anything interesting, give me a call. Then you can take a break."

He shook her hand and agreed. He watched her walk back to the chopper, waving as it lifted off. *What the hell had happened to Pike's rifle?*

7

It had been a long busy weekend. Evan was physically and emotionally tired. Thoughts of Cheree competed for attention with speculations about Pike's murder. He couldn't resolve any of them; they just kept revolving in his head as he drove home from the Saguaro airport. Watching Cheree fly away was depressing. He wished they had been able to spend more time together. Talking leisurely while they lingered over lunch would have been nice. I'll have to be patient, he thought. After all, I got along without her before I met her. He was reminded of something his mother used to tell him when he was young. "All good things come to him who waits." It was one of her favorite homilies. Over the years he'd generally found it to be true, as long as he worked like hell while he waited. He had convinced himself a relationship with Cheree would be a good thing, a great thing even, and he was also convinced he'd have to work at making it happen. Pulling out onto the highway, he hammered the accelerator. The cruiser bucked, sprinting down the road. Evan's thoughts spun around like the symbols in a Las Vegas slot machine, never quite lining up for the payoff.

Like Evan, Buster was playing his own version of the same mental game. As Evan left the airport, Buster was leaving Ruth Pike's place. He'd just finished an hour-long conversation with her and her son, Jason. He knew more now than he knew an hour ago, but the case had become more complicated, not less. Ruth and her son were cooperative. Neither of them had any delusions about Ben Pike's character traits, yet it seemed to Buster, Ruth had actually loved Ben regardless of his flaws. Jason was another matter. Buster hadn't been able to discern Jason's feelings for his father. He appeared to be an emotionally flat character, although he could be in a state of shock. That would easily explain his apparent detachment from the situation. Buster had seen behavior like his before in certain cases where a spouse or family member had met a violent and untimely end. One or more of the survivors would act like a robot, devoid of the normal feelings and responses such a situation normally inspired. Buster hoped this were the case. If not, Jason should have a Guinness record book entry as one of the world's coldest human beings.

"I had some strange visitors about four months ago," Ruth told Buster toward the end of the interview, long after Buster asked her if she knew of anything her husband might have done to anyone that would warrant a death sentence. She appeared to be aware of most of her husband's indiscretions, misdemeanors, and general bad behavior, although none of it included rape or sexual assault. "But," she continued, "I never thought much of it. I still don't know if it's important. I don't exactly remember the date, but it was either toward the end of June or the first part of July."

"Tell me about it, anything could be helpful."

"I don't remember much about them. They asked if Ben was around."

"You say them, how many?"

"There were two of them. They were young men, big men. As big as my son Abel."

"How old would you imagine these big, young men to be?"

She frowned. "That's hard for me to guess, but I'd say they were in their early twenties."

"When you say big, do you mean heavy or big like a football player?"

"Like football players. They weren't fat or anything like that, just big and strong. Well built."

"How tall were they?"

"That I can recall. Ben is..." and she remembered Ben's condition. "Ben was six feet five and both these boys were that tall. One of them was probably two or three inches taller."

"What about the color of their hair and skin? Can you remember that?"

"Oh, sure. They were both blonde and fair skinned. In fact, now that I think about it, one of them had hair that was a little bit red."

"How red is a little bit? Like strawberry blonde, maybe?"

"Yeah, that would describe it. He had a lot of freckles too."

"How long was his hair?"

"Not long, both of them were very clean cut. They were polite too."

"Was the redhead the tall one or the short one?"

"He was the shorter one."

"Do you remember what they wanted?"

"Sure, they asked for Ben."

"Did they say why they wanted him?"

"Not really. When I told them he wasn't around, they asked if I knew where they could find him. I was a little curious. Ben would sometimes hire high school or college boys during the summer to help him in his business. I thought maybe he told these two they could have a job. I asked them why they wanted to talk to Ben."

She paused and seemed to go into deep thought, almost a trance. Buster waited. Prior to this, Ruth had been quite talkative. Suddenly that changed. *Now it's like she's talking to the IRS, don't tell them anything unless specifically asked.* "What was their response?" he asked finally, prodding her.

"Oh, yeah." She came back to the present. "They really wouldn't tell me, exactly. One of them, the taller one, said it was personal."

"Was that it? Was that all they said?"

"Yeah, that was it. I even asked them if I could give Ben a message, but they just smiled and said no."

"Then what happened?"

"Nothing, they just left."

"What were they driving?"

"A real fancy pickup." She smiled at Buster. He had to admit Ruth was still a very attractive woman. "It looked brand new and they were pulling a new horse trailer."

"Any horses in it."

"Yeah, but I couldn't tell what they looked like except one of them had its head and neck out the drop window on the side. It was white and gray and it had a pretty head."

"Do you think it might have been a paint horse?"

"Well, it was looking right at me and it definitely was white and sort of a gray color, although its mane was black, long too. Like I said, a real pretty horse. I've never seen a horse that color before."

"How about when they drove away, were you able to get a better look?"

"No, one of the boys closed up the window before they drove away. I probably only saw the horse for just a few seconds."

"How about the other horse, did you see that one at all?"

"Not really, I could just tell there was another one, but I couldn't see what color it was."

Buster summed it up for her. "Okay ma'am, here's what I have. Two tall, well-built, young men; one about six feet, five inches, the other about six feet, seven inches, visited your premises one day in late June or early July asking for your husband. They were fair skinned, white men, one blonde, one with light red colored hair. They were courteous, clean and neat. They were driving a late model pickup truck and pulling a horse trailer. Ah, I didn't ask you what color the truck was."

"It was two-toned, white and gold."

"Do you remember what make it was?"

"No, I'm afraid not, but they left it running and it was rattling like a diesel. Oh yeah, it had dual rear wheels."

"Good, that helps. Okay, the two men were driving a late model, white and gold, dually pickup, pulling a horse trailer. Do you remember anything in particular about the trailer? How big was it?"

"I remember it as a three or four horse slant, painted to match the truck. Yeah, it was a gooseneck. Looked new."

"Okay." Buster made more notes. "These two men asked about the whereabouts of your husband, but wouldn't tell you why they wanted to see him."

"That's right," Ruth agreed.

"And when you asked about taking a message for them, they politely declined and left."

"Right."

"You noticed two horses in the trailer, one looked to be a gray and white paint, the other you couldn't see. Is there anything else you can recall? Anything unusual they did, or said, or anything unusual about their looks? Any tattoos, scars, anything about their appearance that would help identify them?"

She was silent for a while, thinking. "Nothing about their looks, but one of them, the taller one with the blonde hair, kept looking around. He was the one who did most of the talking and just before they left, he said, 'Nice place you have here. You're fortunate.' I thanked him. Never thought about it until now. You think that's important?"

Buster smiled his most inscrutable smile. "Maybe, maybe not. We'll have to find out." He finished, making some polite conversation to thank her for her cooperation. He handed her his card, "If you think of anything else, contact me immediately. Even if you don't think it's terribly important, call us. Anytime."

Looking as if she were about to break down, she promised she would. Jason put his arm around his mother's shoulders to draw her tight.

"Thank you, sheriff. Please find who killed Ben." She tried to smile her best smile at him, but she was tired and sad. It came off a little flat. "Please tell that other deputy who was here before, thank you for me too."

"I'll do that." He tipped his Stetson to her and nodded to Jason. "Ma'am, Jason. We'll be in touch."

Pulling out of Ruth's driveway and onto the highway, he ran the cruiser up to seventy and started thinking. Being only ten miles apart, on the same highway, going opposite directions, Buster and Evan were now closing the gap between them at a combined speed of almost a hundred and fifty miles per hour. They would meet shortly.

Moments later they passed. They both hammered the brakes as recognition dawned. A short time later they were talking to each other from across the highway. "How'd it go?" Evan asked Buster.

"Fine, I guess. How much can your hair grow in three months?"

"Damn, Buster. Now what are you talking about?"

"Follow me home, I'll get Amy to make us some lunch. We can talk like civilized folks instead of shouting at each other from opposite sides of the road." Buster was grinning as he peeled off back down the highway.

Mumbling under his breath, Evan made a U-turn and followed. "Damn you, Buster, what's this all about?"

Evan had been on his way home, but now, no longer in a hurry to get there, he held to the speed limit. By the time he arrived at Buster's place, Buster's cruiser was parked and he was already in the house. Amy answered Evan's knock on the door. "Well, what a pleasant surprise, twice in the same week. You and

Buster need more of these high profile cases so we can visit more often."

"I don't think Buster can handle the pressure of one high profile case! I think he's losing his grip. He just asked me how much my hair could grow in three months!"

Amy looked at Evan as if he were the crazy one. "So? Seems like a legitimate question to me."

Evan knew when he was beat. "Got any beer?"

"I do, but you look to me like you're on duty. You drove here in a car that says 'Sheriff' on the side, and you're wearing a gun and a uniform. I don't think I can give you a beer. How about a nice cold glass of milk?"

"Okay, anything." He hung his Stetson on the back of a chair and sat down at the kitchen table.

Just as Evan was lifting the glass of milk to his lips, Buster walked in wearing jeans and a Harley Davidson tee shirt. "You didn't want a beer?"

Evan took a long pull on the glass. When it was half empty he set it down on the table. "Of course not, I'm on duty."

"Suit yourself. What did you and the beautiful medical examiner discover?"

After Buster's ridiculous question about the speed at which hair would grow, Evan had all but forgotten about Pike's missing rifle. Now he remembered it. "Ah, I'm not real happy about what we found. Or should I say what we didn't find."

"Sounds cryptic." He waved the bottle of beer Amy had just handed him in Evan's face. "Sure you don't want one of these?"

"No thanks. Actually, I think I'll drink milk from now on. It's much healthier." He took another pull off the glass. "You didn't take Pike's Browning did you?"

"Pike have a Browning in his tent when you found him?"

"Yup."

"It's missing?"

"Yup. There was a BAR .270 propped up in the corner across from his cot when I found him on Friday afternoon. At the time, I was positive it was Pike's. It was the only rifle I found and he was hunting. This morning, I found an empty .270 cartridge in the trees where Pike shot the elk. It had to be his rifle."

"Now it's gone. How about Cheree's crew, could one of them have taken it?"

"She says no, and I'm sure she's right. It had to disappear Friday night—right from under my nose!"

"That means you had a visitor between the time you fell asleep and the time I got up there in the morning."

"That's the way I see it." He paused, "I feel stupid about it, too."

"As long as you don't make a habit of it, feeling stupid can be helpful. My guess is whoever killed Pike wanted his rifle real bad, bad enough to come back and get it after he forgot it. Why?"

"I don't know, Buster. The only thing I can think of is he wanted a trophy. If that's the case, he's either very dangerous or incredibly stupid."

"Or both. But what if he has a plan and needs the rifle?"

"What are you getting at? You think he might use Pike's rifle to commit more crimes?"

"Possibly. We know absolutely nothing about this person other than he apparently had a grudge against Pike."

"We don't even know that for sure."

"I'll bet a month's paycheck on it. You game?"

"No, you're probably right, but the only thing I know about him for certain, is he was riding a grulla paint horse when I scared him off. I'll bet a paycheck on that."

"Did you and Cheree find any proof of that?"

"Yeah, we did." Evan filled him in on the details of his morning romp in the woods with Cheree.

"You know Gordon Mason from Grand Junction?" Buster asked when Evan was finished.

"Of course, I know him. Anybody who knows anything about cutting horses knows who he is. Why?"

"I happen to know he's got a couple of grulla horses."

"Yeah, but they're probably quarter horses. I don't think he has any paints in his barn."

"Normally I'd agree with you, but I happen to know that a number of years ago, one of his mares, a daughter of Smart Little Lena, presented him with a real flashy grulla paint foal. Normally, he'd sell a cropout as soon as it was weaned, but he took a fancy to this horse and he kept it. The last time I saw him, he told me he'd gotten another grulla paint from the same mare. He developed their cutting abilities. He was using both of them for schooling horses."

"So what could Gordon Mason have to do with Pike's murder? He's one of the top cutting horse trainers in the country and probably the most respected horseman in the state. I can't imagine him being involved, although we can't rule out anyone—yet."

Buster shrugged his shoulders. "I'm sure he has nothing to do with Pike, but he knows a lot of people. If he takes an interest in something, like a grulla paint for instance, a lot of other people will take an interest in grulla paints. I think I'll call him."

"Yeah, it can't hurt. It's not like we're drowning in leads. What did Ruth have to say?"

"That was interesting, but I didn't learn anything until the last five minutes." Buster related his interview with Ruth and her mention of what she thought was a pretty, gray and white paint horse. "It would appear there certainly is a grulla paint horse involved in Pike's murder."

"We can do a search on the pickup by color and body style," Evan suggested.

"Yeah, provided it's in the data base. Ruth didn't pay any attention to the license plates. It might not be a Colorado truck."

"We'll check Colorado first. If we draw a blank, we can check surrounding states. There shouldn't be more than five thousand, late model, gold and white dually pickups on the road in the whole country."

"Be a good job for our boss."

"He'd screw it up somehow," and Evan laughed. "What about the two guys? Do we get an artist to work with Ruth on a description?"

"We could, although I think you should get Cheree's opinion on that. Remember, we're officially working for the state. I think we should let her decide the technical stuff."

"Okay, so what do we do? Sit on our hands?"

"No, obviously not, but unlike you, I have formulated a plan."

"Care to share this plan with your partner?"

"The first thing we do is interview Abel Pike. He's a guard at the prison in Buena Vista, and lives very privately in the hills just west of town."

"Ruth tell you that?"

"No, Jason did. He suggested that I talk to Abel even before I brought it up. I got a feeling he either thinks Abel knows something, or he knows Abel knows something."

"Something about dear old dad being a rapist?"

"I don't know. It was nothing he said, just gave me an impression."

"Cheree said he seemed to be detached when she met with the family at the morgue."

"I agree. He seemed the same way to me."

"Maybe it's because he grew up with Ben Pike for a father."

"Could be, there's no denying Ben would be a tough act to follow. Anyway, what do you think about interviewing Abel?"

"Yeah, let's do it, the sooner the better. I'm also going to contact the American Paint Horse Association to get a list of all grulla paints registered in the state."

"That's good. What about the missing rifle?"

"Other than kick myself in the ass, I can't think of anything. I screwed up and it's gone. I'll talk to Cheree to see if her people found it, but I think not."

"When you talk to her, see what she thinks about an artist visiting Ruth. She didn't seem to be able to recall a great deal about their appearances other than they were big. I don't know if it's been too long or not."

"Cheree will know. How do we handle the sheriff until the governor calls?"

"I don't know about you, but I intend to be on the road when he gets in. He can read my report."

"Good idea, I think I'll be out early tomorrow morning investigating reports of cattle rustling."

Amy had been listening without comment all this time, but now she spoke up. "You don't really think the sheriff is stupid enough to believe that cattle rustling story again?"

Evan turned to her, "Sure, I only use it once or twice a year. The sheriff doesn't know which end of a steer to cut a steak from, let alone realize there hasn't been a cow rustled in the county for more than six years."

She shook her head. "If you two want lunch, go wash up and let me set the table."

After lunch, they corroborated on the reports they would submit to the sheriff. They were painstakingly accurate; they didn't want any technicalities open for critique. Their boss was a nitpicker. He didn't know enough to do anything else. He thought if he could find a contradiction or minor mistake, it gave him the upper hand, made him look smart. He was only fooling himself. His private nickname with the troops was "Clouseau", after the bumbling detective popularized by Peter Sellers. However, unlike the movie character, the sheriff was not at all humorous.

"You know, Buster, I've changed my mind," Evan commented when they were satisfied with the reports, "I think I'll be in the office tomorrow when the sheriff shows up. He's going to drag us in anyway."

Buster pondered Evan's statement for a few moments. "Yeah, I believe you're right. I'll be there too. I'd also like to be there when the governor calls. What about the press? Is Pike's murder going to make a splash?"

"Cheree told me she'll try to hold the lid down. Basically the press release will indicate Pike was found dead and the matter is under investigation. The only way the reporters will learn more is if Ruth or her kids start talking."

"I like that. Cheree's a one fine woman."

"I'd like to meet her," Amy said to Evan. "Buster told me all about her yesterday afternoon."

"Maybe we can all go out to dinner."

"Oh good, you boys can get dressed up. We'll go some place real nice."

"I'll try and arrange it," Evan promised.

Buster agreed, "See that you do."

"Okay, but now I'm going home. Unlike you two, I have work to do. Thanks for the great lunch, Amy. Buster, I'll talk to you after I talk to Cheree." Amy gave him a big hug. Next to Buster, he was her best friend.

The first thing he did when he arrived home was call Cheree. When she didn't answer, he briefly considered calling her at her office, but decided against it. Instead he left a message for her at home. "Cheree, this is Evan. I have some information from Buster's interview with Ruth Pike. I'll call you later." He thought about what else he could say. "What are you doing for dinner?" crossed his mind and he glanced at his watch. *Two o'clock. I could be there by six easy. It might be tough getting up for work tomorrow. But, if I left by nine and got back at midnight, I could still get five hours of sleep.* He decided he would get the horses taken care of early and try calling her back in a half-hour. *It's a long way to go for a date, but like Buster said, "She's one fine woman."*

Forty minutes later he had his chores done. He called again. No answer. "Hi, Cheree, it's Evan again. I'll call you later." He hung up and checked his watch. "I'll try again in a bit," he told himself. At three, he called once more and felt stupid when he got the answering machine again. He felt an explanation was in order.

"Cheree, it's me, Evan. Again. I keep calling because I want to ask you to go to dinner, but it's starting to get late. I'll have to try again another time. Talk to you later, bye." After he hung up, he felt even more stupid. He hated talking personal to an answering machine. *Oh well, it's only my first try,* and decided to go for a ride. He hadn't checked the fences lately. Half way to the barn, his phone started ringing behind him, but he never heard it.

Three hours later he was pulling the saddle off Red Max, his big sorrel gelding. Max wasn't fancy, but he was big, strong, and willing to try whatever Evan asked of him. They had ridden the entire perimeter of Evan's property, about two and a half miles. The backside of it was rugged, full of short, steep ravines and breaks where it bordered on the banks of a huge, dry wash. It was hard riding for both man and horse. Evan had fixed a couple of minor problems, but for the most part, the fences were in good shape. He patted Max on the neck. "You're a good boy, Max," he told the animal, giving him an extra ration of oats. He closed the barn for the night.

It was just getting dark as he went in. Autumn had arrived. The twilight air was perfumed with dry sage, dead cottonwood leaves, and cut alfalfa. It was heady stuff. Stopping at the back door, Evan inhaled deeply. It was his favorite time of the year even though it filled him with melancholy for the demise of summer and the approach of winter. He relished the warm days and cool, clear nights when the sky dazzled with incomprehensible numbers of stars. He made a note to come out later with a cigar and an ounce or two of whisky, to sit on the deck and gaze at the moon and stars until he lost his senses. As soon as he thought it, the lyrics of "Don't Fence Me In" came tumbling out of his memory.

"I want to ride to the ridge where the West commences, gaze at the moon 'til I lose my senses. Can't look at hobbles and I can't stand fences. Don't fence me in." He went in the house singing.

His phone was ringing and he hurried to answer. It was Cheree. "Hello, Deputy Coleman."

"Hello, Doctor Nicoletti."

"I'm sorry I missed you earlier, I would have loved to go to dinner. I got your last message right after you called. I called right back, but apparently you'd already left." She sounded apologetic.

"I'm sorry too. But now that I know you're willing, I'll try again."

There was a pause. "Did you think I wouldn't be willing to go to dinner with you?"

Now it was Evan's turn to pause. "Ah, well," he spun mental wheels searching for a clever response, "I'm not the presumptuous type." It was the best he could do.

"Okay, I forgive you—this time."

"It won't happen again."

"What news from the front? Did Buster interview Ruth Pike?"

"Yes, he did. He wants to know how fast your hair grows."

"Me personally or in general?"

"In general I'm sure."

"I don't know. An inch a month, maybe. Why?"

"Several months ago Ruth had two visitors. She described them as big, athletic looking, young men. They were polite, clean cut and were inquiring about Ben, but wouldn't tell her why. One of them had red hair—perhaps strawberry blonde. Problem is, his hair was short. The red hair you found is fourteen inches long, at least twelve inches longer than what this guy was carrying. There is no way it could have grown that much in three months."

"And that's not the only problem. I just heard from the lab. The hair we found is from a woman."

Evan's first thought was to ask her if she were sure, but quickly realized that would be a stupid question. "Okay, that takes care of that. Do you think the hair came from a girl friend of Pike's or a perpetrator?"

"Maybe it's from a woman who was both, an ex-lover who later found a reason to murder him."

"That's an interesting speculation. Gives new meaning to the term 'tough love', but, she couldn't have done it on her own."

"Sure she could. She rides up to see him. Lures him into the tent, zaps him with a stun gun and injects him with ketamine. While he's out, she ties him to the cot and has her way with him, permanently."

Evan shuddered. "What kind of a woman would do that?"

"There are probably a lot of women who would like to do it, and a few who could. Men don't have a monopoly on violent behavior, or the desire for revenge."

"You think revenge is the motive?"

"It could be, considering what she did to him. It's a reasonable guess, but what can we say for certain at this point? The only thing that looks positive is that the perpetrator, the one you scared off, was riding a grulla paint horse. Although I do rather like the idea of a female perpetrator."

"Seriously?"

"Sure. Why not? Women are victims of horrible sex crimes committed by men often enough. Don't you believe in fair, foul play?"

"Well, when you put it like that, how could I disagree? Except, since I didn't see the rider, it could have been a trained monkey on a circus horse." He changed the subject. "What about sending an artist to interview Ruth? A sketch of her visitors might be helpful."

"It depends on her memory. From what you said she told Buster, I doubt if it's worth a try. It doesn't sound as if she remembers much about them except their physical size. Neither of them would tell her why they wanted to see Ben?"

"No, when she asked, the taller one said it was personal."

"You don't suppose he has an older sister do you?" Cheree speculated.

"Good thought, but actually, he wouldn't need a sister. At his and Pike's respective ages, it could be his mother and I'm certain he has one of those."

They discussed the case, including the missing rifle, for another two hours. It was after nine when they finally said goodnight. Cheree promised Evan the governor would call the sheriff first thing in the morning, and Evan promised Cheree he would report back to her just as soon as he knew the sheriff's decision on the assignment.

Evan found it hard to believe he'd been on the phone for two hours. Never had he talked on the phone for that long, to anyone. He hated talking on the phone. To his surprise, the conversation had never stalled or even hesitated. He decided to skip the drink of whisky on the deck. He already felt giddy. He went to bed and fell immediately asleep.

He woke up one time about two AM. Two packs of coyotes were talking trash to each other from opposite sides of the river. They howled and yipped for about twenty minutes. Then they stopped cold. Evan thought about Ben Pike tied to a bunk, immobilized by ropes, paralyzed by drugs, but awake and lucid while the killer had his way with him. He knew he was being killed, and the only thing he could do was sweat and cry. Evan shuddered, feeling a deep chill. Pulling the blankets tighter under his chin, he curled his knees up closer to his groin.

8

The sheriff said, "So tell me again why you called in the state investigators."

Evan sighed audibly. This would be the third time he and Buster had told their story, explaining their actions to the boss. It was eight-thirty in the morning. They had been sitting in the sheriff's office since seven defending their investigation of Pike's murder. The sheriff seemed to be upset with Evan and Buster, but he wouldn't say exactly why. He was looking for something he could criticize. Suspecting as much, Evan was beginning to show his irritation. Buster was also irritated, but he was still wearing an inscrutable expression.

"You're a taxpayer, aren't you Sheriff?" Buster asked.

"Well of course I am. What's that got to do with anything?"

"Do you have any idea how much money the state has pumped into the new crime lab?"

"No, how much?"

"I heard twenty-eight million just for the instruments and furniture. The facility was another thirty-two." Buster was blowing smoke. He had no idea how much the state had spent on the new facilities. What he knew, however, was no finer or more sophisticated lab existed west of the Mississippi, east of the Cascades. He continued on, "Hell, Sheriff, other states and even some foreign countries send samples to us for analysis. Evan and I figured if anybody should be using that new sixty million dollar resource, it should be us, and by us I mean all the hard working, tax paying citizens of Saguaro County." He paused momentarily to stare into the sheriff's eyes. "Wouldn't you agree?"

Sheriff Tate stared back, but only briefly. "Yeah, you're right, but I wish you would have talked to me about it." Now he was entering his whining phase. When all other methods of control failed, he whined.

"Well, sir, it was Friday afternoon, you were in Hawaii, probably on the beach where you could appreciate all those tiny, thong bikinis, and we had a dead man in the middle of a large, outdoor crime scene. Did we do something wrong?"

The sheriff was smart enough to know he had lost. "Next time, inform me."

He would have gone on, but just then Suzy announced he had a phone call. "Sheriff," she said over the intercom on his phone. "You have the governor waiting on line one." Buster looked at Evan and winked.

The sheriff looked at the phone. "What governor?"

"You know, Sheriff, the Governor of Colorado, your boss."

The sheriff waved at Evan and Buster to leave him alone. They were only too happy to oblige. As Evan was closing the door behind them, the sheriff called out, "You two hang around here, we're not done yet."

"Good job, Buster, I was about to detonate on him."

"I could see that. You need to cultivate patience."

"Yeah, especially for dealing with morons. What the hell was his point? I got the feeling he didn't know if he was mad at us or not, and if he was, what, exactly, was he mad about."

"I believe you're right. He doesn't know. He was trying to figure it out as he went along."

"Thank God for Cheree's influence with the governor. We could have been stuck in there until lunch."

"You never would have lasted that long."

Evan slapped Buster on the back, "You're right. Thanks, partner, this is another fine mess you've gotten me out of, although I think maybe you got me into it in the first place."

Buster ignored the comment. Consulting his watch, he asked, "How long do you think he'll be on the phone?"

"Not long. If you were the governor, how long would you want to talk to him?"

"Good point. That means we won't have to hang around here much longer."

Five minutes later they were summoned back to Tate's office. He was all smiles. "That was the governor," he announced as if they hadn't heard. "I've decided to volunteer your services to the State Bureau of Criminal Apprehension." He stood up, clasped his hands behind his back and began pacing behind his desk. "The governor feels we could be, with their help, instrumental in solving Pike's murder quickly. Because of his confidence in us, I felt it would be advantageous for us to have you two detailed to the state. This will allow you to concentrate on this one case only, devoting all your energies to finding Pike's killer. The governor thought my idea was excellent. He'll have the state aid us in every way possible." He stopped lecturing them long enough to consider Evan and Buster seated in front of him. The gesture was calculated to give his next comment the importance he thought it deserved. "Of course, I fully expect both of you to give this assignment your maximum effort— and don't forget, you still work for me." He paused again, "Any questions?"

Evan was going to respond either by laughing or passing gas, he hadn't decided which when Buster beat him to the draw. "Thank you for your confidence, Sheriff, when do we start?"

The sheriff looked at the clock on the wall, again for emphasis. "I told the governor you'd contact the medical examiner, some woman by the name of Nicoletti, by nine o-clock. She apparently has some information that could be useful. You just started." Buster and Evan got up to make their exit. "And deputies," he added, "keep me informed."

"Yes, sir," they replied in unison.

Evan followed Buster out of the office, down the hall, into the outer office past Suzy and right on out the front door of the building. As Evan passed Suzy, he made a circle of his forefinger and thumb, raising his right hand to his lips to indicate they were going down the street to the Stockman's Cafe for coffee. She smiled, "Bring me back a caramel roll." Evan nodded and kept moving.

Seated in a back booth, with their hands wrapped around cups of hot coffee, they talked. "The guy is truly amazing," Evan said. "According to him, this is his idea! What does he take us for?"

"What he takes us for is immaterial, but you're right, he is amazing. He can't imagine anyone being smarter than he is. To me, that indicates a truly stupid individual."

"Yeah, we'd be a lot better off if he would try to be useful instead of trying to be important." Evan was going to continue, but Buster was staring at him. "What?"

"That's very profound. I'm impressed. It would appear some of my insight is finally rubbing off on you."

"Yeah, right. Okay, Mister Insight, what do we do next?"

"I'm not sure what I do, but the next thing you do is to call the state medical examiner, some woman by the name of Nicoletti I believe."

"I'll do that right now." Evan pulled out his cell phone. "And I think what we do next depends on what the Nicoletti woman says. We're working for her now."

"Only technically," Buster reminded him, "You heard the last thing Clouseau told us."

"Doctor Nicoletti please," Evan told the cell phone and waved his hand at Buster for silence. "Yes, please have her call Deputy Evan Coleman as soon as possible. She has my cell phone number." Evan ended the call and placed the phone on the table. "She's out of the office. And since when did you ever pay attention to our boss?"

Buster grinned. "You ever heard the expression 'Do as I say, not as I do?' I can retire any time; you still have twenty or more to go."

"Of all the things you are, I never thought you were a hypocrite." He shook his head in mock grief. "I guess you can never be sure, even about your partner."

He intended to say more but the phone rang. "Deputy Coleman."

"Deputy Evan Coleman?"

"Yes, ma'am. At your service." He rotated the phone up away from his mouth. "It's that Nicoletti woman," he whispered to Buster.

"Evan, this is the Nicoletti woman."

"You weren't supposed to hear that."

"I have exceptional hearing," Cheree told him.

"I'll have to remember that. Our boss referred to you this morning as 'some woman by the name of Nicoletti' and we're still having fun with it."

"He sounds charming. I can't wait to meet him."

"Be careful what you wish for."

"Well, right now, I wish you'd tell me what he said after the governor finished with him."

"As of right now, Buster and I are all yours. And not only that, it was his idea to volunteer our services."

"That's funny, I was in the governor's office when he was talking to him and I could have sworn I heard him tell the sheriff he wanted you two working for the state, no ifs, ands or buts."

"Since you have such exceptional hearing, I'll have to go along with your version. Did the sheriff put up much resistance?"

"No, the governor was very patronizing before he delivered the ultimatum. I don't even think your boss thought about protesting."

"I'm sure he didn't. It was obvious he was happy about the deal. Two years ago he shook the governor's hand at a convention. We heard about it at least a dozen times."

Cheree laughed. "I'll see if I can't get the governor to call him a time or two with progress reports as we proceed."

"Don't do too much; he won't be able to get his hat on."

"I won't. Are you and Buster ready to start?"

"Yeah, in fact, Buster called the warden at the prison in Buena Vista early this morning to request an interview with Abel Pike. We have an appointment with the warden at eleven this morning."

"What time will you get there? I could rearrange my schedule and meet you." Evan could hear the rustle of papers. "If I can get the chopper, I could be there."

"That's good. We'll leave in about a half-hour and see you there at eleven."

"Okay, I have to get moving. I'll call if anything changes. I have to run. Goodbye."

Evan laid the phone down. "Let's have some breakfast or did Amy feed you this morning?"

"No, I was up early, and I let her sleep in. I could stand some nourishment now that you mention it. I think I'll have steak and eggs."

They both had the Rancher's special, a ten-ounce sirloin, three eggs, toast, and hash browns. The cafe's owner had his own herd of Belted Galloway cattle. The Stockman's Café was noted for its lean beef. Buster and Evan had their steaks rare and their eggs over easy with buttered toast and hash browns. They ate seriously for they had a serious job to do, and neither knew when they'd get a chance to eat their next meal. It was only seventy miles to Buena Vista, but they knew that situations can develop quickly and take time to resolve.

They had some time now; later they might be too busy for lunch.

Between mouthfuls Evan said to Buster, "If I ever get too old to appreciate a good breakfast, promise you'll shoot me."

Buster cut a piece of steak, eating it before answering. "If you get that old and I'm still alive, I'll be in no condition to pull the hammer back on my revolver. You'll have to shoot yourself."

Evan finished chewing, took a drink of coffee, and remarked, "Okay, but if you're that bad, I'll have to shoot you first."

"Deal."

When they finished, they paid the bill. Evan didn't forget to buy Suzy an incredibly gooey caramel roll. Strolling back into the office, they met the sheriff coming out. "Where have you two been?" He demanded.

"At the Stockman's eating breakfast," Buster explained. "We're meeting that Nicoletti woman at the Buena Vista prison in about an hour."

"Oh yeah. What for?"

"We're going to talk to Pike's son and she wants to be there."

"Pike's son is a con?"

"No, he's a guard. Remember our discussion this morning? We told you he worked at the prison."

"Oh yeah, that's right. What's she like, the Nicoletti woman?"

There was a pause while Buster waited for Evan to answer. They had told the sheriff the head of the crime lab had been in charge of investigating the scene of Pike's murder, but they had not referred to her by name. Her name did appear in their written reports. Obviously, the sheriff hadn't bothered to read them yet. "I don't know, Sheriff, she sounds demanding," Evan said.

"Probably ugly too. You boys have my sympathies." He walked away whistling.

Evan passed Suzy the bag containing her caramel roll. "Where's the big man headed?"

"Big headed man you mean. I don't know, he didn't tell me, but if you want my opinion, he should be going to buy a new hat. His head's been swelling at an alarming rate ever since he talked to the governor. You two didn't have any thing to do with that did you?" She took Evan's offering and pealed away the waxed paper in which it was wrapped. "And what's the deal with you two working for the state? How did you pull that off?"

"Suzy, I'm appalled at your suspicious nature," Evan said feigning innocence. "I certainly don't know the governor at all, let alone well enough to have him call the sheriff. Buster, do have that kind of influence with the governor?"

"Never met the man."

"There you go, Suzy. We're not guilty. All I did was find a dead man and now I'm working for the state. According to Tate, he volunteered us to the state out of the goodness of his heart."

Suzy rolled her eyes from Evan to Buster. "It's no use, one of you lies and the other swears to it. How long is this going to take?"

"I don't have a clue. Could be a few days, could be a few months."

"It better not take anywhere near a month. I have to get all the other deputies to work overtime to make up for you two." She waved a piece of paper at them. "He's already got me making up a roster. Plus all vacations are canceled effective immediately. Do you know how many guys were planning on going elk hunting?"

"All of them?" Evan asked tentatively

"That's right, all of them! Except you two of course, and I assume that's only because you can shoot one in your back yard any time you want to."

Buster looked at Evan. "Have you noticed how many people keep referring to us as 'you two'? Why do you suppose that is?"

Ignoring her, Evan put his hand on Buster's shoulder and got him moving down the hall, past Suzy. "I don't know, partner, but I've noticed it too. Let's get our stuff and head up to Buena Vista. Maybe the people there will show us a little respect."

They collected what they thought they might need from their desks, notebooks, a few business cards, some extra ammunition just in case, and a set of radios. On their way out, they informed Suzy of their plans. "We'll check in before four-thirty," Evan told her.

"Don't forget," she chastised, "and be careful."

Evan nodded and Buster tipped his hat. They were out the door, leaving her with the job of calling the rest of force, canceling vacations, and requiring overtime. There were only six deputies and they would all be affected. She wasn't happy, and the deputies weren't going to like it either.

"You drive," Buster told Evan. "I think breakfast has affected my driving skills."

"You mean you want a nap?"

"Something like that."

"Do you realize," Evan asked as he slid behind the wheel of his cruiser, "how unpopular we're going to be?"

"Don't give it a thought. The sheriff volunteered us, remember? He's going to be the unpopular one."

"He's already unpopular. Some of it's going to roll downhill."

"Oh well," Buster sighed as Evan pulled away from the curb. He leaned back in his seat, pulling his hat down low over his eyes. "Just try to give me a smooth ride and don't break the speed limit."

When Evan cleared the city limits, he ran the cruiser up to sixty-five, and engaged the cruise control. It was nine-thirty on a fine, clear morning with bright sunshine flooding down on the high prairie. A temperature in the upper fifties with clear skies had been promised. It was a wonderful day to go down the road. Evan thought he might even catch a speeder before they got to Poncha Springs. He turned on the radar. He decided not to stop anyone unless they were going over seventy-five. Two minutes later, the first vehicle he met, was doing seventy-eight. It was a new pickup pulling a goose-neck, horse trailer. Evan decided to let him go, watching the truck shrink in his rear view mirror. "Probably running empty anyway," he told himself. Then he recalled what Buster had told him from his discussion with Ruth Pike. Her mysterious visitors had been driving a late model, white and gold pickup with dual rear wheels. The truck that just passed him was white and gold, and a dually. "What are the odds?" he asked himself. He braked hard and flipped on the lights.

Buster came forward against his seatbelt with the sudden deceleration. "What's up?"

"Speeder, and it's a late model, white and gold dually pulling a horse trailer."

"What are the odds?"

"I don't know, at least five thousand to one. What do you think?" He cranked hard on the steering wheel to make a U-turn in the highway.

"Go get him!"

The driver of the pickup was watching the cruiser in his mirrors. When he saw the brake lights wink at him, he knew he'd been made. He took his foot off the gas and began coasting. By the time Evan got the cruiser pointed at him, his speed was down to fifty. He was stopped on the shoulder before Evan reached him.

Evan and Buster approached the pickup from opposite sides. Evan's right hand rested gently on the butt of his pistol. He glanced in the trailer as he walked past. Over the box of the truck he said to Buster, "Empty." Buster nodded and kept walking. The driver of the pickup was watching Evan in his left-hand mirror as he approached. Evan was watching the driver stare at him in the same mirror. He didn't look much like a young athlete. Suddenly the driver opened the door.

"Hold it right there!" Evan commanded. "Show me your hands and come out slowly!" Evan's pistol was out, leveled at the open door.

A pair of empty hands appeared in the open doorway followed by a short, white-haired, old gentleman. "What's goin' on? I was only doin' seventy-five."

Buster came around the front of the pickup. "Hello, Mack," he addressed the old man, "Actually you were doin' seventy-eight." He waved at Evan to put up his pistol. "Where's the fire?"

The man turned to meet Buster. "Hello, Buster." He jerked his right hand over his shoulder and pointed to Evan with his thumb. "It's in his eyes!"

Buster laughed. "Mack, meet Evan Coleman. Evan, meet Mack Williams. Mack retired from law enforcement about fifteen years ago."

Evan and Mack shook hands. "What's goin' on, or have you guys just got a new method for apprehending speeders?"

"So you admit you were speeding?" Buster asked.

"Of course, I was speeding. What the hell good is this new truck if I can't get down the road in a hurry? But that ain't why you two stopped me now, is it?"

"No, it isn't," Evan admitted. "We're looking for somebody."

"Somebody in a white pickup?"

"Somebody in a white and gold, late model, dually pickup with a matching horse trailer to be exact," Buster told him.

"What do you want this somebody for?"

"Can't tell you that, Mack. Sorry."

"This got anything to do with Pike's murder?" Mack asked innocently.

Evan and Buster were momentarily dumbstruck. Evan responded first. "Maybe, maybe not," he said. *Where had he heard about Pike's murder?*

"Where'd you hear Pike was murdered?" Buster asked.

"I just heard it over the radio about twenty minutes ago. Your boss was talking to the highway patrol, said something about Ben Pike getting whacked on Friday."

"Mack, do have a scanner in your truck?"

"Course I do Buster, I gotta keep up on the news."

Evan turned to Buster, "Jesus, Buster, let's get out of here. We stay here talking to this guy any longer, we're going to have to arrest him." He grabbed Mack's hand and shook it again quickly. "Pleased to meet you, Mister Williams, slow down and leave the scanner at home. You of all people should know it's illegal to have one in your vehicle." He didn't wait for Mack to answer. He turned to start back to the patrol car.

Mack watched him go. "Hasty fella!" he commented to Buster. "You better take care of him."

"I do, Mack, I do. Good to see you again and get that scanner out of your truck. You aren't completely immune you know."

"What an idiot," Evan commented when they were once again headed north towards Buena Vista.

"Mack's harmless."

"I'm not talking about your old buddy. I'm talking about our stupid-ass boss, Clouseau."

"Yeah, apparently he had to tell somebody, and since he only has one friend, he had to tell Trooper Davis. I'll bet it's on the five o-clock news."

"Why did he have to tell him over the radio? If he felt he had to talk, he could have at least met him somewhere semi-private. Damn, that man is dumb."

"I agree, he gives new meaning to the word, but the news was bound to get out sooner or later. As long as we don't have to deal with the press, I'm not going to worry." He slouched down in his seat and tipped his hat forward. "Do me a favor; don't pull over any more speeders."

Evan wanted company. He wanted to talk, even if it was only about the sheriff. He was keyed and he wanted Buster to share his momentum. "What if they're going really fast?" he asked.

"How fast is really fast?"

"Oh, I don't know. Say maybe a hundred and ten."

"That's pretty fast. You'd have to go after them."

"Okay, how about a hundred?"

"What is your problem, boy?"

"I'm only trying to put a relative value on your nap time. I know it's important, I just want to know how important."

Buster sighed. "You can chase anybody doing a hundred. And don't ask me about ninety."

Evan smiled. That would have been his next question. He tried being silent for a while, but he couldn't make it last. "Do you think Pike's wife had anything to do with his murder?"

Buster didn't reply immediately. He'd considered that possibility several times himself. Based on what they had for evidence, she was an unlikely suspect, but he would be the first to admit they didn't have squat for evidence. "You don't want your poor, old partner to get any rest, do you?"

Evan ignored the question. "Based on what we have, she's as good a suspect as any. Seems to me, living with Pike for twenty-five years would be good enough motive."

Buster pushed his hat back into place and sat up straight. "The only problem with that theory is what does Ruth get out of it, other than the obvious?" Buster realized Evan wasn't going to leave him alone. He might as well cooperate. "According to Ben's will, the ranch goes to his son. Under state law she owns it, but she can't sell it, and when she dies it belongs to Abel."

"We don't know that for certain. That's what Pike told you some years ago. How do we know he didn't change his will? Ruth might have somehow persuaded him to leave it all to her."

"Yeah, that's possible. We'll have to wait and see. Maybe just getting rid of her husband was enough, but I didn't get the impression she was glad to see him go. She seems genuinely distressed. Why do you think she's a possibility?"

"I don't even know if I think she is. That's what I'm asking you, if we should consider her a suspect? Her story about the two guys in the pickup with the horse trailer could be a total fabrication."

"Yeah, it could, but there's the matter of the horse she said they had with them. She was describing a grulla paint. That seems to correlate with the horse hair you and Cheree found."

"Yes, it does. If she's telling the truth, should she still be a suspect? I don't want to overlook anything."

Buster was silent, pondering the few facts they had. "Let's assume she made up the story about the two guys in the white pickup with the horse trailer. That would mean she planted the red hair on Pike's body, and made sure the grulla horse left some of his hairs lying around, where you and Cheree could find them. That seems to be a stretch to me." He was quiet again for a short time. "I don't think she's involved."

"I thought you were of the opinion this murder was committed by a woman?"

"I still think there was a woman involved, but I don't think Ruth is the woman."

"Okay, so it's not Pike's old lady who did him in, but I don't think she's telling us everything she knows. Assume her story about the two big guys in the white pickup is true. Maybe the red haired guy who came looking for Pike had a bone to pick with him. Maybe Pike raped his sister, or his mother, or at least one of them claimed he did."

"I like that a lot better than Ruth killing him. I believe he was killed in retribution for something, and rape certainly seems possible considering his wounds." Buster shook his head. "I hope Abel Pike can tell us something because right now, we don't have much."

"I'm not betting we get a lot out of him. If he knows something about his old man raping someone, I don't think he'll talk. Cheree described him as the strong, quiet type. I think he'll take any secrets he has about his father to his grave."

"We'll find out soon enough," Buster replied consulting his wristwatch. "About twenty minutes, we'll be there."

Their conversation ceased abruptly, both of them lost in private thoughts. The last twenty-five miles slipped by uneventfully. Then they were driving up to the front gate of the prison entrance. As they approached, a helicopter was landing on the pad across from the warden's office.

9

Cheree was waiting for Evan and Buster outside the prison administration building. "Good morning, gentlemen, you're right on time."

"What did you expect? You're our new boss," Evan told her while he discreetly gave her the once over. She looked terrific in a dark blue business suit with a skirt that not quite covered her knees. Her legs were as good as he had imagined.

Buster tipped his Stetson, "Morning ma'am, always a pleasure no matter where we meet." He moved to open the door for her.

"Thank you Buster, I'm flattered." She went inside followed by the two deputies.

They announced themselves to the security guard who immediately directed them down the hall to the warden's office. "Go right in, he's expecting you," she told them.

"I don't suppose there's been any earth shattering development in the case during the last two hours?" Cheree asked Evan as they walked down the hall.

"Not on our end. How about on yours?"

"Don't forget about what that speeder you stopped told us," Buster interjected.

Cheree regarded Evan. "Holding out on your new boss already?" Considering the things he would be willing to do for this woman, withholding information from her would not be possible.

"Merely an oversight. On the way up here, we pulled a guy over, but not for speeding. He was driving a late model, two-tone, dually pickup and pulling a horse trailer. The vehicle was a potential match to the truck Ruth Pike's mysterious visitors were driving."

"I assume it wasn't them or you wouldn't be here."

"You're right. As fate would have it, the driver was an old friend of Buster's, a retired cop from Salida. And guess what he asked us about?"

She was quiet for a moment. "Pike's murder?"

Evan was surprised. "A lucky guess? Or have you been holding out on us?"

"Neither, merely a deduction."

"Okay, now deduce how he found out."

"That's a little tougher. I know I haven't talked, so that leaves the governor, my people, you two, Pike's survivors, and your boss. I don't believe my people or the governor leaked it and I'm pretty sure you two haven't said anything. Ruth, her two sons, and your boss are the only others who know. Am I on the right track?"

"Yes, you are and because I don't want you to be wrong, I'm going to give you a hint. The guilty party's initials are Sheriff Tate."

"He didn't waste any time, did he?"

"No. We told him at seven, the governor called at about eight-thirty and we stopped Buster's buddy in the white and gold pickup at about nine-thirty. Tate was going somewhere when we were leaving the shop. He must have gotten on the radio to inform someone at the state patrol before he started the engine on his car. We're betting it's on the evening news."

"It can't be helped, I suppose," Cheree said. "I hope he didn't go into all the gory details."

"Probably not over the radio, but you can bet he will if he gets a call from a reporter. In fact, he'll probably add a few."

"When is he up for re-election?"

"He's got a year and a half left."

"You need to take his job away," Cheree said, looking Evan directly in the eyes.

He stopped abruptly just outside the entrance to the warden's office. "What?"

"You need to run against him and take his job."

"I agree," Buster chimed in.

Evan's hand rested on the knob of the door. He stared back at Cheree. All he could think of was how good she looked. "Now why would I want all those problems?" he finally asked.

"Because, we need the brightest, most honest and competent people in charge, especially in positions of public service. Don't you think you qualify? I think you do."

Evan's hand started turning the doorknob. "I'll have to think about it," he said trying hard not to.

"See that you do," Buster told him as the door opened.

Inside was another office complete with a secretary. Cheree handed her a business card and introduced herself, Buster and Evan. "We have an appointment with Warden Huarrera."

The woman rose, and talking to Cheree, but looking at Evan, said, "Yes, he's expecting you, but I'm afraid you won't be able to talk to Mister Pike."

"Really," Cheree asked, "why would that be? He's the reason we came."

The secretary was about to explain when Warden Huarrera entered the room from his office. "Doctor Nicoletti and Deputies Coleman and Alexander, I presume," he said extending his hand to Cheree first. He was a short, very muscular man with a deep, broad chest. He had practically no neck. His head seemed almost to sprout directly from his powerful shoulders. His face was lined and pocked, but he sported a thick growth of wavy white hair which somewhat softened his hard features. He reminded Evan of a tough, old bulldog with a touch of class. The amazing thing was his voice. Based on his physical appearance, he should have had a deep, gruff voice, but he didn't. His voice was thin and reedy, as if all his chest muscles were squeezing his larynx to produce a sound completely foreign to the way he looked. The prison guards called him 'Squeaky', but not to his face.

After handshakes, Cheree wasted no time. "I understand, Warden, we won't be able to talk to Mister Pike."

Huarrera fired a quick glance towards his secretary. "Please, come into my office," and he lead them past his secretary's desk into his office. He gestured to three chairs arranged in a semicircle in front of a massive desk built from a species of wood Evan didn't recognize. "Have a seat. Anyone care for coffee?" The three of them politely declined.

After the Warden settled in behind his fortress, he leaned back in his chair. "I know I promised you an interview with Abel Pike this morning, however, that was before I knew he didn't show up for work." Evan, Buster and Cheree all briefly looked at each other. It was hard for the Warden not to notice.

"I share your surprise. Mister Pike rarely has a sick day and has never had an unexcused absence. He has never failed to notify his supervisor if he were going to be late. I told his supervisor to contact him. As yet, we haven't been able to reach him."

"Was he aware we were coming to interview him?" Buster asked.

"No, I talked to you at six-thirty and first shift doesn't start until seven. I didn't tell his supervisor until just an hour ago that he would be having visitors. That's when I found out he didn't report for work. He's a model employee. He does his job, he doesn't complain about anything, and he's actually respected by the inmates." He paused for emphasis. If you can believe that."

"So his supervisor hasn't been able to contact him and that's all we know?" Evan asked. "Is there anyone else at home? Does he have a family?"

"I believe he lives alone. According to some of the other guards who know a little about him, he has an ex-wife somewhere, but no children. He lives northwest of town in the hills."

Evan looked at Cheree and Buster. "We better drive out there and take a look."

"We can take the chopper," Cheree volunteered.

"If it's all right with you," Buster said, "I'd rather drive."

"You'll probably have to drive," the Warden said. "My understanding is he has a cabin in the woods. I couldn't guarantee you there's enough room to set the chopper down."

Cheree acquiesced, "Okay, we'll drive. I don't want to scratch up the governor's helicopter."

"I'll have my secretary get you an address and directions." Huarrera punched the intercom button on his phone. "Alice, please get Abel Pike's address and directions to his house for our visitors." He looked back up at them, "I'd really like to go with you, get out of the office for awhile. Problem is, I've got another appointment in a half hour." Evan thought his squeaky voice lacked conviction. "The chief of the State Corrections Bureau is on his way and I have no idea what he wants."

"Well, we'll get out of your hair," Evan told him. "Thanks for your time and assistance."

Huarrera pushed back from his desk to stand. "You're welcome, even though I wasn't much help. Hopefully, you'll find Mister Pike at home and there'll be an easy explanation." They shook hands and left his office.

The warden's secretary handed Evan a piece of paper. It was a computer-generated map of the local area with directions to Pike's house. She was an attractive woman, probably in her mid thirties. She smiled sweetly at Evan. "Here are the directions to Mister Pike's home," she said, managing to touch his fingertips while passing him the paper. "If you need anything else please don't hesitate to call me. My number is on the bottom." The invitation was as overt as any Evan had ever received.

"Well, thank you Alice, I'll keep that in mind," Evan said as politely as he could. He did not return the flirtation. He knew Cheree would not miss Alice's intent.

Outside the building, Cheree asked Evan for the directions. He handed her the map. "I'll navigate," she told him. She looked at the paper to see Alice had not only given Evan her office number, she had included her home phone number. "She must think you're looking for something besides Abel Pike's house. She put her home phone number on here."

"She's obviously confused."

"Confused about what?"

"Thinking I would need something from her.

"Do you have this effect on all women?"

They had reached Evan's cruiser. He opened the door for her. "I don't know. Do I?"

Cheree turned to Buster, "Buster, do you want to sit next to him? I probably should sit in the back. I might swoon if I'm too close."

"No ma'am, you sit up front. I guarantee you'll be just fine. He doesn't have any adverse effect on intelligent women."

"Okay, Buster, I'll trust you." She slid into the passenger side of the front seat. However, Buster was wrong. Evan made her feel emotions she thought had died with her husband three years ago. Jealousy was one of them. She couldn't believe the nerve of the warden's secretary, giving him her home phone number. She had not missed the way Alice had touched Evan's hand when she handed him the directions either. It was incredibly blatant. *What's my problem? Evan and I don't have a relationship. Why am I jealous over some bimbo who makes a pass at him? It probably happens all the time.* And when she thought that, she was even more jealous. *Good, God, I'm acting like a high school sophomore!*

The car starting brought her back to reality. "Cheree, buckle up. We don't want to get pulled over for not wearing seatbelts," Evan told her.

"Oh, yeah, sorry." Buckling her seatbelt, she consulted the map. "Okay, go north on twenty-four through town. About ten miles north of town, take a left on three-eighty-seven and then we have to wind around to the northwest for about three miles until we get to Mountain Lake Drive. Pike's place is at the end of an unnamed road that connects with Mountain Lake, although his address is 19240 Mountain Lake Drive. Oh well, if we don't find it, we can always call Alice."

"I'm sure the three of us can find it with no problem," Evan said. "And not to change the subject, but Buster, how well do you know the warden?"

"Not well. I met him once a few years back and I know he has a good reputation. He runs a tight ship, doesn't tolerate any bad behavior from the inmates or the guards, and he does it without being a hard ass. He commands respect. Not only that, I'd hate to have to wrestle him."

"Yeah, I agree, but what's with his voice? He sounds like a parakeet."

"The story I heard he was shot. He was a lieutenant with the First Infantry Division during the second Gulf War. His platoon walked into an ambush and his radiotelephone operator was wounded. When he got his troops regrouped, Huarrera went back for the RTO and got hit in the throat and the shoulder. He was still able to rescue his RTO and they both survived, although it was two years and several surgeries later before he could talk. You still think he sounds like a parakeet?"

"Well, yeah, I guess I do, but have I ever told you how much respect I have for talking birds, especially when they're built like Huarrera."

"I hope so. He's a good man, although I've heard rumors he's come under criticism from some of the more liberal state officials. They think he's too hard on the inmates."

"He doesn't have to worry about his critics," Cheree said. "As far as the governor is concerned, he's doing just fine. In fact, the visitor he mentioned, the head of the State Corrections Bureau, is coming to see him to tell him just that."

"He sounded like he was dreading it." Evan said.

"Probably because he doesn't know the purpose of the visit."

"How do you know so much?"

"Because I talked to the governor this morning, and when I mentioned I was going to see Abel Pike at the Buena Vista prison, he told me all about the warden. I thought about telling Huarrera the situation, but decided it was none of my business."

Evan glanced at the odometer. "I've got ten miles from town, what county road am I looking for?"

"Three-eighty-seven," she said pointing ahead to an intersection about two hundred yards down the road. "I'll bet that's it up ahead." It was. Evan made the left turn onto the graveled road. "Now follow this for about three miles and we'll eventually come to a road that enters from the left. Pike's house should be on it." She consulted the map again, "I think."

The road twisted and turned, always climbing, and soon they were in the trees, high above the valley. Crossing a rickety old bridge spanning a skinny, dry creek, they continued for another mile and a half. To their left, at a slightly higher altitude, Evan caught a glimpse of a green, metal roof. He remembered the warden had referred to Abel Pike's home as a cabin in the woods. Evan wondered what kind of place it would be. From what he'd heard about Abel, he imagined it would be small and basic. He also wondered what happened to the man. According to the warden, he was an exceptional employee with an exceptional work record. *Maybe after losing his old man, especially the way it went down, he went on a weekend bender and couldn't get up this morning.*

"I think this must be it," Cheree interrupted his thoughts. "Take that left just ahead."

Evan dutifully turned. They started up a narrow winding road. "Must be his driveway," Buster commented.

"How does he get in and out during the winter?" Cheree asked.

As they followed the switchbacks up the hill, the house played peek-a-boo with them. Every time the road turned to the left or the right, they got a glimpse at what appeared to be a log cabin with a green roof. As they drove closer, the trees grew thicker causing them to lose sight of it completely. Suddenly, when they rounded the last corner, the house was in front of them, but it was no cabin. What they had seen from the drive up the hill was only a small portion of the house. Evan stopped the patrol car on the paved parking area next to the attached, three-car garage. From there, they could see the front of the house. It was two stories tall and had a classic western look with a covered porch running the entire length of the front. A huge stone fireplace chase climbing high above the roof separated two large picture windows.

"Not what I expected," Evan commented as he got out of the car.

"Must be close to two thousand square feet on the first floor alone," Buster said.

"If I were going to have a log cabin in the woods," said Cheree, "this would be it. I hope he's home so we can see the inside."

"Let's find out," Evan suggested as he started down the front porch towards the doubled-door entry. Cheree and Buster followed close on his heels.

The doors were carved masterpieces of solid oak. They depicted two brown bears standing on their back legs. Separated by the narrow gap between the doors, the bears regarded each other with hostility. Not finding a doorbell, Evan used the big brass knocker. It made a solid thud that seemed to reverberate all the way down to his feet. When there was no immediate response, he knocked again. After waiting about thirty seconds, he said to Cheree and Buster, "Keep knocking, I'm going to walk around back." He couldn't help looking in the windows as he walked down the porch. From what he could see of the darkened interior, the house was well furnished and neatly kept. He stepped off the porch and rounded the corner. The first thing he saw was a large corral about a hundred feet to the south of the house. Six horses were standing still, watching him. The second thing he saw brought him to a dead stop. He turned and ran.

"Back to the car!" he commanded to Buster and Cheree.

"What? Why?" Cheree demanded.

"Back!" He waved towards the car.

Buster grabbed Cheree by the arm and started moving. Evan came running close behind, hand on his pistol, ready to draw it. Buster hustled Cheree into the back seat as Evan jumped in the driver's seat. By the time Buster got in the passenger side, Evan had the motor running. When Buster slammed his door shut, Evan slammed the cruiser into reverse and rocketed backwards down the driveway. He didn't stop until he had rounded the corner and the house disappeared from view.

"What, Evan?" Cheree demanded. "What did you see?"

"Pike."

"Is he down?" Buster asked.

"Yeah. Flat on his back. Staring at the sky."

"What are you talking about?"

"Pike is laying face up on the ground about fifty feet from the south end of the house. His chest is covered with blood. It appears he's been shot at least once. It looks like he was ambushed on the way to his horses. I don't know if the shooter is still out there or not."

"You think he's dead?" Buster asked.

"Be my guess."

"How do we find out for certain?" asked Cheree

"You don't find out. You stay here with Buster who's going to call for backup. I'll find out. Buster, you call the Buena Vista PD. I'm going to see if Pike's still breathing."

"That's insane," Cheree told him, "If the shooter is still out there, you can't expose yourself."

"I don't intend to. Buster, grab my binoculars out of the glove box."

Buster handed him the glasses. "Where's your rifle?"

"In the trunk." Evan punched the trunk release button and got out of the car, quickly slamming the door behind him.

"Be careful," Cheree told his departing figure as he ran back up the driveway in a low crouch, rifle in hand. Buster already had the Buena Vista police on the radio.

When Evan reached the house he was breathing hard. He stopped at the front corner, waiting long enough to calm down. *We didn't get shot at while we were knocking on the front door. The porch should be safe.* Rifle at the ready, he rounded the corner and moved down the porch, watching for any movement in the trees. He stopped at the far corner of the porch to kneel down. He thoroughly glassed as much of the area to the south of the house as he could see. "Nothing," he whispered to himself after studying the area for several minutes. Taking a deep breath and thinking he didn't get paid enough, he slowly eased part way around the corner until he could see Pike.

The horses in the corral looked to be at ease. He watched them for a while before glassing the trees behind the corral. "Nothing again," he told himself. He moved a little farther around the corner, and brought the binoculars to look on Pike's inert form. From his distance he could tell the man was dead. He could even see the place where a bullet had most likely entered his chest just to the left of his sternum. Right through the heart! He moved the glasses up to see Pike's head. A capital 'R' had been cut in his forehead. The binoculars were sharp enough for him to tell the blood was dried. He lowered the glasses, ducked back around the corner and hurried back to the car. About ten minutes had elapsed. He could hear the faint whoops of sirens on the highway down in the valley.

Cheree was on the radio when he got back in the car. "She's calling in her crime scene people," Buster explained. "She's also upset with you."

"Why?"

"I don't know, something about being foolhardy. Is Abel Pike dead?"

"Yes, if that's Abel on the ground, he's dead. My guess is he was bushwhacked early this morning when he went out to tend to his horses."

"Anything else you noticed?"

"He's got an 'R' scratched in his forehead."

"Seems we're a little late, again."

"Deputy Evan Coleman, you're a damn fool!" Cheree said, handing the microphone back to Buster. Her face was flushed. She was not happy. Evan thought she looked beautiful—perilously so. "Tell me you'll never do anything that stupid again!"

"I didn't think it was all that stupid. I..."

She cut him off. "If you thought it was so critical we get back to car and call for backup, why did you think you wouldn't be in any danger. Do you think you're bullet proof? Or what?"

"This is my job, not...."

She cut him off again. "Your job is what? To get shot?" She was silent for a moment and Evan was about to explain how he could take chances with his life, but not with hers. She didn't give him a chance. "Look, you two are assigned to the state on this case and right now, I'm the state's representative. So I'm your boss and from now on when we're together, I call the shots!"

Evan looked to Buster. Buster raised his hands in surrender. "Yes, ma'am," they said in unison.

"Okay, that's settled. Buster has the Buena Vista police on the way and I've sent the chopper pilot back to pick up a CSI team. By the time they get here, you and the police will probably have the area secured." She exhaled long and slow. "Is he dead?"

"I'm afraid so. There's a hole in the middle of his chest and a lot blood on the ground. Our mystery killer beat us to the punch."

"He was shot?"

"Yeah, and I bet I can tell you the caliber of the bullet."

"A two-seventy?" she asked.

"I'd bet a paycheck on it." In the background they could hear sirens howling their way up the hill. Evan lit up the lights on the cruiser. They waited in silence for the police to arrive.

10

Four units answered Buster's call for back up. There were four cops in two cars from Buena Vista, plus a Chaffee County deputy and a state patrol cop who happened to be in the area when Buster's call for help came through. As they got out of the car to meet the backup, Cheree said to Evan, "You handle the troops and the outside search. I'll go inside and have a look around."

"Deal, but we have to clear the house first."

"Deal."

After Evan made quick introductions, he explained the situation. "Buster and I have been detailed by the governor to work with the state to solve the murder of a citizen, Ben Pike. Ben Pike is the father of Abel Pike who lives here. Doctor Nicoletti is the state medical examiner and has been doing the forensic work on the case. She's also in charge of this investigation. We were supposed to interview Abel Pike this morning at the prison where he's a guard. When we got there, we were informed by Warden Huarrera that Abel Pike didn't show for work. The warden suggested we come up here to see if we could find him. We found him, but he's dead. He's lying outside, at the opposite end of the house, shot through the heart. It looks like he was ambushed on the way to his corral."

Evan paused to consider his audience. He had their undivided attention.

"We don't know if the shooter is still out there. I doubt it, but it's possible." He paused again to study their reaction to his speculation. He had them completely. "The front of the house faces west. The dead man is on the south end about fifty feet out. Beyond where he's lying, another hundred feet to the south, is a large corral. There are at least six horses in it. The area all around the house and corral is wooded. My guess is the shooter was waiting somewhere at the back of the corral and shot Pike from there. The ground rises slightly there. He possibly shot from the prone position. Here's my plan. After you've heard it, if you don't like it, we can discuss alternatives."

Technically, Officer Phillips, the county deputy, should have assumed leadership. It was her county, well outside the Buena Vista city limits. But she was satisfied by Evan's explanation, okay with him being in charge. The four cops from Buena Vista had been instructed by their police chief to take orders from Buster and his partner. The chief and Buster knew each other quite well. The chief trusted him. Trooper Thomas, the state highway cop, had been instructed to assist, not assume command.

"Okay, who's got a rifle?"

Phillips and Thomas raised their hands. "Good," Evan said. "What I'd like is for you two to take up positions at the corners of the house, one of you at the southwest corner and the other at the southeast corner. I want you to watch for movement and provide cover if we come under fire. The rest of us will split into two teams of three each. One team will work through the trees on the west side of the house, the other team on the east. Both teams will head to the south, and we'll meet in the middle behind the corral about two hundred yards due south of the house." He stopped, waiting for comments. There were none. "Okay, one last detail is the house. We haven't been inside. I want to go through it before we sweep the woods."

"What are the chances the killer would be in there?" The question came from one of the Buena Vista cops.

"I was hoping you could tell me that." There was a round of nervous laughter. "I doubt it. Actually, if this perpetrator is the same one that killed the first victim, I think he's long gone. However, we need to check the house first. What I propose is to place two of you on each side of the house and two of you at the back with Doctor Nicoletti. Buster and I will enter through the garage at the back. As soon as we determine the house is empty, the Doctor can go in to start her investigation."

"Are we dealing with a serial killer here?" asked Officer Phillips. "I heard talk over the radio this morning about the first victim being mutilated."

Evan turned to Cheree. "I think Doctor Nicoletti should answer that question."

Cheree groaned inwardly, apparently Sheriff Tate had gone into some detail of Ben Pike's murder over the radio. "I doubt it. Serial killers usually don't go after big, powerful men. Statistically, they pick on small women, but at this instant I can only speculate and instead of speculating, we need to secure the area. We have a scene investigation team on the way. After they finish, I can give you more information."

Evan regarded the assembled troops. He was confident he had a competent group. No one was acting macho and they were all attentive. If they came under fire, he'd find out. "Okay, if everyone is clear, let's move out."

They moved up the driveway at a brisk walk. When they reached the garage, Evan stationed Thomas and Phillips at the back. He sent two of Buena Vista officers along the west side of the house and the other two along the east side. When everyone was in position, he and Buster moved to the passage door at the back of the garage. Evan tried the knob. It turned easily.

"Open," he told Buster. Buster nodded and Evan pushed it hard, stepping back. The door swung inward a hundred and eighty degrees to bang up against the back wall. Obviously there was no one standing behind it to the right. Evan ducked through the door, his rifle at the ready, safety off. He turned to his left. As soon as he was in, Buster entered, facing right. They were back to back.

"Nothing. Let's make an announcement."

"Be my guest."

"This is the Sheriff!" Buster said in his authority voice. "Place your hands on your head and step out where I can see you!" He waited ten seconds before repeating the command. There was no response. "Let's move."

There were two vehicles in the garage, a late model pickup and a partially restored fifty-seven Chevy convertible. Buster and Evan swept through the garage, around the vehicles to meet at the door into the house. Buster tried the knob. "Open," he said, yanking the door while taking a quick step back. "My turn." He ducked into the house. As soon as he turned away, Evan followed him in. Nothing.

Five minutes later they were finished. The most surprising thing Evan saw was a walnut paneled study with shelved books halfway from floor to ceiling. It was a room the home of a college professor would be expected to have. Finding it in the home of a prison guard unnerved both Evan and Buster. It was completely out of context.

"Nobody home," Evan told Cheree and the two lawmen he had posted at the back by the garage. "Doctor Nicoletti you can enter." He pulled his pistol, offering it to Cheree.

"Thanks, but I have my own." She opened her suit jacket and displayed a compact .45 automatic in a shoulder holster

"Okay. Buster, you pick up your two troops from the east side, I'll get mine from the west and we can start searching the trees. We'll meet you out behind the corral." Buster nodded, moving out along the east side. After sending Thomas and Phillips to the south corners of the house, Evan moved his team into the trees along the west side of the house. Once away from the house, both teams turned south, moving towards their rendezvous behind the corral.

The first two hundred yards of the sweep were uneventful, but after the two groups of lawmen turned the corner and started to close in on each other, one of the cops on Buster's side called out, "I've got something over here!" Buster signaled the other cop to hold up while he went to investigate.

"Look there!" the cop pointed to a spot. Buster followed the officer's outstretched arm and finger. He saw the bright twinkle of a brass shell casing. He walked over to it. Bending down, but not picking it up, he examined the casing.

"Looks recent." He could see a slight indent on the open edge. He moved as close to it as he could without disturbing the immediate area. He could make out the caliber number stamped into the back end. "It's a two-seventy, from a semi-automatic, probably a Browning."

"How can you tell it's from a Browning?" the cop asked rather incredulously.

"I'd like you to think I'm that good, but actually a two-seventy BAR is involved in the other murder." Buster stood up, looking towards the house. He had a clear field of view over the corral right into Pike's backyard. He moved to his left two steps and looked down. He could discern the imprint of the shooter's body in the soft earth. He could tell where the toes of his boots had roughed up the ground on one end, and he could see the dimples in the dirt where the shooter's elbows had dug in to support the rifle. He had lain right here in ambush until Pike made his appearance outside his back door. *Cheree can probably figure out how tall this guy is.* He tied a handkerchief to a low hanging branch, and walked back to where the city cop was standing.

"Good work. Let's join up with the rest of the troops."

Evan's team had discovered nothing. "We drew a blank," he told Buster. "You find something?"

"Yeah, unless he's really stupid, the shooter left us a calling card." Buster filled him in on the details. "I believe he intentionally left the brass lay where it was ejected."

"You're probably right, but let's leave it for the scene investigators. I'd like a look at Pike."

All of them moved past the corral, down to where Pike was laying. The county deputy and the state patrol cop left their positions to join the group. They stood back severl feet, almost as if they expected the body to jump up at them. Eight pairs of eyes stared down at Pike as he stared blindly back at them. The blood on his forehead was caked and streaked, but the capital 'R' was clearly legible even if its meaning wasn't. His shirt was blood soaked around the quarter inch hole in his chest, and there was an irregular circle of blood almost three feet in diameter on the ground beneath him. They had all seen bodies, but there's something different about a murder. Accident victims could be a lot messier, yet the fact the deed was intentional, gave the murder victim a distinct finality. Pike seemed to say, "I'm dead. I was killed in cold blood."

"There certainly is a lot of blood," said Officer Phillips.

"I wonder if he knew what hit him," said Trooper Thomas.

"I wonder if he knew who hit him," speculated the Buena Vista cop who had found the spent shell casing.

No one volunteered answers. Evan was thinking how big the guy still looked. Normally death seemed to diminish a person's physical size, or at least it did to Evan. He remembered the first dead body he had ever seen. An older cousin of his was killed in a car accident. Evan remembered thinking how small he looked in death. The dead relative had briefly been on display immediately prior to the funeral service. Evan was only ten and even though his cousin was ten years his senior and over six feet tall, he looked little and forlorn tucked away in the plain casket. Abel Pike, however, was another matter; he still looked big and formidable. *Must be three inches taller than his old man. Probably weighs close to two-eighty. Amazing how a chunk of lead just over a quarter inch in diameter could bring him down. I doubt he was even conscious when he hit the ground, still alive maybe, but for all purposes, dead.* Evan had seen animals shot through the heart travel up to a hundred yards, running hard before they tipped over. That didn't happen with humans, their systems were different. Humans went into shock. Everything shut down to protect the brain, prolong life as long as possible. He was pretty certain Pike didn't feel anything but a massive slap to his chest. Then he was dead. Getting hit with more than two-thousand foot-pounds of energy in a vital spot had a tendency to bring you to a speedy finish.

"We'll leave him for Doctor Nicoletti's investigators," he announced, walking off towards the house to talk to Cheree. The rest of the contingency followed.

Twenty minutes later, Evan and Cheree were alone in the spacious living room of Abel Pike's house. After thanking the lawmen for their help, Evan had sent all of them on their way except Trooper Thomas. He and Buster were taping off the area around Pike's body and the place where the shooter had lain in ambush. Cheree's investigation team had not yet arrived.

"I'm almost positive the killer wasn't in here," Cheree said. "I can't find any evidence that anything was disturbed in any way. The place is almost too neat." She paused briefly to run her hand through her hair, a gesture Evan found to be provocative. "He must have a girl friend living here or at least staying here from time to time. There's a fair amount of women's clothing in his bedroom, plus cosmetics, perfume, and other feminine things in the master bath. Judging by the clothes, she's not a petite woman either. But why would she be?"

"Anything to tell the name of this woman?"

"I believe her name is Raleigh."

"As in North Carolina?"

"Spelled the same way. But I can't find anything to indicate her last name."

"Abel Pike appears to be quite a different man than I expected. The study with the books for instance, that's something I wouldn't ever have guessed any son of Ben Pike to have. Even if he never read any of them, I'd never have expected to find a room full."

"Me either. It also appears he may have been somewhat religious, or at least he was curious about the divine. There's a well-used Bible lying open on the desk in the master bedroom."

"What's it open to? What was he reading?"

"Revelations, chapter six. You familiar with it?"

"The Four Horsemen of the Apocalypse."

"I'm impressed. Verse eight is highlighted."

Evan quoted. "I looked, and behold a pale horse, and the name of him who sat upon it was Death, and Hades followed after him."

"Now I'm really impressed. Have you memorized the entire Bible?"

"Far from it, but there are a few things I know. When I was a kid, I went to Sunday School while my parents went to church. I thought the four horsemen of the apocalypse were pretty cool. The way it's written always impressed me as being mysterious and magical."

"You still think they're cool?"

"No, not now. I realize if they ever show up, they won't be riding Clydesdales pulling a beer wagon."

"Well apparently Abel had some sort of warning or premonition. Saturday, when he, Ruth, and Jason came out to ID Ben, I told them we suspected his father's killer came to his camp on horseback. What color would a pale horse be?"

"I'm not sure, although I seriously doubt the apostle John had grulla paint in mind when he was writing about a pale horse."

"Well, I don't think it was coincidence. It seems obvious to me he sensed something. I doubt if he knew someone was going to take a shot at him this morning, but I'll bet he knew why his father was killed. The fact he's been killed too, leads me to believe he was involved in whatever his father had done."

"I'd have to agree, but what about his mother and brother, you think they might know anything? They're not talking."

"They're not talking, but they could be next in line. This isn't a serial killer. It's someone with a major grudge. We better notify them before it's too late."

"You're right, I'll call Sheriff Tate now and have him send someone out to talk to Ruth."

A commotion at the front door of the house brought Evan and Cheree quickly to their feet while reaching for their weapons. Before they could cross the room to the door, about the tallest woman Evan had ever seen burst in with Buster right behind her.

"Stop, right there!" Evan commanded looking into her eyes. Evan was six-two, but even with his boots on, he was eye to eye with the lady.

She stopped. "What's happened?" she demanded.

Evan took his hand off his weapon. She looked distraught, not dangerous. She was also pretty. "Who are you?"

"Raleigh. Raleigh Pike, Abel's wife." She said 'wife', not ex-wife.

"I wasn't aware he was married."

"Well, he is!" She was defiant. "Who are you and what are you doing here?" She started to get a bad feeling. She moved towards Evan, "What's happened. Where's Abel?" Her voice was rising both in pitch and volume.

Evan took a couple of quick steps towards her, taking her gently by the wrists. He could feel she was strong, fit. He hoped she wouldn't get belligerent. "Please," he said as soothingly as he could, "come over here and sit down. I'm afraid we have bad news."

She allowed herself to be steered to a chair where she sat. Evan moved back a couple of steps. "I'm Deputy Coleman, this is Doctor Nicoletti, the state's chief medical examiner," he indicated, nodding at Cheree. "And the man behind you is Deputy Alexander."

She regarded Cheree and Buster. Evan knew the longer it took to give her the bad news, the worse it would be. "I'm sorry to have to tell you, but your husband is dead. He was shot some time this morning." There wasn't any good way to say it.

She slumped back in the chair as the news took over. Her hands went to her face. She started to cry. Evan looked to Cheree. Cheree moved over to Raleigh, putting a hand on her shoulder. "He said he was in danger," she said between sobs. "If I only would have gotten here sooner."

There was obviously a lot going on that Evan, Cheree and Buster knew nothing about. "Can you help us?" Cheree asked her gently.

"I want to see him! What have you done with him?" she demanded, her voice cracking with grief.

Cheree looked first to Buster, then to Evan. "There is a crime scene investigation team on the way. We don't want to disturb anything."

Raleigh fought for control, starting slowly. "If he's here, I want to see him before a bunch of strangers start poking at him." She looked at Evan. "Please, you have to let me see him." She lost control, sobbing deeply again. "Please let me see him."

Evan looked back to Cheree. Cheree nodded. "Okay, we can let you see him, but we can't let you get too close. If the killer left any trace of anything on or near the body, we have to find it."

"Okay, I understand. Now please let me see him." Rising slowly, she regained a measure of control. Buster and Evan stood, one to each side of her, to lead her from the house to where the body lay.

Buster had taped off a space from ten feet in front of the body in a semicircle and ran the tape all the way back to the corral. He figured the killer may have walked directly through the corral to where he had dropped his victim. Anticipating the arrival of the forensic team, he hadn't covered the body. As soon as they rounded the corner of the house, Raleigh saw her dead husband.

Buster and Evan felt her losing control. They tightened their grip on her arms. When they stopped at the edge of the tape, great sobs shuddered through Raleigh's body. They thought she might collapse.

"Oh, my God, what happened?" Her voice was small, overpowered with grief.

"He was shot, ma'am," Buster told her. "We believe someone with a rifle shot him through the heart this morning when he went out to see after the horses."

"Oh no, Abel," Raleigh called out. In spite of Evan and Buster supporting her, she sagged to her knees. She looked up at Evan imploring, "He can't be dead! Are you sure he's dead."

"Yes ma'am, he is dead. We are certain of that much. I'm very sorry, we don't know anything else yet," Evan told her.

She tried to rise, but her legs wouldn't obey. She remained on her knees, sobbing uncontrollably. "Why? Why? What did he do to get shot?"

Cheree knelt beside her. "We don't know what happened here yet, but we're hoping you can help us." Cheree didn't want to demand answers, but she knew if she could get Raleigh to talk as soon as possible, she might say something she wouldn't say after she had time to think.

"I don't know if I can help. He called me Sunday morning and said he had to talk to me as soon as I could get here. I asked him what was wrong, but he said he didn't want to talk over the phone." She looked at Abel's body again, fighting for control. "The only thing he would tell me is something bad happened to his father because of something that happened years ago. He said he could be in trouble too." She finally noticed the blood on Abel's forehead. "Oh God, what happened to his head?" She turned to Cheree, "Was he shot in the head too?"

"No," Cheree told her and suggested they go back into the house. "I'll explain as much as I can, but why don't we go into the house. As soon as the investigators have finished, you can come back out."

"Okay. They don't have to cut him up, do they?"

Cheree assumed she was talking about an autopsy. "No, they won't do anything like that." She didn't tell her she would have to do it later. Although, based on what she knew now, it might not be necessary. "Can you stand?"

"Yes, I think so." Buster and Evan gently helped her to her feet. She took a last look at Abel and allowed herself to be guided back into the house. In spite of being two inches taller than Evan and almost a head taller than Buster, she now seemed very small and frail.

Once inside they eased her into a chair. "Is there anything I can get for you, ma'am?" Buster asked.

"Maybe a glass of water."

Cheree wasn't sure where to start. She had so many questions. Evan helped her out. "Ma'am, I know this is very difficult, but if we're going to have any success finding your husband's killer, we have to ask some questions." He paused briefly and when she didn't respond, he asked, "Do you think you can answer some questions?"

She waved her hand in the air as a gesture of acceptance. "Yes, okay. I'm okay now."

She didn't sound okay, but Evan started regardless. "Did your husband tell you his father had been murdered?" Brutal perhaps, but this wasn't going to be easy.

He saw a new wave of shock cross her face. "Oh, no! Oh, no! When did that happen?"

"I'm sorry, but I found his body Friday afternoon. He was murdered sometime Friday morning." Evan wondered why Abel hadn't told her.

"Was he shot too, like Abel?" She sounded ready to be hysterical. Buster handed her a glass of water. She drank half of it.

Evan decided to ignore her question as long as he could. He hoped she'd forget it. "I received a call from Ruth Pike just after noon on Friday. She was upset. She told me her husband was up in the mountains elk hunting and his horse had come home without him. I drove over to her place and rode out to look for him. Perhaps you know where he hunted. Ruth told me Abel was supposed to join him later that afternoon."

"I've never been up there, but Abel told me about the place. He liked it. He said he didn't care if he shot an elk or not, it was just a nice place to be. I talked to him on Thursday evening. He said he was going Friday after he got through with work." She shook her head slowly. "I don't believe this is happening."

Outside the house, two Buena Vista police cars drove up with the state's crime scene investigators. Cheree had asked the police to pick them up when they arrived and she excused herself to supervise. Buster went with her. Raleigh watched them leave, new tears brimming from her eyes. When she was gone, Evan started again. "Ma'am, I have to ask if you know why Abel didn't tell you his father had been killed?"

She slumped deeper down into the chair. She waved her hand around the room. "Abel built this place, mostly by himself. His dad helped and I did too, a little bit, but we didn't live together all the time. I grew up in a little town in Nebraska. I was always on the outside looking in, being as tall as I am. As soon as I finished high school, I left home. I tried college for a year and did okay, but the only dates I had were with basketball players who just wanted to score with me. When I was nineteen I went to Las Vegas, lied about my age, got a job as a showgirl. People there liked me because I was tall. I met Abel when I was twenty and I thought he really loved me. We were married three months later."

Okay, this is helpful. She's relaxing, opening up. He was a good listener, and he wasn't about to interrupt to ask where she was going with her thoughts. Eventually, she'd tell him something helpful, provided, of course, she knew anything.

"For about a year, everything was wonderful. Abel worked construction. He made good money. We even bought a little house. But he had a mean streak. He never beat me or even hit me, but he was mean. He started hanging around the casinos, chasing women, probably having affairs, not coming home for days at a time. When I tried to reason with him, he told me it wasn't any of my business. I put up with it for as long as I could until finally I confronted him. I told him if he didn't stop, I was leaving. I didn't want to leave, I loved him, and I was willing to forgive him if he would only stop. Frankly, I didn't think he would, but he did. He said he was sorry, said he would change. He suggested we get out of Vegas, move to Colorado where his folks lived. He said there was too much temptation for him in Vegas. I agreed and we moved." When she paused, a brief smile graced her face.

"We moved here, not this house, but Buena Vista. Abel got a job at the prison. For a while everything was good." Then her smile was gone. "After about a year he was acting up again. He started drinking heavily after work, staying out late, disappearing on the weekends. Sometimes he told me he was going to see his father, but I was never sure that's where he went. So after I had enough, I threatened to leave again, but this time he said, 'Go, ahead, get your ass outta here!' I was hurt, but I wasn't about to live with a man who obviously didn't think enough of me to behave himself."

Evan had been studying her while she talked. Not only was she attractive, she had classic beauty. She should have been on magazine covers. It was hard to imagine Abel Pike chasing other women when she was at home waiting for him. Evan was fairly positive he wouldn't be out looking if he were married to her.

"I packed up everything I had, which wasn't very much. We had two pickup trucks. I took the older one, loaded all my stuff in it, and left. Abel just watched me go, he didn't say a word. I wanted him to beg me to stay or at least ask me to stay, but he wouldn't. He just stood there glaring at me like everything was my fault. I drove out of town thinking I'd go to Vegas and get back my job as a chorus girl. The problem was I didn't have enough gas money to get to Vegas. I drove over to Creede instead.

Abel took me there right after we moved here from Vegas. We stayed a few nights at a very nice bed and breakfast, and I remembered the woman who owned it was very busy. I thought maybe I could go to work for her at least until I got enough money to do something else." She paused to look at Evan.

      He had been listening intently, staring at her profile. She was seemingly unaware of her beauty. "Did that work out for you?" Evan asked, slightly embarrassed for staring.

      She smiled again. "The woman who owned the place was busier than ever. Her husband had died just before I showed up and she hired me on the spot. That was six years ago. I've been there ever since. I own the place now. Three years ago I bought her out on a contract for deed. At the rate I'm going, it'll be paid off in five more years. Anyway, to answer your original question, Abel and I didn't live together, but we never got a divorce. I didn't hear from him until four years after I left him. I dated other guys occasionally, nothing serious. I never felt any pressure to get a divorce. I suppose in the back of my mind I was hoping someday we'd get back together. Finally about three years ago he called me. When I asked what took him so long, he said he spent three years looking for me." She paused to look Evan in the eyes. "Does this make any sense to you?"

      Evan thought briefly about his failed marriage and the little girl he hadn't seen for nine years. He wasn't about to judge anyone else's relationship. "You loved him. He must have eventually realized he had feelings for you, too."

      "Yeah," she admitted sadly. "He said he loved me. Said he was sorry. He wanted me to come back to live with him. I told him I wouldn't do that, not yet anyway. That made him mad. He hung up on me. I figured it was really over. I mean if he had loved me at all, like he said he did, he could have tried a little harder to understand why I wasn't in a big hurry to run back to him. After I didn't hear from him in three months, I filed for divorce. He didn't contest it, but on the day of the hearing, he showed up at the courthouse, begging me to give him another chance. I decided, what the hell, I had waited this long, why not?" She took another long drink of water, emptying the glass.

"Can I get you more water, ma'am?"

"No thanks and you should call me Raleigh. 'Ma'am', makes me feel old."

"Okay, sorry, Raleigh."

"Anyway, after almost seven years of being separated, we started dating again. And I discovered Abel had changed. He was kinder and gentler, you know, softer. Not that he still didn't have some rough edges, but I thought maybe I could be with him and trust him again like I did when we first met. It seemed to me he had come to terms with something inside, like he realized he could forgive himself." She looked around the living room. "He had started building this house. He said it gave him purpose, kept him out of the saloon, and when it was finished, he wanted us to live in it together. Even when I told him I was buying the place I worked at, he didn't get upset. He only said we could still spend as much time together as possible and someday, when I got tired of making beds and cooking breakfast for other people, I could move in here permanently, make his bed, and cook his breakfast."

"Apparently that never happened?" As soon as he said it, he wished he hadn't. "I'm sorry, I didn't mean that the way it sounded."

"No, that's okay. It didn't happen permanently, but I did spend a lot of time here with him. And we were happy when we were together, especially the last two months. I was taking things slowly, but our relationship was getting so good, I stopped trying to meet anyone else, not that I was ever seriously dating. Actually, it was a good arrangement because whenever we were apart for a little while, it was great to be together again."

"You mentioned earlier, the last time you talked to him, he told you something had happened to his father and that he could be in trouble also. Did he ever give you any indication what his father had done or what he and his father might have done together to make someone want to kill them?"

"How well did you know his father?"

"I've had a couple of encounters with him, but personally, not at all. By reputation I knew him as well or better than any other law enforcement official in Saguaro County except maybe Buster, my partner. But I don't know of anything in his past to give anyone a serious enough reason to kill him."

"I'll tell you something you might find hard to believe. I liked Abel's father. I know he was a rounder and got in plenty of trouble, but he was always a gentleman to me. Of course I didn't have to live with him. I don't know how or why his wife stayed with him. I figured she must be a saint."

"So Abel never told you anything about any trouble they could have been in with anyone. Something so serious, they'd eventually pay for it with their lives."

"No. There were times when I thought he wanted to talk about his past, but he would never completely open up. I think maybe this time if I'd have gotten here sooner, he might have." She was silent for a moment. "But obviously I didn't and now it's too late." Tears filled her eyes again. She looked out the window, away from Evan.

11

      Standing with her back to Evan, Raleigh watched from a south-facing window of the house as two investigators examined the body of her dead husband. She was sobbing quietly. Evan watched her shoulders quake as he contemplated their conversation. He wanted to believe she had told him the truth. Abel Pike had not told her what he and his father had done to get themselves murdered. Evan wondered if Ben Pike's other son, Jason, had been involved also. If he had, Evan needed to warn him soon. "Raleigh," he asked, "Are you all right? I have to make a call."

      She didn't turn around, she just waved her hand, "Go ahead, I'll be okay."

      Evan left her and went out the front door. He spotted Buster talking to the Buena Vista police chief, Buddy Banks, and joined them. The chief grabbed his hand, shaking it vigorously. He was a little guy with a grip like a mountain gorilla. "Hello, Evan. Long time no see."

      Anyone who didn't know Buddy could be inclined to think he was a typical two-bit police, chief presiding over a second-rate police force, in a backwater burg a hundred miles from anywhere. Nothing could be farther from the truth. Buddy had an IQ a couple points over genius. Damn little escaped him. His staff was first-rate and there wasn't much they couldn't handle.

"Hello Buddy." Nobody called him "Chief", but nobody forgot he was. "It's been a while, how have you been?"

"Apparently better than you and Buster. I hear you lost one of Saguaro County's finest citizens." He was grinning. Buddy could afford to be flip, both murders were out of his jurisdiction.

"I wouldn't say finest, most notorious would be more like it."

"Yeah, that'd be more accurate. I was just telling Buster how Abel Pike came to own this place."

"I wondered about that. Property up here can't be cheap."

"Not anymore. Today just the land value of this place is well over three hundred, maybe even four hundred thousand. Now with this house here, I can only guess it's close to a mil. But about fifteen years ago, Ben Pike picked it up for a song."

"Why does Ben Pike keep popping up wherever we go?"

"You don't think he confined his antics just to your county do you? I probably had more contact with him than you boys did. He was always trying to screw somebody out of something."

"You know of anything he did worth getting murdered over?"

"Same thing Buster asked me. No, just general mischief and mayhem. Never anything real serious so I could lock him up and weld the door shut. Now take this property for example. It used to be part of the Silver Spoon Ranch. About twenty years ago the old man who owned it died. He had one daughter who wanted no part of it. She tried to sell it, but had the price set so high, nobody would look at it. Then the Colorado Springs Water Board people came along, and talked her into selling the water rights. At first she balked, said the land wouldn't be any good without the water. The guy from the CSWB was pretty slick. He was ready for that. He suggested she sell the water rights, parcel out the land in thirty-five acre chunks. That way, he told her, she could get more than what she was asking for the ranch being intact and according to state law, each property owner could still dig a well. She fell for it. She got a big pile of change for the water, but in order to sell off the thirty-five acre lots, she had to have a survey and put in a road."

Evan interrupted him, "Let me guess. This is where Ben Pike comes in."

"You're readin' my mind, boy. Where and how she met Pike, I don't know, but he told her he could handle the whole transaction for her, including the survey. And actually, he did too. The only problem was the price he charged her was twice as much as what he told her it would cost. Of course she refused to pay so he filed a claim on the property. He maintained what he quoted her was only an estimate. Since he was smart enough not to put the terms in writing and she had been dumb enough not to get it in writing, she was pretty much screwed."

"This woman isn't a redhead by any chance is she?"

"Oh, hell no! She was as gray as an old piebald mare. Besides, she's been dead for ten years. Her father, the old man that left the place to her, was in his nineties when he finally seized up and tipped over. The old gal had to be close to seventy when this happened." Buddy got a funny look on his face. "Why do you ask?"

"We found some long, light red hair on Pike's body."

Buddy jerked his thumb over his shoulder to where Abel lay. "This one or his old man?"

"The old man, we don't know about this one yet."

"Speaking from experience, redheaded women can be trouble," Buddy said with a grin. "But anyway, to settle Pike's claim on the property so she could start selling, she had to give Pike some cash and four of the thirty-five acre parcels. He eventually sold two of them and gave the other two to his son."

"So Abel actually has seventy acres?"

"Yup, two contiguous, thirty-five acre parcels. The nicest two of the whole lot I might add. He's still got some water on this one that the CSWB didn't get. There's a spring out back." He pointed to the south behind the corral. "Puts out about two cubic feet per minute."

"Where does it go?"

"Doesn't go anywhere. Pike set it up to flood irrigate the nicest twenty acre meadow you've ever seen."

"That's a bit much water for twenty acres. Where does the rest go?"

"Any excess goes into a deep trout pond he dug. Whatever is left after that runs off the property onto BLM land. The CSWB can't touch it."

Evan turned to Buster. "Don't ever let me suggest Ben Pike was stupid. And before I forget, I have to call the sheriff to tell him to give Ruth the bad news about what's happened here."

"Already done, Partner," Buster told him. "He didn't want to do it, he said it was our case, but I gently reminded him that Jason Pike or even Ruth could be the next victim. He wasn't happy, but he said he'd go out there and 'Do our job for us,' were his exact words."

"What a guy! I love my boss."

Buddy Banks laughed. "Sheriff Tate is a prince all right, but you could take his job away next fall. Big, handsome, young buck like yourself would get all the women's votes in the county. And if you could get Buster to vote for you too, you'd have a majority. But I'll bet since you're workin' for that good lookin' lady doctor right now, I don't suppose you even want to think about runnin' for office."

"I assure you my interest in this case is strictly to see that justice is done." He had trouble saying it with a straight face.

"Shee-it! You don't expect to be able to lie to me now do you? I was your age once too, you know."

"I'm sure you were, but can you remember that far back?"

Buddy waved the cigar he was smoking in Evan's face. "Go on, get outta here. The doctor is back up behind the corral lookin' for clues. If I were you, I wouldn't leave her alone with Trooper Thomas. He ain't as pretty as you, but he ain't altogether stupid either."

"Well okay, I'll just check on Abel Pike's widow and go shoot it out with Thomas." He shook hands with Buddy again before he started back to the house.

He hadn't gone two steps when Buster called to him, "Evan. Here, catch." He tossed a small plastic bag at Evan. "Give that to Doctor Nicoletti. I pried it out of the front of Abel's house."

Evan looked at what Buster had thrown him. It was a bullet, deformed into a crude mushroom shape by its passage through Abel's body and a subsequent collision with a log. Evan looked at Buster. "You sure this is from Abel?"

"Yup. I found it in one of the logs at the front of the house. I didn't figure the bullet slowed down a whole lot by going through him, but it was barely into a log, about four feet off the ground. I'm guessing a hundred-forty grains, hollow point, plated copper jacket. Appears as if the shooter was going for maximum energy release."

Evan nodded, and slipping the bag containing the bullet into his pocket, continued towards the house. He knocked on the front door; after all it was Raleigh Pike's house now. He heard a faint, "Come in," from Raleigh. She was talking on the telephone in the kitchen.

"You okay?" Evan asked her.

She waved and gave him a brave little smile. "I'm okay. Thanks."

Evan left her alone to go look for Cheree. There were a lot of things here that bothered him. The biggest mystery was still what had Ben and Abel Pike done, and who had they done it to, to get themselves killed. Abel Pike's inability to answer questions certainly didn't help matters. Obviously, the next question was who did it? If this wasn't revenge, none of the events of the last three days made any sense. He needed to find some plausible answers soon, or be ready to turn in his badge before someone asked for it. And if it was revenge, what was the murderer trying to say by carving initials into the victims? Why bother to provide clues, no matter how cryptic? Was this killer toying with them? He didn't like that. It implied the killer had delusions of intellectual superiority. On the other hand, if these were revenge murders, maybe the killer was so full of hate he couldn't stop himself from mutilating his victims. On the bright side, that should make the perpetrator easy to catch. All they had to do was discover what Ben and Abel had done to whom.

He made a mental note to ask Cheree about it, she probably had a lot more knowledge of murderers and their motives than he did. In fact, this was only the sixth murder case he had investigated. Murder was relatively rare in Saguaro County, for which he was grateful.

When Evan caught up with Cheree, she was lying in the dirt on her stomach; toes dug into the ground, her torso propped up, supported on her elbows as if holding a rifle. She had changed from her business suit into the jeans and coveralls her staff had brought along for her. There was a thin white line on the ground around her. She looked up at him. "The shooter could have been a woman. The marks on the ground left by the toes, knees, pelvis and elbows, are consistent with a person about my size and stature. The footprints we're finding indicate shoe size is about the same as mine too."

"Yeah, but you're a tall woman. The average height for a man is what, maybe five ten?"

"True, but look at this." She got up. "This is where the shooter was lying. We got all we could from the site and then we drew an outline." She pointed at the ground.

Again he regarded the white silhouette outlined in the dirt. He handed her the plastic bag containing the slug Buster had pried out of the wall. "Present from Buster."

"Where did he find it?"

"In one of the logs of the house behind where Abel was standing when he was shot. I didn't look at it real close. Buster thinks the shooter picked a bullet for minimum penetration and maximum knock down." Cheree nodded as Evan continued to stare at the painted outline. It looked remarkably feminine around the hips and waist, but considering Cheree was used for the pattern, it was to be expected. "How accurate is this? I mean if I were to lie down on the ground and you painted around me, the silhouette should look masculine."

"Sure it would, but we drew the outline first, based on the pattern on the ground. Then I lay down to see how it fit. Of course it wouldn't stand up in court, but it makes me believe a female perpetrator is possible. We also found another long, strawberry blonde hair. The root is intact. The shooter may have pulled it out while getting into a shooting position."

"How about the body? Anything unusual about it?" Even was still staring at the silhouette. Raleigh was about four inches taller. However with minor adjustments, she could fit the outline. So could Ruth and Jason.

"No, it's clean. I believe the shooter walked up, made certain Abel was dead, cut the initial in his forehead, and quickly departed the scene. Also, we didn't find any evidence anyone other than Abel and Raleigh have been in the house. I think the murderer did his dirty work and left the scene without so much as a look around."

"Would that imply the shooter knew no one else was home?"

"It could, but that wouldn't be too hard to figure out. He could have watched the house yesterday afternoon for some time."

"Yeah, that's true. Could it be we have one, very angry, red-headed woman settling an old score?"

"Could be, but the hair I found bothers me a little. I looked at it with my jeweler's loupe. The root looks somewhat dehydrated."

"What does that mean?"

"Maybe it's not fresh from the killer's head."

"It was planted?"

She shrugged her shoulders. "I'll look at it closer in the lab. One thing I am sure of, whoever pulled the trigger is a good shot. It's two hundred and twenty-one yards from here to where Pike fell. Another thing, he or she came in on horseback. About a hundred yards farther back in the woods we found where the killer had a horse tied to a tree." She paused. "And guess what else?"

"You found hair from a grulla and white paint?"

"It certainly looks similar to what we found yesterday."

My God, Evan thought, was it only yesterday morning he and Cheree had been up at Ben Pike's murder scene for the second time? He looked at his watch. It was just after three. "Show me where the horse was tied. If any of those horses in Abel's corral can ride, I'm going to try to follow the trail."

"Is that a good idea? What if the killer is still out there?"

"He's long gone. I don't believe there's any chance the perpetrator waited around for us to discover the body, but maybe I can tell what direction he came from. If I wait, any trace of the killer's passing will deteriorate. He had to have accessed the property from somewhere fairly close by. Maybe somebody saw a truck and trailer parked on a nearby trailhead or just off the road somewhere in the immediate vicinity."

"You'd better take Buster along."

"You're not worried about me are you?"

She blushed just a little. Two of her people and Trooper Thomas were within earshot. She gave him a look that promised she'd get even. "I'm in charge of this investigation, remember? I don't want anyone getting hurt. Understood?"

"Yes ma'am. I'll see if there are two horses in the corral that can ride."

After Cheree had shown him where the killer had tethered his horse, Evan went back to the house to talk to Raleigh. She was just hanging up the phone when he came in. Her eyes were red and swollen, but dry. "I was talking to my mother in Nebraska," she volunteered. "She wants me to come home for a while. Maybe I will, if I can get someone to take care of the horses."

"Speaking of the horses, are any of them broke to ride?"

She brightened a bit. "Oh yeah, all of them ride. The two geldings are the best behaved, but none of them will give somebody like you any trouble."

Evan was a little puzzled by her comment. "Ah, I'm not sure what you mean by that. Are they afraid of cops?"

Now she laughed. "No, obviously not, but you're not just Deputy Coleman, you're Evan Coleman. Abel told me more than once, if he could train horses like Evan Coleman he could quit his job."

"Did Abel know me somehow, because I'm afraid I don't remember ever meeting him?"

"It took me a while to put it together. Your last name sounded familiar, but I couldn't remember why. When the woman, Doctor Nicoletti, called you Evan, I started thinking about why I knew your name. Abel went to several clinics you put on for people with problem horses. He said your father was there too. I never went, but I know you impressed Abel."

Evan shook his head. "The last time I put on a clinic was several years ago. In fact, come next spring it'll be four years. My dad and I rented the arena at the fairgrounds in Alamosa. As I recall, we had a good turnout, but I sure don't remember meeting Abel there. I can't brag about never forgetting a face. I have a good memory, it's just short."

"That might be, but you were something of an inspiration for him. Several years before we got back together he had an idea. He was a big man and he thought there was a shortage of big, well trained horses for people like him." She paused briefly. "Me too, I guess. I'm big. Anyway, his idea was to find some big horses, train them well and sell them to big riders. He always thought he looked really stupid sitting on a horse that was only fifteen hands high. He figured there were other people like him that would pay good money for a bigger horse."

"Great idea. How'd he do?"

"He sold at least six most years. This year he'd already sold eight. He'd buy the biggest saddle-bred horses he could find, and train them to be the best he could. All the extra money he made went into this," she said looking around the house.

"He did well. He should have been proud of this place."

She choked back a sob. "Oh, he was, but it's funny, the only people who have ever been inside here were him, me, and his father—until today that is. He didn't have much to do with his mother, and I know he didn't associate with his little brother at all, but I don't know why that was. He would never say. After a few times, I quit asking. I was just glad we were getting along so well." She looked Evan in the eyes, "You don't mind me telling you all this do you?"

"No, please continue. I want to listen as long as you want to talk."

"Thanks. Talking helps." She drew the sleeve of her blouse across her eyes. Not terribly classy, although it made her seem vulnerable.

"Anyway, he liked working the horses. He said it kept him out of trouble and if that was true, I was grateful, but I don't think it was the case. I think he stopped hanging out at the bars and chasing women some years ago. Maybe the horses are what got him away from that scene in the beginning. He was a shy person, or maybe insecure, I don't know. He didn't have any good friends that I ever knew of. I think the reason he drank in the bars is because he could socialize without getting too close to anyone. Does that make any sense to you?"

"Perfect sense, I've been in a saloon a time or two myself. What about the people he worked with? Did he have any friends there?" Evan was hoping he might have confided something to one of his co-workers at the prison.

"There were a couple of guys that he would mention on occasion, but I never met any of them. I don't think he was close to them. If he was, I didn't know about it. He was very private. I think I was probably the only person, besides his father, he ever opened up to and now, after this, I'm not sure how well I knew him. I know he admired your abilities. He tried to use the training methods he learned in your clinics. Once or twice, he even mentioned trying to call you, but I think because you were a deputy he never did. You don't do the clinics anymore?"

"No, my dad's health deteriorated and they're too much work for me to do alone. I keep telling myself I should give up being a cop. Become a full time trainer, but the only way to make a million dollars in the horse business is to start with at least two million."

"You should do it. You probably won't get rich, but think of the fun you'd have doing what you want. "

"How much fun did Abel have doing it?" Evan steered the conversation back to her. He didn't want to talk about himself. He wanted her to keep talking about her late husband. He'd already learned a few things. Abel didn't get along with his mother and brother.

"I'm sure he really enjoyed it. I know when I was here with him, he seemed very happy when he was working the horses. I don't really know if his training methods were the greatest. Mostly, once he got them to accept a saddle, he just rode them a lot."

Evan couldn't help it. He had to ask, "How'd he start them?"

"He told me it was the same way you did. He ran them in a round pen 'til they gave up their attitude, saddled them, and climbed on."

"That's the best way I've ever heard anyone explain it! And believe me, I've heard a lot of people try to explain it."

"He was real gentle with them, very patient. The only thing that set him off was if they tried to bite him. If they did that, he got very violent with them for about five seconds. He said he learned that from you too."

"Well I hate to admit that trick is not original with me, but that's the technique. If they bite, you need to convince them they're going to die. The only rules are you can't hit them in the head, and you can't use anything but your hands and feet. No whips or clubs. You can punch and kick and scream at them for four or five seconds, but then you have to stop. Any longer they don't know what it's for. It's about respect not pain. I know other trainers who will lay a biting horse down and tie it up for a while, but I'm certain what I do is more effective. Safer, too."

"Well, your method worked for Abel. Nobody who bought a horse from him ever complained they'd been bit." She laughed a little laugh and looked up the ceiling. Tears began filling her eyes. "We used to ride the hills out back, to train the horses and just for fun, too. I'm going to miss him." She wiped her eyes on her sleeve again. "Did you see all the books?"

"Yes, when we first got here, we had to sweep the house, make certain no one was in here. It's very impressive."

"He'd read a lot of them. He told me he'd started reading heavily about a year after I left him and got addicted to it. It was another thing that he said kept him out of the saloons."

From what he was hearing, Evan was getting an impression of a man who was seriously trying to keep the demons from his door. What had he done, and was there anyone besides the killer who knew? He was pondering these questions when Raleigh asked, "Why did you ask me if any of the horses were broke to ride?"

He had gotten so wrapped up in the conversation; he almost forgot why he started it. "Well, I was wondering if I could borrow a couple. Buster and I would like to ride out back a ways to see if we could track the perpetrator. Doctor Nicoletti believes he came in on horseback."

He was completely unprepared for her response. "Do you and her have a thing going?"

"Ah, I ah," he stammered. "I'm not sure I know what you mean." That was a lie, but he found the question disconcerting.

"Well, if you don't, she wants to. It's obvious by the way she looks at you that she's interested in you. If you can't see it, you're blind."

"That's interesting. I'll have to pay more attention." There was a long embarrassing pause.

"If you really didn't know, don't wait too long to make a move." It seemed to Evan she almost enjoyed watching him squirm. Before he had to say anything, he was rescued by a knock at the door. He practically jumped to get it. It was Buster and Cheree. Raleigh's smile disappeared.

"Ma'am," Buster started carefully, picking his words, "Doctor Nicoletti and the investigation team have completed their work. If you would like to see your husband, this would be a good time; and ma'am, I am very sorry for your loss. We all are. We'll do everything possible to apprehend the guilty party."

Her tears started again. "Thank you, I know you will." Then turning to Cheree she asked, "What are you going to do with him? Do you have to do an autopsy or anything?"

Cheree thought for a moment. She knew what killed Abel. What more could she expect to find by cutting him apart. She wasn't interested in how much his liver weighed or what he had for breakfast. She wished she could tell Raleigh she didn't have to post Abel, but it was impossible. "Yes, that will be required in this situation. We need to examine the body more thoroughly. I'll have my team take your husband's body to Denver with them. I'll do an examination the first thing in the morning. I can help you make the funeral arrangements right after that if you like."

"I don't know what to do about a funeral right now. I'd like to see him first. Will you go with me?"

Cheree put her arm around her, "Of course."

They went out the front door together and started walking to where Abel Pike lay dead. After their inspection, the scene team had cleaned the blood from his face and bagged him. They folded his arms across his chest, and left the bag unzipped from the waist up The letter cut into his forehead was still prominent, but not as rude as it been with the caked and dried blood for emphasis. Pike looked almost peaceful.

Evan watched them go. Cheree was five feet-ten and Raleigh was at least four inches taller. They were two women about the same age, both pretty and shapely. From the back, it appeared to Evan almost as if a beautiful Amazon woman and her equally beautiful, teen-age daughter were going for a pleasant walk.

Buster broke the spell. "I hear we're going for a ride?"

"You up for it? There're two geldings in the corral that are supposed to be bullet proof."

"I'm up for it if you give me the one that is more bullet proof. You and I have a different opinion of what is a well trained horse."

"Okay, let's go take a look at what's out there. According to Raleigh, I shouldn't have any trouble with any of them. You, however, are another matter."

12

Raleigh knelt beside her dead husband. She still couldn't comprehend what she was seeing. *"What happened to him? Who did this? God, what happened?"* Touching his forehead, she lightly traced her finger over the mark cut there by the murderer. She covered the initial with her hand as if by doing so she could erase it. She looked up at Cheree, "Why? What does it mean?" She was pleading for answers.

Cheree knelt beside her and put her arm across her shoulders. "We don't know why it was done or what it means, if anything. I promise you though, we will find out, and we will apprehend whoever did it."

"Who could do such a thing?" She moved her hand from his forehead. The rude R was still there. "Oh Abel," she pleaded with the dead man, "What happened? What did you do?" She hung her head while great sobs shook her body. Her tears fell on her dead husband, mingling with the blood on his shirt. All Cheree could do was feel compassion. No words of solace would come.

After a minute, Raleigh regained a measure of composure. She leaned forward to brush Abel's lips with hers. "Goodbye, friend. It took us a while, but I know we loved each other. Goodbye," she whispered. Reaching down, she took hold of the zipper on the body bag. She pulled it up slowly, carefully as if she were tucking Abel in for the night. When she reached his head, she paused briefly to caress his face one last time before pulling the zipper closed. Partially supported by Cheree, she stood. "Do you have to leave now or do you have a little time to talk."

"I can listen as long as you want to talk, but first we should make arrangements for the body."

"Yeah, that's what I want to talk about. I need you to help me decide what to do." She paused as they walked to the house. "I also want you to tell me what happened to Abel's father."

"I'll tell you everything I can." Cheree dreaded the prospect. She remembered the day her husband had been killed. In the morning he was alive, two hours later she was being told how he'd died. In spite of her grief at the time, she could still sympathize with the man who had to give her the news. Raleigh was getting a double dose.

Evan and Buster did not interrupt Raleigh and Cheree as they made their way past them to the corral. They picked out the two geldings and led them to the east side of the corral where there was a long three-sided shed. The front of the shed provided shelter for the horses. In the back was hay storage, tie stalls, and a tack room. Tying the two horses to the fence separating the shelter from the stalls, they went looking for saddles.

"You notice how big all these horses are?" Buster asked.

"What'd you expect for a man the size of Abel Pike?"

"Well, I guess what I mean is, I hope the one I'm riding really is steady. It's a long way to the ground from the backs of these monsters. I never rode a horse over fifteen-two before."

"What's the tallest horse you've ever come off of, that's the important thing?"

Buster thought for a minute. "Well I once got dumped from the back of a little cutting horse. She was only about fourteen-two."

"You've only been dumped once? In your entire life?"

"Yeah, I like to ride horses, not fall off of them."

"In that case, you can have the shorter gelding. He looks to be about sixteen two. That's only eight inches taller than the one that threw you. If this one tosses you, I doubt if you'll be able to tell the difference when you hit the ground." Evan handed him a saddle. "Throw this on him. See how he reacts. I'll get a bit and bridle and ride him around the corral before you get on."

Ten minutes later they had both horses tacked up. Ten more minutes and Evan had taken both horses on a test drive, deciding they were good to go. The two deputies rode out the back gate of the corral, picked up the trail of the perpetrator, and followed it to the southwest into the hills away from the house. The ground was soft and loamy so the trail was well defined. For the first quarter mile they could clearly see both sets of hoof prints, coming in and going out. Skirting the meadow at the back of the property, they started to drift off towards the south onto BLM land.

"How far do you intend to follow this trail," Buster asked Evan after they had been riding for about fifteen minutes.

"I was hoping to discover where the killer parked his truck. I don't think he rode over the mountains to get here. I'm sure he pulled a horse trailer somewhere close by and rode in early this morning."

"Why do suppose he came in on horseback anyway?"

"I'm not sure. I'm trying to think how I would have done it. I'd want to be here early enough to ambush Abel first thing in the morning. I wouldn't want to drive up the main road because I'd have to leave my car within walking distance and since there are only a few houses up here, everybody knows what everybody drives. A strange vehicle parked on the side of the road is going to be just that—strange. I need to get in and out without anybody seeing anything suspicious."

"Okay, so you park as far away as you can and ride in through the back door. I like that, Evan. You have a fine criminal mind. But, being able to find Pike's place before daylight, from several miles away implies an intimate knowledge of the lay of the land."

"Yeah, that part bothers me. Whoever did it, had to have done some recon. This didn't just happen, it was well planned."

"I agree, but Ben Pike's murder was well planned too. Unless of course the two incidents are unrelated and we're dealing with two different perpetrators."

"What do you think the odds of that are?"

"I've got a better chance of being the next president. What I believe is both murders are part of a single, well developed, and well executed plan by one or several people bent on revenge. I'd guess it's been in the planning stage for quite a while."

Evan considered what Buster had just said. "Yeah, you're right. Until recently, I never thought about an elaborate plan. I figured somebody had a beef with Ben, they knew where he was going to be, they went to his hunting camp, and whacked him. But now when you throw Abel's murder in with Ben's, the logistics get a lot more complicated. The killer had to get from Ben's elk camp on Friday morning over here to murder Abel on Monday morning. He had to know all about Ben's hunting camp as well as Abel's routine."

"Could it be an inside job? Maybe little brother Jason was sore about the old man's will leaving everything to his big brother. Maybe the initial in the forehead is just something to throw us off."

"Maybe," said Evan, "but Jason was the one who suggested we come out to talk to Abel as soon as possible. Seems to me, if he was planning to shoot his brother first thing Monday morning, would he be so quick to suggest we talk to him? Depending on when we got here, we could have foiled his plan."

"I don't agree. The chances of us being here at six o-clock Monday morning were non-existent. And, even if we had talked to Abel on Sunday, Jason could still have shot him the next day. If Jason did it, he didn't do it to stop Abel from talking to us, he did it because he had planned to do it anyway."

"What about the red hair?"

"Yeah, that does seem to be a problem if Jason is the killer. Although, he's the right size."

"I don't think he did it," said Evan. "He might know something about who had a reason to kill him, but I don't believe he killed his brother."

"You don't believe in fratricide?" Buster asked.

"Is that a question designed to remind me you still remember your high school Latin, or you just trying to see if I know any big words?"

"Neither. I merely want to know why you don't think Jason murdered his brother."

"I don't know why. I just don't see the motive. If he killed Abel, it seems to me he would have to be involved in his old man's death too. Let's assume our theory about Ben Pike's will is valid and Abel gets everything. And, don't forget, you admitted you don't know if that's the case. But say it is. So Jason decides he wants what Abel is supposed to have, and he kills his father and his brother. Not to mention chopping off dear old dad's member and scratching initials in everyone's forehead. I'm not buying it because he'll have to kill his mother too. She's going to get everything now."

"He doesn't have to be involved in Ben's murder. Consider that Ben was murdered by somebody he offended sometime in his past. Jason knows the secret so he kills Abel to prevent him from getting all the goods, and gouges the initial in his head so it looks like the same MO. He doesn't have to kill his mother; she's going to leave him everything anyway."

"But you just told me both murders were part of a grand plan. Now you're saying Ben's murder was planned and Abel's murder was merely a result of Jason being an opportunist. Sorry, Buster, you can't have it both ways."

The tracks they were following turned sharply to the left, dropping down a steep embankment. Evan pulled up the reins and stopped. He could hear water running at the bottom of the slope. "Stay here. I'm going down. If you don't hear from me in ten minutes, call the police." He cued his horse ahead, leaning back in the saddle as the animal started down the bank.

Buster whoa'd his horse to watch Evan negotiate the slope. *I'd have gotten off and led the horse down. Although that's what I'd do today. Twenty-five years ago, I'd have ridden down too. That's what getting older does for you. Makes you realize you don't heal as fast as you used to.* Evan quickly disappeared into the draw. Buster checked his watch. It was getting on towards five. In another hour it would be dark. He'd like to be back at Pike's house before then.

"Okay, now tell me as much as you can about what's going on," Raleigh said to Cheree. They were sitting across the kitchen table from each other. Cheree's crew was on its way back to Buena Vista.

"The details are ugly," she warned Raleigh.

"I've seen plenty of ugly already today; I guess I can handle some more."

"You're father-in-law was murdered at approximately ten o-clock on Friday morning. Deputy Coleman was responding to a call from Ruth Pike. Ben was supposed to be at his hunting camp when his horse came home without him. Ruth called the sheriff's department shortly after noon. Deputy Coleman took the call and eventually rode up into the hills where he found Ben Pike dead, lying on a cot in his tent." Cheree paused hoping Raleigh wouldn't ask for details.

"How was he murdered? Was he shot like Abel?"

"No, his femoral artery had been severed and he bled to death."

"You mean somebody just walked into his tent and stabbed him in the leg. I find that hard to believe."

"You're right that would be hard to believe. Actually, he'd been drugged, tied to his cot, and then his femoral artery was severed. His body was also further mutilated. His penis was completely severed and the initial 'R' was branded on his forehead with a hot iron." Raleigh's face had lost all color and she was hugging herself. "I'm sorry to have to tell you this Raleigh."

"No!" Raleigh couldn't believe what she had just heard, "What is going on? What did they do?"

Cheree assumed the "they" Raleigh was referring to were Ben and Abel. "We don't know. We'd hoped Abel could provide some answers as to why his father was murdered, but we were too late. At this point we can only speculate. We think the initial 'R' might refer to rapist," and she was quick to add, "although, there is absolutely no record of Ben Pike ever being involved in a rape."

Raleigh's lips started moving, but she was barely audible. Cheree had to lean across the table to hear her. "Evan asked me if Abel told me anything he might have done in his past to make someone want to kill him. I didn't want to tell Evan what Abel told me over the phone the other night. See, Abel really admired Evan." She swallowed hard. "I couldn't tell him that Abel had done..." There was a long pause. "Something—something bad."

This was a strange twist in an already strange case. "I didn't know Abel and Evan knew each other."

"Evan didn't know Abel, but Abel had been to every horse clinic Evan had ever put on. Abel thought Evan had a tremendous ability to train horses so he tried to copy him. I know I was wrong, but I just didn't want Evan to think less of Abel."

"I understand, but if we're going to catch whoever did this, you have to tell us everything you know."

"Will you explain to Evan why I didn't tell him and that I'm sorry?"

"Of course I will. He'll understand. He's very patient."

"Thanks. I don't want anyone to think I was trying to hide something." Raleigh sat up straighter in her chair. Some of the color had returned to her face. "When Abel called me Sunday morning, he didn't tell me, but obviously he knew about his father's murder. He sounded very troubled over the phone, but he wouldn't say why. I didn't want to keep asking what was wrong, so I promised him I'd come over as soon as I could. He wanted me to come on Sunday, but I still had a couple of guests that wouldn't be leaving until this morning. I told him I'd be there early Monday afternoon and make him a special dinner. I asked him one more time what was wrong. He said, 'My dad and I did something sixteen years ago and he just paid for it. My turn is probably coming soon.' When I asked him what had happened, he told me he'd tell me all about it Monday night. He just didn't want to talk about it over the phone."

"Did you get a sense from talking to him that he was in any kind of danger? I don't mean just trouble, but real danger?"

"Yeah, he sounded scared and I've never seen him afraid of anything, ever. I've been worried about him ever since I talked to him." She put her elbows on the table and buried her face in her hands. "If only I'd got over here Sunday like he wanted, maybe he'd still be alive."

Cheree reached across the table to put a hand on Raleigh's shoulder. She wanted to tell her something that would reassure her none of this was her fault. It had apparently started sixteen years ago. It was unlikely Raleigh could have done anything to prevent the consequences from happening. Cheree didn't tell her that, but she did ask if Abel had given any indication Jason might have also been involved.

"No, he didn't, but if it happened sixteen years ago, Jason would only have been twelve years old. Abel would have been sixteen." Raleigh had a horrible thought. "Do you think it could have been a rape?"

"We don't know, but considering how Ben Pike was mutilated, we believe it's a possibility."

Raleigh put her head on the table and cried. Outside the house, the investigation team had finished. They were loading their equipment into the Buena Vista police cars for the trip back to the airport where the helicopter was waiting. An ambulance arrived to transport Abel's body to the airport for the trip to Denver. Trooper Thomas was officially off duty two hours ago, but he was still there and planned to stay until Evan and Buster returned. Chief Buddy Banks was going back to town with the rest of his force.

Buster was sitting uncomfortably on the tall gelding waiting for Evan to return. Almost fifteen minutes had passed since Evan had ridden out of sight at the bottom of the gully. Buster fished a two-way radio out of his pocket. He was just about to key it when he saw movement below. It was Evan, and when he cleared the creek that had created the gully, he charged up the hill. There was something in his left hand that looked a lot like a rifle.

He pulled up alongside Buster. "Guess what I found?"

"Looks like a rifle to me, Partner. In fact, it looks like a Browning semi-auto-loader. Could it be a two-seventy BAR?"

"Yes it is, and not only that, I believe this very same rifle was stolen right from under my nose about three days ago. This is Ben Pike's rifle. I'd stake your reputation on it."

"How did you come by it, or did you catch the perpetrator and wrestle it away from him?"

Evan gestured over his shoulder with the rifle. He had a handkerchief wrapped around the stock where he held it. "At the bottom of this gully, just on the other side of the creek is an old ranch road through the trees. The trail leads right down the middle of it for about a quarter mile and stops. That's where I saw the rifle just laying there in the middle of the road. When I picked it up, I started looking around and found tire tracks. I believe it's where the killer parked his truck and trailer. From there he came in on horseback."

"Why would he leave the rifle, especially after he went to all the trouble to retrieve it the other night from Pike's camp?"

"Did you ever get up early to go hunting and in the process of packing your truck, you lean your rifle or shotgun against the truck? When you're finished packing, you jump in and drive away, but hopefully, before you get very far, you remember you left your gun leaning against the pickup?"

"You think the killer leaned the rifle against the side of his truck and drove away without it? That would imply a certain level of incompetence."

"Either that or he deliberately left it lay where we'd find it."

"That makes more sense to me."

"Yeah, I agree. But now you've got to wonder why he wants us to find it, unless it has become meaningless. I'm positive there won't be any prints on it except maybe Pike's."

"What do mean by meaningless?"

Evan turned his horse back the way they had come and gave him some leg pressure. The horse started moving and Buster followed. "Maybe the killer has no further use for it. Doesn't mean he won't kill somebody else, but he isn't going to use this rifle. So what if it belongs to Ben Pike and was used to kill Abel? Who cares? It makes no difference that we have it and he's better off not having it in his possession."

"He's giving us the finger. I really don't like this guy."

"I'm with you." Evan laughed. "You okay with that horse? I'd like to open it up a bit. Get back to the house before dark."

"Okay, I won't race, but I think I can keep up."

Evan took his horse to a trot and when he was satisfied Buster could handle it, he urged the powerful gelding into a smooth lope. In the fading light, the two horsemen glided over the soft earth, twisting and turning through the maze of big pines, almost without a sound, chased by ever lengthening shadows.

Cheree sent the investigation team on their way. She had no idea how she was going to get back to Denver, but she wasn't planning to go anywhere until Buster and Evan returned. Buddy had gone with his police officers and only Bill Thomas, the state trooper, still remained. He had joined Cheree and Raleigh at the kitchen table. Cheree had suggested he could leave also, but he said he didn't mind staying. He was a big, tall, capable looking man, and both Cheree and Raleigh were glad he was still there. They were attempting to make light conversation and he was a good storyteller. He had been telling tales about his youthful attempts to be a rodeo cowboy specializing in bull riding. He finally gave it up after two years when he realized he had a handicap.

"I was too tall," he said. "The bull would rear up on its back legs and my forehead would hit the bull's neck. Then it would buck up on its front legs and the back of my head would slam into its rear end. So I'd get this rhythm going, back and forth, alternately smashing my head from front to back and just when I'd think I could last 'til the buzzer rang, the old bull would throw off my timing by leaping straight up in the air. My head didn't know which way to go, I'd lose my rhythm and when the bull hit the ground again, I'd come off. I only had two, eight second rides my whole career."

He kept Raleigh and Cheree smiling until Evan and Buster returned. The knock at the door brought them back to reality. Cheree got up. She opened the door and the first thing she saw was Evan holding a rifle. "Is that the murder weapon?" She stepped outside closing the door behind her. Raleigh and Bill stayed put, staring at the closed door.

"My paycheck against yours, I'm betting it is."

"Where'd you find it?" Evan proceeded to tell her.

"You think he wanted us to find it?"

"I don't like this guy. He doesn't give a rat's ass whether we found it or not. My guess is he's done with it and he could care less." He sounded frustrated. "How's Raleigh doing?"

She quickly filled him in on their conversation. "I think she's okay for now, but..." She looked from Buster to Evan, leaving her statement unfinished.

"But you don't think we should leave her alone up here." Evan finished it for her.

"I don't think we should either," Buster said. "Evan and I can take care of the horses for tonight. I believe Thomas would probably be willing to come by in the morning to look after them. In fact, I'm sure he'd be willing to look after them for a while if Raleigh would ask."

"Now how do you know so much about what the deputy would be willing to do for Raleigh?" Cheree asked him.

"I know he's a horseman. He told me he has three of his own. He lives not far down the road, and most importantly, he told me he's single."

Cheree was standing with her back to the door. "Let me find out. You two can see to the horses." She turned and opened the door.

Ten minutes later Cheree joined Evan and Buster in the shed adjacent to the corral. "Okay, here's the plan. The county is sending out a female deputy to spend the night with Raleigh. Thomas will wait until she gets here. Raleigh is going to stay here until after the funeral. Then she's going back to Creede. Thomas will take care of the animals for a few days, until she decides what she's going to do with them. So, as soon as you're finished, we can leave."

"Do you want a ride back to Denver?" Evan asked knowing it would take him and Buster over five hours to get there and back home.

"Yes I do, but not from you and Buster. You wouldn't get home 'til midnight. I had my crew make arrangements to get the chopper to come back for me. It'll be here at eight. That gives me time to buy you two some dinner. Let's say goodbye and get out of here."

Later, after dinner at a local steakhouse, they sat in Evan's car at the airport waiting for the helicopter. They had discussed the case at great length and were talked out. It had been a long day. Instead of getting a good lead from Abel Pike, they had discovered his body and no leads, only more questions. They were tired, disappointed, and frustrated. There was a night breeze sliding down the eastern slope of the mountains. It was a damp, chilling wind, portending bad weather.

"What now?" Cheree wanted to know.

"Good question," said Buster.

"We'll think of something," Evan promised.

They were quiet again. All three were wondering where to go from here. The arrival of the helicopter broke the silence. It set down at the end of the airport's only runway about fifty yards from where Evan was parked. Evan put on the lights and drove to within thirty feet. He got out to give Cheree a hand with her bag and Pike's rifle.

"Good night, Evan."

Evan took her hand, pulled her close, and hugged her. "Good night, Cheree."

Yeah, why not? She hugged him back and kissed his cheek. Ducking into the cabin of the aircraft, she was gone.

Evan walked back to the car. "It's been a long day, partner." Buster was grinning at him.

13

Evan woke up late. If it were a normal workday, he would never have made it to work on time. On their way home from the latest murder in Buena Vista he and Buster had speculated on what should be their next move. All they had were two bodies, a few wisps of hairs, and a rifle that more than likely was free of prints.

"Let's not be negative," Buster said, "We know there's a redheaded woman somehow involved, and we know one of the horses is a grulla paint. And don't forget Ruth Pike's story about her two visitors. The big guys driving the new, two-tone pickup with matching horse trailer who stopped by looking for Ben back in June."

Initially he'd agreed with Buster; they did have something to work with. However after watching his boss, Sheriff Tate, being interviewed in front of the Saguaro County Courthouse by a reporter from a Denver TV station, he became disheartened. The sheriff, in all his glory, was on the late news. Evan watched incredulously as he discussed the details of the elder Pike's murder, even telling the reporter about the victim's severed penis. Evan groaned when "Clouseau" said it. The reporter immediately named the case, "The Grulla Paint Murder" because the sheriff also related the major lead was the perpetrator may have been riding a grulla and white paint horse. The only good thing about the interview was it had been recorded before the sheriff knew about the second murder, although Evan wouldn't be surprised to see him on TV again tonight spilling his guts about that also.

Evan looked at his bedside clock. He groaned again—six-fifteen. "Gotta get up!" he told himself just as the phone rang. It surprised him and he grabbed it. "Hello!" It wasn't a pleasant salutation.

"Well, good morning to you too," said a warm, soothing voice. It was Cheree.

"Hi, Cheree. Sorry, I'm a little jumpy."

"Jumpy or grumpy? Where are you?"

"Ah, actually I'm still in bed."

"Mmmm, that's interesting. Guess what I just saw on the early morning news?"

Evan rolled back under the blankets. "Oh, I don't know. How about some rancher has a cow that just gave birth to a two headed calf?"

There was some silence. "No, Evan, that wouldn't be news in Denver. Saguaro maybe, but not Denver. Denver has big news, stuff like paint horse murders and severed penises. Does that ring a bell?"

"Yeah, actually it does sound somewhat familiar. In fact I'm investigating a very similar case right now. I wonder if they're somehow related."

"They could be. Do you know a Sheriff Tate?"

"Quite well, I'm sad to say. I saw the whole debacle last night at ten. Was there anything new this morning?"

"I don't know. What did you see last night?"

"I saw my boss, standing tall, wearing a brand new hat, babbling about the murder of Saguaro citizen, Ben Pike. He didn't say anything about Abel only because when the interview was taped, he didn't know much about Abel except we told him he'd been shot."

"Well, I saw what you saw. The guy is a complete fool. I have to tell you I was pretty disgusted with his performance. I'm going to have the governor call him and tell him to keep his mouth shut. We don't need the media wolf-pack after us."

Even at this hour in the morning Evan liked listening to her voice. He liked everything about her. He wanted to tell her that. "Cheree, can I change the subject slightly? At least for just a minute?"

"Sure. What do you want to talk about?"

"I'm curious why you wanted to be involved in this case. It's not standard procedure for the state crime lab boss to be doing what you're doing. This is a police matter and I know you work with the police, but to me, this seems to be out of your orbit and I think you know that too."

The pause at the other end of the line was long, uncomfortably long as far as Evan was concerned, but he waited it out. Finally she spoke. "If you don't know it already, I probably shouldn't be telling you, but I'm attracted to you. The first time I met you I thought you were attractive, but I'm sure you know how women look at you. Under different circumstances, I might have hit on you. At least I would have liked to. I'm not very good about that stuff. But I believe I would have tried. It wasn't just your looks either, you seemed so gentle and caring with your horses, almost like they were your children. However, I was happily married. I forgot about you. When Buster called the lab last Friday and mentioned your name, I remembered you immediately. I decided I wanted very much to see you again. My husband has been dead for almost three years. I've realized it's time to move on and I want to. Seeing you again was like opening a window in a tightly closed room. When I heard you were unattached, I wanted to get close to you to see if there was anything there." She paused. "Is that okay?"

Okay? It's damned outstanding! He couldn't have put better words in her mouth. "It's more than okay; it's what I hoped for. I just didn't want to delude myself thinking you might be interested in me to find out later you were only interested in solving the murder." After he said it he realized it probably sounded stupid. "I mean, not that the case isn't important, but I didn't want to make a big fool of myself believing that maybe you had some feelings for me, because I certainly have some feelings for you. In fact, as long as we're doing true confessions, my feelings for you are dangerous."

"What does that mean? Do I need a body guard?"

"No, they're dangerous to me, not you. You were the woman I was looking for when I sold you that horse and you're still the woman I'm looking for. It's been a long time. I'm not sure what to do."

"Well, we'll just have to work together and see what happens. Hopefully, by the time we get the case under control, we'll have a better idea about what to do with each other. But before I forget why I called and start babbling like a teenager, what are you doing today?"

"Other than sleeping late, you mean?"

"It's only a little after six, is that late for you?"

"Yeah, it is. I should have my horses fed and be in the shower by now."

"Mmmm," she said, contemplating him in the shower. "So after you finally get your lazy self out of bed, do your chores, and take a shower, what are you going to do?"

"Buster and I are going out to talk to Ruth Pike again. She has to have some idea why someone would want to kill her husband and son. We'd also like to talk to Jason if he's available. He could be next whether he knows anything or not. Talk to his girlfriend, Veronica, too if she's with him."

"You'll stay in touch?"

"Of course. You're always on my mind anyway."

"That's good, but since I'm not a mind reader, you need to call if there's something you want me to know."

"When I know, you'll know. What are you going to do?"

"Abel Pike's autopsy. I don't think I'll find much besides his exploded heart. If that's the case, I'm going to release the body to Raleigh. She indicated she wanted his funeral as soon as possible. Apparently, at one time, he told her he didn't want to be embalmed, just buried in a pine box. Then, I'm going to contact my friend in the DMV to see if she can track down the owners of all white, late model, dual-wheeled pickup trucks. After that, I'm going to check police records to see if any veterinary clinics have been robbed in the last few months. I think the ketamine used on Ben Pike possibly came from a vet clinic."

"Why do you think that?"

"Vets use it a lot. It works great on animals, but it can be unpredictable in humans. It's been found to have weird effects on people. Some patients that received it during surgery, reported they couldn't feel anything, but they knew exactly what was happening to them. In some of those cases, it was extremely traumatizing, especially for children. A few of them were affected to the point of temporary mental instability."

"You mean it made them crazy?"

"No, not quite that drastic, but they had horrible nightmares for years."

"Jesus! What do you suppose Pike felt like?"

"I don't think he felt any physical pain. Emotionally he might have been going out of his mind. There was enough of the drug in his system to immobilize him, but maybe not enough to put him totally under. I can't be certain if he was conscious when he was mutilated. If he was, he has my sympathies. The only good thing was he was bleeding fast. His ordeal didn't last more than a few minutes."

"Do you think the perpetrator knew what he was doing with that stuff?"

"I don't really know. If he wanted Pike to suffer, why bother to give him something that would kill the pain? I think he knew it would incapacitate Pike for a short time and that's what he was after. He wanted Pike helpless until he was tied up, but he wanted him awake so he could suffer."

"Okay, who would know this stuff would have the desired effect? Obviously a doctor or a vet, but I'm sure they could get something better. How about some kind of a pharmaceutical sales rep or a vet tech of some kind?"

"Yeah, or maybe anyone else who did a little research. Ketamine isn't that hard to get on the street. It's become a popular party drug. A lot of it is being taken by accident because dealers are selling it as Ecstasy. In the right dosage it's like drinking enough alcohol to put you in a great mood. You won't have a hangover the next day either. The problem is, you get too much, you will become unconscious, maybe permanently."

"If it's so easy to get, why do you think it came from a veterinary clinic? It sounds like anyone who wanted it bad enough could get their hands on it. How many people would know how to administer it properly? The syringe is no problem; I buy them by the dozen at the farm supply store."

"I don't think it's that simple. The stuff you get on the street is usually in solid form. To get the right results, you'd have to know the purity of what you had, put it in solution, know the approximate weight of your victim and be smart enough to do the math. I think whoever drugged Pike was no ordinary dope. He or she had to have some smarts. How much of your own vet work do you do on your horses?"

"Well, I worm them, do the basic inoculations, and if one has an infection, I can give penicillin."

"Do you ever tranquilize them?"

"Occasionally, but only if I have to. Like to clean and stitch a cut that's marginal as far as calling the vet."

"So you've had practice in estimating weight and calculating dosages. You know how to convert from metric and you know what an IU is. You're not average. Most people wouldn't have a clue. I believe whoever administered the ketamine was quite capable. Either he knew or he had someone close by who knew exactly what it would take. I think he also had a source for the unadulterated drug, not the garbage you might get on the street."

"Sounds reasonable. What else are you going to do today?"

"I'm sure I'll stay busy. Do you have a special request?"

"Yeah, although I don't think it's terribly important, but what about the rifle?"

"That should be finished by the time I get to the office. I dropped it off at the lab last night before I went home."

Once again Evan was impressed by her competence. "A hell of a woman," he said softly. It was how Buster had referred to her after he and Evan had first met her. Evan had suddenly remembered it, but he had not intended to say it out loud.

"Is that a compliment?"

"Of course it's a compliment! Actually it's a direct quote Buster made last Saturday. After you had flown off in your chopper, he said that he thought you were one hell of a woman. I was merely agreeing with him."

"Thanks from both of you. Speaking of Buster, he's a very nice looking man, how old is he?"

"Too old for you, I hope. He's sixty."

"I was thinking about my mother. My father died five years ago and she's having trouble meeting a nice guy. I suppose he's married."

"Yes, he is. He's married to a woman not much older than I am. He married her about five years ago."

"I guess that doesn't surprise me. How'd he meet her?"

"Actually, he picked her up off the side of the road."

"She was hitchhiking?"

"Not exactly. He literally picked her up out of the road ditch."

"And I thought my life in the big city was interesting. I've got nothing here compared to what happens in your jurisdiction. Please elaborate. I like talking to you when you're in bed."

Evan momentarily considered the possibilities of that comment. He smiled and told her the story. "Early one morning, Buster was cruising south on highway two-eighty-five about ten miles west of town. He came up on a big green, nineteen-fifty-eight, Pontiac Chieftain pulled way off on the shoulder, almost in the ditch. So he stopped to investigate. The car is unlocked and there's no one around, but there's a trail of oil up to it. When he looked under the car, he could see a hole blown through the right side of the engine block. Other than that, the car was in great shape, as if it had been restored. The only things in the car are some empty Styrofoam cups, a few pop cans, sandwich wrappers, and a two-day-old Boston newspaper. Since the next town of any consequence is another twenty-five miles down the road and he hadn't see any pedestrians so far, Buster figures he'll find the car's owner hoofing it somewhere down the line. He got back in his cruiser and headed south. About two miles later, he spots what appears to be a suitcase lying in the ditch. Now he's definitely interested."

"Did it belong to his future bride?" Cheree couldn't help interrupting.

"Yes it did, but obviously he had no clue at that time what was going on. Anyway, he opened up the suitcase and went through it. He found some woman's clothing and a loaded, thirty-eight, snub nose revolver. Weirder and weirder, he thinks, so he continues down the highway. Just a little farther, maybe a half mile, he sees what appears to be a body in the grass thirty feet off the shoulder. He gets out, draws his gun, and slowly approaches. It's a body all right and a fairly attractive one except her nose looks badly busted, and she's either unconscious or sound asleep. He holsters his revolver, picks her up and carefully lays her in the back seat of his car. Half way to the hospital in Salida, the woman wakes up and freaks out. Buster pulls over, calms her down, and on the way to hospital she tells him her story."

Evan stopped. "How much of this do you have time for?"

"Stop now and I'll never talk to you again!"

"Okay, just checking. She told Buster her name is Amy Maguire and she's from some high buck suburb of Boston. Her husband is a big-time lawyer and a reformed alcoholic. When they started dating, he told her his drinking had destroyed his first marriage, but now he'd been dry for over two years. She was in her late twenties and had been married to a career. She fell in love with the guy and married him. For several years he stayed sober. But one night he didn't come home from the office. She couldn't reach him, was worried sick. She waited up for him until he finally showed up about three AM. He was tighter than a tick and when she tried to talk to him, he backhanded her across the face, knocking her down and out. He apparently booted her a few times when she was down, too. She came to right away, but didn't get up off the floor until he went to bed because she was afraid he'd beat her again. Finally, she heard him snoring. She packed a suitcase, took all the cash they had stashed, his gun, and the old Pontiac he'd restored. She wanted to take the Lexus, but couldn't find the keys. She drove away, never intending to return. She told Buster she stayed off the interstates so she wouldn't be so easy to find. She was going to Albuquerque to stay with a sister until she figured out what to do with the rest of her life. The car died before she made it. She tried to walk to town with her suitcase, but her ribs hurt so badly from getting kicked, she dropped it and kept going until she ran out of steam. She crashed where Buster found her. The rest is history."

"What do you mean the rest is history? You're leaving out a lot of details."

"You'll have to get them from Amy when you meet her. This is as close to a date as we've had, but as much as I like talking to you, I've got work to do."

Two hours later, Evan and Buster pulled into the driveway of the Pike homestead. The yellow morning sun was in the process of subliming away a thick layer of frost that had settled overnight. The ground was flecked with gold and silver sparkles, giving everything a sparkly magical look.

"So who owns this place now?" Evan asked Buster.

"Ruth Pike, of course. Colorado State law wouldn't have it any other way." The look on Evan's face matched the look of the property. "What are you getting at anyway?"

"Just curious. I wonder what she'll do with it. What do you suppose it's worth?"

"More than you or I could afford separately, and probably still more than we could afford together. I'm guessing the water rights alone are worth at least a million. What'd I tell you Ben had here, ten, twelve cubic feet per second? How many gallons is that again?"

"About six million gallons a day, forty-two million a week, two hundred million a month, and that's two and a half billion per year. Enough to irrigate up to a thousand acres."

"Not that you're counting, but that much water alone would have to be worth a million. You don't have designs on the place do you?"

"Man can have dreams, can't he? I can see this place running wild with broodmares and foals."

"What is it with you and horses? I mean, I've had a horse or two around all my life and I like riding as much as anyone, but you've got some kind of obsession with them. I don't think it's natural, or healthy either. You want to have them all."

"Buster, you're full of caca. I don't want all of them. I just want a big herd of them. A big enough herd so I can go out everyday and be surprised by a new personality."

"That's crazy. At best a horse is merely tolerant of you. At worst it'll cave your head in or bite a big chunk off your ass. You're talking like horses are dogs."

"You're talking like a sausage. You've got two horses right now. Tell me you don't love them."

"Of course I do. They're big, powerful, and they love the country. In fact, they love the country so much they'll take me along for a ride. But I don't want any more than I've got right now."

"Yeah, you do, you just don't realize it yet."

"How old do I have to get before this realization hits me? Working with you isn't making me any younger."

As they pulled up to the house, Ruth Pike came out to meet them. She didn't look well, or particularly happy to see them, but they expected that. Buster greeted her first. "I'm very sorry ma'am, to be here again and I know this is a terrible ordeal for you, but we need to talk to you again if we hope to catch who's responsible. Can you spare us a few minutes."

Evan tipped his hat, "Morning ma'am, sorry for your loss."

She flashed him a brief smile. "Thank you. Thank you both. Please come in and we can talk. Would you like coffee?"

"That would be nice," Buster said. When they went in, Ruth motioned for them to sit at the kitchen table.

She poured coffee for them. The kitchen walls needed repainting, the linoleum on the floor was cracked in a few places, and the appliances were of an avocado green period. Otherwise, the room was neat and clean. Great shafts of morning sun flowed in through large east-facing windows making it unexpectedly cheerful.

"Can you tell me anything about the murderer?" Ruth asked as soon as she sat at the table.

"We know a few things," Buster said cautiously, "but I don't mean to imply we're ready to arrest anyone yet. That's why we're here, to see if you could possibly remember anything your husband or son, did or said, that would lead them to believe anyone would have a reason to kill them?"

Ruth made a most unflattering face as if she were about to spit something distasteful from her mouth. "You think my husband and son did something so bad somebody killed them for it?"

"Ma'am," Evan said soothingly, "people commit murder for all sorts of reasons. From an outside perspective most of those reasons make little or no sense. We aren't suggesting your husband and son actually did something to deserve being murdered. We're asking if you know of anything they did that could have provoked an unstable person to kill them. A murderer is generally not a rational person, and an irrational person is tough to figure. The murderer may have only imagined what happened was worth murdering for. That doesn't mean it was."

"Oh." It was all she said.

Evan waited for more, but she had buttoned up tighter than a clam at low tide. "Ah, is it possible ma'am, you have any ideas along the lines I'm talking about? Any ideas at all?"

She looked him in the eyes. "Look, neither my husband nor my son, Abel, was ever going to win a popularity contest. They both made enemies, on their own and probably together too, but I have no idea, and I can't imagine what they could have done to make someone kill them." She looked at him accusingly. "Don't you have any leads or suspects or anything?"

For just a brief instant Evan saw a flash of temper he had not seen before. Ben Pike may have had half a fight if he provoked this woman too much. *Good for her.* "Well, ma'am, we know a few things and we have a lead or two, but truthfully, no, we don't have any suspects. Would it be possible your son Jason could have any ideas that could help us?"

"I doubt it, but you'll have to ask him to be sure. You think he could be in danger too?"

"If I were him I'd be thinking about it. How do we get a hold of him?"

"I'll give you his phone number. He lives in Colorado Springs. Jason was here from Friday night until yesterday morning when we buried Ben. Then he went back home. Two hours later, the sheriff came out to tell me you had found Abel murdered. I called Jason last night to tell him, and he said he'd come back out tomorrow. Right now he should still be home, but if you come back this afternoon you can see him. He's coming to stay with me for a few more days."

"How about his fiancé, is she coming with him?"

"I doubt it. She has to work."

"Do you know where she works?"

"At the college in Colorado Springs."

"The University?"

"Yeah, Jason met her there. He was taking a graduate class."

"Who does Jason work for?"

"He's the city engineer of Colorado Springs." There was pride in her voice.

"How well do you know Abel's wife?" Buster asked her.

"You mean Raleigh? She's his ex-wife."

"Not according to her. She says they never were divorced. It came close, but never happened."

"I didn't know." Ruth looked genuinely puzzled. "The last thing Abel told me was that they were divorced. But I guess I'm really not surprised. I liked her even though we never saw much of each other. I thought she was classy. Way too good for Abel. I told him many times to take care of her and not let her get away. At least he listened to me once in his short life."

"Ma'am, I take it you and Abel were not close?"

Now she regarded Buster the same way she had previously regarded Evan, there was a flash of annoyance at his question. "No, we weren't real close. That should be obvious. I didn't even know he was still married. He was a difficult boy and later, a hard man. He was his father's son. I couldn't do a thing about it." She turned her eyes away from Buster and looked at the table. "Doesn't mean I didn't love him."

The cell phone in Evan's pocket started ringing. He excused himself to take it outside. Caller ID told him it was Suzy, the dispatcher. "Talk to me," he said.

"Have you no couth? You're supposed to answer by saying hello."

"Hello."

"Oh damn you, Evan Coleman! Where are you? And where the hell is Buster? And why doesn't he have his damn phone on?"

"He's here at Ruth Pike's place with me and I have no idea."

"Very funny. Tell Buster some guy by the name of Gordon Mason called. He said it was important. I tried to call Buster, but he must have his damn phone turned off again."

"Suzy, for such a sweet looking, pretty girl you have one nasty vocabulary. Buster is just old and somewhat forgetful. I'll give him the message."

"Yeah, well, I used to be pleasant until I started working with you two clowns. You and Buster did it to me. See you later and be careful."

"Love you, bye."

Evan smiled as he cleared the phone. He had the feeling this interview was going nowhere. He was now of the opinion Ruth really didn't know anything. *Let's get her kid's phone number and get out of here.*

Back in the house, Evan rejoined Buster and Ruth at the table. Buster looked at him questioningly. "Ma'am, would it be possible to get Jason's phone number?"

Without a word she pushed back from the table and disappeared into another room. "What's up?" Buster asked quietly.

"Gordy Mason wants to talk to you. Let's get out of here."

"Good. If she knows anything, she's not about to tell. It could take hours."

"My sentiments exactly. Maybe we can get something out of the kid. If he's coming out here like she says, it'll save us a trip."

Ruth walked back into the room and handed Evan, Jason Pike's business card. He thanked her and they made their exit. She saw them to the door. As they departed she said, "Please let me know what's going on."

Buster replied, "We'll do that, ma'am, and if you think of anything please let us know."

"Turn on your phone so I don't have to take any more heat from Suzy," Evan told Buster as they drove away. "She's extra-specially pleasant this morning."

"Why do you think I don't turn on my phone?"

"Damn it, Buster, call your buddy Gordon. We've got to get our stuff together. The longer this case takes, the worse it'll get."

Pulling the phone from his jacket pocket, he punched it back to life. "You get the number from Suzy?"

"Buster, Gordon is your buddy, don't you know the number?"

Buster smiled and started pushing buttons.

14

As Evan drove back to the courthouse, he could only hear one side of the conversation Buster was having with Gordon Mason, but that side was interesting. It sounded as if Gordon had a grulla paint horse and it had apparently been stolen or strayed, but had been returned, or something like that. Gordon had a training facility in Grand Junction. He was probably the most respected horseman in Colorado, and had a national reputation for being one of the most successful cutting horse trainers anywhere, although he had been quoted as saying, "You can't train cutting horses, you can only encourage them." His methods were copied with varying degrees of success wherever cutting cattle was a popular game. At sixty-five he was still training and still competing; constantly searching for one more good horse.

When Buster ended the call Evan asked, "Should I turn around and head for Grand Junction?"

"You hungry?"

"Yeah, I was running late and I haven't had anything except the coffee Ruth gave us."

"Let's go to the Stockman's. I let Amy sleep in this morning and I could use some chicken eggs and dead cow for breakfast."

"So what's Gordon got for us or was that just a social call?"

"I'm still pondering what he told me. As soon as I get a cup of coffee in front of me, I'll be able to talk."

The sky was blue, the morning sun was bright, the road was clear and straight, Evan nudged the cruiser forward. They were soon going well over the speed limit. He knew Buster wouldn't talk until he got him to the café. His intention was to get him to the café as fast as he could.

"Gordy owned a flashy grulla paint. Two years ago he gave it to his daughter-in-law," Buster told Evan when they had settled into a booth at the café. "His son, Matt, raises paints and trains them in reining and cutting. He apparently has produced some good ones. The one Gordy gave him has won some money. Anyway, Matt is married to a woman who is a pro-rider and she loved the grulla paint so Gordy gave it to her."

"What's her name? I've heard of a rider by the name of Sarah Mason."

"It's probably her. Sarah was the name Gordy mentioned. You ever meet her?"

"No, but if she's the one I'm thinking of, I saw her cutting cattle two years ago at the Denver Stock Show. I remember her because she was a real looker. Slim, great physique, good rider too. At the time I'd wondered if she was a daughter of Gordon's."

"You notice what she was riding, or just her?"

"Yeah, she was riding a sorrel paint gelding. I thought he was a little tall to be a cutter, but as I recall she finished in the money."

"What about the color of her hair?"

"Can't say, she had it all up under her hat and I was on the other side of the arena."

"Too bad. Anyway, Gordy called me because he saw our boss on the news last night talking about Pike's murder. Gordy didn't know Pike, but when he heard Clouseau talking about a grulla paint horse, he started paying attention, especially after what had just happened to his kid. Now, this gets interesting. Last Thursday morning two of Matt's horses went missing. One of them was this grulla paint his wife liked and the other was a sorrel paint, maybe the one you saw her riding. They looked all over to no avail. They couldn't find any a break in the fence either."

"Were there more horses in the area or just those two?"

"There were twenty-five head in there together which is why they got suspicious. They knew if the fence was down somewhere, all of them would have gotten out."

"Yeah, that's what usually happens. And if the rest don't follow, the ones that are out will usually be hanging around somewhere close by."

"Well they weren't. They looked all over the area. Never found a trace. They assumed somebody stole them. Matt's wife was heartbroken, but lo-and-behold, guess what was standing in the pasture in front of their barn this morning?"

"The two paints."

"You got it. Matt was so happy he called Gordy who had seen the story about Pike's murder on the news last night. He didn't say anything to his kid other than to remind him to keep an eye on his horses. Then he called me."

"What'd you tell him?"

"I told him you and I, and probably Cheree, want to talk to Matt and his wife, as soon as he can arrange it. He said he'd call me back in an hour."

"Where's Matt's place?'

"Down where you come from, somewhere between Del Norte and South Fork on the Rio Grande."

"Nice area. I wish I could afford it."

"Gordy has done well. I imagine he's sharing it with his son."

"I hope he calls back soon. We could be there in an hour if I drove."

"Yeah, I noticed. What's with the lead foot lately?"

Evan started to answer, but a cell phone went off. Buster reached for his, but it was Evan's. "Deputy Coleman here."

It was Cheree. "Hi, Evan. Got any good news?"

"Hello, Cheree. Yes I do, but first tell me if you have a list of white dually pickups."

"I have a list of dually pickups, but not by color. That information isn't on the registration. But I've sent the registration numbers to the manufacturers requesting they match the number with a color."

"Can you sort the list alphabetically?"

"Already done, you have a last name?"

"Yeah, Mason."

There was a pause and Evan could hear the rustle of paper. "There are three Masons on the list; Gordon, Mathew and William."

"Where does Mathew live?"

"North River Road, South Fork."

"Bingo!"

"Bingo what? What do you have?"

Evan looked at Buster. "Matt Mason has a one-ton dually." Buster nodded.

"How soon can you get here?" Evan asked Cheree.

"Tell me where you are."

"Downtown Saguaro."

"Hang on," Cheree told him and put him on hold.

Evan started to tell Buster they were going to South Fork when Buster's phone rang. It was Gordy Mason. Buster listened for a while. "Thanks, Gordy we'll be there at one." He shut the phone off and stuffed it in his pocket. "Matt Mason is expecting us at one."

"Good, that gives Cheree plenty of time."

"Evan, I'm back," Cheree said. "I can be there by eleven. Now tell me what's going on."

"Ever heard of Gordon Mason?"

"Other than the fact I just read his name off a list of truck owners, no, I don't think so. Who is he?"

"He's one of the best cutting horse trainers in the country and more important for us, he's a friend of

Buster's. He also had a flashy grulla paint horse that he gave to his daughter-in-law. That horse disappeared for a few days, but now it's back."

"Wait, wait, slow down. Is Mathew Gordon's son?"

"Yeah, and he lives in South Fork. The grulla horse that Gordon gave to Matt's wife disappeared from their pasture last week. They searched the area, but couldn't find it. This morning it was back in the pasture like nothing happened. Gordon saw the sheriff on TV last night talking about Pike's murder and a grulla paint horse. He put two and two together and called Buster this morning. We've got an appointment to interview Matt and his wife this afternoon at one."

"So you think someone stole this horse, committed the murders, and put it back in the pasture?"

"Possibly, but what I'm thinking right now is this could be the closest thing we've had to a lead since I found Ben Pike."

"Okay, I'll be there at eleven. Oh, by the way, the governor talked to Tate this morning. I don't think he'll be doing any more interviews with the press."

Evan smiled. "That might be a mixed blessing. His big mouth produced the call from Gordon Mason, although Buster was going to call him today anyway. Whatever, we'll be waiting at the airport. See you in a bit." Evan hung up the phone. "Cheree will be here at eleven."

After their late breakfast, Buster and Evan had an hour to kill before Cheree arrived. They checked in with the sheriff. He was unusually quiet; didn't seem terribly interested in their progress. About the only thing he told them was not to talk to the press. Evan tried to do some paperwork, but kept watching the clock. He was in a hurry to see Cheree again. He felt like a teenager with a body full of testosterone, barely able to contain it. He couldn't remember feeling this way even about his ex-wife when they first met. He went over to Buster's desk.

"Buster," he asked quietly, "how did you feel when you first met Amy?"

Buster looked at him over the top of the drugstore reading glasses he used when he wanted to see close up. "What's the matter, youngster, you got the hots for the good Doctor Nicoletti?"

"Yeah, I do, bad."

Buster pulled off the specs, tossing them on his desk. "That's certainly understandable; she's a very desirable woman."

"Tell me something I don't know, like how you felt when you first met Amy."

Buster leaned back in his chair. "I can tell you that because, sometimes even now, five years later I still feel the same dizzy way about her. When I picked her up off the roadside and got a good look I remember thinking she was the most beautiful woman I had ever wrapped my arms around, even with her mangled nose. Made me so weak I almost dropped her. I waited at the hospital for two hours while they checked her over. All the while I was nervous, wondering what I was nervous about. After all, she was a stranger and she had a husband. Just because I found her didn't mean I could keep her. I was ecstatic when she decided to stay in Salida while the old Pontiac was being repaired. I called her every day for a week before I got up the nerve to ask her to dinner. When she accepted I damn near fainted. I couldn't believe she would have anything to do with an old fart like me. I told myself I was being stupid, making a fool of myself thinking she might be interested, but that didn't stop me from thinking she might be. A week later, when the car was finally fixed, I thought she'd be moving on, but when she found a job in Salida, I really went nuts. I thought about her constantly, hoping she cared and worrying she didn't." Buster laughed.

"I was crazy with lust and love. I had to know if she had any mutual feelings, so I got another date with her, and basically told her I was crazy about her. When she said she was interested in me, I thought I'd explode. Damn foolish behavior from a man of my age and experience." Buster paused, "Sound familiar?"

"Yeah, almost identical. You'd think when a guy gets to be thirty-five he'd have more sense than to act like a sixteen year old."

"Thirty-five! Hell I was fifty-six! Hormones are powerful things. I wonder if I'll live long enough so they lose control over me. On second thought, maybe I don't want to live that long. The last time I saw my old friend, Woody McPherson, was two years ago, and you know what he said about women?"

Buster occasionally mentioned Woody. He thought Woody was one of the wisest men he had ever met. Evan thought Woody's utterings were usually somewhat cryptic, or maybe he just wasn't smart enough to understand them. "I give up, Buster. What did wise old Woody have to say about women."

"He said it was a marvelous thing that they had between their legs. And Woody was seventy-six at the time. He also said it wasn't love that made the world go 'round, it was hormones."

"I'd like to meet Woody the next time he's in town. For once I understand what he was talking about, although I'm certain I wouldn't have used those words to express that aspect of a lady's charms."

"Yeah, well, me either. I hope he lives long enough I'm able to see him again." Buster checked his watch. "But, hey, I think it's past time we go pick up your friend at the airport."

They arrived at the mostly deserted airport five minutes after eleven, just in time to see Cheree's ride set down. She jumped out, and the chopper lifted off as soon as she cleared the rotor wash. When Evan pulled up, she got in the back seat on the driver's side. She sat there so she could see Evan's eyes in the rear view mirror.

"Hi guys. What kept you?"

"Buster was telling me a story about one of his old friends and we almost forgot the time."

"Is that right, Buster? Can you tell me the story?"

"I think it's a story maybe Evan should tell you," Buster said. "Sometime when you two are alone."

"Mmmm, sounds mysterious. I can't wait to hear it."

Evan was quiet as he pointed the cruiser away from the airport towards South Fork. Glancing in the rear view mirror, he saw Cheree smiling at him. He could feel his neck start to redden.

"How did the rifle check out?" he asked, changing the subject.

"Just like you said it would. The only prints on it belonged to Ben Pike and they were on the barrel, underneath the forearm, probably left from when he last broke it down to clean it. But it's the gun that killed Abel Pike. The rifling marks on the bullet Buster dug out of the wall are a match."

"Interesting," mused Buster, "but unimportant. Funny how things change. Two days ago we didn't have the rifle and we thought it was important. Today we not only have it, we know it was used to kill Abel and it doesn't matter at all."

"What do you suppose your old buddy, Woody, would have to say about it?" Evan asked him.

"He would probably take a big hit off the fine Dominican cigar he just bummed from me, lean way back in his chair, blow a few fat smoke rings, and say, 'Time is the ultimate coin of each and every realm.'"

"Very profound," said Cheree, "I'm not sure I see the connection, but still very profound."

"According to Buster, Woody is full of profundities. From what I've heard, most of them make no sense, or least they don't make any sense to a country bumpkin like me."

"You're hardly a bumpkin," Buster told him, "you're just lacking great wisdom."

The small talk continued as they drove south past the sprawling potato and alfalfa fields flanking US 285 as it cut straight through the valley between the Sangre de Christo mountains to the east and the La Garitas to the west. Heavy snows in the high elevations had blanketed the mountaintops with eye-dazzling whiteness. Under a crystal sky of blue so dark it was almost purple, the valley floor was bathed in saturated yellow sunlight. Evan held the cruiser to the speed limit. They had plenty of time, and the view was spectacular. They stopped for lunch at a café Buster and Evan frequented in the little town of Monte Vista where US 285 intersects US 160. The food was palatable and the service was good. Cheree caused a major stir among the mostly male patrons, farmers and ranchers. This was where Evan had grown up and he visited regularly. Several of his old acquaintances made certain they got a good look at Cheree, easing over to their table to say hello. None of them were terribly subtle about the way they looked at her. After lunch, Evan headed the cruiser west on US 160 for the thirty-mile drive to South Fork.

"You always cause that much commotion in a restaurant?" Evan asked Cheree.

"Not in Denver I don't. Some of your 'friends' acted like they had never seen a woman before."

He looked in the rear-view mirror, noticing her smile. "Well, there are women and then there are other women. All my friends have seen women, but very few of them have seen a woman like you."

"I'll take that as a compliment."

A few miles west of Del Norte, Evan turned north on a county road and a mile after it crossed the Rio Grande; he made a left turn onto North River Road. The road went up a slight rise, then dropped quickly. He slowed the car to turn into a long driveway that wound its way through a pasture towards a house close by the river. Constrained by fences, horses on one side of the driveway and cows on the other side watched them drive past.

"This is it," he announced, slowing the car to a stop about a hundred yards from the house.

"How do you know? You didn't even look at the name on the mailbox," Cheree asked.

"Didn't have to, look at that paint horse over there," he told her pointing to his left at a group of four horses.

"That's the grulla paint? She was looking at a mouse colored horse streaked with big patches of white across its flanks and legs.

"Yeah, that's her. I'd say she was a frame overo, wouldn't you Buster?"

"I'd say. Nice conformation, not too tall, looks like a cutting horse to me. I'm surprised Gordy gave her away."

"She's a paint. Gordy is a quarter horse man."

Cheree was puzzled. "What's the matter with paint horses?"

"Nothing as far as I'm concerned," Evan said as he slowly continued down the driveway, "but Gordon Mason is a traditional quarter horse man. As far as I know, he rides quarter horses exclusively. I don't think he's ever taken a paint into competition."

"But he could if he wanted too, right?"

"Gordy could ride in on a Shetland pony, and if the pony could cut a cow the judges would pay attention."

"I don't get it."

"Tradition is all I can figure. Maybe before this is all over you'll get a chance to ask Gordon himself." Evan drove on, finally stopping in front of the house. There was a gold and white, one-ton, dually pickup truck in the driveway and a four-horse slant, goose-neck trailer painted to match, parked next to a corral to the east of the house. A well-built, young man who looked to be in his early thirties was already coming out to meet them.

He stuck out his hand as Evan got out of the car, "Howdy. I'm Matt Mason and you must be Evan Coleman." He had a no nonsense handshake. "I saw you drive in. You and your dad are somewhat of a legend in this neighborhood. What did you think of the grulla paint?"

"She looks like she can move," Evan told him and turned his attention to Cheree. "Doctor Cheree Nicoletti, meet Matt Mason. Doctor Nicoletti is the head of the state crime lab."

Matt was about an inch shorter than Cheree and had to look up slightly. "My pleasure, Doctor Nicoletti."

She shook his hand. "Please call me Cheree."

"And this guy," Evan said, gesturing to Buster, "you probably know better than you want to."

"Good to see you again, young man," Buster told Matt.

"Yeah, it's been a while; don't you ever get any older? You look the same as when I saw you five years ago."

"Remind me to tell your father what a fine son he raised."

Matt laughed, "Come on in and we'll talk about whatever it is that brings you here."

Matt got everyone seated around the kitchen table and offered coffee. "My wife will be home shortly. She told me to be hospitable 'til she gets here."

"You're doing just fine," Cheree told him. "I'm sure you don't really need prompting to be hospitable."

"No, I reckon not, but it makes her feel good to tell me stuff like that." He put back the coffee pot and asked point blank, "By the way, just exactly what does bring you all here? Dad said something about maybe our grulla paint being involved in some kind of crime."

"Well, Matt," Buster started, "there was a murder last Friday in Saguaro County. We believe a grulla paint horse was ridden to and from the scene by the perpetrator, or at least one of the perpetrators. Early yesterday morning, there was another murder in Buena Vista. We found evidence to believe a grulla paint was involved in that one too. To be honest, the horse is about our only lead to the murders. When your dad called this morning to tell me your grulla paint had disappeared a few days ago, then magically reappeared early this morning, we thought we best check it out. That's why we're here."

"Jeez Buster, that's pretty weird. Am I a suspect?" He asked the question honestly, without hesitation or irritation.

"No, you're not, but your horse might be. It's possible she may have fallen in with bad company during the time she was gone."

"How can we know?"

"I'd like to take some samples from her if I could," Cheree said. "We have hair from the horses that were used during the murders. If they match up, we can attempt to determine who may have borrowed your horse."

"Actually, two of them went missing for about five days, the grulla mare and a sorrel gelding. My wife was sick over it; they were her two favorites."

"We believe both horses could have been involved. We recovered hair from a sorrel horse also. I'll need samples from both of them."

"Sure. Yeah, that'll be no problem. Jeez, Dad didn't tell me anything about this."

"He doesn't know anything about it," Buster said. "Right this instant you know almost as much as we know."

Before Buster could continue Matt's wife, Sarah, made her entrance. She stepped into the kitchen with a brown grocery store bag cradled in the crook of each arm. All three men got to their feet when she entered the room. Matt moved to her side and relieved her of half of her burden; Buster and Evan just stood and stared. She was pretty, but the amazing thing was her hair. She was as tall as her husband and her hair fell in golden waves almost to her waist. There was no hint of red.

"Hi. Sorry I'm late." She sounded genuinely sincere, as if she had missed an appointment of great import.

Her husband quickly introduced Cheree, Buster, and Evan, referring to them not as law enforcement officials, but the friends his father had sent over to talk about their grulla paint horse. She extracted a pie from each of the grocery bags. "There's a woman in Del Norte who bakes the best pies. I can't drive by her place without stopping. The choices are apple or pecan, or both. The only choice you don't have is none."

About the most adorable little girl Buster and Evan had ever seen burst into the room. "I want apple pie," she told her mother, and turning to Buster and Evan both of whom were still standing asked, "Are you guys cops?" She was a miniature of her mother including the long hair, except hers was strawberry blonde. Buster looked at Evan, and Evan looked at Cheree. It suddenly seemed as if their most likely perpetrator might be a five-year old girl.

"Taylor," Matt said, "that's not a polite way for you to talk to our guests." He took her by the hand and gently pulled her over. "This," he said directing her attention to Buster, "is Mister Alexander. He's a good friend of Grandpa Mason. And this is Mister Coleman," he said steering her towards Evan. "He's a famous horse trainer from Alamosa."

"Who's the pretty lady?" Taylor asked pointing at Cheree.

Her father pulled her hand down. The pretty lady's name is Doctor Nicoletti and it's not polite to point."

"Are you really a doctor? You don't look like a doctor."

"Yes, I am. What's a doctor supposed to look like?"

"Older, doctors are supposed to look older. The doctor I go to when I'm sick looks a lot older. He's not very pretty either."

"Well, thank you, Taylor. That's a very nice compliment."

"That's enough now, Taylor," Sarah told her. "Here's your pie."

Taylor took the offered plate. "Can I go outside on the patio and eat it?"

"Yes, that would be good. Thank you."

"Bye people," she called over her shoulder, her hair a rosy blur as she made her hasty exit.

"What a beautiful child," Cheree told Sarah.

"Thank you. She is beautiful most of the time. We won't talk about the other times."

"So tell us, Buster, what's this all about?" Matt asked after Sarah had served fat pie slices all around.

Buster paused with his fork in mid travel from his plate to his mouth. "We have a couple of murders and not much for leads. About the only definite clue we have is that in both cases, the perpetrator may have been riding a grulla paint horse."

"Who was murdered?" asked Sarah.

"No one you know unless you grew up in Saguaro County," Evan said. "A man by the name of Ben Pike and his son Abel."

Sarah dropped her fork. The color left her face. She sat motionless for about ten seconds. All eyes were on her. "Excuse me." Her voice cracked.

"Did you know them?" Evan asked quietly.

"Yes." She lowered her eyes. "Yes, I did." She looked up at Evan and met his eyes straight on. "And I'm glad they're dead!"

15

    The room became painfully quiet. Her head down, Sarah pushed a piece of piecrust around on her plate with her fork. The bit of pastry went back and forth across the plate a couple of times before she mashed it flat. When she lifted her head, they could all see the tears in her eyes.

    "I hated those two bastards." She spat out the words. "I'm glad they're dead. I hope they're burning in hell."

    Her hot, caustic words hung in the air. Evan looked to Matt for a sign of understanding, but he appeared to be as confused as the rest of them. "Sarah, what are you saying? How did you know them?"

    Looking back down at her plate, Sarah resumed the attack on the defenseless bit of piecrust. She poked at the flattened mass with the tines of her fork, tearing it into tiny pieces. "Sixteen years," she said, her voice almost a whisper. "It happened sixteen years ago. I never told anyone. At first, I was too afraid and later, I was too ashamed. I tried to put it out of my mind, but not a day has gone by for sixteen long years that I haven't thought about it at least once."

"Ma'am," Buster asked quietly, "what is it you've been holding inside for so long? Did Ben Pike and his son do something to you sixteen years ago? If that's the case, we're here to talk about it."

She looked back up at Buster. She saw a friendly face there. Then she looked from him to Evan to Cheree and finally to her husband. Everyone was waiting for her. It was too much, her composure collapsed and she started to sob. Matt got up and put his arm around her shoulders. "It's okay, baby," he whispered. "It's okay." He had no idea of what else to say to her for comfort.

Sarah took her hands away from her face and held to Matt's arm. In a breaking voice, between sobs, she said, "I've wanted to tell someone for so long, but I just couldn't. It was horrible and embarrassing. I felt horrible it happened, like it was all my fault."

Cheree suddenly understood Ben and Abel Pike had brutalized this woman sixteen years ago and terrorized her into silence. She had kept quiet until now, but Cheree knew with a little prompting, the dam would burst. "Sarah, could you and I talk about this? Just the two of us?"

Sarah nodded. Cheree looked imploringly at Evan, knowing he was smart enough to realize what she wanted. "Ah, guys," he said, "why don't we all go out and let Sarah and Cheree talk about things in private for a while. I'd like to see that grulla paint close up if I could."

Matt responded slowly, "Yeah, sure. Yeah. Well, let's go do that." He removed his arm from his wife's shoulders. "You okay, Honey?"

"Yes, I'm fine. You go ahead. I want to talk to Cheree alone."

When the three men were outside, Buster turned to Matt. "You have any idea what that's all about?"

"My God, no! You're not thinking she could have killed this Pike character, are you? Sarah could never do anything like that." He was looking at Buster.

"Not for a minute, but obviously she had a serious run in with him and his son."

"How old is your wife, Matt?" Evan asked

"She just turned thirty-two. She would have barely been sixteen when it happened, whatever it was."

"Yeah," Evan said to Buster, "and Abel would have been about sixteen or seventeen and Ben about thirty-nine."

"What is this all about, please?" Matt implored.

For the next ten minutes, Buster and Evan proceeded to tell him most everything they knew about the case, omitting only a few strategic details, like the long, strawberry blonde hairs and Ruth Pike's story about her two big visitors in the white and gold pickup. Matt's pickup? They walked around the pasture, looking at Matt's horses, little Taylor in tow, but they spoke quietly. She was far more interested in the horses than the adults' conversation.

When the men left the house Sarah sat quietly, staring at the table, no longer sobbing, but not talking either. Cheree gently prodded her. "Sarah, both Ben and Abel Pike are dead now. They can't possible hurt you anymore. Whatever they did to you happened sixteen years ago. I think if you tell me the story, you'll finally be able to put it behind you."

Slowly lifting her head, her voice wavered as she started to speak. "My parents had a farm about fifteen miles north of Monte Vista. We raised potatoes and lettuce. In the early spring one year, my dad hired Ben Pike to clear some land. All he did was grade it and run a rock picker over it, but he made a big production of it. He'd come out, do a little bit, then disappear for a few days. When he came back, he'd claim he was busy and couldn't finish, but he'd do a little bit more. He carried on like that for a several weeks until my dad got impatient with him. I couldn't stand him. I was physically well developed for my age, and he'd stare at me like I was naked. I tried to disappear whenever he showed up. Anyway, he was about half done with the field when Dad told him to get finished or he was going to have to find somebody else who wasn't so busy. Pike didn't like that, but he finally finished the job, and my dad paid him off. I hoped we'd never see him again."

Sarah paused to regard her coffee cup. She swirled the contents around without drinking any before she put it back down. She seemed to Cheree to be looking for strength to continue.

"On a Saturday morning almost a month after Pike had finally finished, he showed up again. It was early summer. School had just let out. My mom and dad had gone to Colorado Springs. They weren't going to be back until sometime that night. I was in the kitchen when Pike pulled up in his ratty old pickup. My little brother, Jake, was outside playing or I would have locked the door and refused to open it. I had no idea what Pike wanted, but I wasn't about to leave my brother alone with that creep, so I went out. I can still see him getting out of his truck like it was yesterday. He was grinning and his face was red, like he'd been drinking. He had his two sons with him. The big one, Abel, was taller than he was. The other son, Jason, was small, only a little taller than my brother and almost delicate. I still remember wondering how two brothers could look so different.

"Pike smiled at me when I came out. Said he wanted to talk to my dad. I said, 'About what? He already paid you.' I wanted him the hell gone. That's when Pike said there was a mistake. He had more money coming. I told him I didn't know anything about it and my dad wasn't home. He sort of smiled, and said in that case he wanted to talk to my mother. Then I made a mistake. I said they weren't home and wouldn't be back 'til late. He said, 'Is that so?' I immediately got a bad feeling." Sarah looked down again for a moment and when she looked back up at Cheree, there were fresh tears in her eyes.

"I was standing only about ten feet away from him. He took three quick steps and grabbed me by my arm. He spun me around, pulled my arm up behind my back, and said, 'In that case I'm gonna take it out in trade!' He told Abel to grab some baling twine out of the truck, and said,

'We're gonna have us some sport sex.'" Her voice faltered. She started to sob.

Cheree got out of her chair across the table from Sarah to sit next to her. She put her arm around Sarah's shoulders, and hugged her tightly. "I'm so sorry." Sarah was shaking with grief and anger. Cheree held her until her sobbing subsided.

"He pushed me towards the house, and I started screaming. He told me to shut up or he'd break my arm. I kept screaming and tried to pull away from him, but he was too strong. He told me if I didn't shut up, he'd have his boys beat my brother. I quit screaming, and he forced me into the house. He told Abel to hurry up with the twine and to, 'Bring the little brat too.' Inside the house he demanded to know where my bedroom was. I didn't answer him so he put both his arms around me and lifted me off my feet. I was totally helpless. I started to cry. He laughed while he carried me upstairs. Abel was behind us dragging Jake along by one arm and Jason was behind him."

Sarah paused, taking a deep breath, like a sprinter before the race. "He kicked open the first door at the top of the stairs. It was the bathroom so he moved down the hallway to the next room. It was my bedroom. When he saw the bed, he laughed again. I could feel the son-of-bitch getting hard. He threw me down on my back and straddled me. He stretched my arms out so he and Abel could tie my arms across the bed. I was crying hard, begging him to let me go. He said, 'Shut up you little slut, I'll let you go when we're done!' Then he got up and started to pull down his pants. I pleaded with him. I told him I was having my period. He just laughed. 'Good', he said, 'you'll be nice and wet!'"

Cheree thought back to the tent where Evan had found Pike murdered. It was all beginning to make a perverse kind of sense. "You poor girl. That was horrible!" She was starting to think Pike got what he deserved.

"He didn't even bother to unbutton my blouse, he just ripped it apart. My bra, too. When he got his pants down, he straddled me again. He pulled my pants off. I was wearing a pad, and I started screaming at him again to leave me alone. He told me to shut up, and when I wouldn't; I couldn't stop screaming, he pulled off my panties and stuffed the pad in my mouth. I tried to kick at him so he spread my legs apart, and had Abel tie me down by the ankles too." She stopped and looked away. "Then he raped me."

"My God! What a bastard!"

Sarah wasn't crying anymore. She was spitting out the words. "When he was done, he got off me. Told Abel it was his turn. He already had his pants off. He raped me too. When Abel was done, he told Jason he was next."

"Jason couldn't have been more then twelve!"

"Yeah, I guess, something like that. He said he didn't want too, so Pike grabbed him, and pulled his pants down. He and Abel picked Jason up, and put him on top of me. Then Pike grabbed my little brother, and forced him to watch."

"Jesus!" Cheree couldn't believe what she was hearing.

"I don't think Jesus was anywhere around at the time. If he was, he didn't help me. Jason just laid on me for a little while before he started crying. My brother was crying and screaming, too. Pike was laughing, holding him by his neck. After a minute or so, Pike yelled at Jason, 'If you can't be a man, get the hell off!' When he got off, I thought the two of them would rape me again, but they didn't. Pike took the pad out of my mouth and untied me. He told me I'd better not tell anybody what happened. I'll never forget what he said. 'If you or this little brat ever talk, me and my boys will get you. I'll cut your brother's pecker off and stuff it down his throat so he chokes on it!' Then they walked away. Jake was screaming words at them I didn't realize he knew. Pike just laughed, but Jason pushed him down on the floor and shook his fist in his face before he left the room."

"As soon as they were gone, Jake tried to help me get up. I laid there until I heard their truck leave. I wanted to be hysterical, but I couldn't freak out in front of my brother. I told him to go downstairs and lock the door and wait for me to come down. I got up and pulled myself together. When I went downstairs, Jake was sitting on the kitchen floor with his back against the door. He was just sitting there, quietly sobbing. I comforted him as well as I could. 'I'm okay,' I told him, 'they didn't really hurt me, but we can't tell anyone, ever, what happened.' I made him promise never to tell. I figured in time, he'd forget about it and be all right. I wasn't so sure about me."

"And did either one of you ever tell anyone what Pike did to you?"

Sarah looked at Cheree. "I don't know if Jake ever told anyone. I don't think he did. I know I haven't. Not until now. I didn't ever sleep in that bed again. I slept on the floor for three months. I got a part-time job after school that year and saved my money. When I had enough, I bought a new bed. I burned the old one." She looked at Cheree. "What would you have done?"

"I don't know. It was horrible. I don't know what I would have done." She was thinking she would have hunted Pike down and killed him–slowly.

"Well, I didn't do anything then, and I didn't kill them now either, although I'm glad someone did. When you find who did it, thank him for me."

Cheree got up from the table, and went for the coffee pot. She offered some to Sarah, and filled her own cup. "I'd like to tell you a little bit about what's going on." She proceeded to tell Sarah some of what she knew. She figured she owed Sarah something. She described how Evan found Ben Pike murdered in his tent, omitting the detail of the long, strawberry blonde hair she found on Pike's body. She told her about Abel Pike's murder, and she told her Ruth and Jason Pike were maintaining they knew nothing about a possible motive.

"Jason is lying. That little bastard was there. In fact, I almost felt sorry for him until he pushed my brother down. Then I realized he was a bully too, he just wasn't old enough to rape me."

"I'm not big on suppressed memories, but I think in some cases it's possible. Jason might have put the incident somewhere in the back of his mind and doesn't want to remember, or you're right, he is lying; for obvious reasons. We need to have another talk with him."

Sarah got up, paced across the kitchen and back to the table. "So, am I a suspect?"

Cheree thought for a moment. "You said you didn't do it. I believe you, but you realize I'm going to have to tell your story to Deputies Coleman and Alexander. I'm sure we'll have some more questions. We're also going to want to talk to your brother. Where does he live?"

"He just moved to Colorado Springs. He was here with a buddy of his until two days ago."

"He was here for a visit?"

"Yeah, he and a friend stayed with us for a few weeks. The two of them wanted to be cowboys for a while. In exchange for using some of the horses, they helped out."

"What's he doing now?"

"He went back to school. The company he works for is paying him to get a master's degree."

"That's generous. Who does he work for?"

"I forget the name, it's one of the big veterinary drug companies. He has a degree in animal science from the University of Nebraska, and he went to work for this company right out of college. He was a big football star in college. He probably could have played pro football, but he decided he'd stay healthier if he got a normal job. Anyway, he worked for this company for a couple of years. Now they want to move him into management, so he made a deal with them. They pay him to get his MBA and he signs a five-year contract."

Cheree didn't like where this seemed to be going. "You say Jake had a friend who stayed here too?"

"Yeah, a real nice guy, Dale Kupfer is his name. He and my brother played football together. This was kind of like a vacation for the two of them. They went on trail rides in the mountains and did a lot of fishing. Actually, they stayed here for a few weeks early this summer too. I enjoyed having them around."

"Have you and Jake ever talked to each other about what happened sixteen years ago?"

Sarah shook her head, "No, never. Not even once since the morning it happened when I came downstairs to tell him we could never tell anyone. Neither one of us ever mentioned it again. I honestly don't know if he even remembers it. He was barely eight."

Cheree was silent, contemplating what she had just learned. Was it possible Sarah's brother killed Ben and Abel Pike? He certainly had motive and opportunity. And the bigger question, Cheree thought, is Sarah involved? Cheree desperately wanted to believe she had nothing to do with it, but what if she was just a good liar.

"I suppose you're going to have to talk to him about it," Sarah said flatly.

"Sarah, after what you just told me about Ben Pike, it sounds to me like Ben and Abel got what they deserved. I wouldn't mind dropping the whole investigation, but that's not going to happen. Murder, no matter the reason, is still against the law. I'm obligated to pursue all leads. In fact, even though I believe you, I can't promise that you won't become a suspect. Right this instant, the only thing I'm certain of is that whoever killed Ben Pike knew what he did to you sixteen years ago. That means you, your brother, and Jason Pike for certain. But I will promise you this, I won't settle for anything less than the truth and to get that, we have to talk to your brother."

Wiping her eyes, Sarah sighed, "I'll get you his address and phone number." She walked out of the kitchen, leaving Cheree sitting alone with her private suspicions.

"What do you suppose they're talking about?" Matt asked Buster and Evan after they had explained the murders to him. The three men and Taylor were standing amidst a herd of at least twenty horses. Several of the friendlier ones were quite close. The grulla paint mare and Taylor obviously had a special relationship. The horse had its head down and she had her arms thrown around the mare's neck, practically swinging on her.

"I don't know," Buster admitted "but I'm sure we'll find out soon enough."

"My God, I just can't believe she's involved in this!"

"At this time we have no reason to believe she's involved at all," Evan told him. "She is probably just an innocent bystander who, through no fault of her own, got close to Pike and got hurt. He wasn't a pleasant person. Hurting people came easy to him."

"I'm positive Sarah didn't have anything to do with his murder!"

"Where were you last Friday?" Evan asked. "Pike was murdered sometime before noon."

"Sarah and I were here, all day. My dad was here too. We were working a couple of my horses. We're entered in a cutting at Fort Collins this weekend."

"Anybody else around?"

Matt took his time answering, "No, Sarah's brother, Jake, and a friend of his stayed with us for a while, but they borrowed the truck and trailer and were riding in the hills somewhere down around Pagosa Springs." Matt looked from Buster to Evan. "The two of them wanted to play cowboy. They helped me put in a new arena, and I let them use some horses."

"Well, you and your wife have an alibi. There's no reason to think she had anything to do with Pike's recent problem." The brother and his friend were interesting additions to the equation. Evan thought there were a lot of questions begging, but rather than grilling Matt now, he wanted to hear what Sarah had told Cheree.

"Taylor," said Matt, "quit hanging on Jolena like that!"

"I'm just hugging her tight, Daddy," the little girl protested.

"Yeah, well stop it. You remember what happened the last time. Your Mother will be upset if we have to trim off any more of your hair."

"Okay, Daddy, but you have to tell Jo to stop too."

Matt turned to Buster and Evan. "I don't know what those two have going. That horse will let her do anything. Last Wednesday, the day before the mare disappeared, Taylor got her hair so tangled up in Jolena's halter we had to cut some of it off to get her free. I let her out of my sight while I was shoeing a horse. When I tracked her down, she was standing on Jolena's back doing pirouettes. I almost panicked at first, but then as I watched, I realized she wasn't in any danger, at least from the horse. I was wondering mostly how the hell she got up there. After a few minutes, Taylor sat down, patted the horse on her flank, and I'll be damned if Jolena didn't lay down. Taylor proceeded to crawl all over her, tangling her hair up in the horse's halter."

"Sounds like a horse even I could ride," said Buster.

"Yeah, I suspect even you could," Matt told him smiling. He knew how well Buster could ride. "The only rider I ever saw her protest was Sarah's brother, but I think it was because he's so big. After a little while she settled down though and was okay with him."

"How big is this guy?" Evan asked.

"Oh Jeez, I don't know exactly, maybe six-four, six-five, maybe weighs two-forty. He ain't fat either. His buddy was even bigger. It was fun to go to the saloon with them. You knew nobody was going to hassle you."

Evan copped a peek at Buster. His wheels were turning too. "Were these guys football players, or what?"

"Yeah, in fact, they played for Nebraska. Big stars I guess, although you'd never know it. They're real nice kids. Always polite, very helpful, I got a lot done while they were here."

"Where are they now?"

"You just missed them. They left Monday, just past noon. Jake went to Colorado Springs and his buddy went home to Nebraska."

Buster made a discreet inquiry. "What are their last names? I sorta follow college football." He lied.

"Jake's last name is Lawrence and his buddy's name is Dale Kupfer. Sound familiar?"

Buster did some quick thinking. If they were still in college and playing football, they should have been back at school in training no later than mid-August. He made a guess. "Yeah they do sound familiar, but they played a few years ago, right?"

"Oh yeah, they both graduated two years ago, but Jake just went back to school to get his MBA or something. Sarah knows the details."

Evan was thinking, too. Kupfer was the name of the man who, according to Buster's grandmother, was the original owner of Pike's property. This was becoming far too coincidental to be comfortable. Sarah's brother and his friend sounded a whole lot like Ruth Pike's mysterious visitors. He needed to talk to Cheree. He checked his watch. The time was just after two. Cheree and Sarah had been alone together for a half hour. He hoped Sarah had opened up by now.

Back in the house, Sarah handed Cheree a piece of paper with her brother's address and phone number. "Frankly," she told Sarah, "I hope he doesn't remember anything about it."

"After all this time, don't you want to know?"

"No. Like I said, I'm glad those two sons-of-bitches are dead. I want to forget them and what they did to us. I hope my brother already has."

Cheree could understand that. "I'm probably going to talk to him as soon as possible. I'd really appreciate you not contacting him until I have."

"I won't. I don't want to remind him."

"You're going to have to tell your husband the whole story."

Sarah sighed. "I know. I'm not looking forward to it either."

Cheree looked her in the eyes. "Please, Sarah. What happened was not your fault. You were completely innocent. Your husband will understand. I'm betting you'll feel better after you tell him." Sarah looked away. "Do you feel worse after telling me?"

"No." Cheree waited, but it was all Sarah said.

"Okay. Look, it's a start. Healing has to start somewhere. This is a good place. You have a wonderful family. It's time you give up your hurt. Now let's go find the boys and we can be on our way."

In everyone's life some certain select incidents happen. Good or bad, these things are monumental, and they become indelibly etched on the retina of the mind's eye, to be replayed over and over for as long as consciousness remains. Sarah would never forget the sight of Ben Pike straddling her, eyes raging with lust, ripping off her clothes while she lay helpless, tied to her bed. For sixteen years the pain and shame had haunted her. She assumed it would haunt her until she died. But today, since she and Cheree had talked, she had a fleeting thought. Even though she would never forget it, she might be able to reconcile it.

Sarah smiled briefly. "Maybe you're right. Thanks."

16

They shook hands all around before leaving. Taylor insisted on hugging "The Pretty Doctor", and Cheree was flattered to oblige. Matt stood straight with his arm across Sarah's shoulders. She was managing a smile. It was a friendly departure. The driveway looped past the house and they drove by the one-ton, dually pickup and color-coordinated horse trailer on the way out.

"Almost scary the way things are adding up," Evan commented. They were all looking at the truck and trailer. "What did Sarah have to say?" he asked Cheree.

"Ben and Abel Pike raped her sixteen years ago. It was ugly and brutal. She's been traumatized by it ever since. I don't think she murdered them, but if she had I wouldn't blame her. She then proceeded to give them all the details. They were half way back to Monte Vista when she finished. "So, what do you two think?"

"I can understand her reluctance to talk," Buster said, "I just hope she hasn't taken the law into her own hands."

"She told me she didn't kill them. I believe her, or at least I want to believe her. If she's lying she's damn good at it."

"I believe her," Evan offered. "It was too spontaneous, too unrehearsed, she hadn't even told her husband. I think Pike truly terrorized her into submission. But her brother, now he's got me worried." He looked at Cheree in the rear view mirror. "There's one detail you don't know about yet."

"Holding out again?"

"No, not all. It's something that was totally unrelated to any of this–until now. You tell her, Buster, it's your story."

"I assume you're referring to the story of how Pike's great grandfather came by his property."

"That would be it."

"Well, Cheree," Buster said, "my grandmother told me this almost fifty years ago. I believe most of it is fact, but some could be fiction, there's no way to know for sure. One thing is for certain, it's a very interesting story especially when you consider that the man who first owned Pike's property may be related to Sarah's brother's friend, Dale Kupfer."

"I'm confused," Cheree admitted. "Ben Pike was only fifty-five. How long has he owned the property?"

"Ben wasn't the first Pike to own the property, according to my grandmother, Ben's great grandfather stole the land from a man named Emil Kupfer." Buster proceeded to tell her what his grandmother had told him. By the time he finished, they had passed through Monte Vista and were headed north towards Saguaro on US 285.

Cheree had been spellbound by Buster's tale and when he was through, she shook her head. "I can't believe it! What are the odds?"

"Which odds? The odds that Emil and Dale are related or the odds Dale helped Sarah's brother kill the Pikes."

"Both of course. I don't think you can separate the two."

"You lost me," Evan admitted. "Do you mean that if Dale is the killer or at least one of the killers, he has to be related to Emil?"

"Exactly! Otherwise he has no motive."

"What if was just helping out a friend."

"Helping a friend by murdering two people? Possible, but not probable."

"Okay, what about the converse? If Dale is related to Emil, is he necessarily one of the killers?"

Cheree thought for a moment. "No, maybe not. He could really just be a friend of Jake's and it's only coincidence he's related to Emil Kupfer."

"Maybe the reason they became friends is because they discovered they had the Pike family in common." Both Cheree and Evan looked critically at Buster. "What's so far fetched about that? You two are proposing theories a lot more speculative."

"They became friends because they played on the same team," Evan said.

"Did you play football in high school?"

"Yeah, what's your point?"

"Were you best friends with all your team mates?"

"No, of course not."

"So why would Dale and Jake automatically be friends because they played on the same college team?"

"I see your point, but it's a different situation. College isn't high school. High School is a closed society. When you go off to college you're more open to new people. You're looking to form new friendships."

"Yeah, you're right, but you still form friendships based on things you have in common. Emil Kupfer originally came to Colorado from Nebraska. If he had relatives there, why couldn't Dale be a relative of Emil who knew the story of how his great uncle, or whatever, went off to Colorado and settled some land that ultimately passed to Pike? And when he discovered Jack was from Colorado..."

"Wait! Wait!" Cheree interrupted, "Buster, you said Emil's wife and son disappeared and your grandmother figured Pike killed them."

"Yeah, but she didn't know for sure. She was speculating."

"What if he didn't kill them? What if they ran away from him because they thought he was going to kill them and went back to Nebraska, where Emil was from originally?"

Buster thought about that for a moment. "I like that. If it's what happened, this Dale Kupfer most likely would be Emil's great grandson." He thought for another moment. "More likely his great, great grandson would be correct. So really the only coincidence is that these two end up on the same college football team, and if somehow Dale knew the whole story, he has a motive too! But do he and Sarah's brother ultimately conspire to commit murder? Circumstantially, they look good."

"Good, Hell! Circumstantially, I'd say we don't have to look any farther," Evan said. "They, or at least Sarah's brother for sure, has motive, opportunity, and ability."

Cheree took out a pen and paper. "Tell me what we have so far."

"They have access to a grulla paint horse," said Evan. "Matt gave me hair samples from both the grulla paint and the sorrel paint. Jake and Dale could have easily 'borrowed' the two horses for a few days and made it look like a robbery. We should know if the horses match as soon as your lab analyzes the hair."

"Okay, let's assume Matt's horses are the ones involved. How about the strawberry blonde hair?"

"Something else I forgot to tell you," Evan admitted. "Matt told us his little girl, Taylor, got her hair all tangled up in the buckle on the grulla paint's halter the morning of the day the horse disappeared. She plays with the horse like it's a dog. Matt said Sarah had to cut some of her hair off to get them separated. Probably pulled a few out by roots too. So there were obviously a few of her hairs left in the halter when Jake stole her."

"You don't think he deliberately planted them on Pike's body do you?" Buster asked.

"I doubt it. My guess is in the process of removing the halter and putting on a bridle, some of Taylor's hair stuck to him and was eventually accidentally transferred to Pike. Would that work?"

Cheree answered. "Yeah, I think it could. I can't imagine him wanting Ben's murder to be traced back to his five year old niece."

"It sounds like the two of them would certainly be physically able to handle Pike," offered Buster.

"Yes, easily," agreed Cheree, "and there's something else Sarah told me. Up until a few weeks ago, Jake was selling supplies for an animal pharmaceutical company. That would give him access to ketamine. I'm sure he'd know how to dose it."

"How about the bruise on the back of Pike's neck," Buster asked. "Can we explain that?"

"I'm pretty certain it was caused by a stun gun or a powerful cattle prod. Neither of which is hard to come by."

"Sarah gave you Jake's address, right?" Evan asked Cheree. "I think we should notify the Colorado Springs PD, have him brought in for questioning. They can hold him overnight."

Buster disagreed. "You sure we want to do that just now? I hate to have him arrested. I'd rather we were the ones who picked him up. Let's talk to Jason Pike first. Maybe we can jog his memory."

"I agree with Buster," said Cheree. "Sarah promised me she wouldn't talk to Jake about our visit before we interviewed him. Jason might be able to give us something more."

Evan wasn't so certain Sarah wouldn't try to protect her brother. And in fact, even as they debated it, Sarah was on the phone trying to reach Jake. As soon as they left the ranch, Sarah was putting off a conversation with her husband so she could call Jake.

"Are you okay?" Matt asked her as their visitors drove away.

"Yes, I'm fine."

"What's going on? What did Pike do to you?"

"I'll tell you all about it. Can you give me a few minutes alone first?"

Matt was confused. "Yeah, sure. Ah, I've got a couple of things I could do and then I'll come in and we can talk about it. Okay?"

"Okay." She kissed him quickly and went in the house.

She went to the phone in their bedroom and dialed her brother's number. After the fourth ring his voice mail answered. "Jake, this is Sarah. Call me as soon as you can. It's important." Her hands were shaking. She had promised Doctor Nicoletti she wouldn't contact Jake. She wasn't sure why she was going against her word.

"I don't know if I trust her as much as you do, Cheree," Evan admitted, "and I'm not sure what difference it makes what Jason tells us. Even if he tells us the same story Sarah told you, what would it matter as far as Jake is concerned?"

"I don't know, maybe you're right, maybe it isn't important. The way you found Ben Pike certainly indicates Sarah is telling the truth, but I'd like to hear Jason's version of the story. I think if he freely admits it happened, it could mean he has nothing to hide. That would give us a stronger case against Sarah's brother." She was looking in the rear view mirror, trying to catch Evan's eye, but he was looking down the road. "Does that make any sense to you?"

"Yeah, I guess, although I don't want to ignore Jake for long."

"I'm not suggesting we ignore him at all, just let's talk to Jason first."

Buster agreed with Cheree, "Yeah, also Jason could be next on the list. If he is, we need to get to him before the killer does. Could be Ruth is on the list too; guilt by association?"

"Okay, you're right. We'll hold off on Jake until we talk to Jason. It would be nice if we could prevent a couple more murders instead of discovering more." Evan consulted his watch. It was almost three. He put on the lights and ran the cruiser up to ninety-five. "I think we'll hurry."

"My God, Sarah why didn't you tell me sooner?" Sarah had just finished telling Matt the same story she had told Cheree an hour earlier.

"I was ashamed," her voice faltered. "I felt dirty for a long time. Ben Pike called me a slut and I thought I was. I didn't date anybody until I was nineteen. Until I met you, I never thought I'd have a normal life." She broke down and sobbed uncontrollably. "I was too afraid and too....." She trailed off as she wept.

Matt wrapped his arms around her and hugged her tight. "It's okay, Baby, it's okay. I love you and we'll be just fine. They can't hurt you anymore." He didn't tell her he wished he could have killed them himself.

He held her until her sobbing subsided. "I'm sorry," she said finally.

"You don't have anything to be sorry for, even if you'd killed them you don't have to be sorry." He paused, "I have to ask. You didn't have anything to do with it, did you?"

"No, but I'm afraid Jake might have. I'm worried. I tried to call him a little bit ago and he didn't answer." She pulled back slightly from his embrace to look at him. "Oh Matt, what if Jake killed them? What can we do?"

"What's the chance he evens remembers the incident? He was only eight years old." Matt didn't wait for her answer. "But he looks damn suspicious to me right now. I doubt if Buster and his partner told me everything they know. I can't imagine they would." Matt took Sarah's hand in his. "How well do you know your brother?"

"Right now, I'm not sure I know him at all. All I wanted to do back then was to protect him. I believed Pike was fully capable of coming back to get us. That's why I never told any one and that's why I made him promise not to tell. I can't imagine him understanding Pike's threat, let alone remembering it, but the way Pike was murdered, my God, Matt, it's exactly what he threatened to do to Jake."

"Yeah, that and the horses. He and Dale could have 'borrowed' the horses and just made it look like they were stolen. Hell, they had free access to the truck and trailer anytime they wanted. The last two weeks they were here, they were coming and going all the time."

"Why would Dale have helped him?"

"You're asking me? I never even seriously considered murdering anyone let alone getting my best friend to help me." He laughed nervously. "But you did say Jake was a hell of a salesman."

Just then the phone rang and they both jumped. Sarah got there first. "Hello."

"Hey, Sis, what's up?" It was Jake.

About a mile before they reached Pike's place, Evan cut the lights and started slowing the cruiser. He swung the car to the left, barreled down the driveway and came to an abrupt halt in front of the house, displacing the gravel under the front tires. There was a pickup in the driveway neither he nor Buster had seen before. "Show time!" he announced. "Buster, back me up." He was out of the car and on his way to the door in a heartbeat. Buster and Cheree got out, guns drawn. They took up a position behind the front end of the cruiser. They watched him knock on the door.

"Ruth Pike! This is Deputy Coleman," he announced. "Open the door, please!"

The door opened immediately and Ruth appeared. "Yes, what is it? Is there a problem?"

"Not if you're all right. Is your son here also? We have reason to believe both of you could be in immediate danger."

A grin that Evan remembered later as being silly crossed her face. "Yes, we're fine. What's going on?"

Evan gestured to the pickup parked in the driveway. "Is that your son's truck?"

"Yes. Whatever is the matter?"

"Where is he? We'd like to talk to both of you."

"I'm not exactly sure. He went out to the barn a little bit ago. He was going to saddle up a horse and go for a ride. What's this all about?"

Evan signaled for Buster and Cheree to come up. "I'll have Deputy Alexander and Doctor Nicoletti come in to sit with you while I find your son. We'll explain everything."

He left her standing there with the door opened as he headed for the barn. "I'm going to the barn to look for Jason," he told Buster as they crossed paths. "You and Cheree stay with Ruth."

The big sliding door at the back of the barn was open. Evan stepped in and made a quick right turn. After coming in from the bright sun, he wanted to give his eyes a second to adjust to the dimly lit interior. He stood with his back against the wall, his right hand resting lightly on the butt of his pistol. He saw a man on the back of a horse at the far end of the barn.

"Jason," he called out, "Jason Pike!"

The mounted figure turned in the saddle. "Yeah, who are you?"

"Sheriff's Deputy Coleman, I need to talk to you."

The horse and rider started towards him. "What about?"

About the murder of your father and brother, you moron. "There's been a development in the murder of your father and brother that we need to talk about." He took his hand away from his weapon and started moving towards Jason.

Jason walked the horse up to him, stopping five feet away. The horse was a solid looking, red dun that Evan had not seen before. It must be the horse Ruth had mentioned to him the other day, Ben's latest acquisition. "I've already told you everything I know. I just got this horse saddled up and I'm about to ride her. My father bought it for my girlfriend. I want to check her out before she rides her." His posture was defiant, bordering on threatening.

"As soon as we're finished talking you can go for your test drive. Get down from the horse, now!" It was no longer a request.

Jason sat in the saddle for a long ten seconds, as a slight smirk crossed his face. Evan was mentally preparing to move fast and take him out of the saddle if he didn't comply. He knew how to turn the horse to get at Jason's leg. He'd have him on the ground gasping for breath before he knew what happened. The standoff ended when Jason finally swung down. He led the horse over to the barn wall where there was an eyebolt. He looped the reins loosely through it. He had a paper towel clenched in his left fist.

"What the hell is this all about?"

"We want to test your long term memory is what it's all about. Let's join the others in the house or we can go to the courthouse, it's your choice."

"The house will be fine," Jason answered. The smirk was gone. They walked from the barn and as they passed by an empty feed bag next to the door, Jason dropped the paper towel from his left hand into the bag. "Poked myself with the damn tang on the cinch buckle."

"We have information," Evan started when everyone was seated in the kitchen, "that would indicate Ben and Jason were murdered in revenge for an incident that occurred sixteen years ago. We need your help to confirm this incident."

He started to say more, but Ruth interrupted, "Do you have a suspect?"

"We may, but we still need your cooperation," Evan was not about to be side tracked. "Our information implicates your husband and two sons in the rape of a young woman in southern Saguaro County sixteen years ago." Evan wasn't mincing words. The near incident with Jason had him spooled up.

"What the hell!" Ruth burst out in righteous indignation, "Are you accusing Jason of rape? He wasn't even twelve years old sixteen years ago!"

"I haven't accused anyone of anything at this point, ma'am. I'm trying to determine the facts in this case, all the facts. And hopefully, catch the guilty party while preventing another murder or two."

"Are you telling us you think we're next on the hit list?" Jason asked.

"The way this is going, if your last name is Pike you could be a target. What do you think?"

Jason didn't respond, but Ruth did. "So if you have information, why don't you arrest somebody instead of trying to scare us?"

"First of all, ma'am, I'm not trying to scare you. We came here to discuss what Jason remembers about an alleged incident involving him, his father, and his brother. I'm not accusing him of rape, either. According to the woman involved, he was the only one who didn't rape her." Evan turned towards Jason, "Now, please tell us what you know about the incident." He didn't give him an out by adding an, "if you can remember", or an, "I know it was a long time ago." He was certain Jason remembered. He was demanding that Jason tell them everything he knew about the incident.

The room fell silent. Evan stared at Jason. Jason had tilted his head back to stare at the ceiling. Buster was staring at Ruth and Cheree was staring at Evan. This was the first time she had seen him get tough. The yellow afternoon sunlight was rapidly sliding away, blocked by the mountains to the west. The room had darkened perceptively in just the last few minutes. There was an old electric clock on the kitchen wall, and even Buster could hear its gears not so quietly grinding the time away. The atmosphere bristled with static. Cheree half expected lightning flashes to flicker from the light fixture hanging above the table.

Finally, Jason started to speak. "I remember everything." His voice crackled back and forth between its normal pitch to almost a falsetto, as if he were going through puberty again. "It was early Saturday morning and Dad said to me and Abel, 'Let's go for a little ride.' It wasn't a request so we got in the pickup. When Abel asked where we were going he said, 'I gotta collect on a little debt.' He had a whiskey bottle under the driver's seat. He pulled it out and took a long swig. Then he offered it to Abel. Abel took it, but he just pretended to drink some before handing it back to Dad. He didn't put it down again until it was empty. We drove south on two-eighty-five for a while until Dad turned into the driveway of a big farm. He said the people that owned this farm still owed him money and he was going to get it one way or another. When he parked the car in the driveway in front of the house, a real pretty blonde girl came out. Dad started talking to her, but I couldn't tell what he was saying. The next thing I knew she was screaming. He had a hold of her and was carrying her into the house. He yelled back at Abel to get some twine and for us to come with him." Jason had been contemplating the ceiling as he talked, but now he tilted his head forward to look Evan in the eyes. Evan could see tears beginning to gather.

"He carried the girl upstairs while we followed. Abel had the twine and was dragging the girl's little brother. The kid was crying and the girl was screaming. I thought I must be going to hell. Dad found a bedroom, threw the girl down, and he and Abel tied her so she couldn't get up. He pulled her clothes off and they both raped her. All I could do was stand there and stare. I was so scared I was shaking. When Abel told me it was my turn, I got weak. I thought I was going to pee in my pants." Jason's voice crackled again before he broke down. He put his face in his hands and wept.

His mother stared silently at him from across the table. She had tears in her eyes, too. It appeared to Cheree that Ruth wanted to reach out and touch him in consolation. It certainly seemed as if she had never heard the story before. "Then," Jason started again quietly, "when I told them I didn't want to do it, they pulled my pants down and put me on top of that poor girl. I could feel her shaking. I just laid there, scared. I started to cry. Dad told me I wasn't a man and to get off. I got up and put my pants on as fast as I could. I just wanted to get away. Dad and Abel were laughing at me. Then I did something I'll regret the rest of my life." He looked back up at Evan. "I pushed that little boy down just to show Dad and Abel that I was tough." He stopped, looking imploringly around at his audience, hoping for mercy. "I can't remember a day since it happened, I haven't thought about it." He looked down and was silent.

Evan had to admit he was moved by Jason's confession. It went a long way to explain his apparent detachment from reality that Cheree had commented on when she first met him at the morgue. Buster had also predicted Jason's behavior could be a direct result of having been a member of the Pike household. There was no longer any doubt in Evan's mind that the sons of Ben Pike had grown up in the shadow of a tyrant. He wondered if there were any other dark secrets stuck and festering in Jason's soul. Well, one crime at a time, he thought.

"Thank you," Evan told Jason. "I realize that wasn't an easy story to tell, but we needed to hear it. It's going to be helpful in apprehending the killer of your father and brother."

Jason looked at him through wet eyes. It appeared as if he wanted to say more but couldn't. He merely waved his right hand lamely in acknowledgement of Evan's thank you. Evan's cell phone rang to punctuate the moment.

"Buster, would you take over and explain to Jason and Ruth where we're at in the case? I'm going to step outside and take this call." Buster nodded and Evan excused himself.

"Deputy Coleman," he told the phone when he was outside.

"Evan?" asked a vaguely familiar voice.

"Yes, it's Evan Coleman. Who is this?"

"Thank God! Evan, this is Raleigh. Raleigh Pike!" She sounded somewhat frantic.

"Hello Raleigh, what I can I do for you?"

"You told me to call if anything came up. Somebody just shot at me!"

17

Evan was astounded. "What happened?" He demanded, "Are you hit?"

"No, the bullet missed me."

"Where are you?"

"At Abel's place in Buena Vista. The bullet missed my head by an inch or two. I was sitting in the living room, reading a letter I found from Abel, and somebody shot through the window at me. I grabbed my phone and I'm hiding in the garage."

"Raleigh, did you call the police?"

"Yeah. They're on the way." She forced a nervous laugh. "You said to call you if anything new happened."

"Not exactly what I anticipated. How long since you called the police?"

"About two minutes. I've got them on hold on the land line. Abel has an extension out here so he could answer when he was working on his car."

"Raleigh, put me on hold and get the police back on the line. I sure can't help you from here. Do whatever they tell you. And for God's sake, don't let them in until you're positive it's really them."

"Okay, I'll be fine. I'll get back to you as soon as they get here."

The line went dead. Evan could only hope it was because she had switched back to the police dispatcher. *Why would the killer go after her anyway? Her only connection with the rape of Sarah Coleman was that she had the misfortune of having married into a seemingly cursed family. And this letter from Abel she had just referred to? What was that all about?* Evan was thinking as he moved had just decided he wanted that bloodied paper towel Jason had thrown away. "This whole thing is getting crazier by the minute," he muttered to himself. Keeping the phone to his ear, he waited to hear Raleigh's voice again telling him the police had arrived. He was breathing hard, like he had sprinted a hundred yards.

"I'm sure we'll be just fine," Ruth was telling Buster in response to his offer of protection. "Jason was really an innocent bystander when that poor girl was raped, and I certainly didn't have anything to do with it. No harm will come to us."

Cheree and Buster weren't so certain. "I can have state troopers here around the clock. I'd feel a lot better about you staying out here with them close by," Cheree told Ruth.

Jason's emotional confession had been mostly an act. He felt remorse over the incident, however it was primarily for himself. He remembered it with crystal clarity, but hadn't been terribly concerned about Sarah at the time and he wasn't now. Now, he couldn't help staring at Cheree. She was beautiful and tall. Tall women were his favorite, the taller the better. He wouldn't look twice at a woman shorter than he was no matter how pretty she might be. They had to be tall and leggy. He found himself wondering if she liked that other deputy. He noticed the way she watched him whenever he was talking. He thought he saw adoration in that look. If he didn't have a serious significant other, she would look even better. "We'll be just fine, Doctor Nicoletti," he told her, "and if we decide we're in any danger, I'll take Mom to my place in Colorado Springs until you catch the killer." He did his best to sound authoritative. It was his opinion, that tall beautiful women paid more attention to you if you spoke with authority.

"Okay. I can't force you to accept police protection, but if you should reconsider please contact us. It may take some time to apprehend the perpetrator."

"I thought you had a suspect. Isn't that what the other deputy said?" Ruth asked.

"That's correct, ma'am, we do have a possible suspect," Buster admitted, "however we don't have him in custody. In fact, we haven't located him yet. Until he's actually in custody, you and Jason could be in some danger."

"Yes, but you'll have him soon won't you?"

"I really wish I could promise you that ma'am, but I can't. You have to understand that until your son confirmed the story we heard from the rape victim, we weren't positive the individual in question was definitely suspect."

"I'm afraid I don't understand," Ruth admitted.

Buster didn't want to tell her he really didn't understand either so he basically stiffed her. "I'm sorry I can't tell you any more details. It could compromise the case."

She seemed to accept that. "All right, but you will get him, won't you?"

Evan fished the bloodied paper towel from the empty feed bag in the barn and dropped it into a clean plastic bag. He ran his fingers across the seal of the bag, holding it out in front of him briefly, before putting it in his pocket. "Why do I want this?" he asked out loud. He had a hunch, but it was so vague he was having difficulty explaining it even to himself. Something about Jason bothered him. He believed Jason's story of the rape. It was almost identical to Sarah's version. Yet there was something about Jason he was uncomfortable with. He sounded sincere and his remorse looked real enough, but Evan couldn't help feeling it would be smart to count your fingers after shaking hands with him. Ben Pike was big, coarse, and had usually acted with little concern for anything but his immediate needs at the present instant—future be damned. Evan was developing an impression of Jason. He was shrewd, clever, and calculating. He was so different from his father it had Evan unnerved. It was almost as if Jason couldn't be Ben Pike's son. Although he was probably crazy for thinking it, it's why he went back for the bloody towel. Cheree would be able to determine if Jason was any part of Ben.

"Evan!" Raleigh's voice snapped in his ear.

He winced. "Yeah, Raleigh, are you okay?"

"Fine! I'm fine. Your friend is here, Chief Banks. He wants to talk to you."

"Sure, put him on. You're okay though, right?"

"Yeah, other than still being a little rushed from the adrenaline I'm doing just fine. Here's Buddy."

"You got a suspect yet? I don't like all the lead this guy is throwing around up here. Could hurt somebody else."

"Actually, we do, but we think there could be more than one person involved. Is the girl okay?"

"Yeah, she's fine. Quite a woman she is. If I weren't so old and ugly, I'd sure think about making a move on her."

You ain't that old, Buddy. Wait six months and give it a shot. You might get lucky."

"You're cruel, Evan."

"Maybe, but what have you got for me? Anything that'll help?"

"I doubt it," Banks admitted. "We just arrived, but I'm sure the shooter is long gone. I've got a feeling we're not going to find anything of any consequence. We're searching the area. It could also be a stray round from an elk hunter, although that's a stretch. You think it's the same guy that shot her husband?"

"Gotta be either him or an accomplice. The way this thing is developing, it's hard to speculate on how many people are involved."

"You think there's too much going on for it to be just one man?"

"Yeah, I do. I'm leaning towards at least two. It'd take that to physically handle Ben Pike. Although, I could change my mind at any time."

"Be my guess Pike had a lot more enemies than friends. I'll call you if we find anything here."

"Thanks, Buddy, and take care of Raleigh."

"That's already covered. I've got a couple of female officers who are about to start babysitting the place as long as she stays here or until you catch the killer."

"Good. Let me know when the funeral for her husband is scheduled."

"You gonna show for that?"

"If I can. I'd like to do some people watching."

"Could be interesting. Hey, Evan, I gotta start doin' police stuff. You'll hear from me."

"Thanks, Buddy, later." Evan hung up and started back to the house. He decided they had to get Jake Lawrence into custody as soon as possible. He was the most probable suspect based on the evidence they had. He also had motive, although technically that wasn't Evan's job. Get the evidence and the prosecutor would be responsible for proving the crime. Evan didn't want anyone else, especially Raleigh or the remaining Pikes murdered. He rapped on the back door, but didn't wait for anyone to open it.

"Some one just took a shot at Raleigh Pike," Evan announced without fanfare, looking to Ruth and Jason for reactions.

Jason's expression was impassive, but Ruth came halfway out of her chair. "Raleigh? Oh my God! Is she all right?"

"She's fine. The bullet missed, and the Buena Vista police are there now. But I don't mind telling you, I'm having trouble understanding why your husband and son's killer has her on his list."

Ruth settled back in her chair. "Well, I'm sure I don't know either."

"Look, Deputy," Jason interrupted, "I've told you everything I know. I believe it's your job to catch this clown!" His face was red now and his voice was strained.

Evan stared at him for a brief moment. *Real emotions?* "I don't think whoever is responsible is a clown, and I hope you've told us all you know." He turned to Ruth, "Is there anything else you might tell us?"

Ruth shook her head, "No there isn't. I have no idea what's happening, and I resent the implication you seem to be making. I'm not holding out on you. I didn't know anything about this rape that happened sixteen years ago until just now." Her voice was straining too.

More real emotion. Evan thought she sounded sincere. "Okay, in that case, we'll be leaving. I strongly suggest you allow us to get you some protection out here."

"That's already been offered," Jason said, "and we won't need it. I just decided we'll be going to my place in Colorado Springs. In fact, we'll leave as soon as Mom can pack a few things. We'll be safer there, until you catch the killer." His implication was clear. They weren't doing their job.

"That's certainly your choice. If you don't mind, we'll wait outside until you leave."

"Suit yourself," Jason told Evan. He was talking to Evan, but he was looking at Cheree.

In the car, waiting for Jason and Ruth to leave, Evan asked Cheree. "Do you have Ben Pike's DNA typed yet?"

"Yes, we finished that Sunday. Why?"

Evan pulled the plastic bag containing the paper towel stained with Jason's blood from his pocket. He turned and handed it to her over the back of the seat. "This is Jason's blood. He poked himself in the hand with the tang of the buckle on the cinch strap when he was saddling a horse. He had this paper towel in his hand when I found him and he threw it in the trash before we came into the house. He doesn't know I have it. I'd like you to check the DNA to see how it matches up to Ben's."

"Sure, but why?"

"I don't know, curious I guess."

"Don't you think Ben Pike is Jason's father?" Buster asked.

"I don't know. He sure doesn't act or look like him. I have a feeling there could be more he and Ruth aren't telling us."

"I have the same feeling, not that it necessarily makes any difference to this case, but it could be helpful to know if they're holding out on us."

"So we discover Ben isn't Jason's father, that's not a crime. Ruth may just want to keep that private," Cheree told them. "Jason may not even know it himself. If Ben wasn't his father, it isn't up to us to tell him."

"I agree," Evan assured her, "I don't intend to tell him, but—and maybe my logic is twisted—I think if Ruth had an affair and Jason was the result, that might give her more motive to do away with Ben and Abel."

"You're not suggesting Ruth killed her husband and son are you?"

"At this point, the only people I don't suspect are you, me, and Buster. Everyone else is fair game."

"What about Sarah and her husband?" Cheree was having trouble with the concept Ruth was the killer. She could believe she might be capable of killing Ben, but not Abel—not her son. "And how about Raleigh for that matter?"

"I don't know, Cheree. Personally, I believe Sarah's brother and his friend are the most suspect, but you tell me. Can we definitely rule out everyone else?"

Cheree thought for a moment. She wanted to believe Ruth and Jason, and definitely she wanted to believe Sarah and her husband, and certainly Raleigh's grief seemed genuine, but she had to admit she didn't know any of these people or what they might be capable of. "Okay, you're probably right, it just seems..."

Buster interrupted, "Cheree, this isn't exactly a science. You're used to running sophisticated tests on high-buck instruments that give you, at least as I understand it, incontrovertible evidence. We're dealing with human nature here. That's a lot different. The best we can do, unless someone confesses, is to find enough evidence to point us to the right person. Then it's up to the prosecutor."

Evan smiled, "Yeah, Cheree, nothing personal, but you're way too nice. You're not suspicious enough."

He had his arm draped over the back of the car seat. She slapped him on the shoulder. "Nothing personal. I'm too nice? Or do you mean I'm too naïve? At least I'm comforted to know I'm not on your short list of suspects."

They watched Jason emerge from the house carrying two medium-sized suitcases. They were patterned in a subdued yellow and gray plaid, probably at least forty years old. He walked to his pickup, rather callously tossed the bags in the back seat of the extended cab and continued to the barn. The horse he was going to ride when Evan interrupted him was still in there, saddled up, waiting. Evan hadn't forgotten about the horse and would have taken care of her if Jason had forgotten. He was glad to see Jason remembered. It upped his opinion of him, but only slightly.

Buster commented, "See, Evan, he can't be all bad. He's going to pull the saddle off the horse he was going to ride before you so rudely interrupted him."

"Yeah, I believe you're right. I thought he'd forget her. But now I wonder who's taking care of the horses while he and Mom are holed up in town."

His speculation was answered directly. As soon as Jason was finished in the barn, he walked over to the cruiser. Leaning against the passenger door and looking into the car past Buster and Evan to Cheree sitting in the back, he made a general statement to no one in particular. "Our neighbor, the guy we lease the pasture to, is going to look after the horses for a few days until Mom can come home." He didn't mention the sooner they caught the killer the sooner that would be, but Evan heard it implied.

He looked away from the car, back up towards the house. He saw his mother locking the back door. "We'll be leaving now. You got my number, right?" He looked at Evan.

Evan nodded, but Cheree said, "I don't. Could I have it, too?"

Jason was only too happy to oblige. Fishing a business card out of his shirt pocket, he handed it to Cheree through the open window of the cruiser with what to Evan seemed to be a flourish. "Call me anytime, at work or at home," he told her.

"Thank you. Hopefully, we'll have good news soon." She reached over to accept the proffered card. Jason was grinning like a fool. He figured he had made an impression on the beautiful doctor.

"Would you look at that?" Cheree commented as Ruth and Jason drove away. 'Jason Pike, City Engineer, City of Colorado Springs' and he's only twenty eight years old. How do you suppose that happened?"

"I suppose he applied for the job and was hired," Evan answered. He had to believe she was being facetious, but her comment still caused a twinge of jealousy.

"Am I the only one who thinks he's too young to be the city engineer for a big city? Seems like a lot of responsibility for somebody in his twenties."

"How old are you?" Buster asked.

She stared at him briefly and smiled. "Okay, forget it. I was just trying to be more suspicious, like you two."

At the end of the driveway, Jason's sporty, new, red pickup turned south. Evan turned left, pointing the cruiser north, back to Saguaro. "So who took a shot at Raleigh?" Buster wanted to know.

"Yeah, good question," said Evan.

"How about whoever shot Abel and killed Ben." Cheree suggested.

"Real good, Doc, why didn't I think of that?" and before Cheree could defend herself, he asked, "But, why?"

"Mistaken identity. The killer thought she was Ruth." Both Buster and Evan gave her the look they reserved for stupid statements from intelligent people. "No, listen!" she implored. She picked up on the meaning of the look immediately. "Look, it appears to me someone intends to wipe the Pike family off the face of the planet. Two are down and two are still standing. The killer doesn't know Raleigh's still around. Even Ben's mother was surprised when we told her Raleigh was still Missus Pike. So the killer figures the woman who is now in Ben's house has to be Ruth. She's come to put things in order. He returns after he knows we're gone to shoot a blonde woman he assumes is Ruth." Cheree looked from Evan to Buster.

"Ruth and Raleigh don't look anything alike," Said Buster.

"I disagree. They're both blondes, both attractive and if Raleigh was sitting down, the difference in height wouldn't be noticeable."

"Raleigh hardly looks old enough to be Able and Jason's mother," Evan weighed in.

"Who said the shooter had a scope on his rifle?"

Buster and Evan were silent. She had a point. Evan had shot more than one coyote over a hundred yards off with open sights on his .30-.30. Maybe this guy was some sort of purist. He wanted to take out Ruth the hard way. Although, he had shot Abel with Ben's rifle and it was scoped. Regardless, Cheree's speculation could be accurate, the killer could have mistaken Raleigh for Ruth.

"Okay," Evan admitted, "that's a possibility."

"So what do we have now?" Buster asked and before getting an answer, proceeded to elaborate. "Ben and Abel Pike are killed, seemingly in revenge for an heretofore unknown crime, and the killer, no make that killers, want to do away with the whole family. So in an effort to take out Ruth, they mistakenly take a shot at Raleigh who is Abel's non-existent wife, only she still exists, but it's okay because the bullet missed and Raleigh still lives. Meanwhile, the real Ruth Pike and her son, Jason, whom we have to assume are prime targets, have run off to Colorado Springs to hide from the killers. Furthermore, we have recently learned our number one and most likely suspect, Jake Lawrence, lives in Colorado

Springs where he attends college." Buster raised his hands in the air and dropped them. "Did I leave anything out, because frankly, I don't get it? I have a feeling we're missing something important and should be doing a lot more, but I'm not sure what it is we should be doing."

"Of course we're missing something. We're missing a whole bunch. The bad guys have had sixteen years to work this out. We just started, but we are doing something," Evan said, "and it's the only thing we can do. We're driving back to the office. Then we're going to request the Colorado Springs PD bring in Jake Lawrence. When he's in custody we'll drive over there and have a nice little chat with him."

"Yeah, that's good if that's what happens. What if he's not available? Let's say, for instance, the Colorado Springs PD can't find him. Then what?"

"Then I don't know what. They look for him like we would if we were asked to bring him in." Evan turned to look at Buster. "What are you getting at?"

"I don't know what I'm getting at. It just doesn't seem like we're doing anything. I mean we've been here, we've been there, and we don't have squat. Ben Pike was murdered five days ago. Today, we just learned he raped a girl sixteen years ago. At that rate this case won't be solved before I retire."

"Buster, are you serious or you just pimpin' me again? I've never known you to get frustrated like this."

"I'm not frustrated, I'm merely trying to motivate you two to think harder. I don't want the body count to get any higher."

Both Cheree and Evan were silent as they pondered Buster's comment. Obviously, neither of them wanted more bodies. Other than the one story on television, the press had been unnaturally quiet, but they all knew that wouldn't last if there were more murders. Even the governor, popular as he was, would have a hard time holding the lid down. His handling of the situation could be subject to some serious criticism. He could readily justify Ben Pike's murder investigation being conducted solely by the Saguaro Sheriff's Department, but now that Abel Pike was dead, critics could claim more law enforcement involvement was imperative. And what the hell was the talented Doctor Nicoletti doing flitting from place to place with the two deputies on routine business. All the money she was being paid, she should be back at the lab analyzing clues. And that helicopter cost the Colorado tax payers about a thousand dollars an hour to keep in the air.

"Buster's right," Cheree told Evan.

"Off course he's right. He's always right. Just ask him. The problem is, I don't know what else to do. Do you?"

In the rear view mirror, Evan watched her bite gently on her bottom lip. She looked beautiful even when she was worried. "No, I don't know what else, but getting Jake Lawrence into custody, and his friend for that matter, is a good start." She nibbled her lip a little more. "We should also get a warrant and go through Matt Mason's horse trailer. I thought of it while we were out there. I doubt if we'll find anything of importance, they've had plenty of time to sanitize it."

"Now this is more like it," Buster commented.

Evan looked across the front seat at him. "How about you, Old Man? Got any ideas?"

"Yes I do. I want to talk to Raleigh again. She mentioned she found a letter from Abel, right?"

"Yeah, that's what she said."

"We need to know if there's anything in there that could be helpful. I'm also curious about her relationship with Jason and Ruth. Ruth acted mighty surprised when we told her Raleigh and Abel were still man and wife."

"You think Ruth is lying?" Cheree asked.

"I find it hard to believe Ruth was unaware her son was still married. Or maybe Raleigh is lying and they aren't still married. Once again, it doesn't seem to me we're getting the whole story from either of them."

"What's Raleigh got to hide?" Evan asked.

"I don't know, maybe she's in it with Jake Lawrence."

"Pardon me, Buster," interjected Cheree, "but that really seems to be a stretch. Somebody took a shot at her. And how does she know Jake?"

"Yes, you're right, somebody did take a shot at her, but that somebody also missed. And this is probably the same somebody that drilled Abel Pike through the heart from over two hundred yards out. The shot could have been faked just to mess with our minds. As far as Jake is concerned, how does anyone know anyone?"

"What's her motive?" Evan demanded. "She wouldn't stand anything to gain by murdering Ben, and if what she said about her relationship with Abel is true, she has no reason to want him dead either."

"If what she told us is true, yes, but if she's lying she does have something to gain if both Ben and Abel are dead. She gets Abel's property for sure and depending on how Ben's will is written, she might have some claim on his ranch too."

"Then she would still have to be married to him. Okay, it's a possibility. Any other ideas?"

"We also need to talk to both Ruth and Jason again, but separately. I get the feeling whatever lie either one of them came up with, the other would swear to."

"So," said Cheree, "you two figure the shot at Raleigh wasn't a case of mistaken identity?"

"Not at all," said Buster. "The way I see it there are three possibilities: you're right, the killer mistook her for Ruth and missed; he didn't mistake her for Ruth, and missed; or it's a set up to make us think Raleigh's not involved. At this point, I'm hoping you're guess is right and Raleigh was merely mistaken for Ruth."

Evan lifted his foot from the accelerator as he passed a sign announcing their arrival at the city limits of Saguaro. Cruising up to the old stone county courthouse building, a wicked little grin turned up the corners off Evan's mouth. "Well, Cheree, at least there's an upside to all this."

"And that would be?"

"We're here. Take a deep breath, count to ten, and smile. You get to meet our boss!"

18

Cheree said to Evan from across the table, "There's one good thing about Sheriff Tate you have to realize."

She, Evan, Buster, and Buster's wife, Amy, were sitting around the table in Buster and Amy's kitchen. As they spoke, the Colorado Springs Police Department was looking for Jake Lawrence, and the Omaha Police had issued an APB for Dale Kupfer. Hopefully, by tomorrow morning, their two main suspects would be in custody and available for questioning. Matt Mason readily agreed to have his horse trailer searched. A deputy from Rio Grande County had been sent over to seal it, and a team from Cheree's office was now on its way to perform the search.

When Buster, Cheree and Evan showed up at the office, the sheriff hadn't taken much of an interest in the progress his two deputies had made in the case, but he had certainly taken a keen interest in their new partner. Once he laid eyes on her, Cheree hadn't been able to shake him. When she was informed the helicopter couldn't pick her up until nine that evening, Tate offered to drive her home, promising a stop at an intimate little restaurant he frequented in Colorado Springs. She politely but firmly declined. She had plenty of experience in turning down unwanted offers, but this guy was like a wood tick, practically clinging to her. The only way she could escape was to go to the Ladies' Room. As a last resort, she had Evan fake a call from the governor's office informing her that the pilot was able to change his schedule, and would be there in fifteen minutes. Without further explanation, Evan and Buster hustled her out before Clouseau could make any more unwanted overtures.

"Really, what one good thing would that be?" Evan asked. "For a while there I thought you had developed some kind of kidney or intestinal problem. You went to the Ladies Room four times in an hour."

"Not funny! The last time I thought he was going to follow me in. You two took forever to make a few phone calls. I came real close to decking him." She was smiling, but Evan didn't doubt she was serious. He also didn't doubt she could have knocked the sheriff on his silly ass.

"Yeah, I believe you did. So what's the one good thing about Sheriff Tate besides the fact he's so personable?"

"It'll be easy for you to take his job away."

"I don't know Cheree; I'm just a one-trick pony. Being a deputy suits me fine. Thinking about being the sheriff makes me nervous."

She looked at him critically. It took about five seconds, but then she saw it in his eyes. She started to laugh. He started to laugh. Amy and Buster looked at each other and they started to laugh. Amy rapped gently on her wine glass with the back of her middle finger. "A toast! I propose a toast." She stood up and raised her glass. "To the new Sheriff of Saguaro County, Evan Coleman!"

"Hear! Hear!" and the glasses were clinked together all around.

"You almost had me Evan, but your eyes gave it away. They were just starting to crinkle in the corners."

"I'll have to work on that eye crinkle. I can't run for election without being able to lie with a straight face. What kind of politician would I make?"

"How about an honest one?" Buster asked.

"Is that not a contradiction in terms?"

"No," said Cheree, "I believe our governor is basically an honest politician. He must be. He's always irritating somebody."

"That's a comforting thought, because I know I can irritate people. Should make me a natural." Evan spread his arms wide. "I can see the headlines now. 'HONEST SHERIFF COLEMAN SLIPS IN POLLS—AGAIN.'"

"We don't do polls in Saguaro County," Buster reminded him. "As incompetent as he is, how often have you seen our leader chided by the press?"

Evan agreed, "Good point. I wonder what it cost to buy editorial immunity."

"He wasn't wearing a wedding band so I assume he's not married. Does he have a girlfriend?" Cheree wanted to know.

"You mean here, on this planet?" Evan asked.

"Don't be cruel, Evan," Amy said. "No, this town isn't that big, but apparently he does have a girlfriend in Salida. They just came back from Hawaii. My understanding is she's very nice."

"From where do you get your understanding?" Buster asked.

"From your secretary, Suzy."

"She's never told me anything like that."

"Why would she, it's not guy stuff."

"I don't know about that. Evan and I like to hear juicy gossip once in a while. Actually if you think about it, a big part of our job is hearing gossip and listening to rumors."

"Speaking of your job, your friend from Buena Vista, the police chief called."

"Buddy Banks?"

"Yeah, him. He called about an hour ago. He said the funeral for Abel Pike was tomorrow at two, at the Witt Mortuary."

Buster looked to Evan. "We going?"

"One of us should. You want to flip for it?"

"No, you can go."

"You know that's not what I meant."

"Yeah, but you can go anyway. You look good in a dark suit. Give you a chance to mingle, practice for your campaign and all."

"How about you?" Evan looked to Cheree. "You want to put in an appearance?"

"In spite of the fact I'd love to see how good you look in a dark suit, I have some serious work to do."

"What could be more serious than a funeral?"

"Trying to discover who's responsible for the deceased being in the casket. There's a ton of lab data on this case I need to look at again, plus you gave me another mission; type Jason's DNA. Plus the results from searching Matt Mason's horse trailer will be in, and I think we need to request a DNA sample from his little daughter. You'll have to mourn without me."

Evan drained his wine glass. "Amy, does Buster have any single malt around here? I'd ask Buster, but he'd say no regardless."

"I think you two drank all the Scotch whisky the last time you were here, but we do have a bottle of Patron."

"Terrific! How about pouring me a nice little shot?"

"Sure, anybody else?"

Buster raised his hand. "I'm in."

"What's Patron?" Cheree asked.

"Tequila," Amy told her.

"Sure, why not. I'm not flying the helicopter."

Amy brought out some thick bottomed, low-ball glasses and poured ample shots all around. Evan raised his glass and toasted. "Here's to the successful resolution of the Grulla Paint Murders case." He added, "Hopefully, with the arrest of Jake Lawrence and Dale Kupfer we'll be about done." He didn't sound overly positive.

They drank, everybody but Cheree draining her glass. "Not bad," she said, setting her half finished shot back on the table. Then she noticed the other three glasses were empty. "Sorry, I was unaware of the custom." She finished the tequila.

Amy laughed. "It's okay, it's not really a custom. Evan made us start doing it a couple of years ago. He says it's some kind of brain stem therapy. Apparently guys need to get in touch with their brain stems on a regular basis, maybe to make certain they're still there. Come to think of it, Cheree, I'll bet you're the only one of us who's ever seen a brain stem."

"I'll bet you another shot of tequila she isn't the only one in this room who's seen a medulla oblongata," Evan told Amy as he reached for the bottle.

"I suppose you have too, Mister 'Been Everywhere, Done Everything.' Convince me!" She pulled the bottle back out of his reach.

Evan was quiet. All eyes were on him. "I took Human Anatomy in college. We dissected a cadaver. No big deal."

"What was your major?" Cheree asked him.

"I started out in Pre-Med, but right away I realized there was no way I was going to make it. Too much self-discipline required. The thought of eight years of school and then the struggle of internship; I knew I couldn't do it. The way doctors get treated today, I'm glad I gave it up."

"Did you finish college?"

"Yeah, I had always liked numbers, very predictable you know. I did summer school, got my degree in mathematics in three years and joined the Army. After that I went to work for the County. Brilliant huh?" The disclosure was slightly embarrassing for Evan. He wasn't the boastful type and he didn't want to come off that way in front of Cheree. She was a talented, good-looking woman with a prestigious position. Normally confident, and even though she had told him she was interested, he wondered if he was qualified enough to pursue her. He also wondered what he'd do if he caught her.

Sliding the bottle back in his direction, Amy told him, "Since you're a mathematical genius, I trust you'll know when you've had enough. You have to drive Doctor Nicoletti to the airport after supper."

Evan took the bottle and made a production of pouring a certain amount. "Okay, according to my calculations, the amount I've poured will bring my blood alcohol level to point zero two five, well below the level of any impairment. Anyone else?" He waved the bottle. They all joined him.

Buster tossed his down and stood. "I have to get cooking. The salmon steaks aren't going to grill themselves."

The lighthearted banter continued. By the time they finished eating, Cheree felt as if she had known Buster and Amy for years. She also decided she wanted to get to know Evan much better. He had a quick wit and easy smile. He listened too, and a good listener was a rare thing. Her late husband had been a good listener. They had never argued. There were times when she'd wanted to argue, when she was irritable and stressed, but he always listened calmly to her tirade and with a few words, was able to restore her tranquility. Dignified, that's what he was. He had possessed an uncomplicated, almost careless dignity that was neither pretentious nor stiff. She recognized the same quality in Evan, not to mention he was the best looking man she had ever seen. He could be a movie star, but then she would never have met him. She found herself reaching out to touch him more than once during dinner. The first time she stopped just short of her target, wondering what she was doing. The second time she wondered what she was doing, but didn't stop. After that, it came natural, nothing heavy, just a light touch on his shoulder or arm during the course of conversation, for emphasis. It felt good.

The emphasis did not go unnoticed. Evan wondered how a mere touch could carry such weight. She had his full attention, as if she had clubbed him with a baseball bat. Five days ago he didn't know she existed; now she was the only woman in the world. Buster's friend, Woody, was right when he said hormones make the world go around. If he could only keep from getting dizzy.

When Jake returned Sarah's call earlier in the afternoon, she didn't tell him about her visit from the law, only that she needed to see him as soon as possible. "Are you guys okay?" he asked.

"Oh, sure we're fine, but Taylor's been asking about her 'Big Buddy, Uncle Jake' and," Sarah paused, almost losing her composure, "if you can come out, I'd really appreciate it. I know it's a long way, but you can spend the night and go back early tomorrow." She wanted desperately to tell him to get the hell out because the cops were probably on their way and she didn't want him arrested, handcuffed, and dragged off in the back of a police car. She had to talk to him, tell him what had happened so he could be prepared. If that made her an accessory she didn't care. She owed it to him if he had killed Ben and Abel Pike. Those two bastards deserved to suffer over and over, just like she had for sixteen years.

"Well little sister, you and Taylor are in luck. In fact, even if you hadn't invited me, I was going to stop in. I didn't have a class today and there are a few things I could have done, but I decided to blow them off to go for a ride."

"You're not at home?" Her relief was surely audible.

"No, I'm in Creede. I just called my apartment for messages and got yours."

"You're in Creede?"

"Yeah, Creede. You know where it is, just down the road from you. Used to be a booming, silver mining town a hundred years ago. Now it's a quaint little, artsy-craftsy, tourist trap." He laughed. "Sure you're okay?"

She ignored his question, her relief turning to suspicion. "What are you doing in Creede?"

"Friend of mine owns a bed and breakfast, I thought I'd pay her a visit, but she isn't home. I hung around town for a while, waiting, but I don't think she's going to show." He thought it was odd her place was closed. He had imagined it would be filled with elk hunters, but he didn't tell Sarah that.

"When can you get here?"

By now, Jake knew something was going on, but he also knew his sister wouldn't tell him until she was ready so he might just as well play it her way. "I'm going to give my friend another hour. Then I'll be out. If she gets back, I'll call you. Otherwise I'll see you in about an hour and a half."

"You'll still come, even if she shows up?"

"Yeah, I'll just be a little later is all."

For the next ninety minutes Sarah couldn't sit still. The call from Buster asking if they would agree to having the horse trailer searched without a warrant didn't help her nerves any, especially when Buster told them a deputy from South Fork would be right over to seal it. She prayed the deputy wouldn't be there when Jake arrived. Ten minutes after Buster called, Doctor Nicoletti called informing her an investigation team would be there in four hours to inspect the trailer. That almost finished her off. She was a nervous wreck when Jake finally arrived.

She and Matt met him in the driveway before he could get out of his car. "Park in the machine shed!" she commanded pointing to the large metal pole barn where Matt made repairs to the farm equipment.

"Hello, to you too!" Jake said as he obeyed her order. "What's with her?" he asked himself. He got out of the car and started towards the house. They were still standing there, watching him.

"Close the door!" she called to him.

"What the hell?" he muttered, but he pulled the sliding door closed. She was acting very strange. He thought it was too early for menopause. He remembered their mother becoming momentarily crazy on a periodic basis several years ago. He shook his head, "Hormones!"

he said, "Who needs 'em?" Then he noticed the yellow tape wrapped around the horse trailer. He muttered it again. "What the hell?"

Sarah had always been a direct, no nonsense type. At times she bordered on tactless. Her husband referred to her as prophetic, not because she could foretell the future, but because of her quick, brutal honesty. How she had been able to keep quiet about Pike's assault was unfathomable. Matt stood next to her, gently massaging her shoulders. "It'll be okay," he said. "Try to relax."

Reaching back over her shoulder, she put her hand on his hand. "I'm trying."

"Hey guys, what's up?" His normally fair complexion was bronzed by a summer of high altitude, Colorado sunshine. His reddish blond hair was bleached almost white. He looked like a giant, California surfer boy. He moved easy on a six foot, four inch frame packed with mostly muscle. There was only a little fat. He gave Sarah a quick hug and shook hands with Matt. Sarah turned her back and led him into the house. Taylor jumped into his arms, demanding attention. It wasn't easy for Matt to pry her away from Uncle Jake. He told her they would read until Mommy and Uncle Jake were through talking and she could see him again.

"Promise, Daddy?"

"Promise, T."

Taylor turned back to Jake. "Promise you'll stay Uncle Jake?"

"Of course, Sweetie, you're my best girl. I'll be here."

Taylor finally acquiesced and went off with Matt. Jake didn't notice the tears in Sarah's eyes until she sat him down. He started to ask what was wrong, but she popped the big question before he could get out the words. "Do you remember the day Ben Pike attacked us?" Sarah Mason asked her brother.

Jake's smile instantly evaporated. He stared at her, dazed, as if he'd just been blind-sided by a three hundred pound line backer. He tried to take a deep breath, but all he got was a raspy little gasp. His fists clenched involuntarily and his face lost its color. He couldn't reply. His vocal cords were momentarily paralyzed. Her question had suddenly released a flood of memory he had suppressed for sixteen years. In two heartbeats it was back with a vengeance. Then he couldn't talk. He sat, his breath coming in shallow gulps.

It was hard for Sarah to believe so powerful a man could be incapacitated by just a few words. Sixteen years ago Sarah told him they could never talk about what happened and he hadn't. It stayed fresh in his memory for a time, but he was an eight-year old boy, full of dreams, hope and daring. His sister told him to forget it, so he had, completely. But the memory really wasn't gone, just lying dormant, ready for the right circumstances to awaken. Sarah just turned the key and now it was back, staring him full in the face, and he wasn't a big, powerful man, he was a skinny, little redheaded, boy. His sister was screaming, being attacked by a monster of a man named Pike. With painful clarity the entire incident repeated itself. He could even feel the rough grip of Abel Pike on his arm as he dragged him upstairs to the bedroom where he was forced to witness the rape of his sister.

"All of it," he finally said. "I can remember all of it." His voice was thin and strained. It sounded like it was coming from a scared eight-year old. He lowered his head into his hands as a great sob escaped his chest.

Sarah pulled his hands away from his face and lifted his head. "It's okay, Jake. We're okay," and she added, "but Ben and Abel Pike are dead."

He stared at her through tears. "Good!"

The intensity of his reaction surprised Sarah. She believed it was real and therefore, he couldn't possibly have plotted and committed the murders of Ben and Abel, unless she knew nothing about her younger brother and he was a first class actor. Looking at him now, tears streaking his face, he seemed incapable of violence. She hugged him. "Same thing I said."

He wiped at his eyes with the back of his hand. "What happened to the Pikes; somebody do us a favor?"

"Yeah, it appears as if their sins finally caught up with them. The problem is, I think the police believe the somebody that killed them might have been you."

Again his reaction surprised her. He laughed. "Why'd I wait so long? It's really funny, I wanted to kill them so bad, I used to fall asleep planning different ways I could do it. Then, in the morning, I'd wake up early and lay there, planning new ways to kill them all over again. Sometimes I would use Dad's rifle, carelessly shoot them, leaving them for the crows and buzzards. Another idea was to stab them in their sleep, and oh yeah, I had one plan where I would dig a deep pit and trap them. Once they were in it, I'd fill it up with dirt, burying them alive. I should have written down all my schemes. You'd be surprised how imaginative I was."

"Sometimes life imitates art." Sarah smiled a grim smile. "Want to hear how they died?"

"Love to!" His voice had returned to normal.

"She told him the story as it had been related to her by Evan and Buster. He sat, seemingly spellbound by the tale of death. "I'm certain the two deputies know more than they told us. I got the distinct impression they considered you to be their main suspect, you and Dale."

"Yeah, I can see how they got it too. Do you realize Dale and I actually visited the Pike place early this summer?"

"You never told me that!"

"No, I didn't. I never thought anything of it. Even when Dale said he wanted to see the place, I never remembered the incident. Pike's name didn't even sound familiar. It's strange. Maybe because you were the one who told me I had to forget what happened, you were the only one who could make me remember it. Dale mentioned the name several times since I've known him and it never triggered any response. Maybe if I'd seen him I'd have remembered."

"Good you didn't, you might have killed him on the spot. How does Dale know Pike?"

"He doesn't personally, but his great, great grandparents, at one time may have owned Ben Pike's property. According to a story Dale's father told him just before she died, his great grandmother claimed she and Ben Pike's great grandfather killed her husband to get the land. There was never any proof, just the ravings of a demented old lady. I think Dale wanted to see the place."

"Nothing would surprise me about those bastards. But obviously you and Dale didn't kill the Pikes so who did?"

Jake shrugged his big shoulders. "Don't know, don't care, although I owe them one. But I'll bet that weasel Jason has something to do with it."

"He must have. He's the only one left alive who heard Ben tell me what he'd do to you if I talked. Not even you heard it. That's another reason I believe you couldn't have killed him. And I can understand why you don't care. But you have to care because it appears somebody is trying to frame you."

"Maybe I should look up pretty boy Jason and have a little chat. See what he's got to say for himself."

"Maybe you should just stay here for a few days. Wait and see what happens. You go back to Colorado Springs, I guarantee you'll be in jail in short order."

He smiled. His little, big sister was still trying to protect him. "They might take me in for questioning, but they have no proof, they couldn't hold me." He sounded confident, but he didn't feel it. "Besides, if I stay here, won't it make you an accessory?"

"To what? Nobody told me you were wanted for anything. I just think those deputies don't have anything else going. You and Dale have to be looking real guilty to them right now, is my guess."

"All the more reason for me to go in and enlighten them. I'm innocent. Why should I worry?"

"Humor me. At least stay here tonight. We'll see how you feel in the morning. One of the deputies is a good friend of Matt's father. I'd rather see you go to him than get hauled in by the Colorado Springs police."

Jake agreed. "So where's my little girl, Taylor. I thought she couldn't wait to see me?"

"Taylor," Sarah called out. "Your Uncle Jake wants to see you."

She came running and leaped into his lap. She threw her arms around him. "I missed you so much," she told him. Jake laughed.

Evan and Cheree were sitting in Evan's Grand Victoria police special parked at the edge of the runway of Saguaro County's little airport. They were sitting sideways on the front seat, facing each other, each had an arm on the seatback. They were holding hands. They wanted to get closer, but all the police paraphernalia in the front seat between them made it almost impossible. Amy had offered him her nineteen fifty-eight, Pontiac Chieftain so he could drive Cheree in style, but he had declined the generous offer. Now he was silently cursing his decision. The thing had a front seat like a queen bed. He smiled when he thought it.

"What's so funny?"

He interlaced his fingers with hers. "Just thinking we should have taken Amy's car is all."

"She squeezed his hand. "Yeah? Why might that be?" Her smile matched his.

"It would make something like this a lot easier." He leaned over in her direction to kiss her.

A little while later, she agreed. "Next time we take Amy's car."

"You realize I can have us busted for this?" he said two minutes later.

She ran her fingers through his hair, "What's the charge, Officer?"

"Officially, it would be loitering."

"Could have fooled me. I thought we were kissing in a parked car."

"We are, but kissing in a car isn't illegal, loitering is." Looking over her head and out the window he saw aircraft lights low on the horizon. "I guess I won't have time to arrest you properly, your ride is here."

"Too bad, I was just starting to like this loitering thing." She slowly moved away from his embrace. "Are you going to be up for a while? I'll call you when I get home?"

"I'll stay up all night waiting for the phone to ring." He didn't tell her he wouldn't be able to sleep because he'd be thinking about her.

They stood together next to the car as the helicopter settled on its gear. She gave him a fast, hard hug, a brief kiss on the lips, and she was gone. He stood facing the departing chopper and waved. He didn't walk back to his car until the lights had disappeared.

19

By eleven o'clock that evening, both Evan and Jake were in their respective beds. Cheree had called Evan before ten, and they talked for an hour. Evan fell asleep with a smile on his face. A hundred miles away, Jake was not sleeping and definitely not smiling. First, there was the team of crime scene investigators that worked over Matt's horse trailer. Watching them discreetly from inside the house, he felt guilty as sin. If he hadn't been hanging around Sarah's place half the summer this wouldn't have happened. About ten, after they were finally gone, he tried to call his friend, Dale, several times, but couldn't reach him at home. He wasn't at his fiancée's place either. Finally, he called Dale's parents and talked to his father. Dale's father gave him the bad news. He told Jake he'd received a call from Dale minutes earlier. Dale was in jail. He was being held for questioning in some murder case. Dale's father was rather distraught and wouldn't or couldn't relate any details.

When Jake got off the phone he cursed, referring to the Pikes. "Stupid bastards, they can't even get murdered without involving me!" Lying in bed, he wondered why Dale wanted to visit the Pike ranch back in June. Other than to say he was curious about the place because some distant relative of his might have initially settled it, he'd never explained. That kept Jake's mind working for a long time, pushing away sleep. And when he finally got that thought out of his head, he remembered the reason he'd gone to Creede this morning. It was to visit a woman by the name of Raleigh Pike.

He sat up straight in bed. "Damn! Raleigh Pike! Pike!" He realized he didn't know much about her except she was tall, good looking, and initially seemed to have some interest in him. *Who the hell is she anyway?* He couldn't imagine she was Ben Pike's daughter, or at least he didn't want to imagine it. *Maybe a niece at worst. Hopefully she's unrelated, Pike's not an uncommon name.* Then reality punched him like a fist in the stomach, taking his breath away.

"Damn!" He jumped out of bed. "She could be married to Abel Pike! How could I be so stupid?" he demanded. Not getting an immediate answer, he got back in bed, but now he was really wide awake. The next several hours were spent wrestling with questions and speculations that had no answers and made no sense. How could he put his sister's rape so far back in his mind he'd been able to date a woman with the same last name as the man who had brutalized her, and not even recognize it? On top of everything else, he felt very foolish.

Although he and Raleigh hadn't gotten very far in their relationship, it wasn't for his lack of trying. He met her in a crowded saloon in Creede on a Saturday night in June, almost six months ago. Being as tall as he was, he could easily survey a crowd, picking out the prettiest women, especially tall, pretty women in a matter of minutes. When he and Dale walked into the Silver Lode Saloon back in mid-June, they both spotted Raleigh immediately. "Too bad you're engaged," Jake told Dale and walked directly over to where she stood to get a better look.

When he got there, he found himself staring almost eye to eye at the prettiest woman over six feet tall he'd ever seen. She smiled at him. She'd seen him coming. "Hi," she said, "my name's Raleigh. What's yours?"

They only dated twice in June and once in July, but since then she'd become extremely evasive. In fact, Jake wasn't even certain why he continued to call her periodically, except she was tall, good looking, and interesting. When he went to visit yesterday, he'd decided unless she were receptive, he'd give up the chase. What had he been thinking? When they met, she told him she was separated from her husband and couldn't get into another serious relationship until she had resolved the last one. At the time, Jake thought that was a novel, even noble concept. Now he wondered what the hell her game was. Could she have possibly figured a way to end her relationship with Abel and make it look like Jake murdered him? If she had known the details of the incident, after meeting him, she could have hatched a plan to kill her father-in-law and her husband while framing him and Dale in the process. He thought back on their conversations. He'd told her about his sister and her husband, where they lived, and what they did. *She never told me much of anything. She's a strong, capable woman. She could've easily driven over with a horse trailer, grabbed a couple of horses out of the pasture and ridden into the hills to ambush Ben. According to the story Sarah was told by the deputies, Ben was murdered in his bed inside his tent. No big deal for Raleigh to get him in that position. All she'd need to do was take off her blue jeans. No doubt Pike would come running. She murders him, whacks his peepee so it looks like revenge, rides back down the mountain, and hauls the horses to Buena Vista. Two days later, she rides up to Abel's house early in the morning so she can put a bullet through his heart. She knows the terrain. Nice and neat, no messy divorce, she gets all the property and I get all the blame.*

Jake realized there was at least one important assumption in his logic; Raleigh had to know about his sister's rape. He couldn't imagine Abel would tell her. *But, what if Jason is involved? What if he'd told her about it?*

They could even be partners in crime. That made some ugly sense. Jason would probably also profit by killing them. Except for his mother, he would be the heir to Ben's ranch, and if something were to happen to her, he'd have it all. Jason, or at least another person being involved made sense to Jake. If not two people, why did Raleigh "borrow" two horses? He had to be in on it. For that matter, Ruth could be in on it too. He imagined living with Ben Pike would be like six months of hard winter—you get tired of it. Maybe Ruth had finally gotten her fill of her nasty spouse. Or maybe Raleigh had nothing to do with it. Jason could have stolen the horses as easily as Raleigh. Hell, two, six year-old kids could have stolen those two horses. They came when you called them, and it didn't matter what you called them.

It was three in the morning. Jake's head was reeling with possibilities. He groaned, pulling the pillow over his head, trying to force himself to stop thinking. Sleep would not come. He finally got up and quietly went downstairs to the kitchen. Maybe eating something would take his mind off his troubles.

Sarah was up at six, finding him fast asleep, head down on the kitchen table. She started a pot of coffee, sat down across the table from him, and watched him. A few minutes passed before the smell of the coffee woke him. He sat up slowly, regarding Sarah. She had a smile on her face.

"Good morning," she said. "Rough night?"

"Morning to you, too. The roughest." He yawned and stretched. "That coffee done?"

"Almost. Want a cup?" She was surprised. She didn't think he drank coffee.

"Yeah, but I don't want it, I need it."

She pulled out the pot, sliding a cup under the brew basket. When it was filled, she swapped the cup back for the pot and handed it to him. "Cream, sugar?"

He overlapped his big hands around the cup, "No, thanks. This is the way I hate it most. If I doctor it up, I might start liking it. I don't want to do that."

"So you couldn't sleep?"

"Not a wink. How about you?"

"I remember twelve-thirty, but not much after that. I woke up about five so I got a few hours. When did you come down here?"

"Must have been around three. I couldn't stop thinking. Do you know why I went to Creede yesterday?"

"You said to see a girl friend."

"Yeah, that's right. Guess what her name is."

"I don't have a clue," she said immediately.

"Okay, bad request. Guess what her last name is."

She started to say she couldn't possibly guess, but then it dawned on her. "Not Pike, is it?"

He nodded. "Very astute, little sister. Her name is Raleigh, Raleigh Pike, and she told me she was married."

She looked at him critically. "What are you doing dating a married woman anyway? Didn't Mother teach you anything?"

"My behavior has been beyond reproach." He proceeded to tell her all details, including his speculation she could have been married to Abel Pike.

Her first question after he finished was, "How old is she?"

"I'm not sure, she could be a few years older than me. I didn't ask and she never volunteered the information. Why would that be important?"

"If she's four years older than you, she'd be about Jason's age, twenty-eight, twenty-nine; make her four years younger than Abel. It's possible, but I think it's more likely she's unrelated to the Pikes we know."

"Why is that such a stretch? I remember Ben Pike being huge. Abel at sixteen was even taller. He probably ended up at least six foot-six. I'm six-four and Raleigh's only an inch or two shorter than me. It makes sense that Abel would marry a tall woman and Raleigh is tall."

"So just because she's tall, she's Abel wife?"

"No, because her married name is Pike and she's tall is why she was married to Abel Pike."

"If she's part of the Pike zoo, why couldn't she be married to Jason?"

"She could be, but I have a feeling it's Abel, not Jason. Obviously, neither one of us knows how either one of them turned out stature wise, but I remember Jason being not much bigger than me. I'll bet he's nowhere near as tall as his brother."

"Therefore, Raleigh was married to Abel. After meeting you, she and Jason conspired on how to get rid of both Ben and Abel and then blame it on you?" She shook her head slowly, her long blonde hair slightly twisting left and right with the motion. "I don't know. That seems unlikely. On the other hand, maybe the only thing coincidental was you meeting Raleigh. Once that happened, the rest might have been easy. I don't like it."

"Hey, I don't like it either, but I'll bet I'm right." Then he thought for a minute. "Why aren't you a prime suspect? The two of us should have done this together. In fact, you have more motive than I do."

"I do think I could be a suspect, but like I told you last night, they have more information than they gave us. Besides they haven't talked to you yet, but I think they want to question you bad enough to have you arrested. You said Dale was picked up and brought in. What more do you need than that? Maybe it's because you two were out looking for Ben. You weren't hostile, were you?"

"Hostile? We were incredibly polite. And besides, I had no idea why we were there. I believed Dale just wanted to see the place, period."

"Maybe Dale had ulterior motives."

Jake acknowledged her point, "Yeah, maybe, but from what he said to her, Ruth Pike never would have picked up on them."

"How do you know what Ruth Pike was thinking? She might be incredibly paranoid. Living with Ben Pike all those years, she could be nuttier than a pinion tree. You have no idea what she might have told those two deputies."

"Yeah, I guess you're right." He acquiesced again, "So what do I do?"

"First of all we'll have some breakfast. Then we explain everything to Matt so he can talk to his father. Apparently Matt's father and one of the deputies that was here are good friends. We let those two talk, see what they come up with."

"Why not just call the sheriff in Saguaro and tell him I'm coming in?"

"From what Matt says, the sheriff over there is a moron and I don't trust the other deputy that was here."

"Why not, he have shifty eyes?"

"No, he had beautiful eyes, that's why I don't trust him. Men who look that good can lie too easily and get away with it."

"First time I've heard that one. You trust me don't you?"

"Yes I do, but you're just handsome, not incredibly handsome, besides I know you, or at least I think I do." She got up from her chair, "How do you want your eggs?"

Evan was in the office early. There was a message from a Lieutenant Dirks of the Omaha Police Department stating they'd had Dale Kupfer in custody since last night. He wanted Evan to call him as soon as possible. Evan did, and they discussed the Pike murders at great length. They agreed Dirks would ask Dale certain questions and get back to Evan. Based on Dale's answers and Dirks' impression, they would either release him or hold him until Evan or Buster could get to Omaha. In order to extradite him, they'd have to charge him. Evan didn't want to do that, not just yet anyway.

He'd no more than finished talking to Dirks when Cheree called him. "I have news," she announced.

"Good or bad?"

"Depends on who you are. In your case it's probably good. In Jake Lawrence's case it's probably bad."

"I'm interested."

"The scene investigators found some blood in Matt Mason's horse trailer. It's human, not equine, and they started DNA testing about three this morning. By tomorrow morning, you'll know if it's from Ben Pike or somebody else."

"I'm impressed. What did they find it on?"

"You're not going to believe this."

"I'll believe anything you tell me. You're too pretty to lie."

"Thanks. They found a man's brown, suede work glove, size extra large with one bloodied fingertip. It was in the little dressing room of the trailer, apparently thrown in a corner and forgotten."

"Just one glove? That seems odd, doesn't it?"

"No, not to me. I'm always losing one glove or one stocking."

"Yeah, but don't you think if you had just murdered someone you'd remember to take care of your dirty gloves, not leave one of them laying around where it's sure to be found?"

"Yes, I'd certainly not want to forget that little detail, but if you had just murdered Ben Pike and were on a strict schedule to murder Abel Pike, I can imagine how hectic your life could be for a few days. I believe it would be very easy to forget a detail or two, even a major detail."

Evan considered the murderer running back and forth, stealing horses in South Fork, going from there to Saguaro, then to Buena Vista, and finally back to South Fork, all the while looking over his shoulder as he's loading horses, unloading horses, stealing rifles, and killing people. Cheree had a point. He told her so. "You're absolutely right, I wasn't considering everything the suspect had to do. Now that I think of it, it's amazing if that's the only thing that was overlooked. Does the glove match the leather fibers you found at Ben's camp?"

"Oh yeah, perfectly, but there's probably only a hundred thousand pairs of those things sold state-wide every year. I have a pair myself, and I imagine you have at least one or two pair. No, the beauty of it is the blood. It's not from a horse, it's recent, and we'll know in less than twenty-four more hours if it came from Ben Pike."

"How about the little girl, have you decided to request a DNA sample from her?"

"No, not yet. I really want to keep her out of it as long as possible. I want to see the results on the glove first. Have you heard if they've picked up Jake?"

"Nothing from Colorado Springs, but Omaha PD has his buddy, Dale, in custody. I just talked to a Lieutenant Dirks and he's questioning the lad as we speak. When he's done, he's going to call me back. We'll decide whether we should charge him or let him go."

"Evan, one of my staff is signaling me for a time-out. Can I call you back in a few minutes?"

"You'd better. In the meantime I'll check on Jake."

He hung up and immediately called Colorado Springs PD. He talked to a desk sergeant at the downtown precinct who put him through to a detective. After five minutes of waiting on hold, the detective finally answered. Evan explained who he was, and the detective promised to do some checking and call him right back. "Yeah, sure," Evan muttered as he hung up the phone, "probably never hear from him again."

Five minutes later the phone rang and Evan grabbed it. He thought it was Cheree. "Evan," he stated pleasantly.

"Deputy Coleman?" asked a masculine voice.

"Ah, yeah, this is Coleman," he said warily.

"Detective Samuels from Colorado Springs PD returning your call for information on a Mister Jake Lawrence."

Wrong again. "Yes, thank you. Have you got anything?"

"No, I'm sorry. I just talked to Detective Billis, he's the officer who went to the Lawrence residence yesterday afternoon. Mister Lawrence was not there at the time, nor did he return home last night. Detective Billis was over there again this morning. There's still no sign of him.

Billis wants to know if there is any place else we should be looking, like his place of employment?"

"The only other thing I can tell you right now is that he's a graduate student at CSU, School of Business. I can do some more checking and see if I can find another address, girlfriend or something, but right now it's all I have."

"I'll pass that on to Detective Billis. He said he'll call you as soon as he finds the suspect."

"Thank you," Evan said sincerely, "Thank you, very much."

As he hung up the phone, he was already wondering if Sarah had tipped Jake off. She had promised them she wouldn't contact him, but that was then, and he is her brother. As soon as he and Buster had left, she may have decided something different. Last time Evan checked, blood was still thicker than water. And if Sarah were in on it, she would have definitely contacted him immediately. "I don't like it," he told himself.

"Don't like what?" Evan spun in his chair so fast he almost screwed himself into the floor.

"Damn, Buster! Don't ever sneak up on me like that again!"

Buster stood smiling at the door to the office. "I didn't sneak, I merely walked in and saw you there deep in thought. So what is it you don't like, or is it personal?"

"No, it's not personal. Colorado Springs PD can't find Jake Lawrence and I'm thinking Sarah has told him we're looking for him."

"Understandable, especially if she's involved. How hard have the police in Colorado Springs looked?"

"Hard enough to know he wasn't home yesterday afternoon, all last night, and he's not there now."

"So what are you going to do about it?"

Evan exhaled a long sigh. "I think I'm going to hang around here until about eleven. Then I'm going home to change clothes; after which I intend to attend Abel Pike's funeral. Does that meet with your approval?"

"No need to get testy! I just don't want to duplicate any effort."

"How so? What do you intend to do?"

"Well, I was just thinking, since we don't have Jake Lawrence in custody yet, I'd drive back over to Matt Mason's place again, unannounced that is. See if I could nose around a bit more. Maybe ask a few questions. Maybe get a look at the horse trailer and all."

"Yeah, speaking about the horse trailer, Cheree called me ten minutes ago. They found a glove with some blood on it in the trailer dressing room. She'll know by tomorrow morning if it belongs to Ben Pike."

"It's not horse blood?"

"No, apparently not, but I'm sure you don't want to look at the horse trailer. What are you really up to?"

Buster was sitting at the desk across from Evan. He spread his hands on the desk top and looked up at Evan. "I'm afraid you know me too well. That's good and bad. Good because we make a better team, but bad because I can't get away with as much as I used to. Alas, what's an old deputy to do?"

"An old deputy has to do what an old deputy has to do. I'm so glad you're finally being honest with me." Evan knew Buster wanted to see how Sarah would perceive his return visit, if it pressured her at all. If it did, well, Buster would know what to do. "I think you're going back to squeeze Matt and Sarah a little bit. It's a great plan. A lot better than going to a funeral."

Buster was silent for a moment. He appeared to be deep in thought. He looked at Evan. "I've got to go. Keep your eyes open and be careful. Stay in touch." With that he walked out.

Evan was thinking that was strange behavior for Buster when his phone rang again. It was Cheree. "More good news. We just found a pubic hair in the detritus vacuumed from the horse trailer. Morphologically it matches the samples from Ben's tent."

"With or without the root?"

"You're getting awfully astute. I'll have to hire you as an investigator. The root is attached."

"So you'll check DNA, right?"

"Yes, but I'm not starting it until we sort through the whole pile. There might be other evidence. I can't combine samples of course, but it would be convenient to run everything concurrently."

"In your professional opinion, Doctor Nicoletti, is the evidence you have uncovered up to now pointing to any particular suspect or suspects?"

"Is this on or off the record?"

"Off. I'm looking for a little help here, not an indictment."

"In my humble opinion, based on evidence I've seen so far, I think the victim, Ben Pike, was murdered by one or more persons in revenge for a crime he committed against one or more persons sixteen years ago. How's that for non-committal?"

"So you're saying, in an indefinite way, Jake and Dale or Jake and Sarah, or for that matter, all three of them, killed Ben and Abel Pike?"

"Maybe."

"Maybe? Is that a definite or indefinite maybe?"

"Oh, Evan I don't know. You're the detective not me. I just find and develop evidence, you have to interpret it. Maybe Jake acted alone or maybe he's being framed. You and Buster have to decide that."

"Yes, but what's your intuition telling you. Based on everything you know right this instant, who do you think did it?" There was a long pause during which Evan could here a clicking sound, as if she was tapping her front teeth with her index finger.

"My best guess would be Jake Lawrence, and I think he had help, but I don't know if I feel comfortable with Sarah. She seemed so sincere yesterday. I have trouble believing she could fake that. As far as Dale goes, I can't say, we've never even met him. Could it be Jake and someone else besides those two?"

"Oh yeah, we might not have scratched the surface of possible suspect combinations yet. I'm only trying to determine whether to charge Dale so he can be kept in custody for a while."

"I can't help you out with that. I don't think I would unless the detective in Omaha comes up with a good reason. You have nothing to link him to the victim except the story Buster's grandmother told Buster about how Pike stole Emil Kupfer's land."

"True, except Jake and Dale are good friends and they had borrowed Matt's horse trailer the day in question."

"But the day Abel was shot, Jake was back in Colorado Springs and Dale was headed for Omaha."

"According to Matt and Sarah, Jake and Dale didn't leave their place Monday until noon. That would've given them enough time to shoot Abel in the morning, clean up and still be back at the ranch well before noon. What really would be nice is to have something that puts Jake at the scene of Ben's murder. Even if the glove from the horse trailer has Ben's blood on it, it's still circumstantial evidence."

"But fairly damning I would say. What about the red hair from Ben's tent?"

"At best it belongs to Sarah's little girl, but it's still circumstantial. It will be argued that whoever stole the horse had access to the hair because some of it was still stuck in the horse's halter from when she was playing with the horse. We don't have any hard or what the prosecutor would call incontrovertible evidence yet."

"I'm sorry, Evan, I wish I had something like that, but there doesn't appear to be anything else right now."

"Not your fault, you're doing a great job. I'm whining. I think I know who did it. It would make it easier to prove if I had a set of his fingerprints from Pike's tent."

"You think it was Jake?"

"Yeah, I'm certainly leaning his way, but I'm confused about who helped him. I don't think he acted alone."

"Look on the bright side, you have it narrowed down to three choices; Jake, Sarah, Dale, and perhaps even Matt if he knew and wanted to help his wife get revenge."

"Yeah, or any combination of those. That makes a total of sixteen possibilities, seventeen if I count the possibility it was none of them." He laughed, "At least I'm not bored with my job."

They talked for a while longer, but when Evan hung up, the choices were still there. He just didn't have enough information yet. And when Detective Dirks from Omaha called him back, he still didn't have enough information. Dale told Dirks he was back in Omaha by Monday, early evening. He was also claiming he and Jake were in Pagosa Springs on Friday, and could prove it because they bought dinner in town at a saloon with a credit card. Saturday and Sunday they were in the mountains west of town and by Monday morning they were back at Matt and Sarah's ranch.

"So, you want me to hold him?" Dirks asked.

Evan thought quickly. The time frame for Dale and Jake killing both Ben and Abel would work, although in Abel's case, he felt it was a stretch. Killing Ben Friday morning would have been no problem. They had access to the truck, trailer and horses. The receipt for dinner from the bar in Pagosa Springs was something, but they could easily have driven from Saguaro to Pagosa Springs on Friday after they killed Ben. Nothing was substantial. Evan had the feeling it was still too iffy. He turned his attention back to the phone. "Can you check when he got back Monday?"

"Already have, his bride to be is down here swearing he was with her from Monday eight PM on."

"What do you think?"

"I think the part about being with the girl Monday night is genuine. The part about buying dinner in Pagosa Springs doesn't prove anything, I looked at a map."

"Yeah, you're right." Evan made a decision. "Let him go. I don't feel comfortable charging him with what I have."

"Okay. Don't worry; I can always nail him if you need him."

"Thanks, Detective. I appreciate your help." Evan stared at the wall for a long time after he hung up. He was missing something, but he didn't think it was anything he had overlooked. It was something he didn't know yet.

20

Evan had a proverbial rich uncle in his family. It was his mother's oldest brother who had made it big, first in potatoes, then in the commodities market. Evan didn't know the man well. Twenty-five years earlier he moved to New York. Evan had met him only a handful of times, but what Evan knew of him he liked. Whenever Evan saw him, he was well dressed. The last time was at his mother's funeral, ten years ago. They'd talked about a lot of things and when Evan commented on his stylish clothes, his uncle told him, "Clothes don't make the man, but they can temporarily smooth over a man's rough edges, give him a chance he might not otherwise get."

Evan knew his uncle was a lot more than an empty suit. His statement had made sense. Some years ago, acting on his uncle's advice, Evan took five thousand dollars of his savings to have four suits tailor-made. They were all conservatively cut, of fabric and color that would never be out of style, at least not for the next twenty years. Staring at them now, hanging at attention in his closet, he debated between the black and the dark brown pinstripe.

The tailor who made them was a wrinkled little Chinese man of indeterminate age who owned a shop in Denver. The last thing he told Evan at the final fitting was,

"You have a good body, you wear my suits with pride, nobody look better." Evan smiled. Yeah buddy, if only looks were all it took to be successful. He finally settled on the black suit. It was a medium weight, worsted wool with a two button, no vent jacket that emphasized his broad shoulders.

Evan was going to Abel Pike's funeral hoping, on the off chance, he might accidentally learn something. Stranger things had already happened. He didn't expect the event to be particularly well attended. Abel Pike was apparently something of a recluse, but maybe somebody would say something, anything, to provide a hint as to who the guilty party might be. Next to Jake Lawrence on Evan's list of the most suspicious, were Jason and probably Ruth Pike. Evan knew they would be there and he could at least observe them. He couldn't imagine them spilling any beans at this point, yet their behavior would be interesting to watch. *Good Lord*, he pulled on his pants, *I must be some kind of voyeur. I'm going to the funeral of a murdered rapist to see how his mother responds to her grief! Oh well, it's my job.* Before he finished dressing, he strapped on a form-fitting, ankle holster, that held an eight-shot, .22-magnum revolver. Briefly regarding himself in the mirror, he gave a final adjustment to his maroon and black silk tie before heading out the door.

When he arrived forty-five minutes early on purpose, he was surprised to see the parking lot of the mortuary already half-full. Immediately inside the front door was a member of the staff, maybe the owner himself, who gestured with both hands, in opposite directions asking, "Findely or Pike?"

That explains it, two funerals in one day. Hope it's not a daily occurrence. Looking past the man's extended right hand to a small knot of people talking in hushed voices, making sympathetic noises as they slowly moved forward, he said, "Pike".

The man dropped his right hand. "To your left, sir, around the corner." To the couple who had just entered behind Evan he repeated his routine, "Findely or Pike?"

Evan walked in the indicated direction. Around the corner was a room with about fifteen rows of wooden church pews bisected by an aisle, room for well over one hundred mourners. There was no one else in the room or at least no one else alive. Flanked by several sprays of flowers, was a casket at the front of the room. The lid was open. That was a surprise. He hadn't anticipated there would be a period of visitation prior to the funeral. He walked towards the casket. After the killer, he had been the first one to see Abel in his present condition—dead. He might as well have a last look.

Evan hated to think it, but Abel Pike looked good, really good. Like he was having a restful nap in the middle of the afternoon. The mortician was obviously a genius, cosmetically speaking. The initial that had been etched into his forehead was virtually erased by artfully applied makeup. Evan had to study Abel's face carefully to see any trace of it. Peaceful and serene, the sins and guilt Abel had accumulated in his relatively short life, did not show on his visage. "And who knows," Evan whispered to the dead man, "maybe you have been forgiven."

"Hello Evan," said a quiet voice from behind him.

Startled, he turned quickly. It was Raleigh. "Hello, Raleigh, I didn't realize you were here."

She gestured to an open set of double doors leading to another room to the side of the room they were in. "I was in there with Ruth when I saw you. You're the first one here. I thought I'd say hello."

"I'm very sorry for your loss, Raleigh." Evan thought she looked almost too good; no red eyes, no running eye shadow, no tear streaks down her cheeks. Other than the sedate black dress she was wearing, he'd never suspect she was at her husband's funeral. But as soon as Evan finished making the statement, she started to come apart.

She took a step towards him and spread her arms. He did the same, and they hugged. She rested her head on his shoulder. Her sobbing sounded legitimate to Evan.

"In just the last few months, we'd finally started to really be in love," she sobbed. "It's so unfair."

Evan thought about Sarah Mason's adolescence being brutally terminated the day she was raped and terrorized by Abel and his father. *How fair was that? Not very, but then Raleigh has a different perspective of Abel. Perspective is an amazing thing. It determines everything. We can measure the speed of the wind and calculate the distance between stars using perspective. It also gives us the ability to decide whom to love and whom to hate.* Evan wondered what God's perspective was regarding Abel, but all he could tell her was, "I'm so sorry, Raleigh." And he meant it because her husband had been murdered, and she was a young woman suffering with a load of grief. Evan liked Raleigh. He sincerely hoped she wasn't part of the crime.

Stepping back, Raleigh brushed off his shoulder with her hand, "Sorry, Evan, I didn't mean to cry all over you." Now she looked like a grieving widow. Her eyes welled with tears that tricked down her cheeks, leaving streaks all the way to her chin. She dabbed at her eyes with a tissue. "Any closer to finding out who did it?" Her voice cracked around the edges.

"We have a significant lead, and we're in the process of bringing in a suspect for questioning." He hated to see women cry, it made him feel helpless.

Raleigh sniffled and wiped at her nose. "What's that mean in English, Evan?"

"Ah, it means we know a person with motive and means, but we don't have our hands on him yet. Any more than that I can't tell you." He thought he'd heard a hint of sarcasm in her question.

"Would your suspect be somebody with the last name of Lawrence?" Her eyes had stopped crying, locked on his.

He was surprised, but hid it well and didn't back down. "Could be. What do you know today that you didn't know yesterday?"

"I told you yesterday I discovered a letter to me from Abel. Well, in the letter he said why he was worried. He also says who he thought might be after him for what he had done a long time ago."

It seemed obvious to Evan, Abel had told Raleigh about his part in the rape of Sarah Lawrence. There was no other way she could know the name of Lawrence, short of Ruth or Jason telling her Although, if she were involved in the murders, she might have known about the incident for some time and was playing a game of fish. Either way, Evan realized keeping Jake's identity from her didn't matter.

"I assume you're referring to Jake and Sarah Lawrence."

"He didn't give first names, just said a young boy and a teenaged girl."

"Well, those are their names. I can tell you we talked to Sarah Lawrence yesterday, and we're looking for her brother Jake, right now."

"He's the one with the motive and the means?" She didn't tell him she knew a man with the name Jake Lawrence.

"Yes, the woman is not considered to be suspect, at least not now with what we have for evidence." It was time to take back control of the discussion. "When do I get to see the letter from Abel?"

Raleigh's eyes softened as she put her hand on Evan's arm. "I have it with me because you said you were coming. How about right after the funeral?"

A few visitors had entered at the back of the room and were starting forward, towards the casket. "That would be fine. I'm going to sit down now, you're about to be busy."

"Thanks for coming, Evan." She squeezed his hand briefly. He moved away to choose a seat where he figured he could best see any action that might transpire.

As Evan sat, pondering life's mysteries, what started as a trickle of mourners turned into a steady stream. Some selected seats immediately. Others formed a line that solemnly filed past the casket. Evan was surprised by the turnout. There were people of all ages; men, women, and children, the men outnumbering the women by about two to one. A lot of the men could be Abel's co-workers, guards from the prison. He spotted Warden Huarrera and his secretary who had made the pass at him the other day. He had no idea who the others were, especially the women and children. Ruth had joined Raleigh in front at the casket, and just when he was beginning to think it odd Jason was missing, he walked in through the door from the adjacent room. Evan had selected a seat close to the door leading into that room and slightly behind. From there he could clearly see the faces of the mourners as they walked past the casket. If he shifted slightly in his seat, he could also watch the main entrance. The only blind spot was the door from which Jason entered. With him was a woman slightly taller than he, and had she not turned and looked directly at Evan, he wouldn't have seen her face at all. It was a very interesting face. From the brief look, Evan wouldn't say she was beautiful or even pretty. She certainly wasn't cute either; rather she was striking. Her features were soft and muted, as if sculpted from soft soap. Her complexion was pale, seemingly flawless, and her large, wide set eyes were the intense color of chrome-green tourmalines. She had an innocent, timorous look, like a doe of some exotic species of deer.

It was an appealing face, full of innocence that probably made most men want to wrap her up in their arms to shelter her from the cruel world. The other feature that intrigued Evan was her hair. It was shoulder length, thick, wavy, and the palest shade of red. Their eyes were locked for only a second before she turned with Jason, and walked to the front row where Jason steered her to a seat. He briefly joined his mother and Raleigh standing next to the casket.

As he stared at the back of her head, Evan wished he could see her face again, but he would have to be sitting next to Abel's casket to do that. This must be the woman whom Cheree had said was Jason's bride to be. However Evan was somewhat confused. Cheree had definitely said the woman was a natural, or at least naturally appearing blonde. The woman he was looking at was a strawberry blonde. It wasn't a mistake Cheree would make. He was wondering how he could get a strand of her hair with the root attached. In Evan's mind, Jason's position on the suspect list had jumped up dramatically.

As he watched, Raleigh, Ruth, and Jason conferred intently about something. Raleigh shook her head negatively. Jason moved away from the two women, returning to his green-eyed lady. When he sat to her left, she put her arm across his shoulders. That's when Evan saw the diamond in its solitary setting. They were engaged. It had to be the same woman Cheree had seen. In Evan's mind, perceptions changed causing new possibilities to arise. The service for the deceased hadn't even started and Evan wanted it over. He had to engage Jason and his intended in conversation. He had to know more. He also wanted another look at that face.

The warden and his secretary were two of the last visitors to pay their respects. As they turned away from the casket, Huarrera spotted Evan sitting in a row with two empty seats next to him. The secretary was smiling eagerly at Evan as they joined him. She made a point to brush gently against him even though he stood to allow her and the warden to get to the vacant seats. She sat first, next to Evan. The warden winked at him as he passed by. Evan grabbed Huarrera's hand, pulling him close. He whispered in his ear, "I'll get you for this." The warden shook Evan's hand, smiled, and sat on the other side of his secretary. While Evan was speculating what type of suitable payback he could inflict on Huarrera, the woman was speculating how Evan looked under his fancy suit. She was also fighting a powerful urge to rest her hand on his thigh.

Much to Evan's surprise, by the time the service started, the room was almost filled. A dignified, motherly looking woman with white, page-boy styled hair approached Ruth and Raleigh who were sitting in the front row next to Jason. They talked briefly before she stepped behind the podium to the left of the casket. She appeared to be in her late fifties, early sixties with an easy, gracious smile.

"Family and friends of Abel Pike," she started gently, "we are here to honor the memory and celebrate the life of our departed friend." Evan wondered how Sarah Lawrence would respond to that little introduction. "Even though Abel was taken from us under the most tragic of circumstances, I am confident he now rests easily in the arms of the Creator. Life is not always easy, not always fair, and not always joyful. Sometimes it is hard, cruel, and painful. But I tell you this," her voice increasing in intensity, "it is always meaningful!" She paused briefly. "Even if we can't see it, the purpose is always there and it is clear to God. I met Abel two years ago when he first visited our congregation. He walked in late. I think he was hoping to go unnoticed by sitting in the very last row." She softened her voice and gave her audience a wink. "A man of Abel's stature does not go unnoticed by sitting in the back row." A polite chuckle quickly passed through the audience. It seemed most of the little church's congregation had turned out for Abel's funeral.

"A big man, and as I later came to learn, carrying a big burden. He had struggled with his burden for a long time until finally, the hand of God pushed him through the door of our church and into our midst. I don't know what his burden was. I don't need to know, but I can tell you this for certain; before he died, his burden was removed." Her voice picked up again as she raised her hands. "Our Lord, from whom we can hide nothing, lifted the weight from Abel's shoulders to place it on His own. In so doing, Abel was forgiven and was finally able to forgive himself." Her voice quieted, "Even though I didn't know him long, let me tell you about the forgiven man, Abel Pike."

Evan had to admit she was good. By the time she finished, he believed even Sarah would have been moved. She may not have forgiven Abel on the spot, but she would have certainly given pause to think he had truly undergone a reformation. In two short years, he had apparently become a silent pillar of the small congregation. He found a home. Evan thought back two days ago, to when he'd found Abel lying face up in his back yard, dead with a bullet through his heart. At the time he figured Abel was well on his way to hell, but now it was not hard for him to believe Abel had been forgiven. His old man, Ben, well that was another matter.

Immediately after she gave the benediction, the preacher announced that refreshments would be served at the church directly after the graveside service. As soon as the pallbearers wheeled the casket down the aisle and the family filed out, Evan nodded to Huarrera, ducking out through the double doors to the adjacent room. He not only wanted away from Huarrera's secretary fast, he was hoping he could catch Raleigh before she got in a car. If there wasn't a separate exit from the room, he was going to feel very foolish. There was, and he walked quickly to it. Slowly opening the door, he found himself across the hall from the main entrance to the building. Too late, the pallbearers were already sliding the casket into the back of the hearse, and Raleigh was just getting into the mortuary's limo. As soon as the pallbearers packed up, he went to his truck.

Probably just as well I missed her. He wanted to see the letter, but he didn't want to seem aggressive about it. *I'll have to go drink coffee and eat cake and insubstantial little sandwiches with no crust on the bread.* He started up his truck to slowly enter the line of vehicles for the parade to the cemetery.

"So, is there any other place you might know where he could be?" Buster asked Sarah Mason. He had driven back to Matt and Sarah's ranch shortly after noon. Sarah graciously invited him in for coffee and pie, but she seemed distant or nervous, or both; Buster couldn't decide.

"No," Sarah lied, "but I'm sure he'll turn up shortly."

"No disrespect, ma'am, but what do you mean by shortly?"

"Look, I'm not sure. I can't give you a certain number of hours, but he could be anywhere. I'm just certain he'll show up soon, wherever he is. Do you think he's on the run or something?"

"No, of course not, there's no reason he would even know we're looking for him." Buster noticed her expression changed slightly when he said it, almost like a small wince. Just a slight narrowing of the eyes and tiny clench of her jaw made Buster wonder if she were lying to him. "Could you please tell me if you do hear from him? It would make everything a lot easier if we could question him."

"Is he a suspect?"

"Everybody involved is a suspect." Buster responded to her point blank question with a point blank answer.

"I imagine that includes me, although I certainly didn't ask to be involved." Her tone was seriously bitter.

"I'm afraid so, but if it's any consolation, you're pretty far down my list."

"So my brother is more suspect? He's higher up the list?"

"Yes, that's correct. You see, all you have is motive. He has motive, means, opportunity and at this point, no alibi. You and your husband can account for your whereabouts during the time in question. That's why it's so important I talk to your brother. He may have a perfect explanation also. We can clear him off the list."

Sarah considered Buster's logic. Jake had talked to Dale this morning after he was questioned by the police in Omaha. They had released him. Someone must have believed his alibi. Maybe she should tell Buster that Jake was upstairs, hiding from the law at her insistence.

Maybe the sooner Jake was questioned the better, but for some reason, she didn't want him to go in just yet. She wanted Matt's father, Gordon, to talk to Buster first. Sarah and Matt had talked to Gordon, but he hadn't talked to Buster yet. That was probably because Buster was here and Gordon didn't know that. She considered having Buster call Gordon right now, but then he would know she'd been lying to him. She decided to keep still. "I can't help you, Buster, but I'm sure Jake will turn up soon."

"I believe you're right, ma'am, and I'll be going now." He pushed away from the table. "Thanks again for your time and the pie and coffee."

Sarah felt bad. She liked this man. Deceiving him made her feel guilty. It never occurred to her that he might not believe her. "You're welcome, Buster. You can stop in anytime."

He left, but he didn't go far. Driving back to the highway bridge, he crossed the river and went north back towards town. The western boundary of Matt and Sarah's ranch was the middle of the Rio Grande River. Their house was a hundred yards from the water and from the opposite side, the view of their place was wide open. There were small ranches and farms off the highway on this side of the river too, so when Buster reached the point directly across the river from the Mason property, he picked the closest driveway and paid a visit.

An old man answered Buster's knock on the door. His white hair was braided into a long ponytail, and his brown eyes were clear and intense, like fathomless pools sliding into the depths of his soul. He looked at Buster as if maybe he knew him. "You part Apache?" he asked. Not a "Hi", "Hello", or "How are you"; he just asked if Buster had any Indian blood in him.

Buster nodded, "Yes, sir. One quarter, my grandmother on my mother's side."

The old man looked him up and down, "Well, that's better than none at all. What do you want?"

Buster had been wondering what kind of story he was going to make up to get access to the river, but now he decided to play it straight—more or less. "You know the people on the other side of the river?"

"My son bought a horse from them. My son thinks he is a cowboy. Sixty years old and he buys a cutting horse. I told him he was foolish. I said to him, 'I'm an old Apache and you are not young, nor are you a cowboy.' He did not listen to me. He bought the horse anyway. Now he chases cows with his horse and pretends he is a cowboy."

That was a little more information than Buster needed. He tried an even more direct approach. "I'd like to know if I could go down to the river and take a look at their place from your side."

"Are you asking me or telling me?"

"I'm asking."

"You go ahead, just don't shoot anything, I want to take a nap." There was the tiniest twinkle in his eyes.

Buster nodded his acceptance of the man's terms and got back in his car. He drove part way down a rough field road, finally stopping behind a cluster of big, cottonwoods growing alongside a slough that apparently held water when the river ran high in the spring. It was dry now, but based on the size of the cottonwoods, it was dependable. He walked the rest of the way to the riverbank. This time of year the water was low and clear. Buster could see several fat trout holding in the current behind a gravel bar a third of the way across the river. They were just hanging out, keeping their eyes open, hoping something would come along. *Not much different than what I'm doing.. The stakes are different though, they get to eat, I get to send somebody to jail.* Then, considering his thought to its ultimate conclusion, he decided, because apprehending criminals was his job, and his job provided the means to buy groceries, he was no different than the fish. He smiled. He'd have to try that one on Evan.

He sat on the bank for some time, using his binoculars to spy on Sarah Lawrence. Tall weeds that had grown up over the summer, now yellowed and sere, concealed him. The afternoon sun had heated the river gravel nicely. Buster could feel heat radiating all around him. In spite of the recent forecast for snotty weather, the skies were still crystalline blue. A nap right here would be nice, inappropriate, but nice. He hoped Sarah was telling him the truth about not knowing her brother's whereabouts, but he doubted it. He was fairly certain he was going to be disappointed in her. In less than thirty minutes his suspicions were confirmed when a big man emerged from the house. In one hand, at arm's length he dangled a little red haired girl by her ankles. Buster could hear her giggling from where he sat in the warm sun next to the gurgling river.

"Swing me some more, Uncle Jake," she demanded. "Swing me some more!"

21

Standing next to Raleigh, awkwardly holding a coffee cup with too small a handle to get his finger through, Evan read Abel's letter of confession. Computer generated on plain paper, and unsigned, he thought it was relatively brief for such a ponderous topic. It wasn't dated. Raleigh thought it was written Sunday afternoon, the day before he was killed, two days after Evan discovered his father's body.

In the letter, Abel related the rape of Sarah Lawrence, incriminating himself and his father. His version of the incident was consistent with the version Evan had heard from both Sarah and Jason. He didn't give as many details as the others had, but he did offer some insight into the mind of his father. "My father knew no restraint. He acted on whatever whim he felt at the time. We didn't go there with the intention of raping the Lawrence girl, at least I know I didn't, and I don't think my father had any such premeditation either. He was drinking whiskey from a bottle as we drove over. When he offered it to me I drank some, too. I still believe his only purpose was to get the money Mister Lawrence owed him. But when he saw the girl was home alone, I think he just decided right then, he would rape her. If I had any decency or integrity at the time, I would have tried to stop him. I didn't, I was worse than he was. I regret it more then you can know."

There was more, but nothing revealing. Evan read the entire letter twice to make certain he hadn't missed anything before handing it back to Raleigh. He wondered why she thought it was written Sunday afternoon. Abel made no mention he was afraid of retribution from the Lawrences. There was no speculation about who might have killed his father. If Abel was afraid for his life because of what he had done, nothing he said in the letter gave any indication of it. Evan didn't tell Raleigh the letter really didn't mean anything anymore. They had the same information from two other sources, and now both perpetrators of the attack on Sarah Lawrence were dead. Also, as far as Evan was concerned, it could have been written by anyone who knew the details of the incident, including Raleigh herself.

Evan didn't tell her that. "Where did you find it?"

"It was under the pillow on his bed. It was in a plain, business size envelope with my name on it."

Yesterday, Raleigh told him she was reading the letter in the living room when someone took a shot at her. He wondered what made her look under the pillow. "How'd you happen to find it?"

She spoke deliberately, almost Evan thought, as if she were making certain she got the story straight. "Monday, after you and everyone else were gone, I went upstairs to look around again. I had already decided I would stay for at least that night, but I didn't want to sleep in the bedroom. It didn't feel right without Abel there. Eventually I grabbed a blanket and pillow out of the closet, and I spent the night on the couch in the living room downstairs. I didn't sleep well that night so by the next afternoon I was really tired and I went to take a nap in Abel's bed. That's when I found it. For some reason, I don't know why, I took it downstairs to read. That's when somebody shot at me."

"The letter was typed. Was that normal for Abel?"

"Two years ago it wouldn't have been, but I convinced him to get a computer so we could send emails to each other. He even took a class to learn how to type."

"Was your name on the envelope written or typed?"

"Written, I should have brought it along. Abel had very distinctive writing. Almost too pretty for a man."

Evan thought even if there were an envelope with Raleigh's name on it there was still no proof Abel typed the letter. The envelope could be from anything, maybe just a note Abel had left for her at some other time. It, just like the letter, gave him no new information and proved nothing, unless Raleigh had written it. If that were the case, Raleigh was involved.

"Hang on to it," he told Raleigh, "It may be needed."

Raleigh looked hurt, "You don't think it's important." It was not a question.

"No, it's very important, but probably not to the case. We already have two witnesses who told us the same story. It reinforces what they said, but what makes it important is Abel has attempted to explain things to you. He obviously loved you a great deal and wanted you to know what he had done. Even if it meant the end of everything, he had to tell you. I'd say that would make it very important to you." Evan was being truthful with Raleigh. He knew if he had been Abel Pike, admission of his crime to the woman he loved would be damn near impossible.

"Thanks, Evan. Even if you're just saying that to make me feel better, I still appreciate it."

"No, Raleigh, I mean it. The letter is very important. I think it proves how much he cared about you and also about setting the record straight." He was sincere, only he wondered more now than he had before if Raleigh were telling the truth.

"Confession is good for the soul?"

"I hope so, because from what I've seen, it doesn't do a damn thing for the body."

"I think it must have helped Abel. I knew he was going to church, but I didn't know he was involved to this extent. The minister told me they have a hundred and ten members. It looks at least half of them are here."

"That brings up a question. If you two were together on most weekends, how is it you didn't know about his involvement here? Last time I went to church it was on Sunday."

"You sound suspicious." She wasn't hurt, she was smiling.

"Curious mostly." But she had guessed right.

"He told me over a year ago he had starting going to church, but I thought it was mostly casual because if I was over on a Sunday, he never went and didn't appear to be concerned about not going. Also, we very seldom got to spend the whole weekend together, especially this past summer. I've been busy with the B and B. It's hard to find good help you know." She locked eyes with Evan. "Curiosity satisfied? Oh yeah, and another thing," she grabbed his hand and held it, "he also went to church on Wednesday night. The minister told me he very seldom missed it."

Evan squeezed her hand, "Okay, I believe you." He wanted to believe her, except he wasn't sure. She seemed to be trying hard to convince him. He decided to change the subject. "What do you know about the woman Jason is with?"

Raleigh looked over to where Jason stood with the green-eyed lady. "Not much more than her name. Jason introduced us when he showed up with her right before the funeral." Raleigh was still holding Evan's hand. "Although I know they're engaged."

"So I see. Do you find it odd you didn't know about her until now?"

"God, no! I think Jason is extremely weird. He's always so damn distant. It's like talking to a photograph. Besides, I don't think Abel even told his mother we were still married. She told me how surprised she was when she found out from you." Evan knew that much was true. "So why should I know anything about Jason's love life? I don't think Abel even knew anything about her."

"What's her name?"

"Veronica Valdez. Jason calls her Ronnie."

"Valdez sounds Spanish. She doesn't much look it though."

"Castilian," Raleigh said, "at least one of her parents could be Castilian. They're all blonde."

"She's a strawberry blonde with green eyes."

"You men are all alike. That's not her real color hair. She probably wears colored contacts too."

"How do you know that?

"The hair is easy, look at her eyebrows. They don't really match the color of the hair on her head. I'm not sure about her eyes though."

Evan looked over to where Jason stood with his bride to be. She was looking his way. From his location, her eyebrows did appear to be blonde; not quite the same color as her hair. He wanted a closer look. "Can you introduce me?"

"She a suspect too?" She pulled on his hand. "Come on."

From his hiding place on the opposite side of the river, Buster watched Jake Lawrence play with his little niece. He smiled as Jake swung her around like a leaf. The faster he went, the harder she laughed. Then when he claimed he was dizzy, she demanded a horsy-back ride. Lifting her easily to his shoulders, he proceeded to gallop around the yard until Buster was tired from just watching. *I sure hope you didn't do it because that little girl will probably be a young woman with kids of her own when you get out of jail. Now what do I do about you?*

There were only a couple of alternatives. He could go back and arrest Jake on the spot, he could notify the sheriff of Chaffee County and have him arrest Jake, or he could drive back to Saguaro to talk it over with Evan. Gravel crunched behind him. He'd been sitting with his knees up, elbows propped against his thighs for support as he watched through the binoculars. He immediately spun around into a crouch while reaching for his revolver. He was looking at the old Indian.

"You move pretty good for an old man," the Indian told him. "Why are you spying on my neighbors?"

Buster got to his feet. "Look who's talking? Spying is part of my job. Why'd you sneak up on me?"

"I didn't sneak. You've been down here for over an hour."

"I thought you were going to take a nap."

"I tried, but I couldn't sleep. I was concerned about you."

"You mean you wanted to know what I was doing."

The old man shrugged. "Concern, curiosity, what's the difference. What are you doing down here?"

"Spying on your neighbors." Buster started walking away. "But I'm done now. Thank you for allowing me on your land."

"You're welcome. You know, some people don't think my ancestors were particularly contemplative. However, I like to come down here by the water to sit and think, especially in the evening when the air is cool and the river is talking quietly."

Buster stopped and regarded the old man. *Where was he headed with this?*

"Sometimes I see things that have no logical explanation."

"Really? What things would that be?" Buster asked, strongly suspecting the old man came here, fell asleep, and dreamed dreams.

"Just two nights ago I was sitting there, right where you were sitting. There was not much moon left, but the stars were bright and just there, by that big cottonwood at the bend," he pointed to a spot at least fifty yards downstream, "I saw the most amazing thing."

Two nights ago would have been Monday night. "And what was this amazing thing?"

"It was a black cat, a large black cat. It came down to the river, slowly entered the water, and swam across the river. I saw it come out on the other side. It disappeared into the night. I waited a long time watching, but I never saw it come back."

"Okay, that was an amazing thing," Buster admitted, humoring the old man.

The old Indian looked at Buster. "You don't understand. The cat I saw walked on two legs like a human being."

Buster was right; the old man had been sleeping and dreaming. "Thanks again," Buster said and walked away, back to his car.

Watching him leave, the old man couldn't help thinking how hasty he was. There was more he would have told him. He looked across the river to where Jake was still galloping around. From her perch, high on Jake's shoulders, Taylor saw him standing there and waved. The old man waved back. Buster was out of sight.

Demure was a word Evan never had much cause to use, but meeting Ronnie, Jason's fiancé, the word came immediately to mind. Close up, she was prettier than he'd originally thought from his first quick look. Her face was of classic oval shape, and her nose was straight and small. Her mouth was small also, but her lips were full. Her face was soft, the only truly prominent feature was her piercing green eyes. She was conservatively dressed, but even if she were wearing a feed sack, her figure would be hard to conceal. She had a very nice physique, no angles, all curves. She stood about four inches taller than Jason, but she was wearing high heels. Evan figured her to about five-nine, maybe an inch taller than Jason. Her hair didn't look dyed to him. When Evan shook her hand, her grip was politely firm. The diamond of the engagement ring she wore was big enough to choke a chicken.

"Pleased to meet you," was all she said. Jason immediately took over the conversation. He wanted to know if they had made any progress in apprehending a suspect. All Evan could tell him was that they were close.

As the two men talked, Ronnie smiled politely. Evan was not sure she was even listening.

Evan wished Cheree were here. He'd really like another opinion on the woman's hair. Then a minor miracle happened. Ronnie tilted her head and reached up under her hair to check on a dangling earring. In the process, her diamond engagement ring became tangled in a wayward tress of her hair. As she pulled her hand away, several strands were snagged in the ring setting and came along. She absently pulled them from the ring, letting them fall to the floor.

Evan watched with amazement. Now how do I pick them up? He obviously couldn't see them lying on the floor, but unless static electricity had pulled them over to her dress on the way to the floor, they had to be right at her feet. He had to act fast if he wanted a shot at retrieving them. He started blinking in one eye, as if it were irritating him. Raising his right hand to his eye, he feigned dropping a contact lens. He had excellent vision and no clue as to how you go about losing a contact. He hoped his performance wasn't too hokey. "Damn," he quietly cursed and announced a little louder, "I'm afraid I dropped a contact. I don't know why the right one gives me so much trouble." Everyone immediately took a step backwards, looking to the floor.

Evan took a short step forward towards Ronnie, and went down to his knees. He made a production of feeling around on the floor for the non-existent contact until he saw what he was looking for. "Ah, there it is," he said as picked up one of the long red hairs Ronnie had just discarded. He put his hand in his suit jacket pocket before he stood up. "Excuse me please, I have to go reinstall this thing." He left them to find the men's room.

The men's room was vacant, and Evan pulled a paper towel out of the dispenser. Extracting his hand from his jacket pocket, he laid the hair on the towel. That's when he noticed he had another long red hair clinging to the cuff of his suit jacket. It must have attached itself by static as he searched around on the floor.

Both hairs were approximately the same length, and appeared to be the same color. Evan decided they must both have come from the same head, Ronnie's. He wrapped them together in the same towel. He checked his watch; just after four. He had to call Cheree.

Returning to the gathering, Evan found that Ruth Pike had joined Raleigh, Jason, and Ronnie. Evan hadn't spoken to Ruth yet, and decided this would be a good time to offer his condolences. Extending his hand he said, "My sympathies, ma'am, I'm very sorry for your loss." He wished there was something better, or at least as good and different, he could say, but if there was it eluded him.

"Thank you, Sheriff," she said, "Are you any closer to arresting a suspect?" She looked tired, not with grief–her eyes weren't red or swollen–just simply tired, as if she had been up all night.

Evan told her the same thing he'd told Jason five minutes earlier. Her response was neutral; she accepted his answer without comment. Ruth was numb. She had entered the state of grief where nothing much matters. It was typical and would probably last for several days. He'd seen it in his father when his mother died. It was sensory overload. Rather than trying to process new information, the mind began ignoring things, especially more bad news. Evan felt he could have told her a huge meteorite was about to impact the entire state of Colorado and she would not have reacted. He wondered what she would say if he told her he now considered Jason and his girl friend to be high on his list of prime suspects. Of course he didn't tell her that, but what he did was to once again offer condolences before politely excusing himself. He wanted to talk to the minister before he left.

He located her with a small group of teenagers. There were eight of them, five girls and three boys. Evan guessed they ranged in age from thirteen to sixteen, although the older he got, the harder it was to guess the age of anyone younger. Approaching them, he heard one of the girls saying, "I still don't believe it, he was such a nice man. Who would do such a thing?"

My question exactly, thought Evan. *Who indeed would do such a thing?*

The minister saw him coming. She wondered who he was. He seemed to know the family quite well, especially Raleigh. She also had noticed him sitting by the warden and his secretary during the service. He seemed to know the warden too. "I'm sure we'll know the answer to that question in good time," she told the girl. And then turning towards Evan, she asked, "Yes, sir. Can I help you?"

He gave her his card. "Deputy Evan Coleman," he said extending his hand. "Could I talk to you privately for just a minute?"

"Of course." She turned back to the group of kids. "You'll have to excuse me for a while. We'll talk more later." The kids left them alone. Evan noticed two of the girls were well on their way to becoming pretty young ladies. He couldn't help but wonder exactly what type of relationship Abel Pike had with these kids.

"Abel was very good with our young people," the minister told Evan when the kids walked away. "He was a helper in the youth group." She studied Evan's face. "You're skeptical aren't you, Deputy?"

Her question caught Evan off guard. The woman was quite perceptive. He decided to ignore it. "During the sermon you mentioned Abel came to you with a big weight on his shoulders. Did he ever tell you the source of that weight?"

"No, but I believe he would have if I'd asked. The only thing I asked was if he had done something the authorities should know about."

"What was his response?"

"He didn't answer directly. He indicated the statute of limitations had run out. I didn't press him, but clearly it wasn't murder because that has no limit. I think his intention was ultimately to come forward. For most people, deep-seated guilt is a terrible thing. It eats away the soul. I know Abel had confessed his sin to God and was forgiven. I'm certain he would have confessed publicly had he lived." She continued studying Evan's face. "You know the reason for his guilt, don't you Deputy Coleman?"

Evan was betting this woman hadn't started out with the idea of becoming a preacher. You don't get as perceptive as she was merely by attending college. She had been around the block a time or two. "You're very perceptive. And if you tell me that you believe God has forgiven Abel, who am I to judge him? However, I'd really like to catch his killer. Anything you could tell me might be helpful."

"I can tell you a lot about him from the past two years, but I'm afraid it's all positive. I don't think he ever suspected someone was out to get him for what he had done. His guilt drove his conversion, not his fear of retribution."

"Did he ever talk about his wife?"

"Raleigh? Yes he did, but only in the last few months. He told me all about their rather complicated relationship, but he was very hopeful it was going to finally work out. He said he'd be bringing her soon for me to meet."

"Did he say when?"

"No, but I believed it would happen in due time. What he had been earlier in his life, I can't say, but he had become very deliberate and thoughtful. I was confident when he was ready, he would bring Raleigh along."

"So you never met her prior to this?"

"No, but I wish I had. I liked her immediately. I believe she genuinely loved him in spite of all they had gone through."

What was it about Abel and Ben Pike that could inspire love? Evan felt Ruth loved her husband too, in spite of his behavior. It must be true; what you don't know won't hurt you. Maybe it was also true; what you don't acknowledge won't hurt you. Even Hitler had a girlfriend. Evan smiled. "So basically you're telling me you're no help to me at all?"

The minister smiled back. "It's not my job to share your suspicions. I know nothing bad about Abel Pike. He came to us to find relief and I'm sure he did. He was a valuable member of this congregation. We will miss him." And then she winked at him, "But I believe you're good at what you do. I have no doubt you will find his killer. I'll also keep my ears open and if I hear anything," she held up the card he had just given her, "I have your number. You'll be the first person I tell."

"I'd appreciate it," however, he doubted she would come up with anything. From what she said about Abel, he'd been a model parishioner. Evan said goodbye to beat a hasty retreat from the church back to his truck. Wanting badly to talk to Cheree, he even considered driving to Denver. He could be there by about six-thirty if he hurried. The strawberry blonde hairs from the head of Veronica Valdez were burning a hole in his pocket.

He called her office first and was told by a member of her staff she was unavailable. "Does that mean she's in and not taking calls or she's out and can't take calls?"

There was a long pause before the staff member asked, "Who's calling please?"

"Deputy Evan Coleman, it's important."

"Yes, sir, she left a message for you. She requested that you call her on her cell phone. Would you like that number, sir?" Suzy could take lessons from this secretary, Evan thought.

"No thanks, I have it." He broke the connection to dial Cheree's cell phone. She answered on the first ring.

"Hey, Doc, you sneaked out early." He thought he heard a horse whinny in the background. "I thought you had so much work to do."

"Hi, Evan. Yeah, I did and I still do. The stable manager where I board my horse called to tell me my horse had cut himself. They wanted to know if I would authorize the vet to come out and stitch him up. I decided to come and see for myself."

"How bad is it?"

"Not that bad really, seventeen stitches below his left knee. No tendons were cut. It really irritates me though; they can't tell me how it happened."

"Hell, he's a horse. Some horses can cut themselves on their own shadow."

"What about the old expression, 'healthy as a horse'? Where does that come from?"

"Whoever came up with that never owned a horse. Most likely never even got near one. You do the stitching yourself?"

"Oh no, I just watched. I hate to admit it; I'm not very good with a needle. I don't get much practice."

Evan thought about it. She probably did a lot more cutting than sewing. "How about splitting hairs. How difficult is it to tell if a hair has been colored?"

"Not hard. Now what do you have?"

"Remembered when you said you met Jason's girlfriend? You told me she was a blonde."

"Yes. I remember. She's a green-eyed blonde. Pretty in a different sort of way."

"She's a strawberry blonde today. That makes me wonder what color she really is, or was on the day Ben Pike was murdered." Evan proceeded to tell her all about his adventure at the funeral of Abel Pike. "If I hit the road now, I can meet you at the lab by six-thirty with the hair sample. We can grab some dinner and I can be back home by ten."

"Oh, Evan, that's a wonderful plan, but I promised my mother I'd meet her later. She wants me to go shopping with her. I don't want to put her off, she gets out so seldom."

Evan was disappointed but tried not to show it. "Not a problem. Sooner or later you'll have to go out with me."

"Sooner I hope. In fact, what are you doing Saturday? You promised me a free tune up on this horse you sold me."

"We're supposed to have a blizzard this weekend. What do you have in mind?" Getting snowed in somewhere, anywhere, with her would be a good thing.

"I was just thinking maybe you could come out Saturday, and although I'm sure my horse can't be worked, maybe you could take a look at him anyway. I'd also like to make dinner for you, but, if you think the weather will be bad. We can wait."

"That sounds good to me. I don't believe the weatherman anyway. But how do I get you this vital new evidence? I had to act like a fool to get it."

She thought for a minute. "You're in Buena Vista?"

"Yes."

Give it to your friend, what's his name? The police chief."

"Buddy Banks."

"Yeah, give it to him. I'll do some calling and have the highway patrol pick it up. They can have it here in a few hours, and you won't have to drive to Denver."

They agreed on the plan. By the time Evan got to the police station, Buddy was waiting for him. They discussed the case briefly before Evan pointed his truck south towards Saguaro. He was tired, not physically, but emotionally. Almost every waking moment since he had discovered Ben Pike's body, his mind had been processing information and sifting possibilities. Just when he thought he had an answer, something changed. Now he had Jason's red-haired girlfriend to consider. She looked a bit fragile to be helping Jason murder people, but looks could be deceiving. It wouldn't be the first time he'd underestimated a pretty face. *And what about Raleigh? She was also a pretty face.* He didn't want to underestimate her either.

Shaking his head as he drove south, he tried to chase away all the thoughts competing for his attention. "Hopefully, Cheree will have some answers for me by tomorrow morning," he told himself. "If I can hold out that long." He forced himself to concentrate on Saturday, when he would see Cheree, rather than speculating on the identity of the grulla paint murderer.

22

It was quitting time when Evan stopped in front of the courthouse in downtown Saguaro. He was hoping to check in with Buster before he went home. Suzy was leaving as he came up the front steps. She stopped to whistle at him. "Damn, look at you. Why don't you come home with me? I'll tell Allen to go out with the boys for a while, a long while." Allen was her husband.

"Careful, Suzy, I'd hate to file sexual harassment charges against you."

"Ha. Ha. I should be so lucky. Anyway, you don't have time to fool around right now; Buster's been waiting for you."

"You can harass me some other time then."

"Sure, I'll be waiting." He walked past and she turned to watch him. She shook her head as the door closed behind him. "That is one damn, fine looking suit!" she said to herself.

Feet on his desk, leaning way back in his wooden swivel chair, Buster was comfortably waiting when Evan walked into the office. Evan looked at Buster and then across the hall to the sheriff's office. His door was open, and he could see Tate was still in there. "Kind of casual, aren't you?"

Buster slowly uncrossed his legs, removing his feet from the desk. He rocked forward in his chair. "I'm on my own time now," he said. "Waiting for you."

"You're always on your own time. What have you got?"

"What have I got? What have you got?"

"Another suspect."

"I'm sorry to hear that." Buster was eyeing him critically. "Don't you think this thing is complicated enough already?"

"This one has possibilities and what's wrong with a little more diversity? What do you have?"

"I have Jake Lawrence."

"Where? Here, in custody?"

"No, not quite, but I know where he is."

"Well, let's go get him!"

"Not so fast, fashion boy. He's coming in all by himself." Buster was smirking. "Nice threads by the way."

Evan ignored the shot. "What do you mean, he's coming in by himself? He's our prime suspect. You know where he is. Let's pick him up!"

"We can't."

"Why the hell not? Where is he? Havana?"

"No, he's in South Fork at his sister's. I promised Gordon Mason I'd give him until noon tomorrow to show up here." Buster punched the top of his desk with his index finger for emphasis.

Sighing deeply, Evan sat down. "Why don't you tell me all about it?"

Buster gave him the long version; complete with the details of his encounter with the old Indian and the phone call from Gordon Mason requesting Jake be allowed to turn himself in tomorrow morning. "At first I wouldn't agree to it, but Gordy personally guaranteed me the boy would be here. So," Buster raised his hands in the air, "what could I do?"

"I hope Gordy's word is better than his daughter-in-law's. She promised she wouldn't tell Jake we wanted him. She must have been on the phone before we got off the property."

"I suspect, but consider it from her perspective. Ben and Abel Pike raped her and got away with it. Then the damn fools get themselves murdered sixteen years later and she gets dragged into it. If she's innocent, it's mighty inconvenient."

Once again the omniscient finger of perspective, was pointing its crooked finger in Evan's face. "What about from my perspective? It looks damn suspicious from where I'm at!" Evan countered.

"You really think Sarah and Jake did it? You just told me you had another suspect. What's that all about?"

Evan proceeded to tell him all about the funeral and Jason's redheaded fiancé. Buster was particularly amused by Evan's account of his performance to retrieve Ronnie's discarded hair. "Cheree thought she'd be able to tell right away if the hair was similar to what we found on Ben."

"That would be handy. I'd much rather charge Jason and his girlfriend for the murders than Jake and his buddy, Dale; and maybe even Sarah, too."

Evan slouched back in his chair. "I'm tired. Not sleepy tired, but I'm tired of thinking about this case. We don't solve it soon, I'll be a babbling idiot with drool running down my chin."

Buster stood up. "Change your clothes first, that suit's too nice to drool on. Come on, follow me home. I'll get Amy to buy us a drink."

Much later that evening, in the barn, when he finished feeding his horses, Evan sat down on a hay bale, leaning back against another. Although the night sky was clear, the forecast for the early morning was windy and wet. The horses were all in their stalls making clunking noises as they foraged around in their plastic pails eating their grain rations. Evan liked the noise it made. It comforted him. They were eating and therefore happy. That made Evan happy. It was a very simple pleasure, like the rush of aroma from the hay when he broke open a fresh bale, or the soft feel of the horse's hide when he patted one of them on the hip. He liked them nuzzling his hands when he petted their noses. He loved to watch them run together when they played. After all these years, it was still a major thrill to see them galloping, racing each other in a thundering herd. Lying back on the stacked bales, he breathed in the scent of dead grass and living horses. He didn't expect anybody else to understand. He didn't care. He couldn't imagine living anywhere he couldn't keep at least one horse and have enough real estate around him to be able to ride. He got claustrophobic just driving through Denver on the freeway. Living in a high-rise or condo would be his version of hell on earth. The words to 'Don't Fence Me In' started trickling through his thoughts. *"Let me ride to the ridge where the West commences; gaze at the moon 'til I lose my senses."*

He sat up with a jolt. It was one in the morning. He had fallen asleep four hours ago. "Damn," he cursed, "I wanted to call Cheree." He slowly got up from his bed of hay bales. He was stiff and cold. A thin, moaning wind chased him from the barn to the house. He kicked off his boots as he pulled off his tee shirt and then his jeans. He left everything where it hit the floor. Pulling back the bed covers, he crawled in under them, shivered once, and was back to sleep. The murderer of Ben and Abel Pike was not a matter of consideration.

High cirrus clouds in the east gave the dawn a pale pink light. Based on the old adage, "Red in the morning, sailor take warning", Evan thought maybe the bad weather being predicted might actually happen. Grinning a wicked little grin, he thought if he could time it right, maybe he could get snowed in somewhere with Cheree. He could probably even tolerate an apartment in downtown Denver for a day or two if he were alone with her. He'd have to work on that.

Buster was waiting for him when he got to the courthouse. "You okay?" he wanted to know.

"Sure, I feel great. Why?"

"You give up answering the phone?"

"Buster, don't mess with my mind. What are you talking about?"

"Doctor Nicoletti called me last night. Said she couldn't reach you. The poor woman was so worried I had to drive over to check on you." Buster had a wicked little grin of his own on his face. "Were you sleeping in the barn for a reason or was that as far as you got before you collapsed from exhaustion?"

"You were over last night?" and before Buster could answer, "Why didn't you wake me up so I could go in and go to bed?"

"Think about it. You wanted me to wake you up so you could go to sleep? You were already sleeping pretty as could be. I didn't want to disturb you."

"How'd you get in the barn without the horses making a fuss?"

"They were all talking, especially Diablo, but you were dead to the world. You gave new meaning to the expression, 'In the arms of Morpheus'. In fact, I'll bet you sucked all the cobwebs off the rafters. You were snoring so hard, I could feel a draft pulling me towards the barn as soon as I got out of my car."

"So you just looked at me and left?"

"Yup. I called Cheree when I got home, and told her you were fine. What are friends for?"

Evan shook his head slowly. "What did Cheree have to say?"

She said to forget about Jason's girlfriend. She went into the lab last night just to examine the sample you sent her. That hair and the hair found on Ben aren't even close. She's going to run DNA on it, but she's ninety-nine per cent certain they won't match."

"So much for Ronnie Valdez it would appear. What else did Cheree say?"

"She said she'd call this morning as soon as she had the results of the test on the blood from the glove they found in the horse trailer, and now she wants a DNA sample from the little girl."

"Makes sense. If the blood on the glove is Pike's, the hair probably belongs to the little girl. If so, I believe we have enough circumstantial evidence to arrest Jake." He looked at Buster waiting for consensus.

"What if the blood doesn't belong to Pike?"

"I don't know. I'd be less suspicious of Jake. We should still get a DNA sample from the little girl. Did Cheree say she was coming down here today?"

"Depends. She did say she'd like to be here when we question Jake Lawrence."

"If he shows."

"Don't worry, he'll be here," Buster assured him. "I trust Gordy Mason as much as I trust you. Gordy will ride the kid down, rope him, and personally drag his ass in here if he has to."

"Yeah, well, I certainly hope you're right." Evan yawned. "You hungry?"

"No, but I'll watch you eat."

They both looked up at the sky as they left the building. "Think we'll get snowed on?" Evan asked Buster.

"Yeah, but not today and maybe not even tomorrow."

From across the street they saw Suzy going into the café. "Tell me how she can eat all those rolls and stay in such good shape?"

"She's young, she's got two little kids, and a full time job." Evan told him. "She burns carbs faster than a loaded pack horse going up a steep trail."

"Nice metaphor, I'll tell her she reminds you of a horse."

"Go ahead. Lots of people remind me of horses. I think of it as a compliment."

Buster was curious. "Does Cheree remind you of a horse?"

"In a way. She's like a sleek thoroughbred, with long legs, a beautiful head, and a lot of spirit."

"Interesting. Do I remind you of a horse?"

"No, actually Buster, you remind me of a donkey." Evan smiled. He couldn't remember the last time he had been able to get a decent, cheap shot at his friend.

Buster pulled open the door to the café and held it for Evan. "Good one. I think I will have some breakfast. You can buy."

Suzy was at the front counter, paying for her purchase. "Hey guys, I got us a treat." She held up a bag.

"Save it for us. We're going to get breakfast and be right back," Buster told her. "Oh yeah, if a big guy by the name of Jake Lawrence shows up, come and get us."

"You expecting him soon?"

"Buster is," Evan said, "I'm not."

"Don't mind him, Suzy. Jake Lawrence will be in sometime before noon. I'm just not sure when." He looked at Evan, "But he will be in."

Evan was already headed for their usual booth in the corner. Suzy wasn't sure if she had just witnessed a disagreement between the two men or if they were only joking. She had worked for the county, in the sheriff's office almost six years. There were still times she didn't have a clue whether Buster and Evan were serious or just pulling her chain. Coming from a family of four brothers and being the only girl, she thought she understood men. Buster and Evan constantly reminded her that men are not from this planet. "I'll come get you if he shows. Have a nice breakfast."

Twenty minutes later, Evan pushed his empty plate away. The waitress came by with a coffee pot. She filled his cup and took the plate. "How was it?" she asked.

"Spoiled my appetite," Evan told her.

"Good," she fired back, "That's why you came in here, ain't it?"

As she walked away with the dirty dishes, Buster looked up to see Suzy and Cheree walk in the front door. Suzy pointed to them, and said something to Cheree.

When Suzy left, Cheree started towards them. There were several men sitting at the front counter. They swiveled on their stools to gawk at her as she walked by. "Hey Evan," Buster asked, "You ever seen a thoroughbred in a restaurant before?"

Evan was about to chastise Buster for making another ridiculous comment, when he suddenly figured out what he meant. He turned to see Cheree approaching their booth. She was wearing blue jeans, boots, and a suede jacket with a sheepskin lining. Her hair was pulled back into a ponytail that stuck out the back of a baseball cap that said, "DCSI" across the crown. The only makeup she wore was a big smile. "Hi guys."

Evan almost hurt himself getting out of the booth as fast as he did. She hugged him briefly before gracefully sliding into the booth on the inside next to the wall. Evan sat down beside her. She put her right hand under the table to give his knee a squeeze. Evan was at a loss for words. "How'd you get here?" was all he could think of saying.

"Helicopter. The governor was on his way to Pagosa Springs so I hitched a ride. Suzy picked me up at the airport. She said you two were having a spat and she didn't want to interrupt." Cheree looked from Evan to Buster and asked, "Is she right?"

Evan answered first, "If we are, or were, I must have missed it."

"Suzy has a very active imagination," Buster confided. "I think it's stimulated by all the caramel rolls she eats. Sugar can do that you know."

Cheree shook her head. "You two are bad. I can see why the poor girl is confused. You probably make it a contest to see who can mess with her mind the most."

"Not true," Evan said. "We don't have time for foolishness."

"Good, because I have serious news. And you're probably not going to like any of it."

The waitress showed up at their booth, "You want anything, miss?"

Cheree took a taste from Evan's coffee cup. "Yes, the coffee's good. I'll have a cup. Do you have any fresh bakery?"

"We got some fresh, gooey caramel rolls. They're still warm."

"I'll have one, please." The waitress left, and Cheree opened her jacket and pulled a notebook out of an inside pocket. "Okay, here's what I know," she looked from Buster to Evan. "For all practical purposes, this is one hundred per cent certain. The blood on the glove found in Matt Mason's horse trailer belongs to Ben Pike. The pubic hair found in Matt Mason's horse trailer belongs to Ben Pike. The DNA of the horse hair from the grulla paint horse found at the scenes of both Ben Pike's and Abel Pike's murder, matches the DNA from the sample we took from Matt Mason's grulla paint horse. The DNA from the red hair found at the scene of Ben Pike's murder is from a female," she looked at Evan, "morphologically, it doesn't resemble the hair sample from Jason Pike's girlfriend. It appears to be from a younger person, and its color has not been altered in any way. No human DNA other than Ben Pike's was found at his murder scene and no human DNA other than Abel Pike's was found on or about his body. The red hair found in the woods at Abel's place, matches the red hair found on Ben Pike's body. We did find additional DNA inside Abel's house, but we believe it belongs to Raleigh. She's providing a sample of her DNA, and we'll know in forty-eight hours if my assumption is correct. Based on what I saw at Abel Pike's residence, there was absolutely no reason to believe the killer went inside." She paused. "That's what I have for certain. Oh yeah, Ben Pike isn't, or more correctly, wasn't Jason's father. So, based on what I just told you, who killed Ben and Abel?"

Buster and Evan looked at each other. They were both thinking the same thing. "I hate to admit it," Buster said, "but it would appear the case against Jake Lawrence is circumstantially very strong."

"I agree," said Evan. "When he gets here, we should charge him. He's got motive, means and opportunity. Who else is involved?"

Cheree offered her opinion. "I don't like the thought, but wouldn't Sarah be the most obvious? She's got the best reason in the world. I told you this before. If it had been me they raped, I'd have gone after them immediately."

"She was barely sixteen," Evan said. "If it were you now, you'd do something immediately, but at her age you might have done the same thing; nothing."

When Cheree tugged at her caramel roll, warm caramel and melted butter oozed over her fingers. "I suppose, but I don't think I'd have let it stand sixteen years." She licked her fingers.

"I believe we have to question Jake's friend, Dale, again," Buster said. "I suspect him more than Sarah."

"What about Matt?" Cheree asked. "Could he be involved?"

"Yeah," said Evan, "He and Sarah have alibis to their whereabouts, but that doesn't mean they didn't have a hand in the planning or support." Then he thought a bit. "No, that makes no sense. If they all were in on it, they would make sure they all had an alibi. I think it's Jake alone or Jake and Dale together."

The three of them were silent for a while, thinking similar thoughts. Even though all the evidence pointed to Jake Lawrence, none of them were convinced he did it, but facts were facts. The ones they had indicated he was guilty.

"How long are you going to be in town?" Evan asked Cheree.

"The governor's cutting a ribbon in Pagosa Springs at ten, some kind of park. They're picking me up on the way back, probably right around noon. I told them I'd be waiting at the airport at eleven thirty."

"You might miss Jake's arrival," Buster said.

"I still think we should go pick him up considering the evidence," Evan said.

"We'll probably pass him on the way."

"You and Cheree stay here and wait, I'll go to his sister's," Evan volunteered.

"Could do it that way," Buster mused. He checked his watch. "It's just after eight. If he doesn't show by ten, okay, we'll go get him."

"I'd rather go now."

"Suit yourself, but I guarantee he'll be here."

Jake Lawrence had spent another mostly sleepless night. He tossed and turned, flopping in bed like a fish out of water. At five-thirty he got up, showered, and dressed quietly. The plan was for Matt and him to drive to Saguaro about eight, but Jake had thought about it all night long. He decided he didn't want anyone else around when he presented himself for questioning. Shortly before six, he left the house. Sarah, Matt, and Taylor didn't hear him leave. He left a note, "Sarah, Matt: Thanks for everything. I have to do this alone. I'll talk to you as soon as I'm done. Please stay home. Love, Jake."

"I'd better get something to eat," Jake told himself as he went down the road, "This could get to be a long morning." He stopped at the same café for breakfast where Buster, Cheree, and Evan had stopped for lunch two days earlier. The counter was full so he took a booth toward the back. Feeling paranoid, he sat so he could watch the doorway. He ordered eggs, toast, pancakes, and pork chops. He was hungry. At first, he tried to take his time, eating slowly, but his apprehension was mounting. He started wolfing the food. By seven he was back on the highway. He wanted to get this over with.

He had to force himself to keep to the speed limit. Don't need to get picked up for speeding. They'll never believe I was in a hurry to turn myself in. Then the realization of his thought hit him. *Turn myself in! I sound like some kind of criminal. I didn't do a damn thing!* He briefly considered turning around, going back to Colorado Springs. "Let the bastards come and get me!" he said out loud. It quickly passed. He didn't want to involve Sarah and Matt anymore then they already were. Besides Matt's father had supposedly guaranteed his deputy buddy he'd show up. Actually, it's what he wanted to do from the beginning. He never should have let Sarah talk him into waiting. He glanced at the speedometer and lifted his foot slightly.

Cheree finished the caramel roll. "That was wonderful. I'd take some home with me, but I'm afraid they wouldn't taste the same tomorrow."

"Yeah, they don't," Evan agreed. "I've taken them home lots of times and they're not the same after I microwave them. Not bad, but not as good. I figure they have a thirty minute half life."

Buster prodded them, "I think we really should get back to the office; I have a feeling our company is coming early."

Evan paid the bill and they walked back across the street. As the door to the courthouse closed behind them, Jake glided his car to a stop at the curb in front of the building. He found his way to the sheriff's office. Suzy looked up at the biggest man she'd ever seen in person. "Can I help you?"

He smiled at her. Suzy was cute. "I'm sure you can. My name is Jake Lawrence, I believe I'm expected."

Suzy jumped up, "Don't move, I'll be right back." She hurried down the hallway. "The biggest guy in the world is here," she announced to Buster, Evan and Cheree. They had just sat down to discuss strategy.

Buster winked at Cheree and said to Evan, "What'd I tell you?"

"Yeah, yeah, let's go get him in here." Evan was already on his feet and moving.

They escorted Jake down the hall, Buster in front, Evan behind. When they went into the office, Jake heard Evan lock the door behind him. He got a sinking feeling deep in his chest. He sat down on the chair Buster indicated. Evan pulled a tape recorder out of a desk drawer. Announcing the date and time, he told Jake that he was recording the conversation. Then Jake got another jolt. Evan read him his rights. "Now, Mister Lawrence," Evan said, "What can you tell us about the murder of Ben Pike?"

Jake started to feel panicky. "You just read me my rights, right?"

"Yes, I did."

"Why?"

"It's a technical matter."

"Did you read my sister her rights before you talked to her the other day?"

"No, I did not."

"Why not?"

"At the time we questioned your sister we didn't have as much information as we do now."

"So today I'm a suspect?"

Evan saw no reason to hedge. "That's correct." He also saw no reason to elaborate on his answers.

"What kind of information do you have today that makes me a suspect?"

"Excuse me Mister Lawrence, but my understanding was you turned yourself in so you could make a statement in hopes of clearing yourself from suspicion. I believe that requires you answer the questions, not ask them."

Jake's fists clenched, his face flushed red. Both Buster and Evan moved their hands towards their weapons. "I want to talk to a lawyer." Jake spit out the words.

Evan pushed the phone across the desk towards him. "Be my guest. Do you have someone in mind or would you like a public defender?"

Jake wanted to say he had the phone number of who he wanted to call in his wallet, but all that came out was, "In my wallet."

Buster was standing behind Jake, "Go ahead you can take your wallet out."

Jake got his wallet out of his back pocket, extricating a small piece of paper from it. The last thing

Gordon Mason had promised him was help if he needed it. He told him if there was any trouble to call him immediately. Jake was about to find out if Gordon's word was good.

He dialed the number. Buster wasn't too surprised when Jake asked for Gordon Mason, and he could guess what Gordon would tell the young man.

"Sit tight, keep your mouth closed, and I'll be right there," Gordon told Jake.

"Yes sir, but what about a lawyer."

"Leave that to me. I'll be there before noon."

Jake hung up the phone. He felt like a freshman at his first day on the practice field with the varsity football team. "What happens now," he asked.

"We have to lock you up until your lawyer gets here," Evan told him. "Unless, of course, you want to talk to us now."

"Am I being charged with something?"

"No, not yet, but we have the authority to hold you for questioning for twenty-four hours."

"Then what?"

"Then we have to either charge you or let you go."

Jake considered his options. He never thought they'd arrest him. They let Dale go after a few questions, although they'd held him overnight. If he cooperated now, maybe he could walk out of here in an hour or two. But something didn't feel right; he sensed a tension in Evan's posture. He was getting an impression. He was going to be charged no matter what he said. He might as well tough it out while he waited for Gordon to show with a lawyer.

"I'm going to wait for a lawyer. You guys sound as if you've already made up your minds."

"This is a murder investigation. Some of our evidence ties you to the victim. I'm not sure how we're supposed to sound to you."

Jake didn't want to irritate this guy any more than he already seemed to be. "I'll wait for the lawyer."

"Please come with me," Evan said and it was not a request.

They put him in one of the two cells in the detention room. The building was not designed to hold a criminal for any extended period of time. The cells had plumbing and a bunk. The last guest was a drunk driver who stayed only half the night before he was transferred to detox in Salida. That was three weeks ago. The door clanged shut, and Buster turned the key. "Can I get you anything? You had breakfast?"

"Yeah, I had breakfast. Thanks. Just a glass of water."

Buster put the key on the desk across the room. *Just like an old western movie,* Jake thought.

"Be right back with that water."

23

"Your deputy friend, Buster, he doesn't think Jake did it either right?"

"That's what he told me yesterday. He said he didn't feel Jake or Sarah were involved. He said it smelled like a frame-up, but they needed to talk to Jake." Gordon Mason was talking to his lawyer friend.

"How well do you trust Buster?"

"As well as I trust you."

"Is there any possibility your son and daughter-in-law are involved?"

Gordon thought about it; not that he hadn't considered it before, but now the stakes had been upped. *Could she be involved and if she was, what about my son?* "I don't know how they could be, at least directly. I was with them most of Friday." he said finally.

"Good! Let me clear my desk. I need a half hour. You're place is on the way to Saguaro, I'll pick you up about nine, you can fill me in on the way down. When we get there, we'll have a chat with the young man and the sheriff."

After Jake was locked up, Buster, Evan, and Cheree debated Dale Kupfer. Charging someone with murder was not something to be done without good reason. In Jake's case, they had good circumstantial evidence, maybe as good as they would ever get. So far the only thing they had to implicate Dale was his statement to the Omaha police that he and Jake were together for the weekend, although he said they were in Pagosa Springs at the time of Ben Pike's murder. Evan thought that was enough. Buster had misgivings.

"Look, Buster, if Jake kills Ben Pike on Friday, and all the evidence points to him, and his buddy swears they were together on Friday; doesn't that mean they both killed Pike on Friday?"

"Dale maintains they were in Pagosa Springs on Friday."

"So what? Either he's lying or after they both killed Pike, they went to Pagosa Springs, and bought dinner and drinks in a local restaurant. Pike was killed about ten on Friday morning. That gave them plenty of time to get down from the mountain and drive to Pagosa Springs. They could have spent the whole weekend there just like Dale said."

Buster waved his hand in the air. "All right, all right, I realize that. I just think we're missing something, and I can't figure out what it is. I don't even want to charge Jake with murder."

"You want to let him go?"

"Of course not! At least not until he talks to us, and if he doesn't have an airtight alibi, we'll have to keep him. I just don't like the way this has gone."

"That's not our fault or our problem. We responded, we investigated, and we found what there was to find. We're not responsible for who did it. We just have to find them and bring them in. We don't have to explain why they did it or how they did it either. That's the prosecutor's problem."

"I know all that, but I'm not happy about it. I'm not positive we've got the right people. I'd hate to have a slick prosecutor convince a jury an innocent man is guilty."

"Me too, but if Jake didn't do it, who did?"

Buster sighed, ignoring the question. "Look, the evidence we found to implicate Jake is easy. We find some hair at the scene that matches his little niece. We know some of her hair was tangled in the grulla paint's halter. Whoever borrowed the horse could have accidentally or deliberately left that hair at the scene. A glove with Ben's blood on it is found in Matt's horse trailer, and Jake was the last one to use the trailer. Jake is a big man. The glove is extra large, and it matches the fibers found at the scene. So what? That glove could have been put in the trailer any time after Ben was murdered. Same for the pubic hair. I know it's a stretch, but somebody who was determined, could be framing our prime suspects."

"I agree with you, Buster," said Cheree, "at least in theory, but I think it would be very difficult. According to what Sarah told us, Dale and Jake took the trailer and three horses Thursday afternoon. They drove to Pagosa Springs to pack up into the mountains. Now that's their story and they could have been anywhere, but regardless, they didn't get back to the ranch until Monday mid-morning. Monday shortly after noon they drove to Colorado Springs in Jake's car. Dale flew home to Omaha while Jake went back to his apartment so he could go to school on Tuesday. My team searched the trailer early Tuesday evening. That didn't give anyone much opportunity to plant false evidence in the trailer. In fact, the way I see it, Monday night was the only opportunity. I'm not saying it's impossible, just difficult."

"I know you're right, it would be tricky. But if someone were determined enough to go to all the other trouble, why not a little extra to make it look really good?"

"Care to speculate on that special someone?" Evan asked.

"I'm suspicious of Jason. His mother didn't know her husband and son had raped Sarah Lawrence. Sarah never told anyone, and she doesn't think Jake ever told anyone. Jason is the only other person who knew."

"He said he never told anyone either. Why assume Sarah and Ruth are telling the truth and Jason is lying? To be honest I don't like him much, but that doesn't mean he's the one who's lying. Besides, we really haven't talked to Jake yet."

Buster ignored the dig. "What about the fact Jason isn't Ben's son? Doesn't that bother you just a little? You were the suspicious one the other day when you obtained his DNA. He's got motive. With Ben and Abel out of the way, he'll likely inherit the ranch."

"You're right, Ruth probably will leave it to him and yes, I am suspicious. My problem is, I don't have anything else, just suspicion. Yesterday, after meeting his redheaded girlfriend, I thought we might have a shot at him." Evan looked to Cheree. "That's not going to happen, is it?"

She shook her head. "No, it isn't. Not with the hair sample you sent me, but there is something else here that bothers me a lot. Who shot at Raleigh on Tuesday afternoon?"

"Could have easily been Jake," Evan speculated. "He was supposed to be at school in Colorado Springs, but he could have been anywhere. He's a grad student not a freshman. He pays his tuition, but nobody keeps an attendance record on him. He's got a car, and he lives off campus. The way I understand grad school, he might not even have any classes yet. Another thing, when I dropped that hair sample off at the Buena Vista station yesterday, Buddy Banks told me he had interviewed Abel Pike's closest neighbors. Nobody saw or heard anything unusual on Monday or Tuesday."

"Did they recover the bullet that was shot at Raleigh?" Buster asked.

"Yeah, they found the bullet, but not the brass. Buddy said it was a thirty caliber, hundred and fifty grain bullet. He said he'd send it to the lab with the hair sample I brought to him. There are probably a hundred thousand rifles in the state capable of firing that cartridge, including mine."

"I have the bullet," said Cheree, "but you're right, it tells us next to nothing."

"That bullet's a little light for elk, don't you think?" asked Buster. "I doubt if it was a stray round from an elk hunter."

"Wouldn't be my choice. Buddy is certain the shot was deliberate. He also thinks the shooter was fairly close. The bullet went through the window, the living room wall, and across the kitchen before burying itself half way into the kitchen wall, and that's an outside wall, eight inch logs."

"What does Buddy consider to be fairly close?" Buster asked.

"His best guess is something under a hundred yards."

"So the shooter would have been in the corral?"

"Yeah, or even closer."

"Why didn't Raleigh see him?"

"I don't know. How about you enlighten me?"

"Do Raleigh and Jake Lawrence know each other?"

"At this point, she at least knows his name," Evan said. "The last name Lawrence was in Abel's confession letter. I gave her both first names."

"Are you thinking Jake and Raleigh might be in this together?" Cheree asked.

"What if they knew each other well, intimately, let's say? Jake wants to kill Ben Pike for revenge, and Raleigh wants to get rid of Abel so she can have his property. Jake kills Ben, Raleigh shoots Abel, a day later, she walks out in the corral to fire a shot through her window just to throw us off."

"What about Dale?" Cheree asked.

"Hell, I don't know. Maybe the deal was that Jake and Dale were responsible for killing Ben, and Raleigh was supposed to kill Abel. Except afterwards Raleigh was a little smarter then her accomplices." Buster looked frustrated. "No, that scenario doesn't work at all. Jake would have to be incredibly stupid to kill Ben Pike in the fashion he was killed, and Jake isn't stupid."

"Maybe Raleigh did it all by herself," Evan offered. "Abel was killed Monday, and she buried him on Wednesday. Seems like she was in hurry to get him in the ground."

"That doesn't mean a thing," Cheree said. "When my husband was killed, I buried him two days later."

"Yeah, you're right, sorry. It doesn't mean anything and if she did it, she's about the best actress I've ever seen." Evan leaned back in his chair, looking to Buster. "Sorry, partner, I've got to go with Jake, and I think we should get Dale in custody too."

Buster acquiesced, "Yeah, okay, but there's a few more things we need to check out. I want to know the financial condition of Raleigh's B and B. I want to know if Jake spent any time at school on Tuesday, and I want to know where Jason's girlfriend works."

"I'm with you on the first two, but what's your thought about Ronnie Valdez?"

"I'd like to know if Jason or Miss Valdez took any vacation last week or the first part of this week."

Evan nodded agreement. "Yeah, that's a good idea. Ronnie could be doing the red hair thing just to mess with our minds."

The three of them went to work on the phone and the Internet, Buster and Evan on the phones and Cheree on the computer. Two hours later they knew Raleigh's credit rating was excellent. Her business appeared to be in excellent condition. If she were in on the murders, she didn't need to do it for the money. They also knew Veronica Valdez worked at the Admissions Office of the University of Colorado, Colorado Springs. She was presently on a two-week vacation. Jason worked the entire previous week except he left early Friday afternoon when his mother called with the news of his father's murder. Ben Pike was buried early Monday afternoon in a brief, private ceremony. Jason hadn't been back to work since Friday. And Jake Lawrence had been at the university for at least a little while on Tuesday; long enough to pay his tuition at nine-thirty in the morning. Nothing they learned was enough to change their minds about anything they previously thought. The only thing of consequence they did was to issue a warrant for Dale Kupfer's arrest.

By the time they finished, it was after eleven. "I hate to leave," Cheree told them, "but I have to be at the airport in a few minutes."

"It was a pleasure as always," Buster told her. "Come back and see us soon." She promised she would.

Evan had hoped for a little face time alone with Cheree when he took her to the airport, but as they arrived, the governor's helicopter was just sitting down. He took her hand. "I'd like us to take tomorrow off. I could drive to Denver and we could spend the day together, maybe even look at your horse, but even if we charge Jake, we're missing something. I can't do it, I need to keep looking."

She squeezed his hand. "I think you're right. Where else do you plan to look?"

"I'm not sure yet, I'll call you at home later." He put the lights on, and drove as close as he could to the chopper.

She gave him a quick kiss. "I'll do better next time." She got in the aircraft, it lifted, and she was gone.

Returning to the courthouse, Evan found Gordon Mason in the office with Buster. Buster made introductions. "Pleased to meet you, sir," Evan said to Gordy, "I've admired you for years."

"Thank you. Buster tells me you're something of a wizard with horses yourself. You get tired of chasing bad guys, you can always come see me."

Evan was flattered. It sounded like the most successful cutting horse trainer in the country had just offered him a job. "Thank you, I might have to do that someday, maybe real soon if we don't solve this case."

Gordy frowned. "I don't believe you've solved it yet, but you'll solve it I'm sure." The comment offered the opinion that Gordy didn't think they had the right man.

Evan let it pass. He wasn't convinced Jake was the right man either, but evidence was evidence, and the stuff they had incriminated Jake. "Did you bring a lawyer with you?"

Buster answered for Gordy, "He's in with Jake; fellow by the name of Asa Emmings. He's a good friend of Gordy's. I've met him before."

Evan nodded. He wondered how much Buster had told Gordy about the situation. He was positive Gordy had asked what they had on Jake to make them feel they could charge him. He was also fairly certain Buster would have been tight lipped about what they knew. In spite of his friendship with Gordy, Evan knew Buster remembered the rules.

"Can you tell me anything about what's going on here?" Gordy asked Evan. "Buster won't give me squat, he says you're the primary investigating officer, and it's your call on what I can hear."

Evan looked at Buster. Buster winked. "I'm afraid I can't tell you anymore than he did. Maybe if we get some cooperation from Mister Lawrence, we can clear up this whole thing. Other than that, I can't offer you anything. Sorry."

Gordy was built like a gymnast, broad shoulders, thick neck, powerful arms, and a skinny waist. Even at sixty-five years old, Evan wouldn't want to wrestle him. Right now, it was plain to see he was upset. His whole body was tight. His concern was understandable. If Jake were guilty, what about Sarah and Matt? Were they involved, too?

"Damn!" Gordy cursed, "I don't like this. Seems to me what I've heard about the two victims, whoever killed them should get a medal, not be looking at hard time."

Evan suddenly felt a huge pang of guilt. They had a primary suspect whom he fully intended to arrest unless he had an airtight alibi. They also had a warrant out for the arrest of his accomplice. They had been working seven days straight, and he knew he could use a break. Evan was no fan of Ben Pike, but his killer would get prison time not a medal. If Jake was the man, fine, he could do the time. However, Evan was not convinced he was the man. If Ben had assaulted Evan's sister and he went after him for revenge, he wouldn't have played with him the way the killer had. He would have sat him down, had a little chat, then put a bullet through his heart. He wouldn't have tortured him. Or better yet, he would have engaged him in a fight, killing him with his bare hands; afterward claiming it had been self-defense. Either method would have worked for Jake Lawrence too. Lord knows he's big enough to handle Ben Pike all by himself, Evan thought. So why kill Pike and make it so obvious? If Jake killed him, revenge was the motive, but Buster was right, he couldn't be so stupid as to implicate himself and certainly not his sister. It had to have been someone else. They were missing something, and the only place Evan could think to look was at Ben's hunting camp. Whether they held Jake or not, he decided he would ride up there early tomorrow morning to have another long, slow look. Maybe something would come to him.

  Evan's phone rang and he flinched. It was Suzy. "Mister Emmings just notified me, he's finished with Mister Lawrence."

  "Thanks Suzy." Evan hung up and nodded at Buster. "You ready to talk to Jake?"

  "Yes, I am. Gordy you're going to have to excuse us for a while. You can stay here or maybe if you're hungry at all you can go across the street to the café. I'll come round you up when we're done."

  Gordy stood and picked his Stetson off the hat rack. "Yeah the café sounds good. I could use something to eat."

  "You go on over there and we'll be along when we've finished here," Buster said.

  "He doesn't look real happy," Evan commented to Buster as they walked down the hall to the detention room.

"Can you blame him? He's got to be thinking if Jake is involved, maybe his son and daughter-in-law are too. I've known him for over forty years and even though I don't see him often, I've never seen him shook up 'til now."

Evan unlocked the door and the two deputies went in. Jake and Ace sat at the table across from each other. Ace stood briefly when Buster introduced him to Evan. "Gentlemen," Ace stayed standing when Buster and Evan sat down, "my client wishes to cooperate with your investigation, but we'd also like to know what makes him a suspect."

"Will it change his answers?" Evan asked.

"No, it won't, but it may delay the process." Ace looked at Evan. "Look, Deputy Coleman, I'm not a criminal lawyer, which is fine because I don't believe Mister Lawrence is a criminal. However, if you intend to arrest him, I recommend he doesn't make a statement at this time."

"Why would that be?"

"You obviously have some sort of evidence that would appear to incriminate Mister Lawrence. I told you I'm not a criminal lawyer, therefore, I'm not familiar with all the tricks of the trade. I certainly wouldn't want to compromise his defense with bad advice."

Evan sighed. He felt like arresting Jake and telling this two-bit shyster to go home. "Look, Mister Emmings, we're investigating a murder and you're right, we do have some evidence that appears to incriminate Mister Lawrence. Now if he cooperates, maybe we can clear this up and all go home. If he can't explain things to our satisfaction, we may have to arrest him and then most of us can go home. It's your choice, yours and his."

Ace turned to Jake. "I believe the deputy has given us an ultimatum. I think you should answer the questions, but pretend he's an IRS auditor and don't elaborate your answers. Just answer the question."

Evan had to smile. He'd never been compared to a tax man before. "Mister Lawrence, according to your sister, you were present sixteen years ago when she was raped by Ben and Abel Pike. Is that correct?"

"Yes, I was there."

"Would you please tell us what happened that day?"

Jake gave them a brief account of the incident. It matched what they had heard from both Sarah and Jason. It was also consistent with what Abel had told Raleigh in his letter of confession.

"Are you aware Ben Pike was murdered on Friday of last week?"

"Yes, my sister told me."

"Can you account for your whereabouts on Friday of last week and Monday of this week?"

"A friend and I went to Pagosa Springs Thursday afternoon. We were there all weekend. We came back to my sister's place Monday morning about ten."

"Would that friend be Dale Kupfer?"

"Yes."

"Did you borrow Matt Mason's horse trailer and three of his horses for this trip to Pagosa Springs?"

"Yes, but we didn't borrow the grulla paint or the sorrel paint."

Evan ignored Jake's reference to the two specific horses that were tied to the crime scene. "Is there anybody in Pagosa Springs who can attest to your presence there?"

"I don't know. We didn't stay in a motel. We went up in the mountains and camped."

"Do you own a rifle?"

"Yes."

"What caliber?"

"It's a model ninety-four, thirty-thirty Winchester."

"Where is that rifle now."

"In Matt Lawrence's gun safe."

"Did you have it with you last weekend when you went to Pagosa Springs?"

"Yes."

"Do you have the combination to Matt Lawrence's gun safe?"

"No."

"How do you know your rifle is in that safe?"

"I watched Matt put it in."

"Do you know if it's still in there?"

"No, not for certain, but I assume it is."

So far Evan had been easy on Jake. Now he gave the ratchet handle a pull. "Do you have any idea how a glove with Ben Pike's blood on it got into Matt Lawrence's horse trailer?"

Jake's face started to pale. "No, no, I don't have any idea how that could be."

"Do you know what condition Ben Pike's body was in when I found him?"

"Only what my sister told me. The same as you told her."

"Do you have access to the animal tranquilizer, ketamine?"

"Yes, I mean no. I used to sell vet medical supplies, but I don't any more so I no longer can get it."

"But when you sold vet supplies you did have access to it?"

"Yes." There were tiny beads of perspiration forming on Jake's forehead.

"Can you tell me how a pubic hair from Ben Pike came to be in Matt Lawrence's horse trailer?"

"Good God, no! I have no idea."

"Can you tell me how a hair from Sarah Lawrence's daughter, your niece, Taylor, was found at the scene of Ben Pike's murder?"

Jake went from pale to white. He shook his head. "No, I have no idea how that could be."

Evan paused briefly, but only briefly. "Do you know a woman by the name of Raleigh Pike?"

Jake swallowed hard. "Yes, I do."

It had been a long shot on Evan's part. Even he was surprised by Jake's answer. "How do you know her? What's the nature of your relationship?"

"We're friends?"

"How friendly?"

Jake regained his color quickly. "We've had a couple dates. I'm not sleeping with her. In fact, I haven't seen her for almost two months."

"When did you meet Raleigh Pike?"

"Last June, at a bar in Creede. I didn't know she was married to Abel Pike. Her last name didn't even ring a bell for me."

Ace spoke up. "Jake, nothing extra, just answer the question."

Evan ignored Ace. "Why is that, Jake? Why didn't her name ring a bell?"

"I was only eight when the incident happened. My sister told me we could never tell anyone what happened. She told me to forget it. I forgot it—completely."

"You're saying you didn't remember the incident? You had completely forgotten it? How could that be? You just related it to me."

"Yes. I didn't remember it until my sister reminded me."

"Did you ever tell Raleigh the story about Ben and Abel assaulting you and your sister?"

"No. How could I? I didn't remember it."

Evan paused to allow Buster to start. "Jake, did Raleigh ever confide in you about her relationship with her husband." Buster's tone was soft and conciliatory.

"No, she didn't. We only went out twice. She told me she didn't want to get too deep in a relationship because she had to see if her marriage still had a chance."

"What did you think about that?"

"I respected her for it. I thought she was being honest."

"Jake, I'm going to be honest with you too. We have evidence that incriminates you. You and your friend, Dale, had Matt's horse trailer during the period when Ben Pike was murdered. We found Ben's DNA in the trailer when it was searched Tuesday evening. We found a strand of hair from your little niece at the scene of Ben's murder. We found hair from a horse owned by your sister at the murder scenes of both Ben and Abel. Someone fired a shot at Raleigh Pike with a thirty caliber rifle. Ben's body contained traces of the drug ketamine. All these things tend to give us the impression you were involved in two murders. Can you help me out here?"

Jake looked from Buster to Evan and finally to Ace. Ace nodded to him. "You can speak freely Jake." He now knew all the evidence against Jake was circumstantial. It was incriminating, but based on what Jake had told him in private, he was certain he could deal with it.

"I didn't kill anyone, and I have no ideas on how this evidence against me came to be. I didn't even remember anything about my sister being raped sixteen years ago until she reminded me of it the other day. Dale and I borrowed the trailer Thursday afternoon. The two horses you say were involved had already disappeared. We drove straight to Pagosa Springs. We had a couple of beers and a steak in one of the local salons, I don't remember the name, but Dale put the tab on a credit card. Then we drove to a trailhead, and rode up into the mountains. At daybreak Monday we rode back to Pagosa Springs, packed up, and drove back to South Fork. That's all that happened."

"Were you hunting?"

"Not seriously. I have an elk tag, but Dale didn't want to spend the money for a non-resident license. Besides that area is on a draw; he couldn't have gotten one anyway. If I had come across a nice bull, I might have shot it, but I didn't. We were just up there for the fun of it. We fished mostly. The last time we were up there we found some beaver ponds full of trout. We went back to see if they were still hungry."

"At the time you borrowed the three horses you took to Pagosa Springs, were you aware the grulla paint horse your sister owned had been stolen and then later returned?"

"Yes, I already told you, we all knew. Dale and I helped Matt look for her on Thursday. That horse is so friendly an untrained monkey could steal it."

The questions and answers continued for another ten minutes, but in the end Evan and Buster were right where they started. They had the evidence, Jake couldn't refute it, nor could he offer solid proof of his whereabouts. They had to arrest him or let him go. There was a long pause when they finished. Jake looked at the table. Evan looked at Buster and Ace looked from one deputy to the other. It seemed like everybody knew what was coming.

"Jake Lawrence," said Evan in a clear and steady voice, "You're under arrest for the murder of Ben Pike."

24

Jake didn't flinch. He was through being afraid. Now he was mad. "So now what?"

"So now we have to lock you up. You'll stay here until you can be transferred to either the courthouse in Salida or most likely, Denver. I have to call the state prosecutor to find out. It's my guess you'll be transferred to Denver."

"What about bail?" asked Ace.

"The prosecutor's office will have to decide that, but I'll call right now and explain the situation. On any account, you won't be able to post bail here."

Evan opened the door to the cell Jake had been held in for most of the morning. "How long will I be in here?" Jake asked when Evan twisted the key to the lock.

"No longer than necessary. Overnight at the maximum." Evan handed Buster the key ring. "I'll go make the calls."

Buster nodded. "Jake, are you hungry at all? I know I am. The café across the street has pretty good food. How about I get you some lunch?"

Jake sat down on the cot at the back of the cell. "Unbelievable! That stupid bastard Ben Pike gets murdered and I get arrested for it. Yeah, I'm hungry. Bring me something good."

Buster said he would, and left Jake alone with his lawyer. "I'll get you out as soon as possible. Try not to worry. From what I've heard, all the evidence is strictly circumstantial. There's nothing that physically puts you at the crime scene."

Jake was upset. "That's because I wasn't physically at the damn crime scene!"

"I believe that, and I also think both these deputies believe that."

"Then why'd they arrest me?"

"They had to. Even though the evidence is only circumstantial, all of it points to you and Dale. They probably issued a warrant for him too."

"That's comforting. I'll bet he's as thrilled as I am. Maybe we'll get consecutive convict numbers and share a cell."

Ace smiled. "I know you think it's bad, but trust me. I don't believe those deputies are ready to quit the case. Try to relax." Ace doubted that would be easy for Jake. "Is there anything I can do for you in the meantime?"

"Just get my young ass out of here as soon as possible is all."

After Evan brought the state prosecutor up to speed, he called Cheree. "We charged Jake," he told her. "I don't feel real good about it, but at least now I can forget about him and keep going on the investigation. I want to ride up to Pike's camp again tomorrow morning. There has to be something up there I missed."

"You want some company?"

"Don't get me wrong, I'd love your company, but I need to do this alone. I want to sit there and think with no distractions."

"I'd be a distraction? You don't think I could be helpful at all."

"Your being a distraction is a problem with me not you. You're about the most desirable distraction I could possibly imagine."

She knew he was right. She wasn't sure what would happen if they were alone together right now. Getting anything productive done might be difficult. "What about the bad weather that's due? You could get into trouble up there if we get snow."

"You looked out your window lately? It's beautiful."

"You know that can change in a hurry."

"Yeah, there's a chance, but I doubt anything serious is going to happen. I'll go at first light. If I don't do it now and it does snow, I'll never see anything."

She wished him luck, demanding he promise to call her in the evening. After he hung up, he sat thinking. *What was missing? Who rode away on horseback through the woods when I first showed up at Pike's camp? Who came back that night to retrieve Pike's rifle, the same rifle that was used to shoot Abel Pike through the heart less than three days later? The clues to the answer have to be there.* Evan was feeling like he had mishandled this case from the beginning. He smiled grimly at Buster as he came through the door.

"You don't look happy."

"I'm not, but it's not important. The prosecutor's office says they'll be back to us in an hour with answers."

"Want to get some lunch?"

"Yeah, let's go to Gordo's, not the Stockman's. I don't want to talk to Gordon or his lawyer buddy."

"You're not impressed with Ace Emmings? I thought he did well by Jake, and he didn't shut us down."

"Yeah, he's okay, for a lawyer. I just don't want to talk to them. Gordy will ask questions, and we'll have to make excuses, and I just don't want to deal with it."

"Okay, how's this? I promised Jake I'd get him some lunch. I'll go to the Stockman's, get something for Jake, and make the excuses. When I get back you and I can go to Gordo's."

Later, after Jake had lunch and Gordon and Ace left town, Buster and Evan were sitting in El Gordo Ricaro. They were the only two in the place except for the cook and one waitress. The hands of the clock over the bar were had pushed past two, half the lights were turned off and lacking a crowd, the place was depressing. However, the food was still good. The two men had finished eating and were talking.

"We need to look at Ben Pike's will and any other legal agreements he and Ruth had," Buster said when he had finished eating.

"Yeah, can you handle that?"

"Sure, what've you got planned?"

"You seen the sheriff around at all today?"

"He was in for a while when you took Cheree to the airport. He said he had some personal business to attend to and he'd be back around five."

"Can you wait for him to fill him in?"

"Sure, you want to leave any time soon, go ahead."

"Thanks, I've got a few things I need to get ready. I'm going up to Pike's camp early tomorrow. I can't help it. I think I missed something up there. It's apparent the perpetrator spent some time there after Ben was murdered. He, she, or they must have hung around somewhere in the general vicinity. If I can find the place, maybe I can learn something."

"You want company?"

"No thanks. Cheree offered the same thing. No offense, I'd take her company over yours, but I need to be alone up there. I don't want any distractions."

Buster nodded. "Yeah, she could be a distraction. Weather might get ugly, better go prepared."

"I intend to, although the way it looks right now, I'll be in my shirtsleeves."

"How long do you plan to be up there?"

Evan shrugged. "Until I find what I'm looking for or I'm satisfied there's nothing to find. I'd like to come down while there's still daylight. What are your plans for tomorrow?"

Buster leaned back in his chair. "Well, I guess I'll just hang around the office, at least until eight when they move Jake out. After that, I'll see if I can get Ruth to let me see Ben's will without a subpoena."

Evan grabbed the check. "My turn. I've got to spend some of this big money I've been making."

When Evan went home, Buster went back to the office. "Anything happening, Suzy?"

"Yeah, Max is here. He wants to know what you want him to do with the prisoner." Suzy made a face. "Jeez, prisoner sounds weird. We so seldom have anybody locked up."

"That's a good thing. I'm too old to have to deal with many prisoners. I'll go talk to Max."

Geoffrey Maximillian, One in a Million Max, or Max for short, was a second shift deputy. Max followed orders exactly and wanted exact orders. He was a stickler for details, fastidious in his appearance, and in Evan's words, "the most anal son-of-a-bitch I ever met." Buster liked him. He could be depended on to do whatever you told him without fail. Even Evan admitted he was a good deputy. Buster spent a half hour with Max going over details.

"His sister and brother-in-law from South Fork will be here around six. They're bringing him supper and some clothes. Look through anything they want to give him, and don't unlock the cell unless you have to evacuate the building. We haven't lost a prisoner in the forty years I've been here."

"How many we had in here in that forty years?"

"Never mind. If you have any questions at all, call me at home?"

"What if it's after ten?" Max asked.

"Call me."

"What if Billy has questions I can't answer?"

Billy was the deputy who would be on duty in the office from midnight until seven in the morning. "There are two marshals coming from Denver to pick up the prisoner at eight. Tell Billy I'll be in by six-thirty. Tell him to call me if he's got problems."

"What if we can't get you?"

"Call Evan, and don't ask me what you should do if you can't get him either."

"Call the sheriff, right?"

"Right, that's why he gets paid the high salary. Make him earn it. I'll fill him in before I leave."

After he had Max squared away, he sat down at his desk. It had been a long day. He hoped there were no problems tonight. *Now, if Clouseau would show up so I could leave, I'd be a happy man.*

The sheriff had been almost invisible since the governor rebuked him for shooting off his mouth to the TV reporter from Denver. Except for the other day when he followed Cheree around the office like a freshly weaned colt chasing its mama, he'd made himself scarce. Buster didn't have much time to think about it until now, and now he thought it was odd. It wasn't like him to keep his nose out of the daily business of his deputies. Actually, his job demanded he be involved enough to effectively supervise and manage the department. The problem with this particular sheriff was he didn't know how to manage, he only knew how to interfere. However, for the past few days, he had seemingly ignored the department or at least he had ignored Buster and Evan. *Maybe he's out looking for a new job. That wouldn't break my heart.*

True to his word, the sheriff returned to his office at five. Buster spent almost an hour with him informing him of all the events that had transpired during the past two days. He supplied every important detail, even expressing his doubts of Jake's guilt. He unintentionally speculated, "If Jake really were guilty, it would be nice if someone could get him to confess. If he did it, I don't know why he won't admit it," Buster told his boss. "With the mountain of evidence we have, it seems to me he'd be smart to cooperate. Considering who was murdered and what they did to him and his sister, a jury would probably be very sympathetic if he'd just own up to it." Buster slowly shook his head. "I don't get it. Either he's innocent or I guess Evan and I just couldn't get through to him. Too bad, would have saved everybody a lot of trouble."

Normally Buster never confided in the sheriff, he just didn't trust the man, but he was frustrated and tired. Talking, even to his boss, was therapeutic. He had no idea what the sheriff would do with the information he'd shared with him. If he had any idea how Jake Lawrence would be thinking by six-o-clock tomorrow morning, he wouldn't have done it. It did, however, get things moving.

"Maybe you two just haven't said the proper words to convince Mister Lawrence of his difficult situation." The contempt in Sheriff Tate's voice was notable.

Buster ignored the thinly veiled insult. "Yeah, I guess you're right. Well, he won't be our problem after eight-o-clock tomorrow. I'm going home." Buster got up to leave, "Good night, Sheriff."

"Yeah, see you in the morning, Buster," the sheriff said to his back. Buster didn't see the malicious grin on his face.

By eight that evening Evan was ready, everything he thought he'd need and more was packed in the little horse trailer. His plan was to saddle Diablo first, and trailer him to the Pike place. Ordinarily he never hauled a saddled horse. He considered it risky, but this was only for a few miles. Saddling Diablo in the barn before he left meant he wouldn't be doing it in the dark at the Pike place. He wanted to be on the trail at first light, about a half hour before sunrise. *If all goes well, I'll be on the scene before nine and have six hours to look. For what? I don't know what I'm looking for!*

Ever since Abel Pike's funeral, he'd felt a growing uneasiness that something was very wrong with his perception of the case. The idea Ben Pike was murdered in revenge for the rape of Sarah Lawrence was just too convenient. It was looking too good to be true, therefore it wasn't. Someone was framing Jake, and so far there was no serious evidence of any kind to indicate who that might be. The only possible hint was the shot fired at Raleigh.

She could have easily done that herself. If she had, she either craved attention or was doing her best to look innocent. If he couldn't find any answers on the mountain tomorrow, he and Buster would have to go back over Abel's homestead with a fine tooth comb. He hoped any big weather would hold off for a few more days. A heavy snowfall would wipe out any clues left on the ground. He poured himself three fingers worth of single malt and called Cheree.

Amy was waiting for Buster when he got home. A few years more than half his age, she had a lithe, lean physique, eyes so brown they were almost black, and short dark hair framing a pretty face. She was wearing black tights and a black silk blouse unbuttoned to the waist over a skimpy, sleeveless, black tee shirt. She embraced him as soon as he came through the door. "I was feeling very amorous," she told him.

He threw his hat on the table. "Was?"

She smiled. "Still am."

She looked like a sleek, slinky cat. "Your place or mine?"

"Look, if we're going to argue about it, the deal is off."

He scooped her up effortlessly and carried her into the bedroom. Much later, after they had eaten supper and gone to bed for a second time, Buster woke. He couldn't get back to sleep. He kept thinking about Jake Lawrence being in jail. Buster was certain Jake was being framed, but who was the framer. He tossed and turned until Amy woke.

"What's the matter, buddy," she asked sleepily.

He kissed the back of her neck and patted her hip. "Go back to sleep." He waited a few minutes before sliding out of bed. She obeyed immediately and was asleep again before he got out of the room.

Buster stumbled into the kitchen. The clock on the wall told him it was early, only four-thirty. Considering his options, he decided to stay up. He began ransacking the refrigerator, grabbing four eggs, half a small onion, a chunk of green pepper, and six slices of thick bacon. He chopped the bacon, pepper and onion, and scrambled everything together with the eggs. He toasted four slices of bread, buttered them heavily, combining everything into two hearty Denver sandwiches. The kitchen smelled like the grill at the Stockman's Café when he was finished. The way Buster ate, his cholesterol should have been measured in pounds per gallon, but it was actually under one eighty. He was strong and fit with a better physique than most forty-year old men. The only thing that gave any indication of his age was his white head of hair. However, there was a still a big fire in his furnace, to which Amy could attest.

While he ate, he was thinking about Amy and the way she looked last night. Half-way through the second sandwich, he almost choked. "Cat!" he said out loud. "That old man across the river from the Lawrence place said he saw a big, black cat! He didn't see any damn cat, he saw a woman in a cat suit." He took a drink of coffee to help the last bite of sandwich on its way down. *No, not a cat suit, a black wet suit. She parked her car on the old man's side of the river, swam across to Matt's side of the river, and planted the phony evidence in his horse trailer. Now who's the woman?*

By the time Buster finished eating and cleaned the kitchen, it was well after five. He decided he might just as well get dressed and go to the office. As soon as the marshals took Jake away, he would drive back to South Fork to talk to the old man again; maybe have another look around to see what he could see.

Buster wasn't the only one having trouble sleeping. Jake was as restless in his little cell as a fresh caught mustang on his first night in a corral. Sarah cried when she saw him in jail, and that hadn't helped his disposition at all. He had slept fitfully since midnight, waking every few minutes to consider his situation. Young, strong, and extremely self-confident, great patience might someday be one of his virtues, but it wasn't now. He wanted out, and he was cursing Jason Pike for putting him where he was. "It had to be that miserable, little weasel," he told himself. Since Sarah had reminded him of that fateful day sixteen years ago, all the hatred he'd felt for the Pikes had come back. However, now that two of them were dead, all Jake's rancor was directed towards the sole survivor, Jason. *I didn't kill Ben and Abel, but if I get my hands on that little son-of-a-bitch Jason, I'll tear off body parts until he confesses.* Physically, Jake probably could tear Jason limb from limb, but he wasn't strong enough to bend the steel bars of his cell. He squeezed his eyes shut. *Think, Jake, think! How the hell can I get out of here?* He'd convinced himself if he could get to Jason, he could use him to prove his innocence.

    The early morning hours passed slowly as he alternated between pacing the floor and trying to sleep. By five he had a plan. He knew where he was going when he broke out, but he would have to wait for another deputy to arrive before his simple plan would work. Only one deputy, Billy, was in the office, but there were two more deputies out patrolling. When one of them returned, Jake could act.

    While Buster was cleaning up the mess he made cooking breakfast, Evan was in the shower. He'd slept well, but wanted to be on the trail by six-thirty. When he was dressed, he would eat something before he saddled and loaded Diablo in the trailer. He wanted to leave the house by six-fifteen at the latest. He didn't intend to stop by Ruth's house on the way in. She was still in Colorado Springs with Jason anyway. He'd drive past the house all the way to the back fence line, and ride the trail into the mountains. He estimated he'd be at the camp well before nine.

    Evan didn't like the smell of the air when he went out to the barn. It had the damp, tangy aroma of dead, wet leaves, but looking up, he could see dim stars through thin, high clouds. There was only a slight breeze. "It's going to blow over," he told himself in an effort to make it happen.

The sheriff was also up early. He'd been considering what Buster told him last night. If Jake Lawrence was guilty and he could get him to talk, he'd be the hero. Sure Buster and Evan had brought him in, but he'd be the one who got the confession. Solving the case would be his doing and actually Buster and Evan hadn't even picked Jake up, he turned himself in. This would get him big points with the governor.

Now if the sheriff had been thinking straight, he might have considered why a guilty suspect would turn himself in and then be unwilling to talk, but the sheriff wasn't thinking straight. He was only thinking about the glory that would be his.

There were others awake at this hour also. Ruth, Jason, and Veronica Valdez had decided to ride up to Ben's camp before it was snowed in to collect his personal effects. As the sheriff drove to the courthouse, Jason was in the barn preparing to saddle horses.

The sheriff arrived at the office before Buster, and went straight to the detention room. Billy was sitting at the desk reading the Denver newspaper. The prisoner was fully dressed, lying on the bunk at the back of the cell.

"Mornin" Sheriff. You're in early," Billy announced as if the sheriff might not know where he was or what time it was.

He nodded. "Billy, I want to talk to the prisoner in private."

"You bet, Sheriff." He got up from his chair. "Holler if you need me."

When Billy was out of the room, the sheriff moved close to the door of Jake's cell. Jake got up from the bunk, and slowly ambled to the front of the little cell. Show time!

The two men stared through the bars at each other. The sheriff was more than just a little intimidated by Jake's size. Jake was thinking how easy this could be.

He lightly wrapped his big hands on the bars directly opposite the sheriff's neck.

"I'm the sheriff. I can help you or I can hurt you," he told Jake.

"Yeah?" Jake replied wondering what kind of bozo is this guy. "How might that be?"

"It's like this," the sheriff took a step closer to the bars and lowered his voice. "You've only been talking to my deputies. You want to tell me what really happened, I can cut you a deal. Make things a lot easier for yourself. Hell, with a sympathetic jury, you could probably walk away a free man."

Perfect, Jake thought. He took a long slow deep breath. With his right hand, he snatched the sheriff's left arm at the wrist and pulled hard. The sheriff suddenly found himself flying face forward into the bars. He instinctively raised his right hand to catch a bar. He missed and his head banged against cold steel instead. A brilliant white light flashed behind his eyes. He almost passed out. Jake immediately grabbed the sheriff's sidearm with his left hand and took a short, quick step backwards. The sheriff's left arm, up to his shoulder, was pulled up tight into the cell. Jake tucked the sheriff's gun into the waistband of his pants. Bending Tate's arm at the elbow, Jake began twisting his forearm up, backwards, against Tate's elbow. The sheriff was suddenly in great pain and a cold sweat. He was stuck against the cell. He couldn't move backward or sideways to take the pressure of his arm, and he damn sure couldn't pull away from Jake. Jake glanced down at the pistol he had confiscated. It was a .44 magnum with a seven and a half-inch barrel.

"You been watching too many Dirty Harry movies, Sheriff." Pulling it from his waistband, he pointed it at the sheriff's forehead as he pulled back the hammer. The sheriff watched cross-eyed as the cylinder rotated a fifth of a turn. Now there was a live round in front of the hammer.

"Get Billy back in here. Make things a lot easier for yourself."

The sheriff yelled for Billy so loud he lost control of his bladder. Billy came at a dead run, drawing his gun as he entered the room. Billy was probably the only deputy on the force who had any affection whatsoever for the sheriff, mostly because he very seldom had to deal with him. Some of the other deputies might have considered different alternatives. When Billy burst into the room and saw the situation, he immediately lowered his revolver. "Easy, Jake," he cooed. "Just take it easy. You're in enough trouble the way it is."

"Thanks for the concern, now get the key and unlock the door. And put your gun down on the desk."

Billy complied. The sheriff was grateful. Keeping a firm grip on the sheriff's wrist, Jake ordered Billy into the cell. "All the way to the back!" He motioned with the pistol. "Lay down on the floor!" When Billy was on the floor, Jake released his grip on the sheriff, stepped through the door, and grabbed him at the back of the neck before he could get away. The sheriff couldn't believe how fast Jake could move. Jake eased the hammer down on the big pistol, stuffing it back into the waistband of his trousers. He took the sheriff's cell phone from the case on his belt, none too gently pushing him into the cell with his deputy.

Stumbling forward two steps, the sheriff spun around. "You're a damn fool!"

Jake smiled at him. "Probably, but you just wet your pants." Swinging the cylinder open on the sheriff's hand cannon, he dumped the bullets on the floor, and threw the gun on the desk next to Billy's. Then he rifled through the drawers until he found the envelope in which Evan had put his wallet and keys. He held up the envelope for the cell's new occupants to see. "My stuff!" He grabbed his jacket from the coat rack to beat his retreat.

Out on the street he looked for his car. It was nowhere in sight. He cursed. The sheriff's SUV was parked in front of the building. Jake looked in the window. The keys were in it. "What the hell have I got too lose at this point?" he asked himself. He jumped in and roared off to the south, towards the Pike ranch.

25

Jake made a U-turn in the street and drove south on 285. He knew where the Pikes lived. He'd been there with Dale. His plan was to drag Jason's sorry ass out of bed and make him confess. Then he would continue to drag him into Saguaro where he could confess again, this time for Buster to hear. "Better get it in writing first," he said out loud. As he cleared town and began to accelerate, he noticed the gas gauge. The needle was below the empty mark. Sheriff Tate had a bad habit. He always ran his vehicle almost out of gas before he refilled. He'd started doing it as a teenager. He always had a car, but seldom enough money to fill the tank. Now as an adult, even with the credit card in the county's name, he was still constantly running on empty.

Jake banged his fist down on the steering wheel. "Son-of–a bitch! I'm surrounded by incompetents!" He wondered how far he would get before the tank was empty.

Nine miles down the road he got his answer. The vehicle bucked twice and started to die. Jake rotated the steering wheel from side to side. The truck swerved back and forth, and the engine came to life as the fuel pump found a little wave of gas. Jake took his foot off the accelerator and when the vehicle slowed enough, he drove as far off the road as he could. He killed the headlights. He estimated he was still about two miles from his destination. *No problem, I can do that in twenty minutes.* He got out, walked back to the road, and started jogging south. It was six fifteen when he stopped running and started slowly walking up the driveway to the Pike house. He was surprised to see lights on in the barn.

    The waning moon was only a silver sliver above the mountaintops to the west, and the sun was still an hour away from clearing the mountaintops to the east. It was almost as dark now as it had been at midnight, but there was a light on in the barn. Jake walked boldly up the driveway towards the barn. He was hoping the Pikes didn't own a dog. Only when he came close to the pool of light spilling out the back door of the barn, did he start to move cautiously. There were no windows on the side of the barn from which he approached. He slid quietly along the wall until he came to the back corner. Listened intently and hearing nothing, he slowly crept around the corner towards the big sliding door. He noticed his heart was pounding and it wasn't all from his recent exertion. Reaching the edge of the door opening, he dropped to his knees to very carefully peer around the corner. Jason stood towards the center of the barn, his back to Jake. He was saddling a horse.

    Jake pulled back around the corner before he slowly exhaled. *What the hell?* He took another peek. Jason was saddling a horse all right. *But why? Why the hell would you want to go riding at this time of the morning, especially during elk hunting season? Unless he's going elk hunting, but if he is, he should already be where he wants to hunt.* It made no sense to Jake. He shivered involuntarily as he had another thought. Buster had told him about somebody firing a shot at Raleigh. *Maybe that son-of-a-bitch is going to kill Raleigh. Maybe he's going to haul the horse down to South Fork, ride through the woods to her B&B and murder her too.* There was no way Jake could know Raleigh was at Abel's house in Buena Vista.

Jake peered around the corner again to watch Jason make an adjustment to the cinch strap. There was a rifle scabbard hanging from the saddle, and Jason had a holstered pistol hanging from his belt. He noticed two more horses tied against the far wall. They were already tacked up, waiting. *What the hell were they for—accomplices? Who were they and where were they?* Considering what he had done to be here, Jake was in an extremely bad position and he realized it. If he didn't stop Jason, he could imagine himself getting blamed for whatever else Jason did. Breaking out of jail wouldn't exactly increase his credibility either. Jake pushed himself to his feet sliding his back up the barn wall as he rose. *I'll just have to stop the little bastard!*

He took a last look around the corner at Jason. He was no more than fifty feet away. Jason had his hands on the saddle horn and was just lifting his left foot into the stirrup. *Gotta get him before he mounts up.* Jake sprinted for his target.

As Jason stepped up to swing his right leg over the horse, he saw movement out of his left eye. Sixteen years had passed since he'd seen Jake. He couldn't possibly recognize him. What Jason saw when he turned, was a huge apparition with fiery eyes and flaring nostrils coming at him. It was as if his brother had come back from hell to attack him. His heart jumped and as he dropped his butt into the saddle, he reached for the revolver that hung from his belt. Jake's arms and legs were pumping like pistons in an Indy car. He'd be there before Jason could point the gun his way, but he'd have to leave his feet to get to him. The horse hadn't spooked yet, but what it would do when Jake knocked Jason out of the saddle was anybody's guess.

Another step and he was six feet closer. Jason had his hand wrapped around the gun butt. In slow motion, Jake watched him start to pull it from the holster. *Now,* and stretching forth his arms, he launched himself at Jason's mid-section. Tucking his head behind Jason's back, Jake tried to encircle his upper torso and hopefully restrict the use of his arms. Too bad the horse didn't cooperate. Normally steady, this was too much for the animal. When Jake left his feet, the horse reared and leaped forward. Jake's missed his tackle, crashing to the floor on his right shoulder behind the departing horse. He tucked into a ball, converting some of his inertia into a roll that carried him over and back onto his feet.

When the horse reared, Jason was thrown up and back. Jake's glancing blow gave him a twist to the left and when he departed the saddle, his right hand came up bringing the gun with it. As he was going down, he instinctively extended both arms to break his fall. He hit the ground and tried to roll.

The rude concussion of the pistol's discharge, roared in Jake's ears as he bounced to his feet. He thought Jason was shooting at him. He spun around and charged forward. Hopefully, he could knock him down before he could fire again.

Buster had a lot on his mind as he drove to the courthouse. He was eager for the marshals to move Jake out so he could get down to South Fork. He needed to talk to the old man across the river from Matt and Sarah's place again and look around some more. He also had done some thinking about Raleigh and Jason's girlfriend, Veronica. He had some questions for both of them. It was going to be a busy day.

He parked directly across the street from the courthouse. A raindrop hit him in the face when he got out of the car. He thought about Evan and wondered how far he'd get before the snow started.

As soon as he entered the building, he heard the yelling. Billy was calling for help. "Hey! Down here! Help! We need help!"

Drawing his revolver, Buster slowly walked down the hall to the detention room. "Billy, is that you?"

Billy recognized Buster's voice. "Yeah, Buster it's me! We're locked in the cell."

Buster entered the room in a crouch, gun in both hands, hammer back, ready to shoot. He scanned around the room, and stopped at the cell. Jake was gone. Billy and the sheriff had taken his place. "Get us the hell out of here!" the sheriff demanded. Buster noted the wet spot at the crotch of his trousers that ran half way down both legs.

Retrieving the keys off the desk where Jake had left them, next to the sheriff's gun, Buster unlocked the door to the cell. Sheriff Tate grabbed his gun and phone off the desk, and hurried out of the room.

Billy just finished explaining what had happened when the sheriff burst back into the room. "The son-of-a-bitch stole my truck!"

Buster looked at Billy. "Call the state patrol. Tell them the situation and see if they can get a chopper in the air." Then he used his phone to call Evan. He let it ring until the answering machine came on. He hung up and dialed Evan's cell phone. "Where are you?" he demanded when Evan answered.

"Good morning to you too. On the road."

"On the road where?"

"About six miles from the Pike place. What's going on?"

"Jake busted out of jail. He stole the sheriff's truck."

"Not starting off to be a good morning for Clouseau I'd say," Evan said after Buster gave him the details. "You think Jake could be headed for the Pike ranch?

"He could be. I believe he blames Jason for the mess he's in."

"I'll call you as soon as I get there. Better alert the State Patrol and the Salida PD just in case."

"Already done. The State Patrol is going to try to get a chopper in the air. Maybe we can recover him before he gets too far."

Evan hung up and stepped on the gas. The pickup had no emergency lights and he was pulling the trailer so he couldn't go too fast. A raindrop spattered against the windshield. "Great!" he said. "Just great." He eased back when he hit eighty. "No sense going any faster," he told himself.

    Jake took two steps in Jason's direction and stopped. Jason was piled up ten feet in front of him. He was on his hands and knees, head hanging down almost as if he were trying to look under him, at his chest. As Jake stood and watched, Jason attempted to stand, but it seemed as if his body wouldn't obey. Jake eased closer. Jason slowly lifted his head. He tried feebly to reach out with one hand. That wasn't working for him either. He stared at Jake for a brief instant, and collapsed in the sand of the barn floor. Cautiously knelling beside him, Jake put a hand on his shoulder to roll him over. He involuntarily jerked back. Jason had a bloody red hole in the center of his chest. The revolver was lying underneath him. Jason had his finger on the trigger when he hit the ground. His arm folded up under him, and he shot himself through the heart.

    Jake slowly rose to his feet. This wasn't going at all the way he planned. *What to do now?* He wanted to run; get as far away as possible just as fast as possible. If no one ever knew he was here, no one would ever know he had a hand in it. He wasn't thinking all that clearly when a shrill scream split his thoughts. Turning quickly, he saw Ruth Pike wearing blue jeans, a robe and slippers, standing in the open doorway. She had obviously heard the shot and come running.

    "What have you done?" she wailed at him louder than he thought was possible. "What have you done?" she screamed again. "You killed him! You killed them all!"

    He held out his hands in a feeble gesture of submission. "No, you're wrong. It was an accident. I only wanted to talk to him."

    "You lying, bastard! You killed him! Are you going to kill me too?" she demanded. Then she saw Jason's horse standing still, it had only gone twenty feet before it stopped. Ruth looked at the rifle scabbard hanging from the saddle.

Jake followed her gaze, instantly reading her mind. He sprang to the horse, and grabbed the reins. "No, I didn't kill him!" he told her, leading the horse outside the barn, away from Ruth. "I didn't kill anybody!" His intention was only to get the rifle out of Ruth's reach, but when he got outside the barn, he saw headlights coming up the driveway. "Damn it," he cursed, and without thinking, he swung into the saddle, galloping away; across the field to the west towards the mountains ahead. The back gate was open, and the horse recognized the trail to Ben Pike's camp in the hills. Over his shoulder the lights from the vehicle stopped dancing. The car had come to a stop.

When Evan turned into the driveway, he was surprised to see lights on in the house and the barn. Assuming Ruth and Jason must have returned from Colorado Springs, he wasn't prepared for what he found. First he knocked on the door of the house. After a minute without a response, he walked over to the barn. Scattered raindrops were falling. Evan looked up, "Just hold off for a few more hours," he pleaded. He swore he could hear faint hoof beats in the distance.

Walking into the barn, he saw Ruth on her back staring up at the ceiling. Her robe was open to the waist, blood covering her chest. Immediately behind her was another body lying face down. *Jason.* Both bodies looked lifeless.

Drawing his revolver, he slowly backed out of the barn. Pulling out his cell phone, he dialed the office. The sheriff answered. "I want Buster," Evan snapped at him. The sheriff didn't say anything, but Buster came on the line immediately.

"Yes, Evan."

"I'm at Ruth Pike's. It looks like Jake got here before I did. Jason and Ruth have been shot and I heard somebody ride off into the hills. If they're both dead, I'm going after Jake. Get out here now. Send an ambulance, and get the coroner out here too."

"Jake killed Jason and Ruth and rode off—on horseback?"

"Don't ask me to explain, but that's what it looks like. He's only got a couple of minutes on me. I'm going now. Call Cheree and get out here now!" Evan hung up and returned to the bodies. Each was shot once in the chest. Neither had a discernable pulse. Jason was dressed to ride, but his mother certainly wasn't. He quickly inspected the horse tied to the back wall of the barn. It didn't appear to have been recently ridden. Why it was saddled was a mystery that would have to wait. Jason must have planned on going somewhere when Jake caught up to him and shot him. Ruth must have heard the shot, come running from the house and Jake shot her too. "Why would Jake do this?" Evan asked himself. Not getting an answer, he decided there was no reason to hang around until Buster got there. *I'm going after him. If I can catch him, he damn sure will answer my questions.* Leaving the two bodies lying on the floor and the horse tied to the wall, he ran back to his truck.

Evan was thinking furiously. The hoof beats he imagined he'd heard were real. He must have missed Jake by scant seconds. He drove across the field to the west. The back gate was open and shifting into four-wheel drive, he kept going. The halogen, high-beams, pierced what was left of the night, but there was no horse and rider in sight. The trail through this little meadow was flat and fairly smooth. Even with the trailer hanging on the back, Evan could do thirty. He should be gaining on Jake. An occasional snowflake flickered through the swath cut by the headlights.

Evan quickly reached the end of the line, the place where the meadow ended and the trail turned to the left into the hills. He stopped the truck, killed the lights, and got out, listening, but hearing nothing. *Maybe I should have stayed at the barn with Jason and Ruth, waited for backup and the sunrise. Maybe Jake didn't go this way, maybe he turned off and doubled back. Maybe.... There!* He heard it; the dull metallic scrape of iron horseshoes against rock! Then he heard it again. Jake was going up the trail, probably no more than a hundred yards ahead of him. Evan smiled. "Gotcha, you miserable son-of-a-bitch."

It only took only minutes to get Diablo out of the trailer, but by the time he mounted up, the snow had started in earnest. The fat flakes were wet and heavy, falling so hard Evan could hear them hit the dry grass. That would change in a hurry. Soon the snow would get drier, finer, and come much faster. Evan grabbed his long drovers coat from the pickup. Made of heavy waxed canvas by a company in Seattle, it shed water better than the back of a loon. It also had a full sheepskin liner, and had kept Evan warm in all types of snotty weather. Throwing it on, he mounted up, pointing Diablo's head at the trail.

Leaving Billy and the sheriff to sort out what to do about the sheriff's pants and missing vehicle, Buster hurried to get to the Pike place. He wheeled into Pike's driveway ten minutes after talking to Evan, driving directly into the open door at the back of the barn. The headlights from the cruiser augmented the marginal light coming from the barn's overhead light fixtures. He checked Jason first. No question there, he was dead. It also appeared as if he had been shot at very close range. Moving to Ruth, he got a surprise. Laying his finger alongside her jugular, he saw her eyelids quiver, but it took a minute to find a faint pulse. She was still alive! He quickly dialed the State Patrol in Salida. He wanted a chopper. Hopefully, they could get here before the snow shut them down. All the dispatcher in Salida could tell him was they already had a request and they'd be there ASAP, weather permitting. Buster gave Ruth all the first aid he could, and held her hand while he waited.

There was no perceptible sunrise, the day merely started to lighten. Slowly, the vague shapes of trees and rocks began to coalesce from the gray mush of the snowy dawning. As the trail became discernable, Evan picked up his pace. He could see partial hoof prints in the damp dirt of the trail. And sometimes, he swore he could smell the flinty tang of sparks caused by horseshoes striking rock. That wouldn't be uncommon; more than one forest fire had been started by horse hooves, shod with iron, sparking against rocks on a tinder dry trail. He knew he was getting close. The wind picked up a notch. The snowflakes were smaller and falling faster.

Ten minutes later, Evan dismounted. The trail crossed a stretch of solid rock that wasn't cold enough yet for the snow to accumulate. Evan led Diablo across the slippery wet rock. The last thing he needed was for his horse to fall. On the other side, he found the trail again. There were fresh tracks. Remounting, he couldn't help thinking he was going to enjoy taking Jake down. In his haste, he failed to see the tracks that turned off into the woods to the right.

After grabbing the horse away from Ruth and riding off, Jake's plan, if it could be called a plan, was first to get out of sight. Then call his lawyer. He wanted to tell Asa Emmings what happened before he was captured. Then he would turn himself in again.

When he reached the gate at the west end of the property, he stopped his mount. He was about a quarter mile from the barn; close enough to see activity, but too far to discern details. He was breathing harder than the horse. Trying his phone, he had no signal. This was not turning out to be a good morning. He laughed grimly, "And breaking out of jail had been so easy!" He had no doubt the headlights coming down Pike's driveway belonged to the sheriff. Maybe the best thing to do would be to go back and give up now. He could explain to the sheriff a lot better than he could to Jason's mother. He hung his head, shutting his eyes. *Somehow*, he thought, *I'll get out of this mess.* He gave the horse some leg pressure while reining it around back towards the barn.

Just then the flat crack of a pistol shot swept past, reverberating into the nearby hills behind him. He checked the horse. "What the hell?" He strained his eyes to see into the pool of light surrounding the back door of the barn. To his amazement he saw a horse and rider exit the barn pointing in his direction. He didn't hesitate. He spun the horse around, rode through the gate, and followed the trail that led into the mountains.

The lighter the day became, the faster the snow fell. Visibility did not improve as the sunrise progressed, it merely became brighter. Evan could see no more than thirty yards in any direction. His only consolation was Jake couldn't see any better either. Very soon Evan figured he would have to dismount and continue on foot. He wouldn't be able to go any faster on horseback, and there'd be less chance of walking into an ambush. He knew Jake was dangerous, maybe even crazy, and he was certainly armed. Evan had no desire to become his fifth victim.

Ahead of Evan, just beyond the limit of visibility, Jake's horse was plodding steadily forward. It had been on this trail many times and knew it well. It also knew that at the end of the trail there would be good pasture and a ration of oats. That had always been the case, and the animal had no reason to think this trip would be any different. It was snowy, but he had done this trail in conditions far worse than this. The horse was confident. Jake, however, was not. He wore only a short jacket, and his pant legs were wet from the snow. He wasn't cold yet, but he would be soon. He had no idea where this trail was leading him, although the horse seemed to know. That gave him some comfort.

Jake also knew pursuit was close behind. He'd stopped a couple of times to hear muffled hoof falls on the rocks to his back. The shot from the barn troubled him greatly. He couldn't imagine what that was all about. The only thing he could rationalize was that whoever showed up at Pike's was not the sheriff. It was whoever killed Ben and Abel and when he had seen the situation, he shot Ruth and now was after him. Tying up loose ends. Or even worse, maybe it was that deputy, Evan. Maybe he killed the Pikes and is framing me! Jake didn't like that thought, but in his panicked state of mind it made a certain amount of sense. He urged the horse to go a little faster.

A gust of wind spilled down the mountain, swirling snow tight around Evan. He checked Diablo, deciding to dismount. He would continue on foot, leading the horse. Just as he started to pull his right foot out of the stirrup, the snow stopped. It didn't taper off or gradually diminish, it quit, instantly. The hand of God rolled up the shade and sixty yards ahead, Evan saw a man on horseback. He pulled his .30.30 Winchester out of the scabbard and raising it to his shoulder, loudly announced, "Jake Lawrence! This is the sheriff. Stop now or I'll shoot!" It was an easy shot.

Jake's day had gone from bad to worse and now to horrible. He tugged back on the reins. He exhaled a long, deep sigh. *It's still early. How much worse can it get?*

Evan remounted, and rode up behind him. "Get off the horse, lay down on your belly, and put your hands behind your back."

Jake slowly got off the horse and turned to face Evan. "I surrender." He put up his hands. "I won't be any more trouble." The horse took a couple steps and stopped.

Evan stopped twenty feet in front of Jake. "Lay down on your belly, and put your hands behind your back."

"I didn't kill Jason."

"I'm tired of talking to you. You can get down on your belly," Evan pulled the hammer back on the carbine for effect, "or I can shoot you in the leg. It's your choice."

Jake complied. He had no doubt Evan was serious. "I didn't kill Jason," he said again, this time from the prone position.

Evan dismounted, stepped forward, put the rifle barrel behind Jake's head while cuffing his hands behind his back. He patted Jake down looking for a weapon.

Finding none, he took his lariat, dropped the noose over Jake's head, and snugged the slack out of it. He called Diablo over, and wrapped the lariat's free end around the saddle horn. "I'd advise you, to relax for a few minutes." He then walked over to where Jake's horse was standing to relieve Jason's rifle and scabbard from the horse. Returning to Diablo, he hung the scabbard from his saddle.

"Now," he told Jake, "I'm going to take off the cuffs. I want you to roll over, and you're going to put them back on so your hands are cuffed in front. If you do anything stupid in the meantime, I'll have my horse break your neck. Understand?"

Jake figured he was stronger than Evan, but he knew he didn't stand a chance against his horse. He nodded. When Evan unlocked the cuffs, he rolled over. Evan handed them to him, and he put them back on. "Now you can ride. Get up." He stepped back as Jake got up. "Oh, and by the way, I'm arresting you for the murders of Jason and Ruth Pike."

"Ruth Pike?" Jake was incredulous. "She was alive when I left her."

"Yeah, and I suppose you didn't shoot Jason either."

"No, it was an accident. I swear it!"

"You're going to get a chance to explain it all to a jury." Evan stepped back. He eased the hammer of the rifle down. "Get back on your horse and shut up. I'm not feeling real charitable right now."

Jake did as he was told. When they were headed back down the mountain, Jake in the lead, Evan told him to lift the rope from around his neck. "Just remember, I'm right behind you and you're easier to rope than a lame steer. I'd hate to have to bring you in with a broken neck." Jake removed the rope, letting it drop. Behind him, Evan recoiled it, and hung it on the saddle horn, ready to throw if need be. He kept his rifle cradled in the crook of his left arm.

The snow had started again, not with great intensity, but enough to blot out the background. Evan was in a hurry to get down the mountain, and was riding close behind Jake's mount, encouraging him along. When they came to the rock where Evan had dismounted and walked, Diablo lifted his head to sniff the air. He nickered a warning. Just as Evan turned his head to the left to see what had gotten the horse's attention, the killer fired. A brilliant blast of white light exploded in Evan's head, spilling him from the saddle. Only one of his feet came out of the stirrups, the other was hung up. He never felt his ankle break when the weight of his body twisted his leg into an impossible angle. As the report from the rifle echoed across the valley below, he came to rest on his back, eyes shut, his left foot still hanging in the stirrup.

26

Startled by the shot, Jake pulled his horse around to see what had happened. Watching Evan hit the ground, blood running freely from his forehead, Jake stared, immobilized, not knowing what to do. A woman stepped out of the tree line, rifle in hand. She was pointing it at him. A broad-brimmed Stetson, pulled low on her forehead, partially hooded her face, but she looked vaguely familiar.

"Get off the horse, Jake!"

"You killed the deputy!" he told her as if she didn't know.

She looked at him sharply, green eyes sparkling. "No, I'd say you were wrong." She walked towards where Evan lay. As the woman approached Evan, Diablo started backing away. When he did, Evan's foot fell from the stirrup. The woman made a quick grab for Diablo's bridle, but he turned and bolted as he'd been trained. "It doesn't matter," she said to herself and then poked Evan in the ribs with the rifle barrel. There was no movement. *Too bad, you were so good looking.* Pulling his pistol from its holster, she rummaged through his pockets until she found the keys to the handcuffs. Jake watched her, frozen in amazement.

She picked up Evan's rifle and left him where he lay. She walked over to Jake. "You're still on the horse. I told you to get off." Holding her rifle and Evan's in her left hand, she raised Evan's .45 with her right and squeezed the trigger. Jake felt a heavy punch to his shoulder, and his torso twisted with the impact. He slumped to his left and toppled from the saddle, crashing to the ground. The woman lowered the gun to her side. "Actually, it looks to me like you killed the deputy after he shot you for resisting arrest."

Jake moaned as the pain locked into his shoulder. He looked up at Veronica Valdez. "You are one crazy bitch." She smiled, ignoring the comment and walked over to where Jake lay. She looked down at him. "Who the hell are you?" He attempted to hold both his cuffed hands to his shoulder, trying to put pressure on the bleeding wound.

"Don't you know me, Jake Lawrence? I know all about you." She smiled sweetly. "I even know all about your sister."

Jake moaned again as gray waves of nausea swept over him. He tried to speak, but it hurt too much. He settled down on the ground, looking for a position that would ease his pain. Trying to force himself to breathe deeply and evenly, cold perspiration beaded on his forehead. "How many people do you intend to kill before you're done?"

"Oh, I don't know," she said nonchalantly, "maybe just one more, but I doubt it. I don't think I need to kill Raleigh."

Jake painfully raised his head to get a better look. He just figured out why she looked familiar. "You work in the college admissions office."

"Very good, Jake, you're still lucid. That's why I know so much about you. I have access to all your personal records. Or actually, I had access, I'm officially on vacation. Jason and I went to Vegas and got married two weeks ago. Big secret, no one in the family knew about it. I guess now none of them ever will. Technically Jason and I are still on our honeymoon, although I'm afraid he's not enjoying it at all."

"So why are you doing all this? Just for kicks?" He wanted to scream obscenities at her, but was afraid she'd shoot him again.

In the far off distance Evan could hear voices. The words weren't making much sense, but he could hear them. There was a burning pain in his head and an intense ache in his lower left leg that was getting more powerful every second. When Diablo nickered and Evan turned his head, his life was spared. The bullet that was intended to take him in the center of his forehead, struck him at an oblique angle. It cut a quarter inch deep groove across the right third of his forehead and continued on its way, releasing only a hundred foot-pounds of energy as opposed to the two thousand it was packing when it left the muzzle of Veronica's rifle.

He opened his eyes to regard snowflakes falling on his face. He wanted to groan, but a little voice in the very back of his head, in his brainstem actually, told him to be very quiet and lie very still. As recognition of his situation slowly returned, he closed his eyes and listened. He could hear a woman talking quietly.

"Don't be stupid, even though I admit it hasn't been without its kicks, I did it for the money. Do you have any idea how much the Pike ranch is worth?"

"No, but obviously you do."

"You know, Jake, I think while I wait for you to bleed to death, I'm going to tell you all about it. I hope you understand, if I don't tell you, I can't tell anyone and it's been too good to keep all to myself. She sat down in front of him, her back to Evan. "Where to start is the problem. I don't know how much time you've got left. And frankly, even though I don't expect the authorities will be up here for a while, I'm going to have to leave soon."

Jake looked at his shoulder. It was bleeding all right, but even though it was his shoulder and hurt like hell, he wasn't worried about bleeding to death. Freezing into a block of ice during a blizzard concerned him more. Between his wet clothes and shock, he was starting to shiver. Hypothermia would get him first. "Were you born cold-blooded or are you the innocent victim of some kind of traumatic childhood." The venom in his voice was unmistakable.

Veronica laughed. "Oh, I was a victim all right, but I got over it after I stabbed my father through the heart in his sleep. He wasn't very nice to me, although he did teach me how to ride and shoot. That's an interesting story too, but I'm afraid we don't have time for it. I'll just stick to recent events if it's okay with you."

The way his shoulder hurt, Jake was thinking he'd rather be dead, but maybe if she let her guard down, he could do something. He wasn't sure what, but he knew he'd have to try. "Start anywhere, I'm pretty much a captive audience."

Evan cautiously opened his eyes again. He was fully conscious now, and he needed to know where everyone was. From the sound of the voices, he was guessing the woman was between him and Jake with her back to him. If that was the case, he had a chance to make a move. The problem was, even with his eyes open, all he could see was a snowy sky. He had to get his head up. Evan was trying to place the voice. He'd heard it before. It was a quiet, demure voice. Slowly lifting his head until he could see the back of the woman doing the talking, he saw a long, strawberry blonde, ponytail spilling from under the hat of Veronica Valdez. *Nothing is ever easy.* He contemplated his next move.

"I met Jason about six months ago," Veronica told Jake. "He wanted to take me home to meet his mother after the first date. I figured what the hell, he wasn't bad looking and had a decent job, I thought I'd humor him. I wasn't too impressed with the ranch until Jason told me how much just the water rights were worth. He said two million, which I doubted, but I did a little checking and found out he was right. That got me interested so I decided to hang around with Jason for a while just to see if I could make something from it. After our third date he told me about how his father and brother raped your sister—gave me all the gory details." She smiled. "Jason thought I was an innocent little flower, and he wanted me to understand his sordid past. He was very happy when I told him, I didn't think any less of him for what happened. I told him he was a little young at the time to be his brother's keeper. He also told me, Ben Pike wasn't his real father. His biological father was the man who is the head of the Colorado Springs water department. Seems as if his mother had a brief affair with the guy when he was a field agent. He helped get Jason his job. Ben never knew, although I'm certain he wondered how he could have a son like Jason. From what I could see, he barely tolerated Jason. Now I was really interested in the whole family. I realized there were some serious possibilities here. Jason by himself didn't thrill me that much, but Jason with two or three million dollars was much more appealing."

She watched Jake as blood slowly seeped past his fingers. "Finding your name on the admissions list for graduate school four months ago was more luck than I could have asked for. It really was what got me started. It made getting information so much easier."

Evan put his head down, closing his eyes against the pain. He slowly worked his right hand over to his holster. It was empty. Not surprising; after all the planning Veronica put into this operation, Evan couldn't imagine her forgetting to disarm him even if she thought he was dead. And it was obvious she had aimed to kill him. A little smile briefly turned up the corners of Evan's mouth. *With some luck, I'll have a chance to fire a warning shot to her head in return.* He slowly started shifting his position to get at the pistol in the holster strapped to his ankle.

"It took me almost four months to develop the plan, but when I was done, I realized it was just too good not to work." Veronica had a smug smile on her face as she talked. "I hope you're paying attention, I won't have time to repeat myself."

"Will there be a test?"

"No, but if you're still alive, I might have to enhance your wound just a bit. Maybe another bullet will do it."

Evan worked up the cuff of his trousers and unsnapped the restraining strap of the holster. He slowly eased the pistol out of hiding. It was an eight shot, .22 magnum revolver, and the bullet it fired was a nasty little round packing a big wallop. At close range, in the right location, it produced fatal results. Evan had put over two thousand rounds through this particular pistol in practice. He could hit a quarter-sized target twenty feet away, each and every time. Veronica was less than twenty feet from him. Pulling his pant leg back over his boot, he rested his head back on the ground. He held the gun in his right hand, below his waist, concealed against his leg.

Veronica chatted on, as if she were talking to a good friend about a pleasant vacation. "So the first thing I had to do was steal two of your sister's horses. I knew where she lived because she was the name in your personnel file to notify in case you had an emergency. Another great help, thank you."

"Don't mention it, bitch." If she wanted to shoot him some more, he'd give her a reason. "How'd you even know she had a horse?"

She ignored his venom. He had no fangs. "You're not paying attention. I told you it took four months to work out the plan. I drove out to South Fork and checked on that little detail. I discovered she had lots of horses. I knew Ben was going elk hunting, in fact I told him I might be up to visit him. I had been teasing him behind Jason's back for five or six weeks, hinting at sexual delights he couldn't possibly imagine. He even bought me a horse to ride. When I showed up at his camp and stood in the doorway of his tent without my clothes, he came running. He was more than willing to let me take off his clothes and tie him to his bunk. The only reason I zapped him with a taser and injected him with ketamine was for effect. I thought it would make the scenario of a revenge killing more believable. What do you think?"

"Do you know what ketamine does? I think you're a sadistic lunatic!"

She didn't bat an eyelash. "Maybe, but I prefer to think of myself as edgy. Well anyway, you should have seen the expression on his face when I sliced off his manhood. His eyes got so big he looked like a hoot owl. Then he started to cry. I finally cut his femoral artery to put him out of his misery. He was taking too long to die anyway." Jake felt very ill and only part of it was due to his wound, but Chatty Ronnie continued on. "The way it was, that damn deputy almost caught me in the act. I barely had time to plant the hair from your sister on Ben's body and get the hell out. Forgot to take his rifle, too. I had to sneak back at night and get it. That spooked me out a little."

"Wasn't my sister's hair," Jake said.

"Pardon me. Whose hair was it tangled in the paint horse's halter?"

"My niece's."

Veronica waved her hand in a gesture of dismissal. "Whatever. It wasn't mine. Nice color though. I liked it so much I dyed mine the same shade. I also figured seeing me for the first time, it would give the sheriff something to think about. I even provided the deputy with a sample. He put on a pretty good performance retrieving it."

Blood had soaked the entire left front of Jake's jacket. Maybe, he thought, I will bleed to death. He had no idea what her last comment meant, but she didn't slow down.

"I had planned to shoot Abel the next day, but I realized Monday morning would work better for me." Veronica figured at the rate he was leaking, Jake had another fifteen minutes.

In spite of his situation, Jake found himself extremely interested. "Where'd you keep the horses over the weekend?"

"No place in particular, but I'm getting ahead of myself, let me back up." It was obvious to Jake she was enjoying this. "I told Jason last Thursday morning, that I had to visit my sick mother in Albuquerque. He didn't want me to go alone, but I told him my mother and I had never gotten along very well, and I wanted to spare him the pain of an uncomfortable situation. I told him I needed to do this by myself. He believed me. He really was a tenderhearted sap. I borrowed the horses from your sister early Thursday morning. From her place, I drove to the trailhead on the BLM land next to Pike's place. I camped near there for the night and got to Ben's camp at nine in the morning. When I was through with him, I chased his horse home and started doctoring the scene. It took a lot longer than I thought it would, but everything had to be just right. I almost got caught. I was planting horsehair in the trees when the damned deputy showed up."

"Jeez, I'll bet that was a big inconvenience for you."

"Yeah, it really was, I had to come back later and get Ben's rifle."

"What'd you want it for, you could have shot Abel with the one you just killed the deputy with?"

"This old thing?" She picked up the rifle lying at her side and waved it at him. The way she said it, one would have thought it was a party dress she had worn more than once. "It's not that accurate. I had to shoot Abel from two hundred yards out."

"Excuse me, I should have realized that. By the way, why the hell did you take two horses?"

"I still haven't answered your last question."

"Sorry, I'm having trouble concentrating."

"I took two, because I wanted it to look like there were two perpetrators. I put hair from both horses in Ben's tent too. And before you interrupt me again, after I got Ben's rifle, I rode back to the trailer and drove to Albuquerque. I put the horses in a mare motel Saturday morning and visited my mother—briefly. Saturday afternoon I test fired Ben's rifle, and by late Sunday afternoon I was in the hills behind Abel's house. When the sun came up Monday morning, I was waiting for him. He never knew what hit him."

"I'll bet that broke your heart."

She shrugged, "Sort of, I liked him, big and strong like you. My kind of man, but Jason said Ben's will left everything to Abel so he had to go."

"Did you shoot at Raleigh too?"

"Yeah, but that was just for fun, I didn't want to kill her. It was intended to keep everyone guessing. Did I tell you I liked living on the edge?"

"Yeah, at least three times. When did you plant the phony evidence in my sister's horse trailer?"

"Monday night, after I put the horses back in your sister's pasture. They really should lock that back gate, the one you can't see from the house."

"I'll be sure and tell her."

"I don't think so, but let me finish. After I dropped off the horses, I went to Creede, had some dinner and waited until it was dark. I drove back to South Fork, parked my car on the far side of the river across from your sister's place, and swam across about eleven. That was real spooky, although it could have just been the amphetamines. I had the feeling someone was watching me. But I got away with it, so it must have just been my imagination." She paused. "What do you think? I was pretty busy for a few days."

"Yeah, you've been busy, but what the hell makes you think you can get away with it?"

"I've already gotten away with it. They arrested you or don't you remember?"

"How did you know that, it just happened last night?"

"I had a feeling that deputy," and she jerked her thumb over her shoulder towards Evan, "was getting close so I had Jason call the sheriff last night to see if any progress had been made. He was only too happy to provide all the details. I have to thank you for your help though. I couldn't have done any better killing Jason and

Ruth myself. It made things so much easier for me. My plan was a little different. I figured I'd actually have to live with Jason for at least a little while before I could kill him and his mother. Your way was so much cleaner for me."

"I didn't kill Jason or Ruth." If he were going to attack her, he would have to do it soon. He felt himself weakening.

"Gee, that's funny. Your fingerprints are going to be all over Jason's pistol, which incidentally is the one that killed both of them. How do you explain that?"

"How do you explain how I killed the deputy?"

"Oh that'll be easy. When the deputy arrived, he found me in the barn with two bodies. I was badly traumatized by finding Jason and Ruth both dead. The Deputy told me to stay put and he went after you. I tried to wait, but I was so upset I wanted to help him find you so I followed him. When I got up here, I heard shots and when I finally found you, both of you were dead. He shot you with his pistol, and you shot him with the rifle from the scabbard on Jason's saddle. She waved the rifle she had used to shoot Evan at him. Oh that reminds me, I have to leave this rifle in Jason's scabbard."

"That's not Jason's rifle, you moron. It's the deputy's. He put Jason's rifle and scabbard on his horse. You remember, moron, the horse that ran away from you."

Veronica laughed. "It doesn't matter. Jason's rifle is a thirty-thirty Winchester. My rifle is a thirty-thirty Winchester, and so is the deputy's. Nobody's ever going to find the bullet that hit him. I'll leave my rifle next to you with your prints all over it, and I'll take the Deputy's with me. I'll also put Jason's pistol on your body, and leave the deputy's pistol with him." She smiled sweetly. "Any other stupid questions?"

"I don't suppose you know where Jason was going this morning?"

"Yeah, he and Ruth, and I were going to ride up to Ben's camp. Ruth wanted to get some of his stuff before the place got snowed in. Jason and I were also going to tell her about our marriage. It's so sad you spoiled everything." She laughed, "Not."

Jake stared at her, trying hard to concentrate. She had the rifle in one hand and Evan's pistol was lying in front of her. He didn't know how he could cross the distance separating them without getting shot again. "So how did you get up here ahead of the deputy?" The longer he kept her talking the longer he would live.

"That was touchy. He was right on my ass all the way. I waited as long as I thought I could and turned off the trail. He passed by me at no more than fifty feet."

"You're quite the ninja. Too bad you're going to get caught. It may take a while but they'll figure it out."

She laughed again. Jake was entertaining her. "Wishful thinking on your part. You don't know anything I don't." She looked up at the sky, "Well, I'm afraid I have to leave."

Jake knew what that meant. "Indulge me with one last question. Where'd you get the rig to haul the horses with? You don't look much like a pickup truck kind of woman, more like a Lexus or Mercedes babe.

"You're too kind, Jake Lawrence. We should have met under different circumstances. The rig belongs to an acquaintance of mine who owes me big time."

"Obviously somebody will remember seeing it parked somewhere in the vicinity of the murders. Won't he get suspicious if the police should check out his truck and trailer or is he a moron too?"

"You know, Jake, I've been ignoring your nasty little insults, but that one's going to cost you another bullet hole, maybe a little closer to your heart. As far as him talking, let me just say, I've got video tapes, and he's got a family."

Evan had been fascinated listening to her explain everything, but he figured it was now or never. He wanted to bring Jake back alive, and the snow was starting to intensify again. If he had any hope of getting Jake and himself off the mountain, he had to act now. He worked his left hand, palm down, under the small of his back.

Keeping his left leg as still as possible, he pushed himself into a sitting position. Contemplating a gunfight had kicked in the adrenalin, and it was holding the pain at bay. He'd never shot anyone in the line of duty before, but in this case he was ready. He'd even contemplated shooting her without a warning, but in spite of everything, like shooting a duck on the water, it didn't feel right. He extended his right arm towards Veronica and spoke in the toughest voice he could summon.

"Veronica Valdez, put down the rifle and turn around slowly or I'll put a bullet through your head."

Jake was just as surprised as Veronica was. He saw her blink and for the first time, her silly ass smile disappeared. It took her several seconds to speak. "Why Deputy Coleman, I thought you were dead. Strange to hear from you and apparently you've got a gun too; very resourceful." She didn't move.

"I'm not dead, but you will be in three more seconds. Put the gun down, turn around slowly." He eased back the hammer of the revolver. "I'm not going to tell you again."

The click of the hammer locking back was audible to Veronica. In an instant her beautiful plan had gone awry. This is what it had come down to. If she surrendered, it was over. If she gambled and got lucky, she could kill Evan and still get away with it. She made a split second decision. "Okay, Deputy, don't shoot, I'm putting the gun down." She glanced at Evan's pistol in front of her, the muzzle towards Jake. She was certain Evan couldn't see it. She had nothing to lose, everything to gain. Her life was standing, balanced on a knife-edge and doing a pirouette, no less. She was almost home free. Very slowly she reached out with her right hand to lay down the rifle.

"Now turn around, and put your hands down on the ground!"

As she started to turn, she snatched up the Evan's .45. The hammer was back and there was a round in the chamber. She spun around to her left as fast as she could.

As she turned, she brought her left hand under the butt of the .45 to steady it. She would fire as soon as she had Evan lined up with the barrel.

"She's got a gun!" Jake yelled.

It didn't matter. Evan saw the muzzle of his own .45 swinging towards him. He knew her head would have to be turned directly towards him before she had the gun lined up. He waited the split second it took until she faced him. Then he willed his finger to pull the trigger. The trigger and sear on the little revolver had been carefully honed to the point it required only a pound of effort to drop the hammer. Jake heard a loud crack. Veronica's head tilted back. In the instant of time between pulling the trigger and the hole appearing in her forehead, Veronica's malevolent green eyes blazed hatred at Evan. She tipped over backwards. The back of her head hit the ground with a dull thud. Her hat fell off, spilling her bogus strawberry blonde hair across the snow. Mouth gaping, she stared stupidly at the sky.

"Nice shot, Deputy. I thought you were dead. Actually, I thought we were both dead."

Evan ignored the comment and painfully sat up, groaning as he rolled over on his left hip. The snow was falling faster. He pulled the cell phone out of the carrier hanging from his belt. It came out and a major chunk fell off. *Damn, now I know why my hip hurts.* He tossed the broken phone over his shoulder and turned to Jake. "I've got a broken ankle. How bad are you hit? Can you stand?"

Jake was optimistic. "Yeah, I think so. What do you want me to do?"

"We have to get down off this mountain or we'll die up here. Where's your horse?"

Jake struggled to his feet. "Hell, I don't know. Where's yours?" As soon as he stood up he sat back down, hard. The ground was spinning.

"Damn," Evan cursed. Jake must have lost more blood than it appeared. It was obvious he was weak.

Evan crawled over to where he sat. "Open up your jacket. I want to see how bad you're hit."

Jake's world was whirling gray. "What for? There's nothing you can do about it."

Evan whistled loudly. "Don't be a pansy ass, we ain't dead yet." A minute later Diablo materialized out of the swirling white gloom. Evan called him. "Walk here, D." The horse came to his side and stopped.

"Now there's a trick I've only seen in the movies. Can you send him to get help?"

"He's a horse, not Lassie the Wonder Dog." Evan used the saddle stirrup to pull himself to his feet. He dug deep into one of the saddle bags hanging across the horse's back. He pulled out a heavy plastic bag containing some non-standard first aid supplies like morphine auto-injectors and industrial strength pain pills. Removing two compress bandages and a roll of tape, he turned back to Jake. "How's the pain?"

"On a scale of one to ten, it's about fourteen."

Evan shook seven, five milligram valiums out of a bottle. It was enough to make them both loopy, but not incoherent. "You allergic to any medications?"

"Alcohol makes me goofy."

Evan pulled a bottle of Wild Turkey out of the other bag, and sat down next to Jake. "Here take these." He stuck four of the pills in Jake's mouth and took three himself. He handed him the bottle of whisky.

"What the hell is this?"

"Bourbon. Can't you read the label? If you want something else, eat snow, I didn't bring any water."

Jake flushed down the pills, making a face. "Don't you know you're not supposed to mix drugs and alcohol?"

Evan took his three pills and didn't make a face after drinking. "Let's not make a habit of it then." He opened up Jake's jacket and shirt. The bullet had entered at the outside edge of his pectoral, exiting just under his clavicle. It had only grazed the rib cage, but blasted through the scapula leaving a jagged exit wound. Jake had probably lost at most, two pints of blood. "Missus

Pike, nee Valdez, would have had to shoot you again if she wanted you to bleed to death any time soon." He doctored Jake as well as he could with what he had. By the time he had finished, both of them were still in pain, but not overly concerned about it.

Evan's plan had been to find Jake's horse and get off the mountain, but in the last ten minutes that had become impossible. The snow was coming fast and furious. Visibility was down to twenty feet. He'd never find the horse Jake rode in on and Diablo couldn't carry them both. "Get your ass up, big boy. We're moving."

"Oh yeah? Where to?"

"Into the trees and out of the snow, at least some of it." Leaning against Diablo, Evan started to hobble away. When he turned back, Jake hadn't moved. "Look, I thought you were some kind of tough guy. Get up."

Jake struggled to his feet. He stood swaying like a palm tree in a full gale. It was obvious he needed help. Evan and Diablo went back to him. "Put your good arm over the horse. Lean on him." Jake did as he was told, and they slowly moved off into the trees, one on either side of the steady horse.

Out of the wind, Evan picked a spot for them to rest. He didn't want to be too far from the trail. He knew Buster would be looking for him, eventually he would find them. Picking the biggest tree within sight of the trail for their crash site, he pulled the saddle off Diablo's back and the bridle from his head. He cued the horse to lie down and Diablo obeyed, settling down like a huge dog. "Lay down with your back against the horse's belly," he told Jake. Jake was only too happy to comply. Next, he put the saddle blanket over Jake's torso. After tucking Jake in, he flopped down next to him, and pulled his canvas drover's coat over both of them. It would keep all three of them warm.

"With a little luck we won't freeze to death before they find us. And don't forget, you're still under arrest."

"What for? You heard that crazy bitch. She killed everybody, not me."

"You're under arrest for breaking out of jail. You don't think the sheriff is going to let that go, do you?"

"I suppose not after peeing in his pants and all."

Evan couldn't help laughing. "Wish I could have seen it."

"Yeah, it was pretty great. By the way, how come you're not dead?"

"She shot me in my least vulnerable spot."

"Damned impressive! Got any more of that whisky?"

"Yeah, but you're not getting it."

"What are you saving it for? A special occasion?"

"Shut up and rest. Save your strength."

Jake was quiet then and Evan closed his eyes. In time, Evan fell asleep and began to dream. He was lying on his back in a field of tall grass. He heard horses and when he sat up, he was in the midst of a herd of horses that stretched to the horizon. Everywhere he looked were mares with fat foals by their sides. Rising to his feet, he stood and walked among them. The mares nickered to him, and the foals took turns nuzzling his outstretched hands. He imagined he had died and gone to heaven. Tiring after playing with the foals, he lied back down in the soft fragrant grass. He quickly fell asleep, only to be awakened by the faint buzzing of a fly. He tried to ignore it, but it grew louder and louder as it buzzed around his head. He finally sat up to see if he could swat this pesky fly. As it passed over his head, he snatched at it and caught it. Slowly he opened his hand to peek at it. The fly was wearing Buster's face!

27

Buster was still kneeling next to Ruth holding her hand when help arrived. Billy was first, the sheriff following only a few minutes later. The first thing Buster noticed was his boss had changed his trousers. Wouldn't do his image any good for any more people to know he had wet his pants. "You got any choppers on the way?" Buster asked the sheriff. It was now snowing in earnest.

Sheriff Tate shook his head. "No, nobody can fly in this crap. But the paramedics from Salida said they would be here as fast as the road would allow." He looked at Ruth, "She still alive?"

"Barely. I've got the bleeding stopped, but that could be just because there's not much left. Nothing else we can do."

"How about the other one?" Billy motioned towards Jason.

"Dead. He looks like he was shot point blank. Take a look. See what you think."

Billy walked over to Jason. "Looks like he shot himself," he called back to Buster.

Buster was about to say, "Why would he shoot himself in the heart?" But Billy was right, it did look as if he'd shot himself—unintentionally. "You might be onto something, maybe he and Jake were struggling for the gun. Maybe he was trying to kill Jake." Buster didn't want to believe Jake was responsible for this carnage. He was hoping there was a reasonable explanation other than Jake being charged to answer for maybe another two more murders.

Billy agreed, "Could be, but then who shot Mom? Not Jason."

"Damn if I know. Try calling Evan. See where he's at."

Billy got on his cell phone and tried Evan's number three times. He shrugged his shoulders. "He's not answering."

"Okay, do me another favor. Can you and the sheriff check the house? I'm pretty sure it's clear, but I haven't been in there, and I don't think Evan was either."

"You got it." Billy was up for that. "Come on, Sheriff, let's go do some real work. It'll be fun. You'll get to draw your piece."

Five minutes later they were back. "Cleaner 'n a whistle." Billy reported.

The sheriff's phone rang. It was the paramedics. They had a highway patrol escort front and back, and called to say it would be only a few more minutes. Then Buster's phone rang. It was Cheree. They were forced to land in Buena Vista and would have to wait for better visibility before they could fly any farther.

"What did we do before we had these things?" Buster asked when he hung up.

"We were uninformed and happier for it," said Billy.

Billy and the sheriff watched over Ruth, and Buster wrote his notes while they waited. Outside the snow was thickening. It swirled past the open door, behind the lawmen, in great billowing clouds as the wind whipped around the corners of the barn. The paramedics, who left Salida traveling at ninety miles per hour, were quickly slowed to twenty. It took as long to travel the last three miles as it took to travel the first thirteen. Ruth had been down for a long time when they finally arrived. They worked on her even as they loaded her, but they were not optimistic. Yet there was some hope, she still had vitals when they drove away with her.

After the paramedics left, the coroner arrived, officially pronouncing Jason dead. That was no big surprise, everybody present, including the sheriff, had agreed to it. The coroner did however make one perceptive observation. When he opened Jason's jacket and shirt to inspect the entrance wound, he discovered a semi-circular shaped welt immediately below the bullet hole. He pointed it out to the sheriff and deputies. "What do you make of that?" he asked.

"Looks like the gun barrel was jabbed into his chest when the shot was fired," speculated the sheriff.

"Or, maybe he fell on it and it went off," Buster suggested.

The coroner spread apart the fingers of Jason's right hand. The web between his thumb and forefinger was cut and bloodied. "How strong was the guy you think killed him?"

"Real strong," said Billy.

"Strong enough to take the victim's hand, holding the gun, and slam it into his chest hard enough to do this kind of damage?"

"No," Billy admitted. "So what happened?"

"It looks to me as if he fell and somehow landed with his right hand up under his chest, and the gun went off. Where's the gun?"

"I don't know," Buster told him. "It wasn't laying around when I got here."

"Interesting, but unless he has to stay here, I'd like to pack him out."

Buster looked at his boss. "What do you think, Sheriff? You think we need to leave the scene intact."

Clouseau didn't hesitate an instant, "It's your call, Deputy."

Buster knew that would be his response. It didn't matter, he felt comfortable with his notes, and the coroner had photographed the body from all angles. The barn floor was a uniform mixture of sand, clay and horse manure. Soft and impressionable, it was a hodgepodge of foot and hoof prints. Absolutely nothing of the recent struggles could be discerned by studying it. There was no reason to leave the scene intact.

"No, take him with you, everything's been noted. I have a feeling we'll know before too much longer what happened here." Buster hoped he was right.

The coroner zipped Jason into a green body bag and the four of them loaded the body into the coroner's modified sport utility vehicle. Switching on the flashing lights, he crept away through the swirling snow. The three lawmen watched the blizzard devour the vehicle.

"I'm going back to the office to coordinate the operation," the sheriff announced. "What about you two?"

"I'm staying here," Buster said. "I'm going after Evan as soon as the snow lets up."

"How, on foot?"

Buster pointed to the saddled horse tied to the back wall. "I'm assuming that horse rides."

The sheriff didn't ride at all. Horses scared him. "Good luck. What about you, Billy?"

"I'm staying with Buster. I figure as soon as the snow lets up, we'll be surrounded by state patrol choppers." Then Billy turned to Buster. "I'm sure we've got a little time, how about I fight my way into town quick, get us some coffee and steak sandwiches?"

"That'd be good. Get some of those gooey caramel rolls too." Buster suddenly realized how hungry he was.

The sheriff turned his back on his deputies and walked off. "Keep me informed," he called over his shoulder.

When he was out of hearing, Billy asked, "If he's coordinating the operation, shouldn't he be keeping us informed?"

"Try not to think too much about anything he says and you'll be happier." Buster pushed Billy on the shoulder. "Get moving so you can get back here. I've got a serious craving for a caramel roll."

Billy nodded and suddenly Buster was alone again. Billy put on the siren for the trip back to Saguaro and as the rise and fall of the wailing faded into the distance, Buster felt a chill. The horse still tethered to the back wall of the barn nickered for attention. Walking over, Buster stared hard, thinking. He pulled off the saddle. He'd made a decision. As much as he hated flying, he would go up with the state patrol to search for Evan and Jake. He led the horse into a stall, made sure she had water and threw her a flake of hay. He scratched the dun mare on the head, between her ears. "All you're people are either dead or dying. I can't tell you where you'll be tomorrow. I'll guarantee you one thing though, I won't let you go to the kill buyer. You're not going to end up on some Frenchman's dinner plate." The horse set into the hay. She appeared incredibly unconcerned.

Buster watched her eat. What was Evan doing? He hoped he was all right. After a few minutes, Buster decided the barn was too cold and lonely. The horse was not much company. He went into the house to sit down at the kitchen table and wait.

He alternated between staring out the window at the swirling snow and staring at the clock on the wall with the hands that moved in extreme slow motion. Every two minutes he dialed Evan's number. It was never answered, although one time he got a busy signal; that was pretty exciting until Cheree called. "I'm worried about him," she said, "I've been calling him every few minutes, and he doesn't answer." Buster knew why he had gotten the busy signal.

"He'll be okay. He's probably just out of signal range. I'm sure he went into the trees to hole up somewhere. Maybe he went to Pike's camp."

There was a pause while Cheree considered Buster's speculation. "God I hope you're right, he owes me a date."

"Cheree, I know for a fact that's one debt he intends to pay." There was more he could have told her on that subject, but he'd never meddled in anyone's love life, and he wasn't starting now. He did like talking to her however, it made his vigil less intense, and he kept her on the line until Billy arrived with the groceries. They agreed to inform each other whenever the snow quit and they could move again.

Along with the coffee and sandwiches, Billy brought some good news. "The snow's supposed to let up in about two hours. I was talking to the state patrol. They said they'd have at least one, maybe two choppers up as soon as they could."

"The snow will be over in two hours or it's just taking a time out?"

Billy shrugged, "I don't know where the state patrol gets their weather information. I was listening to the radio and it's supposed to keep snowing all day and through the night."

"Nothing about a break in two hours?"

Billy shook his head. "Not according to the radio." He looked around the kitchen. There was a radio on top of the refrigerator. He turned it on, and the two of them listened for weather news while they drank coffee and ate caramel rolls.

Two hours later, Cheree called. "We're in the air and headed your way."

Buster looked out the window. The snow was a curtain of white, flowing past unimpeded by his wish for a letup. "It's still snowing here."

"We're betting it clears as we go. There's supposed to be a break for maybe an hour."

"I don't know where you're getting your information, but I hope it's right." Then they were disconnected.

Buster tossed the phone on the table. The clock was inching its way to eleven AM. "What a morning," Buster said. "It feels like I've put in a whole day already."

"What time did you get up?"

Then Buster remembered he had been awake since four. "Jeez, I have put in a whole day already."

Billy pointed to the window. "Check it out. The snow's stopped."

Buster looked. He could see all the way to the barn. He reached across the table and grabbed his phone. Trying Evan's number first with still no success, he dialed Cheree and was elated when she answered. "We're in the clear! I'll put the lights of my cruiser on so you get the right place."

"Okay we're just coming up on Saguaro. We'll follow 285 south until we see your lights."

"Keep an eye out for other aircraft; the state patrol said they were coming as soon as the snow stopped. We don't need a midair."

"Thanks, Buster, I'll tell the pilot. See you in about ten minutes."

The two deputies went out and started both cars. They had to trudge through a foot of snow to get to them. Neither one of them liked the thought of Evan being on the mountain, but neither of them said anything. Ten minutes later the Pike ranch looked like the parking lot at the local Helicopters-R-Us store.

Cheree's aircraft was the first to arrive, followed by two State Patrol aircraft and a medevac chopper from Colorado Springs. It had been dispatched per Billy's request early in the morning, but was forced down in Salida when the snow got thick. When the weather broke, they decided to proceed to their destination to see if they could help. Buster got everybody in the kitchen and briefed them. It was quickly decided that the governor's aircraft would stay on the ground with the medevac aircraft. Buster and Cheree would go in one state patrol helicopter and Billy would go in the other. They would search the area above the ranch until they found Evan or the weather turned ugly. Buster suspended his intense dislike for aircraft at least until they were airborne, and then he remembered why he hated flying.

"You okay with this?" Cheree asked him as they whisked up the mountainside. They were close enough to the ground that the downwash from the blades flushed the snow from the pines.
"I won't do it on a regular basis."

The fly in Evan's hand looked him in the eye. Dreaming he was shaking his head in disbelief, he woke up shaking his head. He heard engines, and Diablo was starting to fidget; moving his legs. He wanted up. "Easy, D," Evan cooed to the horse. "Jake, Jake, we have to move." Jake stayed inert. Evan hoped he was still alive. "Jake!" He shook his good shoulder. Jake moved.

"What?" He looked at Evan. "What the hell?" He was disoriented. "Where? What?" And then he felt the ache in his shoulder and remembered. "Just leave me lay here."

"Yeah, I'd like to, but my horse is going to get up, and I don't need you to get kicked in the head when he does."

Evan pushed off their makeshift blanket, dislodging a small avalanche of snow. He tried to stand, thought better of it and crawled away. Jake followed. As soon as they were away from the horse, Diablo got to his feet, shaking off snow. He whinnied and Evan was surprised when the call was answered. He turned to see two horses a hundred feet back in the woods behind them. One of the horses was tied to a tree. Must be the one Veronica rode in on, Evan thought.

"There's a horse for you. If the choppers miss us we've got a ride home." He said it mostly to make Jake feel good. There was probably no way either of them could get in the saddle. Evan resumed crawling. He wanted to get out in the open so they'd be spotted. It was slow going, but the cushion of snow under his broken ankle eased its contact with the ground. Jake stayed where he was, too weak to go any further.

As Evan emerged from the trees, the choppers passed directly overhead. One continued climbing up the mountain, the other banked hard left, circling around for another look. Buster thought he saw some color besides white and green at the edge of the trees. Roaring back to cross in front of Evan, the second chopper banked hard right over the trees. Evan collapsed face down in the snow. They had seen him.

The instant the chopper set down, Buster jumped out and ran, if you could call it running, through two feet of snow, to where Evan lay. He could tell from the weird angle his left foot met his left leg, that something was broken. He shook Evan's shoulder gently. "Hey, Partner, it's me, Buster."

Evan slowly turned his head to regard Buster. "Hey, Buddy, I dreamed about you. I can't believe you flew up here to rescue me."

"You're hit. Where?" Evan's face was liberally decorated with caked blood. He could have been the guest of honor at some satanic ritual.

Before Evan could answer Buster, Cheree came up and dropped to her knees in the snow beside Evan. He smiled lamely at her. "Hi, Babe."

"My God, Evan, are you okay? What happened?" She took off her glove and gently caressed his bloody forehead.

"Jason's girlfriend tried to kill me. She shot me in the head." He could swear he saw tears in Cheree's eyes. He smiled some more. "It's okay, I'm not going to die."

"Veronica Valdez shot you?" Buster asked.

"Yeah, and I returned the favor. Oh, by the way, it's Veronica Pike. She and Jason were married two weeks ago."

"Where is she now?"

"Right where I dropped her." He pointed at a spot. "Buried under the snow over there. Jake's back in the woods, she shot him too. In fact, she shot Abel and killed Ben too."

Buster looked over his shoulder. He saw no trace of Veronica. "Is she dead?"

"I hope so."

"You okay?"

"Yeah, I don't think I'm going to need grief counseling over it."

Then Buster saw Jake sprawled out in snow. "He dead?"

"He was alive two minutes ago. He lost some blood, but I'm sure he'll be fine. He's just not as tough as he looks."

"Your leg looks weird. You break it?

"Yeah, the ankle's broke."

"I'm going to look at Jake," Buster told Cheree. "Stay here with Evan, okay?" It was a stupid request. She wasn't about to leave his side.

"Oh, Evan, I'm so sorry."

"What for? You didn't shoot me."

She actually laughed. "No, I didn't, but I'm still sorry. Can I do anything right now?"

He grinned. "Yeah, you could kiss me a little bit, and tell me again how sorry you are that I got shot."

"I can do that." His face was cold, but his lips were warm.

Billy wallowed through the snow over to them. "Sorry to interrupt, but we gotta get our act outta here. The snow's gonna start again real soon."

Cheree pulled slowly away and stood up. Her cheeks were rosy, but it was difficult to tell if it was embarrassment or something else. "Okay, you're right. I'll get the medevac chopper up here."

"On the way, ma'am." Billy grinned. "Be here in two minutes." Then Buster called for Billy and they were alone.

"I'm going to need a lot of attention to get better," Evan told Cheree.

She knelt back down beside him. "I think I can manage that." She was about to expound on a recommended course of treatment when she heard the medevac chopper arrive, postponing all conversation.

The medics checked both Evan and Jake, and decided Jake was in more serious condition. He would go with them. Cheree didn't want Evan in Colorado Springs, she wanted him in a Denver hospital where she could watch over him. The medics couldn't argue with her, not only was she a doctor, she said she was Evan's personal physician. They gave Evan nitrous oxide until he was giggling like a lunatic, put an air splint on his leg, and stuffed him in one of the state patrol choppers with Cheree. Two state troopers dug Veronica out of the snow and loaded her into the remaining chopper for a one way trip to the morgue.

Before Evan took off, Buster stuck his head in the door, "Billy and I are taking the horses down. Got any last requests?"

The laughing gas had worn off. Evan knew Buster would take care of all the details. "Thanks, Buddy, be careful. Oh yeah, in case you get a chill, there's a Wild Turkey in one of the saddle bags."

"I think Billy might have found that already." He patted Evan's shoulder and closed the door. The blades began to spool up as Buster hurried away. He was glad he had other transportation for the trip back. The snow was starting again. It wouldn't stop until late the next morning.

As the two deputies watched the last chopper whirl away, Billy turned to Buster, "Now that's what I call a happy ending."

Buster thought he knew what Billy meant, but he wanted to make certain. "How so? Four people are dead, another one might be dead, two are shot up, and we're stuck on a damn mountain in a damn snow storm."

"Well yeah, there is a little bit of collateral damage, but look on the bright side. Evan and Jake will be fine, the case is solved, Evan gets the girl, it ain't snowin' that bad yet, we're finally off duty, and oh yeah," he uncorked the whisky bottle, "there's this!" He put it to his lips and took a healthy pull. After smacking his lips, he offered it to Buster.

Buster accepted. "Yeah, you're right. I just hope Ruth Pike survives. If there's an innocent member of the

Pike family in this mess, it's her." Then they mounted up, Buster on Diablo, leading the mare Veronica had ridden and behind them, Billy on the gelding Jake had ridden.

"What about Jason? You don't consider him innocent?"

"Maybe innocent by reason of stupidity. He let that little, green-eyed, wench dance him around as if he were a puppet on a string."

"Hey, give the guy a break. That's what women do with men, unless of course you're like Ben Pike, and then you hit 'em over the head and drag 'em back to your cave."

Buster briefly considered trying to explain to Billy about loving, adult relationships in which both partners give and take, and respect each other, however, it had been a long morning and there was a lot left to do. Once he got down off the mountain, he had several horses to take care of, both Pike's and Evan's. He didn't know if he could easily explain to Billy what love was supposed to be, and he certainly didn't feel in the mood for extensive mentoring. *To hell with it.* He took another long pull off the bottle. Passing it back to Billy, he gave Diablo a tiny bit of leg pressure, and they started back down the trail. Life was short, he wanted to get home to Amy and enjoy some more of it.

Epilogue

    The Monday following the snowy conclusion of the case of the Grulla Paint Murders, Sheriff Tate resigned. He took a job in administration with the Colorado State Patrol in Salida. It was a position where he could do only minimal damage. He had considered pressing charges against Jake for assaulting an officer and breaking jail, but quickly dismissed it. He didn't want the issue of his untimely urination to come up. Buster was elated, or was until the governor appointed him interim sheriff. Two weeks later, Evan was back on the job wearing a cast on his ankle. An excellent surgeon had stitched Evan's forehead and in time, the scar became negligible. Since it was difficult for Evan to get around, Buster conned him into doing most of the office work. He told him it would be good on the job training for when he was elected sheriff.

    After a long, difficult struggle, Ruth Pike survived. Veronica had shot her with Jason's pistol, a .357 magnum. Ordinarily, one does not survive being shot close to the heart with such a bullet, however Jason never fired .357 factory ammo in the pistol, he didn't like the recoil. He always used less powerful .38 caliber bullets that worked just fine, but carried less than half the energy. All hunters worth their powder know the old adage, "The smaller the bullet, the more critical the shot." Jason took his bullet directly through the heart. Ruth took hers a little to the right. Ruth lived, Jason didn't.

Raleigh sold her B and B in Creede and moved into Abel's place in Buena Vista. A year later, she started dating the county deputy, Bill Thomas, whom she met the day Abel was discovered dead in the back yard. Eventually they were married, and they continue to raise and train big horses for big riders.

Jake spent a week in intensive care, and had a complete recovery. As fate would have it, Jake met Ruth for the second time while they were both in the hospital. After learning the full story, she forgave Jake. A year later, she sold him and Dale Kupfer the ranch, and went to live with Jason's father.

Foregoing his MBA, Jake went back to work selling vet supplies. He and Dale, and Dale's wife mortgaged themselves to the hilt to buy the Pike ranch from Ruth at a very reasonable price. They bought some Piedmontese cattle from a rancher in western Montana, and started raising low cholesterol beef for health conscious, Denver yuppies. Every fall, Evan receives a side of beef from Jake for saving his life.

Veronica Valdez was buried in a cemetery in Albuquerque with no one in attendance other than her mother. Ronnie had been a bad girl most of her youth and all of her adult life. She actually had murdered her father and gotten away with it. She claimed he was sexually abusing her. He never had. When police searched her apartment in Colorado Springs, they found evidence of her participation in many nefarious activities. There were detailed notes of how she planned the murder of the entire Pike family as well as an extensive library of videos featuring her and a number of male friends. There was also evidence that immediately prior to meeting Jason, she and a graduate chemistry student had manufactured and sold the anesthetic, ketamine. According to her notes, they were producing ketamine and marketing it as the illicit party drug, Ecstasy. The raw materials were easier to get, and the process was simpler. The graduate student had since disappeared. There were some vague references that eventually led police to a partially decomposed body in the hills north of Albuquerque. Veronica's last caper came close to being successful. Jason was the only real friend she ever had.

Diablo continues to sire good horses. Although Evan acquired more horses, Diablo remains his favorite. As long as they get their daily oats, none of the others mind.

****

Cheree was trying on dresses. It was late the afternoon of New Year's Eve day. Evan, Buster and Amy were on their way to meet her. They were to be guests of the governor at the most posh restaurant in Denver. Cheree couldn't decide what to wear. Just for this occasion, she purchased a slinky, satin number with an Oriental look. It was slit up both sides to mid thigh, emphasizing her great legs. She thought it looked good at the store, but now that she had it home, she changed her mind—too obvious. It was also too late to return it and try again. She exhaled a sigh, and plunged back into her closet. She started shoving hangers to one side, going deeper into her wardrobe and farther back in time. Almost at the back she found it, draped in a clear bag; a little black party dress she had worn only once. Made of the finest silk, it was clingy and short. The only time she'd worn it, it had driven her husband wild with desire.

Five years ago they had been invited to a gala affair. Seeing her in that dress, he couldn't control himself. They arrived at the party beyond fashionably late. She smiled as she thought about it. Then, when she thought about wearing it for another man, the smiled faded. Nevertheless, she slipped off her robe and held the dress in front of her. It should still fit. She tried it on. It fit her as well as it had the day she bought it.

She stared at her reflection in the mirror. Her husband died three years ago. She'd loved him dearly, and now she knew it was time to move on. She never thought she would find another man to love like she had loved him, but it had happened.

She was not a vain person, but turning slowly from side to side in front of the mirror, she knew she looked good. The smile returned. She hoped the dress would have the same effect on Evan as it had on the first true love of her life five years ago. There was no need for concern. It did. They were married six months later. Buster was the best man.

In the words of Woody MacPherson, Buster's old buddy, "Hormones make the world go 'round."

Made in the USA
Monee, IL
02 December 2019